Night of
the Nyctalope

IN THE SAME SERIES

Jean de La Hire. *Enter the Nyctalope*
Jean de La Hire. *The Nyctalope on Mars*
Jean de La Hire. *The Nyctalope vs. Lucifer*
Jean de La Hire. *The Nyctalope Steps In*

Jean de LA HIRE

Night of
the Nyctalope

With additional stories by
Matthew Dennion, Martin Gately,
Emmanuel Gorlier, Julien Heylbroeck,
Travis Hiltz, Roman Leary,
Jean-Marc Lofficier, David McDonald,
Chris Nigro and Philippe Ward.

Edited and translated by
Jean-Marc & Randy Lofficier
and Matthew Baugh

BLACK COAT PRESS

Visit our website at www.blackcoatpress.com

ISBN 978-1-61227-102-6. Printing. July 2012. Published by Black Coat Press, an imprint of Hollywood Comics.com, LLC, P.O. Box 17270, Encino, CA 91416. All rights reserved.

TABLE OF CONTENTS

Introduction 7
Jean de La Hire: *Night of the Nyctalope* 9
Travis Hiltz: *First Steps* 53
Matthew Dennion: *The Angel and the Exorcist* 79
Matthew Dennion: *Dangerous Territory* 87
Martin Gately: *Dam Busters of Mars* 100
Chris Nigro: *Justice and Power* 121
David McDonald: *The Girl from Odessa* 135
Emmanuel Gorlier: *Una Voce Poco Fa* 153
Philippe Ward: *The Hour of the Grail* 161
Julien Heylbroeck: *Blood and Weapons* 173
Matthew Dennion: *The Road Not Taken* 201
Chris Nigro: *Requiem for a Regime* 206
Travis Hiltz: *Showdown at Steam Town* 218
Emmanuel Gorlier: *Madison Square Garden* 238
Roman Leary: *The Devil You Know* 249
Emmanuel Gorlier: *The Algerian Dilemma* 272
Jean-Marc Lofficier: *The Ides of Mars* 282
Credits and Sources 295

Introduction

Rien qu'une Nuit (translated here as *Night of the Nyctalope*), sub-titled *Une Aventure du Nyctalope*, was published in booklet form by Trémoine as the first issue of its "Cyclope" imprint in 1944. It is the last of the WWII Nyctalope stories, coming after *La Croix de Sang*, serialized in *Le Matin* in 1941, *L'Enfant Perdu* (translated as *The Nyctalope Steps In*),[1] serialized in *L'Actu* in 1942 and *Le Roi de la Nuit* (to be translated in our forthcoming book, *Return of the Nyctalope*), published in 1943.

To contextualize this troubled period of Jean de La Hire's life, in early 1941, as the result of the Nazis' efforts to "aryanize" French publishing and expropriate Jewish owners, he and André Bertrand were given editorial control of publisher Ferenczi, which had issued paperback editions of many of his serial novels. In April 1941, Ferenczi was conveniently renamed "Editions du Livre Moderne." Ironically, La Hire proved to be a less than competent publisher and was subsequently fired in December 1941, which didn't prevent the company from putting out *Le Roi de la Nuit* in October 1943.

After the War, La Hire was arrested in March 1945; he was tried and found guilty in December 1945. He then escaped in February 1946, while being transferred to a hospital, and further condemned *in absentia* to ten years' imprisonment in April 1948. He eventually surrendered in December 1951, but never served his sentence. Still in disgrace, he wrote under various pseudonyms until his death on September 6, 1956. His son-in-law published "refried" versions of several Nyctalope stories, plus two that had remained unpublished until then: *La Sorcière Nue* (1954) and *L'Énigme du Squelette* (1955).

---

[1] ISBN 978-1-61227-028-9.

Plot-wise, *Night of the Nyctalope* is very similar to both *La Croix de Sang* and *La Sorcière Nue,* bolstering the theory that the last two books were, in fact, written during the 1940s, and merely updated for publication by La Hire's son-in-law.

All the other stories published in this collection have never been published before. They illustrate, rather well, the charm and enduring power of the character of the Nyctalope over a century of story-telling. The first tale takes place early in Leo's adventurous career, in the 1900s, and the last is contemporary to the publication of this book.

Like Steve (Captain America) Rogers, Leo Saint-Clair is more than a simple superhero; he is the incarnation of a somewhat naive patriotic ideal, torn from his roots both in time and space. The Nyctalope has had to grapple with the passing of time and adapt to changing values; he is never far from the past, yet is a man of the future. Even more poignantly than Steve Rogers, he has undergone a Fall from Grace, and fought to earn his subsequent redemption. In that, he is truly unique in the annals of popular literature.

Long live the Nyctalope!

Jean-Marc & Randy Lofficier

The following story takes place during the month of January 1941. The Nyctalope does not seem to be particularly bothered by the German Occupation. At that time, it was possible to legally cross the demarcation line between Occupied France in the North and Vichy France in the south only by obtaining an Ausweis *(identity card) or a* Passierschein *(pass) from the Nazi occupation authorities after completing a certain number of formalities. This was quite difficult and even the ministers of the Petain regime had no permanent passes— only Pierre Laval, the Head of the Vichy Government, had this privilege. Yet, as indicated at the start of Chapter IV, Leo has all the necessary papers with him, which leaves one to wonder about his position during those dark times...*

Jean de La Hire: *Night of the Nyctalope*

Chapter I
Attraction and Foreboding

Madeleine d'Evires dropped the newspaper onto her knees. She had been staring at the same two lines for several minutes while her mind wandered.

She continued to daydream a while longer, giving her gold-speckled, green eyes a soulful expression, one that was much more profound than usual. In fact, more than ever, the young woman showed nothing in her beautiful eyes, except youth, intelligence and a real *joie de vivre*.

"How strange," she said. "I feel like going to the next gala at the Palais de Chaillot!"

"No!" exclaimed Madame d'Evires, pushing her glasses up on her nose and staring directly at her daughter.

When there was no response, she continued: "You? You hate crowds! It's a charity performance, you know. Imagine it, that huge theater, full of endless corridors, staircases and concert halls will be dark and swarming with people. Think what it will be like when..."

"Yes, Mother, yes, I can well imagine it. And that's precisely what's so strange. Despite my hatred of crowds, as you just pointed out, I feel suddenly possessed, attracted and compelled by some mysterious desire to go. It's bizarre, but it's becoming stronger by the minute. Yes, I feel a profound and almost painful desire to go to this gala..."

"Painful?" exclaimed Madame d'Evires, suddenly frightened.

"And also, if you can understand, Mother, also, almost... sensual."

"Sensual? Are you mad, Madeleine?"

"No, Mother, because I see it all very clearly and I'm able to analyze it perfectly well," responded Madeleine in a calm, firm voice. "I'm perfectly logical, as you can't help but proudly brag about to all our friends, Mother. And it's precisely because I am logical that I can clearly see within myself. My whole being, body and soul, is irresistibly pulled and attracted to this gala, even though my reason and tastes have always been diametrically opposed to events of this type. Not only are they crowded, but also the variety of acts is usually disappointing, and even boring, to many of the attendees..."

"Well then?" said Madame d'Evires.

"Well then, Mother... I don't want to go, but I feel and predict and even know that I will! How odd it is... Why do I feel this compulsion?"

"What do you want me to say, my dear? Let me think about it."

Madame d'Evires smiled. In the warm, cozy room, there was once again silence. The mother had gone back to her knitting, and the daughter to her vague reverie, interrupted only by moments of lucid introspection.

The gala at the Palais de Chaillot was scheduled for the following day, Saturday, January 25. It was to begin at 7:30 p.m. Every newspaper and a poster laid out a program that was filled with a variety of stars from music, theater, and night-clubs. But the program's abundance of riches didn't impress Madeleine d'Evires in the least. There was something else that astonished her!

As her stated indifference to the ball grew, so did the mysterious depth and even violent nature of her desire to attend it.

It was indeed a mystery, for Madeleine had the definite feeling that this strange compulsion, so contrary to her nature, had been artificially provoked within her... As soon as she thought about it, that word came from her lips. It was the evening of Friday, January 24. Madeleine was in her bathroom, finishing her nightly routine: a brief, lukewarm bath, five minutes of gymnastics, rubbing cologne on her body, then putting on her silk pajamas...

"Provoked?" she murmured, sitting on the edge of her bed after having turned back the sheets.

She looked at herself in the beautiful, large mirror that stood above her dressing-table and noticed that her otherwise flawless face looked a litte more emaciated, and her green eyes speckled with gold were a little more dilated than usual.

"Provoked?" she repeated. "But by what?"

She remained there, motionless, meditative, her arms hanging stiffly by her sides, her hands flat on the edge of the bed. She looked in the mirror and had the impression of seeing another human being who was not herself and who had replaced the Madeleine Evires whom she knew so intimately.

And soon she no longer said: "Provoked by what?" but, in a voice that had lost its firmness, in a voice that betrayed fear, she said instead: "Provoked by whom? Yes, by whom?"

Having experienced the physical sensation that she was sinking into some inescapable abyss, she suddenly straightened up with a burst of energy and free will. She forced herself to do some breathing exercises for several minutes. Then she went to bed, turned off the bedside lamp, lay down on her right side, as she usually did, and, while consciously and willfully closing her eyes, she uttered a loud, firm and decisive:

"I shan't go!"

But, moments later, she knew that she would be going to the wretched gala! She stopped fighting the mysterious compulsion. Then, feeling miserable and yet, at the same time, relaxed and relieved by her acceptance, she wept. She began to examine, in a confused and indistinct fashion, the feeling that had dawned in her mind, and which soon filled her whole being: the feeling that, until that very day, and even the next day, she had lived all her life as a girl, a maiden... Although she had successively reached puberty, and then her real freedom, her legal majority, she still remained a "little girl!" But now she felt that the next day, or rather the next night, she would be entering a new phase of her life, when a young girl becomes a woman. Finally, overwhelmed, exhausted by the opposite emotions of despair and hope, voluptuous attraction and repulsion of pain, desire and fear, Madeleine Evires fell asleep.

For a year, ever since Madeleine had reached her legal majority, Madame d'Evires had always given her daughter her full freedom.

Only three months before, in an intimate ceremony attended only by family and close friends, the young woman had become engaged to Lucien Délévard a virtually penniless medical student, but who was gifted with the kind of genius that would ensure him a brilliant career, either as a researcher or a practitioner.

Was Madeleine truly in love with Lucien? Sometimes, Madame d'Evires wondered about that. But a strong bond of affection united them, being both "cousins" in the fashion of Brittany, and childhood friends. The great estate of the d'Evires in Normandy was adjacent to the farm and stables owned by Lucien's father. Long ago, a Délévard grandmother had married the stepfather of a d'Evires grandfather and that was enough to unite the two families.

This this engagement had been as natural as knotting a piece of string after twisting it into a tangle.

Madame d'Evires had made no objection, although she had thought her daughter's engagement rather hasty. But she followed the rule that she had imposed upon herself, because of the rather rebellious character of her daughter, which was to not interfere with her life in any way after Madeleine had reached her majority. She truly believed that her daughter should now be responsible for all her actions. As a matter of fact, Madeleine was on her own, managing a rather large fortune in real estate and stocks which she had inherited from her father, who had died in an automobile accident in 1937.

So, with respect to the gala at the Palais de Chaillot, on Saturday, January 25, Madame d'Evires asked her daughter, just after lunch:

"Despite the repugnance and fear that you confided in me this morning, are you definitely resolved to go to the performance?"

"Yes, Mother!" Madeleine replied without hesitation.

True to her rule of conduct, which had become an ingrained habit, Madame d'Evires did not say: "Then I will go with you," but instead, asked: "Do you want me to go with you?"

There, Madeleine hesitated. She looked tenderly at her mother, whom she truly loved with all her heart. And Madame d'Evires thought that only a few words or a maternal gesture would be enough for her daughter to acquiesce, but she was mistaken. Upon hearing Madeleine's first words, her mother realized that her hesitation had only been about how to best express her rejection, not the decision itself. Madeleine's statement was frank and honest, as usual, but was accompanied by a sudden flush of confusion and, perhaps, regret.

"I'm sorry, Mother," she said, "but I called the box office and only made a reservation for one person... And I booked only one seat, which I specified should be far enough from the stage and on an aisle, so I can easily get up and leave at any time without disturbing my neighbors."

Madame d'Evires raised an eyebrow.

"Why did you do that?" she asked. "Normally, you like to be near the stage and in the middle because of your eyes—I mean, they're beautiful, but your sight isn't the best in the world."

"I know, Mother. And I wondderdd about that myself, but in the same way that, I believe, I have been compelled, even provoked, to attend, when I called the box office, I felt a similar compulsion to book an aisle seat far from the stage..."

She paused, visibly upset and filled with an odd mixture of curiosity, anxiety and anger.

"This is all very strange and not at all like you!" pronounced Madame d'Evires with conviction.

"You're right, Mother, and I don't understand it myself."

Mother and daughter were sitting in a small salon adjoining the dining room, taking coffee after lunch. Madeleine was distractedly smoking a cigarette. After having said "I do not understand it myself," there was a long, meditative silence between them, during which Madeleine, with the purity of a soul without artifices, looked straight into her mother's eyes several times.

"What is the number of your seat?" Madame d'Evires finally asked.

"I don't know off-hand," replied Madeleine, "but I wrote it down. Wait..."

Her purse was on a small coffee table beside her. She took out a tiny notebook, and offered it to her mother, opened at the right place. Madame d'Evires read a number, a word, and a letter.

"Good!" she said, rising. "I won't go with you, but I'll go by myself. I'm going to call the box office and reserve an orchestra seat or a box placed in such a way that I'm able to see you all the time. What do you think?"

Madeleine got up right after her mother. The words she had just heard moved her with such emotion that her beautiful face was pale and her body trembled. Her heart and mind could not blame a mother who only wanted, in such strange circumstances, to watch over her child. So she nodded her approval, with her gaze, her head, and her gestures. But, strangely, she could not express her feelings with words. She uttered the following with great difficulty, as if she was fighting a hidden and invisible will:

"Dearest Mother... Yes... You're probably right... Perhaps it is better... But we can't go out together... It's important that.... Yes ... I must be there alone ... Alone..."

"Of course, darling."

And with the determination of a mother entirely resolved to watch over her daughter, Madame d'Evires picked up the telephone to call the box office.

Chapter II
The Nyctalope

In January 1941, Leo Saint-Clair, a.k.a. the Nyctalope, had the pleasure of enteraining his dear friend Gnô Mitang in his current Parisian mansion on the rue Montbrun.

Leo Saint-Clair, a Frenchman justly famous for his travels, his adventures, his public and secret missions undertaken in honor and in the best interests of his native country, was nicknamed the "Nyctalope" because of his rare ability to see as well in total darkness as in full daylight, whether under natural or artificial light.

Less well known was Gnô Mitang. This high caste Japanese man had been a close friend of the Nyctalope since his battle with Leonid Zattan, and had often accompanied him on his many adventures across the world. But His Excellency Gnô Mitang was also one of the most energetic and subtle of Japan's diplomats, with the rank of ambassador and the often crucial role of Privy Councilor to the Emperor himself.

Physically, Gnô was a small, stocky man, strong but nimble, both vigorous and healthy, with a Buddha-like face. His ever-present smile could be, in turn, good-humored, ironic, mysterious, severe, and even terrifying.

On the evening of Saturday, January 25, 1941, Leo Saint-Clair and Gnô Mitang had decided to attend the gala at the Palais de Chaillot, to which they had been officially invited.

The program itself did not interest them much. They had spent too many years traveling in too many countries, watching and listening to too many singers and dancers, musicians and comedians, magicians and acrobats! But they knew that there would be enough time during the two intermissions to meet and talk with a variety of prominent politicians, military leaders and diplomats, discreetly, freely and without formalities.

On stage, a dozen dancers had just interpreted for the hundredth time a famous ballet that everyone had already seen a hundred times, when Gnô Mitang leaned towards Saint-Clair and said:

"I spy a very pretty woman!"

"Where?"

"To our left, near the aisle, two rows of seats ahead of ours."

And the Nyctalope's eyes, which saw everything in great detail, spotted the woman in question. She had beautiful black hair, whose twists and curls, under a diadem of flowers, shone with blue reflections in the dim lights. Her neck was fine and slender, forming an elegant and noble curve with her pale, bare shoulders. Her head was resting on her open right hand, her fingers delicately spread between her forehead and temple. Saint-Clair saw three quarters of her face which looked pale and a little too thin. Her long eyelashes veiled her eyes. Two rubies that looked like bright red drops of blood hung from almost invisible platinum wires from her ears. Her left hand, lying on the armrest, was perfect in shape and complexion. A strange combination of power and delicacy, modesty and voluptuousness, emanated from her body, obviously the product of the sports and gymnastics in which modern youth indulge frequently.

"She looks very young," said the Nyctalope to his Japanese friend.

Suddenly, without anything happening on the stage that might explain her change of attitude and emotion, the young woman stood up, turned her head, and looked around indecisively, as if she was searching for someone whom she might recognize... Saint-Clair and Gnô were struck by the contrast between her dark hair, eyebrows and long eyelashes and her bright, green eyes speckled with gold, deep and translucent, projecting a feeling of infinity.

Almost immediately, their color darkened. They seemed to focus on some incalculably distant vision, and expressed a kind of surprise that was at once childlike and terrifying... Her lovely face grew pale and contracted...

"Uh-oh!" whispered Saint-Clair. "What did she see?"

"Strange!" remarked Gnô.

They quickly turned their heads to follow the direction of the woman's gaze.

They saw a man sitting stiffly, his body tense, his head leaning slightly forward, looking at the girl. He was sitting in the opposite direction, also two rows ahead of them, thus closer to the young woman. His attitude, and her response, were evocative of the classical picture of a bird being fascinated by a snake.

"Hey! Hey!" said Saint-Clair. "You're right. This is indeed strange, my dear Gnô. "But does she recognize him, or is she seeing him for the first time?"

"The first time," Gnô Mitang said softly. "I have the same thought as you, Leo. I remember the hypnotic powers of the Brahmin of Bombay..."

"Precisely, Gnô!"

At that instant, the young woman, whom he never lost sight of while watching the man, blushed, closed her eyes, bowed her head, turned again to face the stage, leaned on both armrests, and appeared to pay attention only to the ballet.

Mentally and visually, the communication between the "snake" and the "bird" had not lasted more than a minute.

"This time," said Gnô, "I think that man only wanted to demonstrate his power over his victim. But the strangest thing is that..."

"...he looked nothing like the Brahmin of Bombay," finished Saint-Clair.

"Indeed. Watch out! He's looking at us."

"I see it."

Saint-Clair and Gnô Mitang instantly played the part of two ordinary spectators entertained by the sprightly ballet that unfolded reasonably well despite the stage that was a little too big for the four small dancers.

But they had seen, and committed to their memories, the face of the man whose gaze had transfixed that of the young woman, so suddenly and violently that he had torn her away from her role as a quiet spectator, indifferent and yet attentive.

He was a man whose only remarkable features were his forehead, eyes, and lips. Otherwise, the general set of his face, his complexion, his size, his very attitude, dressed in a banal tuxedo with a discreet shirt underneath, all seemed beyond ordinary, and showed no signs whatsoever of the exotic. And even if one had been drawn to the face of this man, even his forehead, eyes, and lips were not, in and of themselves, sufficient to provoke curiosity. In short, no one would have paid any special attention to this man!

But the Nyctalope wasn't just anyone. For him, and Gnô Mitang, both well versed in science and psychology, the forehead, eyes and lips of that man were significant clues. They spoke of his superior intelligence, his base desires, his depraved sensuality—and, further, of his power to focus his will and strike other human beings at a distance. This is a power rarely given to men by Nature, at least in the course of ordinary life. But such powers do exist, even in the modern world, and thousands of cases have been recorded and, sometimes, scientifically studied.

Suddenly, Gnô Mitang, while pretending to be interested in the ballet, said:

"The successful imposition of his will from afar seems obvious," he murmured. "That woman is suffering under his spell".

"And for the first time, too," added the Nyctalope.

"Yes, I agree."

"It's very interesting. Of course, we're going to investigate it."

"Certainly, my friend."

And forminf the famous smile known and feared in all the chancelleries of the world, Gnô Mitang added:

"In coming to this commonplace variety show tonight, I certainly was not expecting to encounter a rival of the Brahmin of Bombay!"

"Nothing is ever new under the Sun," said St. Clair, also smiling.

"And wisdom is to never be surprised by what life throws at you!" ended the Japanese.

After that exchange, they remained silent. They knew they had no further need for conversation, and that their observations and thoughts, as a result of their long, intellectual and emotional relationship, would be shared between one another without having to utter a word. This is what allowed them, when they did speak, to omit preliminary or intermediate sentences and to use only the most essential words.

But their silence was not idle. It was only in appearance that they seemed interested in what was occurring on stage, to the tumultuous and unanimous applause of the audience. In reality, Saint-Clair and Gnô Mitang saw only the beautiful young woman and the man who, unquestionably, had "fascinated" her. In this case, the verb "fascinate" was taken in its occult sense, meaning "select by intelligence, possess by thought, control by will, attract by using the eyes and the imperceptible sounds made by a barely moving mouth."

Saint-Clair had visited the secret temples and colleges of Tibet, learned at the feet of ancient scholars and masters in psychophysiology; he had been the guest of the scholars of Medina and Fez, and of the venerable Egyptian Gypsy of the

Albayzin district of Granada, among whom are transmitted by word of mouth, over the centuries, the wonderful and terrible secrets of Ancient Chaldea and of the priests of Isis and Osiris. The Nyctalope and Gnô Mitang were too aware of the rituals and powers of the occult sciences to doubt, even for a moment, the seriousness and reality of the scene that, by pure chance, they had just witnessed.

Even though this was happened in 1941, in France, in Paris, during the first act of a gala performance, in the concert hall of the very modern Palais de Chaillot, in an audience of several thousand people, they knew that the mysteries of the human soul and the human body remained far beyond the understanding of western science!

"Even if one were to live for a thousand years," murmured Saint-Clair wistfully, "one would not see everything there is to see on Earth!"

"Indeed," replied Gnô.

Eventually, the curtain fell on the end of the first part of the show. The management of the Palais had set up a bar and a number of smaller rooms arranged to make up a *foyer* for the night. Many spectators were keen to be seen and to see other celebrities than those performing on stage. So, as soon as the applause ended, there was a great deal of talk and movement as the public left the concert hall and flocked towards the many exits.

"Watch out!" said Gnô.

The young woman had gotten up, taking a fur coat that she had not left at the cloakroom on her arm, and started moving quickly towards the door of the nearest exit.

"She is following that man," said Saint-Clair.

"That man" was, in fact, already moving in the stream of people passing through a door held open by attendants.

But because of where they had been sitting, the Nyctalope and his Japanese friend had to make a long detour to reach this same exit. They were slowed down by the crowd and the need to stop and murmur constant "Pardon me, Monsieur... Excuse me, Madame" as they worked their way through the throng. When they reached the exit, they found themselves in a small vestibule located between two grand staircases. They eagerly looked around, left and right, but they were unable to find the girl and the man.

The mysterious hypnotist had gotten out first and likely gone up one of the two staircases, and the young woman, irresistibly drawn to him, must have followed him. As she was young and beautiful, she probably had had no difficulty making her way quickly through the gallant crowd...

But unlike Gnô Mitang, Saint-Clair was no longer absorbed by the search for the man and the girl. While walking through the crowd, he had noticed a remarkable-looking woman in her forties, very distinguished, who, like them, was hurrying toward the exit and whose face was showing a great deal of concern, even anguish.

And now, in the same vestibule where their pursuit had reached its logical end, this woman also stopped and paused, just as perplexed and visibly distressed as Saint-Clair.

The Nyctalope looked her straight in the face, and he no longer doubted that the idea that had had taken shape in his mind a minute ago was correct.

"Madame..." he said, in a respectful tone, bowing.

Immediately, he introduced himself, and Gnô Mitang, and before the woman could react in surprise, he continued:

"Madame, are you not, like us, looking for a young and beautiful dark-haired girl with green eyes who left the concert hall as if she was being pulled from afar by an invisible wire?"

"Oh! Monsieur!" exclaimed the woman in a voice trembling with emotion. "Have you seen her?"

"And, if I may be so bold, judging by a certain resemblance, might you not be a close relative of that woman, an older sister perhaps, or maybe her mother?"

"Yes, yes, Monsieur!" exclaimed Madame d'Evires, overwhelmed with emotion. "I am her mother!"

"In that case, Madame, would you do us the honor to allow us to take you home in our car? This will give us an opportunity to talk to you. And I assure you that we will spare

21

nothing, my friend and I, to unravel the mystery that we have just seen and find your daughter."

Madame d'Evires was a worldly and well educated woman, and knew the names of the famous Leo Saint-Clair, a.k.a. the Nyctalope, and Gnô Mitang, the Japanese diplomat. She saw their faces and their eyes. She had confidence in them.

"I agree, gentlemen—and thank you."

Chapter III
Madeleine

When Madeleine d'Evires had left her apartment, alone and without giving a thought for her mother, to go to the Palais de Chaillot, a new phenomenon had occurred: it seemed to her that the obsession that had held her in its grasp for several days, which had weighed on her and penetrated the very depths of her soul, had suddenly left her, dissipating into thin air as she walked along Boulevard Raspail, towards the Denfert-Rochereau metro station.

Soon, the feeling was so strong that the girl said to herself:

"If I wanted to, I could change my mind!"

She was at the subway entrance. She knew that she had no tickets in her purse, so she had to stop at the counter to purchase, as was her habit, a booklet of ten first-class tickets, as it was less expensive. Besides, her purse contained a section that seemed to have been made to measure to carry a booklet of Metro tickets!

All this was at the forefront of her mind, while at the bottom, she thought that she could, if she wanted to, not take the subway at all, turn around, and and simply return home instead of going to the Palais de Chaillot.

Almost immediately, however, Madeleine d'Evires had a new thought that overrode the other two:

"What if I were to go anyway?"

Was it curiosity? Perhaps—but not the foolish character flaw that is arbitrarily attributed to Eve, but the same sort of compulsion that drives the minds of scientists. Without such curiosity, the brain of man would remain inert, and no progress would ever happen on Earth.

So, driven by this curiosity, Madeleine d'Evires did, of her own free will, what, for two days, she had been mysteriously compelled to do!

Thirty-five minutes later, she entered the Palais de Chaillot, and took her seat. The orchestra had finished the prelude. Almost immediately, the curtain rose. Still free, and conscious of being such, Madeleine began to focus on the performance. It succeeded. How long did that state last? She did not know and wasn't even thinking about it.

Suddenly, she felt her mind become strangely indifferent to what was happening on stage, and her eyes became unfocused, as if the crowd of spectators and the performers had turned into a vague, shifting and nebulous mass. Soon, all that surrounded her disappeared from her consciousness and she turned her head to the left. She saw the face of a man with a high forehead, curly black hair, and a hard but beautiful mouth with lips so red that one might have thought them painted... But no... They were only thick and blood-filled... And his eyes... In those immense eyes she recognized her own, as if in a mirror! She knew instinctively that this was the man who had been holding her spellbound for the last forty-eight hours...

The most remarkable thing was that Madeleine d'Evires, again under the mysterious influence, that was now more powerful than ever, still retained her ability to reason, and this quite consciously, that is to say, with the cold clarity of logic derived from pure observation.

Gradually, she felt fascinated again, just like a small bird before a hawk. She realized, with horror, that she felt both shame and a kind of new, voluptuous thrill, a purely physical passion that was something quite unknown to a young woman whose mind had been enriched by books and plays.

She thought she could never turn away from this man, with his bulging forehead, his hungry lips and those eyes in which she felt herself swallowed whole...

Then, as suddenly as she had been captured, she was freed again; the man had turned his head and was watching the stage. Madeleine d'Evires resumed her normal position and again became interested in the spectacle.

Once again, she felt free.

When the curtain began to slide heralding the end of the first part of the spectacle, Madeleine d'Evires clearly heard a voice inside her mind commanding her:

"*Get up and follow me!*"

She turned her head and again saw his eyes, his lips, his forehead, the once more his eyes, only his eyes... And she whispered distinctly:

"Yes... I obey... I am terrified and yet happy to obey... I'm coming!"

Quickly and with small, precise gestures, she grabbed her fur coat and placed her purse under her left arm. Then, she left the hall at a brisk pace, with firm steps, without any hesitation, even with a feverish haste that caused her to shudder simultaneously with both delight and pain.

She immediately saw the man, who had managed to be only a few steps ahead of her. But, almost immediately, the influx of spectators converging towards the exits was such that Madeleine lost sight of him—at least with her eyes. Because, in her mind, she still saw him, as if they were connected by an invisible and yet unbreakable wire. She walked quickly without hesitation, weaving her way deftly between couples in motion and spectators standing still, talking about the performance. She was rushing towards the unknown with a joyful eagerness, all the time being well aware of the strangeness of her behavior!

Madeleine wasn't thinking about her mother, who had been in the hall, watching her, and who had followed her. She had no thoughts other than those, clearly expressed, whose silent utterance caused her lips to move imperceptibly:

"Who is this man? What does he want from me? Why do I obey his will without fear, without reluctance, without rebellion?"

And she continuously repeated the same questions to herself, over and over, which left no room for anything else in her mind.

With a light, fast and sure step, Madeleine d'Evires climbed a stairway, followed a wide corridor, turned the first corner, and found herself finally alone... when, suddenly, the man who had fascinated her appeared just in front of her.

He had been waiting by an exit door alongside which two policemen stood on duty.

She went straight to him. She instinctively buttoned her fur coat and pulled up the collar. The man was wearing a black overcoat, with a large white silk scarf around his neck, and a black felt hat. He offered his left arm to Madeleine, while opening the door with his right hand. She grabbed his arm, almost clinging to him and, together, they left.

Twenty yards further, he helped her into a car, and followed her inside. The driver must have had standing orders, for he drove off without a word being said.

Now stuck in the corner of the warm and comfortable car, Madeleine had no thought for anything or anyone because her mind was numb as if from a narcotic. She felt the man taking off her gloves, taking her bare hands in his and caressing them with his hot palms. She looked at only his eyes in which she felt that her whole being was drowning. Soon, her entire body was weakening, growing more relaxed... She leaned her head against him and her cheek came to rest on the woolly fabric of his coat...

Not a word was spoken.

This lasted until the car at last stopped.

Then, the man propped her up again and said:

"We've arrived, Madeleine. Come with me."

He opened the car door and stepped out. She followed him docilely. Together, they entered a house, the exterior of which she failed to see.

The man was holding a small pocket flashlight. This was the only source of light she saw, that thin beam that preceded them, crossing a vestibule, climbing a flight of stairs, entering a room...

There, she heard the muffled sound of a door closing behind her, then the click of an electrical switch. Suddenly, a bright light lit up a living room filled with cozy furniture, rugs, paintings, objets d'art...

Madeleine d'Evires once again felt her free will return. That is to say, she suddenly experienced a kind of rebirth, a total release that was both mental and physical. Immediately, as if she was watching a film of her life in fast forward, she relived the events of the last three days: falling victim to the mysterious influence, its increase in power hour by hour, it compelling her to go to the gala at the Palais de Chaillot, her conversations with her mother, her inner struggle, her terrified submission, her sense of revolt at her utter loss of free will, and, finally, encountering the gaze of the magician when he had appeared at last...

Then, a black hole...

And now!

Tense and quivering, her eyes flashing with fury, she drew back, leaning against a book case, and, after a brief moment of hesitation, she spat in an angry and icy voice:

"Monsieur! What you've done to me is intolerable! I do not know you. I want to leave at once!"

He dropped his gloves, as well as hers, his hat and his overcoat on a couch. Dressed in a simple tuxedo, he was a man of medium height but powerfully built, with a kind of severe elegance about him. His smiled, and his dark eyes were very soft under his serene brow. In a deep voice full of emotion, he replied:

"Mademoiselle, except for not leaving this apartment, you are free in every respect. I warn you that the windows, which are double-glazed, are locked, and you have no way to open the door leading to the hallway and the landing. As for the other doors which lead to the other six rooms of this apartment, they are open, or you can open them with a mere push of the handles...

Madeleine shuddered, but still felt furious and cold as ice:

"So I am your prisoner?"

"Oh!" he said with an apologetic gesture of his hands, "you are much less so now than you were earlier in the theater or inside my car! You may be my prisoner physically, but mentally and morally, you are free. Yes, Mademoiselle, I have decided to return your free..."

He suspended his sentence, nodded, his smile deepened, and he added:

"At least until..."

Again, he interrupted himself. But Madeleine, still angry, yet forcing herself to be calm, insisted:

"Until what? Come, Monsieur, tell me everything!"

"Oh! There is not much to tell!" he replied with a non-chalant smile. "Let's say, until I determine that your resistance towards me remains inflexible. Do you follow me?"

"No!"

"Let me explain then, even though, Mademoiselle, I suspect that your 'No' is almost a lie. When I decide that you are stubbornly determined to not overcome your own resistance towards me, then I will replace your will with mine... And then, you will be even less free than you were at home while I compelled you to go to the gala at the Palais de Chaillot, or in the concert hall when I ordered you to follow me, or inside my car when, barely conscious, you abandoned your hands in mine and rested your head on my shoulders... Do you follow me now?"

This time, Madeleine did not answer right away. She understood that she now faced a threat far more serious and terrible than even the worst physical violence inflicted by a man against a woman. She also realized that, against this threat, she would be utterly helpless when the man would want her to be so. It was evident from the very fact that she, Madeleine d'Evires, was there, at night, in a strange house, alone with this mysterious stranger who had used no ouward physical co-ercion to bring her there. Yes, it was indisputable.

But Madeleine had a proud and noble character. She was brave. She was intelligent and resourceful, still capable of gathering information about her enemy's intentions and pow-ers—powers which, she knew, seemed irresistible. But what were they exactly? As for his intentions, she understood them all too well. Was there anything else beyond the obvious? *Well, let the duel continue*, she thought, *but in another way.*

And Madeleine d'Evires, suddenly relaxed, took a couple of steps forward, took off her coat, looked around, chose a chair, and sat down. Having regained her inner strength, with her beautiful, musical voice, full of determination, she said:

"Please sit down, Monsieur. Let us talk, not as the pro-tagonists of some kind of devilish melodrama, but as two or-dinary persons... sensible opponents, if you will! Enemies even, perhaps, but sensible... First, who are you?"

"That's wonderful!" exclaimed the man, visibly pleased. "I was certain you were of superior human stock, something quite rare. Thank you! And you're right, I should introduce myself to you..."

Standing still, he bowed, put a hand on his chest, as in some Eastern ceremony, and slowly, said:

"I am Godfroy, Baron de Montluc, the last direct de-scendant of the famous Blaise de Montluc, Maréchal of France..."

"...Who was glorious defender of Siena in 1555, proved horribly cruel to the Calvinists, and wrote some noteworthy Commentaries," Madeleine finished coolly.

And ironically, she added:

"I learned that in high school.

With a smile, he remarked:

"I'd be surprised if you had forgotten it."

He pulled out a chair and sat down, facing Madeleine.

There was a long silence, during which the two duelists observed each other. It was finally bravely broken by the young woman.

"Monsieur," she said in an even tone of voice, "you have twice used the word 'resistance' by giving it the meaning of an act of free will from my part. So, naturally, the question arises: 'resistance' against what? In other words, and going straight to the point: why have you brought me here? What exactly do you want from me?"

Even though he was in control of himself, Baron de Montluc could not fail to react to an attack that was, indeed, straight to the point. Madeleine instantly became aware of it and was amazed. This was one more little mystery to be added to the list of the great enigmas raised by this strange man. Why was her opponent not answering her right away?

Obviously, he hesitated. And to Mademoiselle d'Evires, watching him keenly, his face, that had seemed energetic and virile, suddenly assumed an air of fatigue: His eyes lost their luster, his cheeks grew hollow, a small wrinkle of bitter weariness appeared at the corner of his mouth. Increasingly surprised, she asked herself what it all meant...

But she did not express that thought aloud. Rather, she kept her calm and almost impassive attitude, her only expression being one of expectation, waiting for the answer to her primary question which, for the time being, rendered other questions such as: "Where did you see me for the first time?" and "Why did you choose me?" obsolete.

The silence continued. And the face of the Baron de Montluc became increasingly weary with such a speed and intensity, that Madeleine, despite her resolution, finally felt obliged to say:

"Well, Monsieur, why do you not respond?"

What happened next was the very last thing that the young woman would have expected.

With a groan, the Baron rose, with a visible effort of all his muscles, his hands trembling. In a stiff and jerky fashion, he drew back several steps, leaning on the various pieces of furniture within his reach. When he reached the other end of the room, near a large door framed by a set of curtains, he made a sudden and brief nod and said, in a low, husky, and slightly breathless voice:

"I will see you tomorrow, Madeleine. This room is your bedroom. The bathroom and toilets are over there..."

He made a short, painful gesture, pointing towards another door on the opposite side of the room. After taking another long breath, he added:

"I have thought of everything. This cabinet contains lingerie, pajamas, slippers... In that other piece of furniture, there are wines, liquors, biscuits, chocolate, cigarettes, fruits... The shelves are full of books... Finally, there's a wireless set and a phonograph, with an excellent record collection... Now, please, excuse me. I will see you tomorrow!"

With a supreme effort, he stepped between the curtains and disappeared.

Moved by a sudden inspiration, Madeleine d'Evires leapt towards the door...

But too late!

Beyond the curtains, which she parted with both hands, the door was already slamming shut, and the young woman could see that there were, at least on her side of it, several locks which were being bolted as she watched.

"Oh!" she said dispiritedly. "If I had the idea a few seconds earlier, I could have reached him, pushed him out of the way with a punch, or used jiu-jitsu on him..."

For Madeleine d'Evires was very athletic, being a volunteer instructor in a sports center for girls, and she had strong muscles, some boxing experience and the knowledge of a dozen basic, but effective, jiu-jitsu holds, jiu-jitsu being at the same time a sport, an art, and a perfect way to attack and defend oneself.

She let the curtains drop slowly and stood there for a moment, motionless and thoughtful. Despite it all, she felt a renewed sense of hope, and even relief.

She turned, dropped onto the couch, and pulled some cushions to her, on which she leaned comfortably.

She was convinced now that her terrifying adversary was subject to powerful weaknesses... The reason was still mysterious, but the fact was obvious. She therefore felt that she could fight him, and even win... Yes! Win! Why not? It was only a matter of waiting until her enemy was again weak...

"But will he display such weakness before me again?" she said to herself. If I try to understand what's happening to me, it seems that I am the victim, the prey, of some kind of sorcerer who, by projecting his strong desire for me, has succeeded in annihilating my free will for three days. I have read many books on the occult, and magazine articles, too. I must remember what I read, and try to understand... For three days, that man held me prisoner of his will, but surely at a huge expense to his own vital fluids. That's why he was exhausted! So much so that he couldn't answer my questions, he couldn't hide his fatigue... So, he fled! He ran away from me! From the weak girl he thinks I am—and which I am in the mysterious psychic realms that I have never explored. But he, the hypnotist, the spell-caster, the sorcerer, he, too, has limitations, weaknesses... Good! I may have a chance to fight back, after all, and not be totally forced to submit to his desires..."

Suddenly, another thought occurred to her and her beautiful face became sad. Tears welled up in her eyes and she murmured:

"What about my mother? If she came to the theater, if she saw me... What must she have thought? How she must suffer! And what is she doing, my God, what is she doing?"

Chapter IV
A name?

Naturally, Leo Saint-Clair had all the *Ausweis* and other papers that enabled him to travel freely in both French zones, and even in many other European countries. The night he went to the Palais de Chaillot, however, he had used Gnô Mitang's car, having left his own in its garage on the Rue de Montbrun.

This was because his driver, Lucien, had been suffering from a violent attack of rheumatism for several days.

The Japanese's car was an anonymous-looking sedan with four seats. It was small but very fast, and its interior had been specially, and ingeniously, designed for comfortable travel, even over long distances, both at night and during the day.

Following her two new acquaintances, Madame d'Evires left the Palais de Chaillot and got into Gnô's car. Once they reached Boulevard Raspail, she gave directions to Gnô Mitang so he could park in the garage belonging to her large and luxurious apartment.

Without standing on ceremony, Madame d'Evires then took the two "investigators" to her daughter's rooms: a small office/library, her bedroom, beyond which was a small walk-in dressing room and a large bathroom with toilet and bath.

All the windows were closed and the curtains drawn shut, as was required by Civil Defense. With Madame d'Evires' permission, Saint-Clair and Gnô Mitang conducted a methodical and meticulous search, which disturbed nothing in appearance, and yet left no stone unturned. Madeleine's mother had said:

"I doubt that you'll find anything useful. My daughter's daily life has always been an open book. She never received any letters that she didn't read to me, never made any visits that she didn't discuss with me, and always gave me a thousand details about her life if my affection or curiosity demanded them. The same was true of her incomprehensible obsession with going to the Palais de Chaillot. For three days, she shared all her thoughts with me, from her initial astonishment about the mysterious compulsion she felt, to her mixture of disgust, fear and an odd attraction... As I said, she shared with me every detail of her intimate life. You will find that all the keys to the cabinets and drawers in her rooms are still in their locks...

"Do you have any servants?" asked Gnô.

"Two. Gertrude, our cook, and Flavia, our maid. we We haven't had a chauffeur since September 1939. Gertrude is 48 and has been in my service for 24 years. When I hired her, she had just lost her husband and had a two-years-old daughter. The child grew up with us, with her mother, and she is as close to me as my own daughter."

"They can't be suspects," said Saint-Clair.

"Absolutely not!" approved Madame d'Evires.

The search lasted no more than half an hour. Everything was open, transparent, simple and natural. Madeleine concealed nothing from her mother; they learned that she was engaged to a childhood friend, with the unanimous blessing of both families.

The search produced no results.

The whole time it lasted, not a word was spoken, neither by the two investigators, nor by Madame d'Evires. She preceded them, opening the furniture and all the drawers, dispensing the occasional, brief explanation. No object or paper was found that provided any clues to the mystery.

After Madeleine's rooms had been searched, they returned to the main living-room. Madame d'Evires invited them to sit, but Saint-Clair said resolutely:

"I'm afraid we can't stay, Madame. We have to leave at once. I have an idea which I must pursue…"

Gnô Mitang knew his friend and his manner of speaking and acting, always in the most direct fashion, often without preliminaries or digressions, so he wasn't surprised. But Madame d'Evires was, and did not conceal her curiosity:

"Did you find something that…" she asked.

"Yes, I did, Madame, but I don't yet know if it means anything. Perhaps it does, and perhaps it doesn't… I assure you, however, that if my idea produces results, Gnô and I will promptly inform you. But first, let me explain. Do you recognize this, Madame?"

From the right pocket of his jacket, he pulled a rectangle of white bristol paper, on which was written in blue ink on a dotted line: *Madame and Mademoiselle d'Evires.*

"I found this amongst a pile of letters in a drawer," explained Saint-Clair.

Madame d'Evires read half-aloud:

"*Monsieur and Madame Levault d'Alnay would be honored if Madame and Mademoiselle d'Evires were to join them for their private concert of chamber music on Saturday, January 18, 1941. RSVP. Please do not arrive after 4 p.m. Avenue d'Iena, 25a.*"

Looking up at Saint-Clair, Madame d'Evires added simply:

"Yes, I recognize this invitation. The Levault d'Alnays are only vague social relations, but Madeleine and I love music, and their concerts are always extremely good and well executed."

"So you went?" asked Saint-Clair.

"Yes."

"Just the two of you?"

"Yes, but..."

"What do you know of the Levault d'Alnays?" Saint-Clair continued.

"He is a wonderful cellist and a perfect gentleman, married to a rather unimpressive woman, who always seems a bit lost, but otherwise appears to be a fine hostess."

"And that's all you know?" insisted the Nyctalope.

"Yes, I think so."

"Very well."

Saint-Clair turned towards Gnô, who had listened to the conversation attentively, then looking at Madame d'Evires again, he continued:

"I know something more, and which might be perhaps of the utmost importance. Monsieur Levault d'Alnay, cellist and gentleman, is also the president of the First Esoteric Order of France. They used to hold meetings on a regular basis, although I presume more infrequently these days, but always in the strictest secrecy. In 1938, I attended three of these. Nothing was done or discussed that was either legally or morally wrong. But they studied and experimented with certain occult practices which would account for what happened to your daughter."

"My God!" exclaimed Madame d'Evires. "But then..."

"Yes, Madame, when you and your daughter went to this private chamber music concert, did you notice anything strange or unusual? Was your attention drawn to any of the guests? Remember—anything at all might be useful."

Madame d'Evires frowned, and her whole face expressed all the concentration of which she was capable. A minute, maybe two passed. Then, suddenly, with a tone of certainty, she said:

"No, nothing at all! But it was the very next day that Madeleine began feeling her strange compulsion..."

"I think that's enough for me, don't you agree, my dear Gnô?" Saint-Clair said.

"I do," said the Japanese. Immediately, he added: "We must pay a visit to Monsieur Levault d'Alnay."

"Immediately!" said Saint-Clair. "The time is not propitious for a social call, but never mind! I'll find an excuse! As for you, Madame, try to get some rest. Trust us. My friend and I are determined to get to the bottom of this strange adventure in which your daughter is involved. You will understand that we can't waste a moment's time."

"Of course, I understand, Messieurs. I understand. And with all my heart, I thank you. I will be quiet and trust in your efforts, I promise. Still, I don't think I'll be able to sleep... I'll stay by the phone. If you learn anything, will you please call me right away?"

"Of course, we will, Madame. On what floor is Monsieur Levault d'Alnay's apartment?"

"On the mezzanine."

Some twenty minutes later, Saint-Clair and Gnô Mitang parked their car outside 25 bis Avenue d'Iena. The Nyctalope pressed the bell. The concierge opened the door and Saint-Clair announced which tenant he was visiting. He then turned on the light on the timer in the staircase, because Gnô Mitang,

35

unlike him, did not have the power to see in the dark as if it were daylight.

Even in that winter of 1941, one could, at 11 p.m., still find people staying up late. This was the case. Saint-Clair handed two business cards to the servant who opened the door, not hiding his surprise, he said:

"Please give these to Monsieur Levault d'Alnay and tell him I must see him on an extremely important matter."

The visitors did not have to wait for more than three minutes in the salon where they had been asked to remain when the servant reappeared, bowed respectfully and said:

"If these gentlemen will follow me..."

They were taken to smaller room which served as a study. Behind a table covered with books of music stood a tall, lanky, older man, with light blue eyes, full of intelligence, a mane of white-hair, and a short white beard trimmed in the square fashion.

"Monsieur Saint-Clair," he said, in a friendly tone, "excuse my surprise at seeing you at such an hour and so unexpectedly after three years...And His Excellency Gnô Mitang... Your name is so illustrious that even I, a humble student in music and philosophy, recognize it... Please, sit down, please... And tell me to what I owe the great honor and very pleasant surprise of your visit...

It took only five minutes for Saint-Clair to tell Monsieur Levault of the strange adventure of Mademoiselle d'Evires. He concluded by saying:

"I suppose this is not so mysterious as to astound you, Monsieur, but the plight of this young woman should, no doubt, offend a man such as you, who has respect for individual human freedom and morality. Thus, on behalf of Madame d'Evires and her daughter, my friend Gnô Mitang and I have come to ask you to assist us in the task we have undertaken— simply, to locate Mademoiselle d'Evires as soon as possible, and deliver her from the mental clutches of the unknown sorcerer who has her in his power."

After a short pause, he added:

"Unknown to us, that is, but is it also the case for you, Monsieur?"

Levault d'Alnay had listened to Saint-Clair without interrupting him once, but also without displaying any visible signs of surprise, or indignation. Obviously, in terms of the occult, what the Nyctalope had described was quite familiar to him. After the Nyctalope had finished speaking, the older man rubbed at his neat and elegant white beard for a while, his clear, blue eyes sparkling with interest. He had not expected his nocturnal visitors to present him with such a challenge. Finally, with the same tone as if he were casually reporting a trivial anecdote to one of his social relations, he said, in the most cordial way:

"My dear Saint-Clair, while I listened to you, I mentally reviewed all the people whom we had invited to the very concert that Madame and Mademoiselle d'Evires did me the honor of attending, and I also kept in mind the succinct but striking description of the man you and His Excellency Gnô Mitang observed at the Palais de Chaillot. I see only one possible suspect..."

He, too, marked a pause, then, no less direct than Saint-Clair, concluded:

"Baron Godfroy de Montluc."

Even though they had felt optimistic about their visit to Levault d'Alnay, Saint-Clair and Gnô had not expected to receive an answer to their initial inquiry that was so specific and categorical.

"Damn!" said Saint-Clair.

"Ah," said the Japanese simply.

"Yes," continued Monsieur Levault d'Alnay with the same simplicity. "Baron de Montluc was amongst our guests. He's a great traveler, who'd just returned from a long stay in India. That he was able to make the trip from Bombay to Paris under our current circumstances did not surprise me too much, because he was always a man of considerable resources, although I never tried to learn exactly what he does. I wouldn't be surprised, either, if he were the sorcerer that you're looking for, because, three years ago, in Lisbon, the last time I saw him before the war, he demonstrated, before a panel of experts, a remarkable array of mental powers involving the projection and imposition of one's will at a distance, hypnosis, fascination, etc. But..."

Here, Levault d'Alnay raised both hands open in a kind of exorcising and disapproving gesture, while continuing in a very serious voice:

"...But we, at the First Esoteric Order of France, have taken a solemn oath never to use our science or our findings, contrary to divine and human morality, and against the full accord of human free will. To this oath, we have added another, that of unmasking, prosecuting and punishing any abuses of esoteric powers for personal interest and gain, even if only for scientific research. In the case of the spell of which Mademoiselle d'Evires is the victim, the instance of such abuse is indisputable. Therefore, Messieurs, I have not hesitated in revealing the name of the alleged perpetrator: Baron Godfroy de Montluc."

Having said this, the noble scientist returned to being the courteous, smiling, and somewhat skeptical man of the world.

"Thank you," said Saint-Clair, with as much ease as if that revelation had been the most ordinary thing in the world.

Gnô Mitang acknowledged Levault d'Alnay's disclosure with a bow of the head and chest, but then immediately asked:

"Where can we find this Baron de Montluc?"

"I have his address," replied Monsieur d'Alnay.

He opened a drawer, took out an address book, leafed through it and said:

"At least, this is the address and telephone he gave me, soon after his arrival in Paris, precisely on the eve of the concert in question. Here it is: Hotel Bonaparte, 20, rue des Pyramides."

"What?" said Saint-Clair.

Gnô Mitang and Monsieur d'Alnay stared at the Nyctalope with the same questioning look.

38

"I flatter myself on my thorough knowledge of Paris. Yet, if I'm not mistaken, there is no Hotel Bonaparte in the rue des Pyramides..." And on a different tone, he added: "Did you send your invitation to the Baron de Montluc by regular mail?"

"No. As he was on the phone informing me of his arrival in Paris and giving me this address, I invited him to come on the following day."

"You haven't written to him since then?"

"No."

"So you don't have any evidence that the address he gave you so spontaneously is authentic? Will you allow me?..."

"By all means, please."

The Nyctalope grabbed a telephone book from a small shelf next to the desk that also contained a Who's Who of Paris.

Two minutes later, they had the proof that Saint-Clair's knowledge of Paris was correct: there was no Hotel Bonaparte on the Rue des Pyramides!

"No matter!" Gnô Mitang said gently. "Let's still check what's at No. 20 Rue des Pyramides. We'll talk to the concierge, if there is one. We should also investigate if there are any other hotels on that street."

"Right!" said Saint-Clair, getting up.

As he rose, he added:

"My dear Monsieur d'Alnay, can you think of any other information that might be useful to us?"

The scientist was also standing. With an expression of sincere regret, he replied:

"By my faith, no! Except to say that, other than his indisputable abilities and knowledge in the field of occult sciences, I know absolutely nothing about this Baron Godfroy de Montluc. I confess I don't even know if that is his real name. Until today, I had no reason to question him. I'd always met him in irreproachable company, and no complaints were ever lodged against him in our circles, so why should I have suspected him? But now, after what you've told me... Well, I now doubt that his beautiful French patronym is legitimately his!"

He shook his head sadly, and concluded:

"I'm sorry, truly sorry not to be more helpful. And I wish with all my heart that you..."

Monsieur d'Alnay did not finish his sentence, as he was suddenly struck by the direct and piercing gaze of the Nyctalope staring at him.

"Monsieur," said Saint-Clair in a steely voice, "I know that the control of human thought—and yes, even animal thought—is a familiar exercise for you, and that you have done it yourself in the past. This is not a theoretical exercise. We are trying to rescue a young woman, who could be your daughter, or mine, from a truly abominable fate, and deliver her back to her mother, who is almost overwhelmed by despair..."

Levault d'Alnay, stiff and stern, frowned and began to make a gesture of apology, but Saint-Clair continued:

"Yes, I know! To use your powers to help us would involve extreme fatigue, and possibly a threat to your very life... But think of our goal, a mission of pure mercy and justice..."

This time, it was the Nyctalope's turn to be interrupted. He saw such infinite distress in the clear eyes of the old man that he stopped.

Monsieur d'Alnay spoke in a low voice:

"Alas! My life force is no longer that of an active Master. I haven't done anything of this nature in two years, gentlemen. I am now an old man, growing older with every day that passes... See in me a scientist, who can still learn and teach, but not a soldier who can fight, even with the terrible weapons he once controlled, and which he was still able to use with some success not so long ago..."

He slumped in his chair, and in a tired voice, he added:

"No, I can do nothing to help Mademoiselle d'Evires, nothing more than what I have already done by giving you this name: Godfroy de Montluc. There is no one else presently in

Paris, other than this so-called Baron and me, capable of such feats. So, gentlemen, so..."

Saint-Clair and Gnô bowed deeply. The old man held out a trembling hand. They shook it one after the other, and said together:

"Thank you, Monsieur."

Three minutes later they were back in the street.

Chapter V
The Sorcerer

Meanwhile, Madeleine d'Evires continued to meditate on her predicaement from the cushions of the couch where she was lying, calmly and the most comfortably she could.

"Naturally," she said to herself, "I won't undress, I won't go to bed, and I will not let myself go to sleep, or even doze off. I will remain alert, strong, and calm. I could continue like this for 48 hours, as long as I eat and drink. And he told me that there was everything I might want in that buffet. Good!"

Having reached a decision about what to do, the young woman transferred her thoughts to the man who held her captive.

"I appear to be his prisoner only physically," she said to herself again. "For him to capture me mentally again, he must first regain his strength, his 'fluid,' as I think they call it. How long will that take? I don't know. Do I run the risk of seeing him return in only a few hours, once again in possession of all his formidable power...?"

Madeleine considered the problem.

"What if...?" she said breathlessly.

Her beautiful eyes, wide open, were fixed on the door behind which her mysterious aggressor had disappeared. She continued speaking to herself in a low voice:

"...If he returns, I won't be myself anymore. Will I be aware that I've again lost my free will? Or will I welcome him with open arms, happy and totally submissive?... My God, that would be awful!"

41

She shuddered with her entire being, but immediately admonished herself strongly:

"Come on, Madeleine, stay calm and don't panic! After all, I don't know what he really wants from me. If he only wanted to take me against my will, he could have done it a hundred times already, at anytime and anywhere, since he first mentally enslaved me three days ago. I'm now beginning to fully appreciate the extent of his power over me. So, this man wants me for some other reason, but what...?"

She spent a long time pondering that question, but any assumptions she made were without any basis in fact, and therefore she was unable to reach a clear conclusion.

"This is a waste of time," she finally said to herself. "But if I can't find an answer, at least I can defend myself... I'll turn my mind into a fortress that he will have to attack and take by force, instead of finding it unconsciously open to any intrusion of his will as it was three days ago... Ah! That is something on which I can work, and perhaps even succeed..."

The intelligent and brave young woman smiled—and when she realized that she was doing so despite circumstances so bleak and so threatening, she felt proud and strong.

"That's good!" she murmured. "Now I just have to continue feeling this resolved and build up my mental defenses!"

For half an hour, she remained perfectly still, meditating, concentrating her will and all her energies. Finally, with a sort of silent laughter, the kind that was featured on the beautiful face of Diana in antique sculptures, she again felt mistress of herself and was secretly invigorated.

"That's it!" she uttered aloud. "Now I'm ready for him!"

With a quick gesture, she set aside the cushions on which she had been leaning and got up. A few firm steps took her to a beautiful buffet, designated by Montluc as containing "wines, liquors, biscuits, chocolate, cigarettes, and fruits." She opened its large double doors and indeed saw boxes of biscuits and chocolates, fruit bowls, cartons of cigarettes and small bottles of wine. She also saw napkins, silverware and glasses. A small coffee table stood close, between two chairs, and

Madeleine sat there, with great care, trying to discipline her every move to follow the pattern of her thoughts and her will.

She was hungry, so she ate and drank slowly, with pleasure. Every item was of the highest quality, and tasted delicious. Then, taking a cigarette and a lighter, she returned to the sofa and again settled comfortably. After lighting a cigarette, she thought:

"What if they are opium? Or saturated with another drug, even more subtle and dangerous? Bah! I know the taste of tobacco. I couldn't be deceived that easily…"

She smoked slowly, trying to analyze the flavor of the tobacco and the smell of the smoke. After smoking a third of the small, gold-tipped cigarette, of a brand that she knew but might have been faked, she felt reassured. They were not intended to harm her.

Madeleine d'Evires chain-smoked half-a-dozen cigarettes, with long pauses between each. This eventually calmed her nerves and made her feel more at peace.

Satisfied, she stood up, went to the book shelves, and read the titles of all the books. She was undecided:

"I need a book interesting enough to stop me from falling asleep—or even thinking too much," she thought.

Finally, she decided on a beautiful hardcover book, leather-bound and lavishly illustrated; it was an edition of *La Princesse de Cleves* by Madame de La Fayette, printed in Holland sometime in the early 19th century, judging from the illustrations. Madeleine had read this incomparable psychological novel, a masterpiece of delicacy and noble melancholy, twenty times already, but its style, both penetrating and caressing, was so captivating that she knew she could still reread it and find it just as captivating. Having turned down the lights so that only one bedside lamp projected its soft beam on the pages, Madeleine d'Evires began to read.

Several hours later, having read, looked at the illustrations, but also day-dreamed and smoked more cigarettes between chapters, Madeleine was roughly two-thirds of the way through *La Princesse de Cleves*.

Suddenly, she dropped the book, sat up straight, and turned her head. She had heard a noise to her left.

"It's him! He's coming!" she whispered, immediately ready, her soul, nerves and muscles armed against her enemy.

She did not rise, but moved to the side, remaining seated, facing the door, her feet firmly planted on the ground, her body free from the sensual softness of the cushions. She reached with her left hand, pressed the switch and flooded the room with bright light. And as she readied herself for what was to come next, the door opened silently and the curtains were parted...

Baron de Montluc had returned!

Immediately, Madeleine knew that she would need all her strength.

He was wearing a suit of brushed black velvet and his neck was bare under an opened white silk shirt. The expression on his pale face was in turn noble and cunning, brutal and sweet, very cold and full of sardonic cruelty. But there were no traces of fatigue...

Without saying a word, he took a few steps forward.

Madeleine did not move; she did not open her mouth.

Standing three feet from her, he looked at her, straight in the eye, with a kind of heaviness.

She met his gaze, remaining calm and cold, without trembling or fear.

The battle is about to start, she thought. *I must not falter. I will not be controlled by this man. I must win!*

One, two, three minutes went by...

Their gazes clashed, challenged each other. He tried to penetrate her shield, but was met only by a wall of smooth, compact, tense will.

Finally, the Baron made a gesture of peace, inclined his head and, in a normal voice, said:

"Good morning, Mademoiselle. Didn't you sleep at all?"

She had just decided that she would answer, but briefly, with as few words as possible, in order to not release any vital fluid from her mind.

"No!"

He smiled.

"You are strong."

"I must be."

"I congratulate you; I expected no less from you, frankly. For the power that you display shows that you are worthy."

"Worthy of what?" she replied curtly:

"Exactly. That's what I came to tell you. Will you allow me to sit?"

"You're in your own home."

"No. It is you who are in your home, Mademoiselle, since last night."

She knew that she was strong, because she wanted to laugh so as to heap scorn upon his lie. She did laugh. She did even more: she shrugged.

"Ridiculous! A prisoner is only at home if he agrees, in his soul, to remain in his prison. This is certainly not the case with me."

"Perhaps you will agree soon," the Baron said softly.

Remaining in control of herself, Madeleine made a face and replied simply in a mocking tone:

"I doubt it."

Baron de Montluc sat. He had chosen a chair that was a little higher than the couch upon which Madeleine was sitting, and pulled it towards himself in a slow movement. Without paying attention the young woman's last challenge, he spoke, immediately going straight to the heart of the matter:

"Madeleine, I have no great merit in guessing that you must have understood the reason for my extreme weakness last night, which seemed to occur suddenly, but actually had been worsening for several hours prior in the car. To control you and force you to follow me, I had to use my last ounces of strength. As you probably have guessed, I had gradually exhausted all my power from the first moment I began to exercise it over you..."

Very quietly, Madeleine said:

"It was during the private concert held at Monsieur Levault d'Alnay's, wasn't it?"

"Very perceptive! Yes. Did you notice me there?"

"No. I didn't even see you. But last night, I thought it over and relived and examined every moment of my life backwards hour by hour. And I remembered that it was during the trip home from the d'Alnays that I saw an advertising poster for the gala at the Palais de Chaillot, and I first felt that sudden and mysterious compulsion to attend it, despite all my tastes and habits to the contrary... But please, continue."

"Since I saw you and, within minutes, knew everything about you without your knowledge, at Monsieur d'Alnay's concert, I gathered all my will, and used all my fluidic powers, exhausting myself with every hour, to control your mind from afar and force you to go to that gala... Last night, at the Palais de Chaillot, I felt that I had no more strength, because, consciously or not, your resistance was almost overwhelming! I used the very last ounces of my power to get you to follow me and step inside the car that brought us here. Then, I was so totally exhausted that I had to leave you. But after a few hours' sleep, and the intravenous injection of a serum, the secret of which I am the only one in all of Europe to know, I am again ready to test my strength against yours!"

"Sorcerer!" spat Madeleine quietly.

"Sorcery?" said Montluc, surprised and smiling. "Good Heavens, no! We, Initiates, prefer to use the word 'Power.'"

"Pure semantics. So what happens next?" Mademoiselle d'Evires asked.

He replied, suddenly very serious:

"I have come to reassert my control over you."

But she, serious, tense, looking straight at his face, in a firm and inflexible voice, responded:

"Again, why? What do you want from me? What are you doing this to me? Why me and not another?"

Silence ensued, which would have been tantalizing for any present but invisible observer—a silence full of secret meanings and thoughts...

Finally, Baron de Montluc, not without visible emotion, replied:

"First, as soon as I saw you, Madeleine, I fell in love with you—love at first sight, that 'thunderbolt' that Stendhal so perfectly described and analyzed in his book about love. Yes, I fell in love with you. I am well over 40, Mademoiselle, and this is the first time that I have felt a passion like this, do you understand me?"

He paused.

She had turned pale but her eyes sparkled; her lips, her beautiful lips, which were usually a normal, healthy red, became almost blue. But she remained strong. She could speak. With a quiet tone of indignation, that was more powerful than an angry invective, she said, slowly:

"You said 'First,' Monsieur, and followed it with a declaration of love. I'll answer you with a question. What comes after 'First'? What is your 'Then'?"

He shivered; his entire body seemed to acquire a sudden hard coldness; all his features turned white as well, even his thin lips; and his eyes became a metallic grey.

However, he controlled himself and, with the same calm as before, in the same neutral tone that she had used, continued:

"*Then*, Mademoiselle, since you insist, or rather in parallel to it, I knew, with total certainty, by means of psychic penetration, of which my mind has the highest capabilities, that you had all the powers and psychophysiological qualities of the perfect medium! Absolutely! You did not know that, did you? And if you hadn't met me, perhaps you would have remained ignorant of that fact until your death—or rather the end of your present incarnation through the eternal cycle of life... Because I must tell you that I am also a believer—in fact, a priest—in the cult and dogma of the transmigration of souls from one body to another, what we call *metempsycho-sis...*"

Suddenly, there was the pearly sound of laughter. Yes, Madeleine d'Evires laughed! The youngest, freshest, cruelest of laughs! But instead of being surprised, or becoming angry, Godfroy de Montluc smiled, indulgently and even amusedly. Instead, he said:

"You laugh because it amuses you to see that I've gone from a passionate declaration of love to the most ridiculous bit of pedantry. And yet..."

Her insolent laughter stopped short; her eyes, her face, her entire body froze in a strange sort of immobility.

The Baron had risen from his chair.

He held his hands forward, making passes in the air in front of Madeleine's face. His gaze was now threatening and even brutal as he advanced towards the young woman, obviously preparing to crush her. When his knees touched those of Madeleine, who was sitting stiffly on the edge of the couch, he said in a loud and incantative voice:

"Madeleine d'Evires, you shall henceforth be mine, in the known and the unknown worlds. You shall be my wife on Earth and my sister on the astral planes. Through you, I shall live my life on Earth to the utmost, and through you again, I will complete the endless cycle of my spiritual life, forever and ever."

He bent over the young woman, trembling and ecstatic, who now stood on her tiptoes, raising her hands in a gesture of offering, murmuring:

"Yes, master... You are my teacher and my husband..."

Suddenly, the door opened...

Yes, at that very minute, a door opened, because real life is, if one can only see it, just like an endless drama, and the most amazing twists we read abiut in the novels that we devour are just like unimaginative nonsense compared with the most logical and simplest events of everyday real life. Therefore...

Suddenly, the door opened...

Chapter VI
Deliverance

Two men entered.

Godfroy de Montluc recognized them at once, as he had seen them at the Palais de Chaillot.

It was Leo Saint-Clair, the Nyctalope, and the Japanese diplomat, Gnô Mitang!

Montluc must have felt defeated, because he immediately jumped back, turned, and ran towards another hidden door...

But Saint-Clair's voice, compelling and chilling, stopped him:

"Stop, Godfrey Cultnom! The house is surrounded. You'd better surrender quietly. An international criminal such as yourself owes it to himself to show a bit of class, especially when he is in reality a Brahmin Great Initiate and a professional spell caster... What?"

That exclamation had been provoked by the fact that the sorcerer, far from stopping, turning around and surrendering, had continued to run.

But suddenly, he'd been thrown to the ground by Gnô Mitang, who had sprung forward with the speed of a panther, and jumped on their enemy just as the other man was about to go through the hidden door...

Gnô was a consummate wrestler and, with a few passes of jiu-jitsu, he forced the sorcerer back on his knees, moaning and twisting.

Meanwhile, Saint-Clair checked on Mademoiselle d'Evires, who had been brutally freed from the spell that held her captive and who, though surprised and perplexed, had quickly recovered her calm composure.

"Madeleine, this gentleman made the mistake of knowing French history too well and playing with anagrams, believing we were all idiots. Still, I have to admit that others investigating this case, besides my friend Gnô and I, might have noticed that the name 'Montluc' used by the perpetrator was but

49

an anagram of 'Cultnom,' and 'Godfroy' the French version of 'Godfrey.' And even fewer people might have realized that Godrey Cultnom is a name well known to the police forces and criminal underworld of several continents... especially those of India and China. You now see how simple it was for Godfrey Cultnom, with false papers, to rent a small, furnished private residence in Passy, a car, two servants, and impersonate the very respectable French aristocrat Godfroy de Montluc. It was an expensive proposition, but this gentleman is very rich. Ah! The chase was quite a thrill. That honest and excellent French scholar, Monsieur Levault d'Alnay, could not provide us with additional clues regarding your persecutor, but my contacts at the Préfecture de Police were very helpful...Mr. Cultnom hadn't escaped their attention... It was child's play to find out his lair... Someday, I'll tell you all the details, Mademoiselle, because it's quite entertaining... But, first, you must call your mother, who is surely in agony! Come, come, there's a telephone in the next room..."

Madeleine was so relieved that she felt a childish glee, and couldn't help herself asking:

"But you, Monsieur, how did you get in here?"

Saint-Clair replied with a smile:

"I have two faithful servants. One, Soca, hasn't yet met a lock that could resist his talents; the other, Vitto, knows how to use the kind of arguments that easily disarmed our enemy's servants. With such help, Mademoiselle, my friend Gnô and I were easily able to enter and rescue you with the greatest of ease. Your terrifying adventure only lasted one night. And, in the end, except for the fear you must have felt, you're not worse for the wear. You can return to your daily life as if nothing had happened."

"Return to my daily life... yes..." murmured Madeleine d'Evires.

It is commonplace to say that women are an unfathomable mystery, as much for themselves as for others. Did Madeleine recognize the note of disappointment and perhaps even regret in her own words?... But Saint-Clair and Gnô, wiser and more experienced, heard it. They looked at each other and smiled. They knew that the daily realities of life would soon bury whatever disappointment or regrets, conscious or not, that the young woman felt at this very moment.

The Nyctalope pointed at Godrey Cultnom, still dazed by the effects of Gnô's jiu-jitsu, and said:

"As for this gentleman, he must be held accountable for many more crimes than what he had plotted against you. Within our police force, we have a specialized unit that knows how to handle cases like his. Godfrey Cultnom will be tried, convicted, and dealt with accordingly... Gnô, keep an eye on him... I'll call the police to come and rid us of this loathsome individual."

Ten minutes later, Madeleine d'Evires sat in a large, comfortable automobile, between Saint-Clair and Gnô Mitang. They drove her home, where Madame d'Evires was waiting.

They quickly left, leaving mother and daughter hugging and kissing each other, amidst peals of laughter and tears of happiness.

As the two friends were settling back in their car, Gnô Mitang said with that spontaneous and surprising naiveté that he sometimes displayed, when the interests of his country were not at stake:

"Still, this adventure of one night could have ended up very badly for that young woman... In fact, I believe it was just about to take a turn for the worse when we broke in..."

The Nyctalope was an avid reader of Montaigne, the great philosopher, and said:

"Evil never truly wins, Gnô... You know that as well as I... And it is especially true where women are concerned... Especially a girl as strong as Madeleine d'Evires..."

Nevertheless, after a brief pause, he corrected himself and added, in a grave tone:

"Still, she might have suffered much... But Cultnom was a mongrel, and I can't imagine a woman of pure French stock becoming fully subservient, with or without sorcery, to a man such as he."

"I suppose you're right," said Gnô.

"Of course, I am!"

And Saint-Clair, happy, laughed. He was sure that he would always remember that adventure of a single night with great amusement, and would take pleasure in seeing Madeleine d'Evires again from time to time.

(July-August 1941)

The rest of the stories presented in this volume are arranged in chronological order. We begin with a tale by Travis Hiltz that takes place barely a year after the events narrated in Enter the Nyctalope. *Leo is 21 and doing his military service at the Saint-Cyr Military Academy; his father, struck by the evil Sadi Khan, is but a shadow of his former self, and will, in fact, pass away the following year. Robert Champeau is one of Leo's friends from the rugby club who assisted him in* Enter the Nyctalope. *This is the adventure that will determine Leo's future and propel him towards a life of adventure...*

Travis Hiltz: *First Steps*

Paris, 1900

Robert Champeau turned his roadster through the gates of the manor house and parked at the curve of the gravel driveway. He nodded a greeting to the gardener as he strode up to the front door.

This was not his home, but Robert was such a regular feature that the maid merely smiled and greeted him with a "He's in the library."

The stocky young Frenchman strode through the foyer and down a corridor paneled in dark wood. He entered a library, lined with bookcases, which contained three good armchairs, one of which was occupied.

Leo Saint-Clair sat at the far end. He was a tall, athletic young man with dark hair. He sat, hunched forward, a nearly empty glass in his hand with a smoldering ashtray perched precariously on one of the chair's arms.

"Leo?" Robert asked, tapping against the doorframe.

Saint-Clair blinked and looked up.

"What...? Oh, Robert, come in, man, come in!"

Robert went to perch on the armchair closest to Leo's and started a cigarette of his own.

"How have you been?" he asked, quietly.

"Checking up on me?" Leo asked with a smile.

"Well, let's be honest, you've been through a great deal in the last few months, enough to lay any ten other men low. The fellows and I were concerned…"

"…And you drew the short straw?" Leo asked.

"Something like that," Robert smirked. He sat back, relaxing at the sign that his friend was acting like his old self. "So, how are your parents?"

"Fine," Leo nodded. "Father is recuperating. He and mother have gone to stay with relatives in Banyuls."

"So, you've been playing lord of the manor, have you?" Robert asked.

'Something like that," Leo shrugged. "I've been overseeing the repairs to the house and thinking…"

"Really?"

"No jokes," Leo chided, good-naturedly. "After all we went through, I needed to think about what comes next."

"Next? What do you mean?"

"Come, now," Leo said. "I can see in the dark and I have not just been given a new lease on life, but this extra…vitality, I guess you'd call it… from my new heart… I should be doing something worthwhile…"

Robert nodded and sat, smoking and contemplating his friend.

"Is this because you believe that with great power comes great responsibility?" he asked, thoughtfully, "or having had an adventure, you now find ordinary life a bit too quiet for your tastes?"

"It's most likely something in between the two," replied Leo. "I may be looking for that next adventure, but I can still help people, do some good in the meanwhile. We made a difference, Robert, and I think I am still needed."

"It's very noble sounding," Robert said, "but how do you propose to go about it? Place an ad in the paper? Get yourself an office and hang out your shingle?"

"Yes, I see what you mean... There'd be a little too much sitting around and waiting," Leo nodded. "I could approach my father's friends in the government..."

"...And you'd also end up sitting and waiting," Robert said. "Look, Leo, you're my friend, and whatever you decide, the gang will follow you, but it's not as though you can just go looking for trouble in order to continue this... calling..."

"That's it!" Leo exclaimed, pounding his fist against the arm of his chair. "We won't sit around, waiting! We'll find someone who needs help, and then, in time, people will come to us!"

He leapt up from his chair, his earlier contemplative mood banished by a call to action.

"And I know just the place to look!"

"What...? Where...?"

"Where else? The newspapers!'

Three hours, a plate of sandwiches and a pot of coffee later, Robert and Leo had made their way through every newspaper they could lay their hands on. The large dining room table was covered with discarded pages, giving it the appearance of a field after the first snow of winter. Next to Leo's plate was a small pile of articles that had seemed full of promise.

Robert leaned back in his chair, rubbing at his weary eyes. He pulled his hand away and noticed it was coated with newsprint. Pulling a handkerchief from his pocket, he dipped it in his water glass and cleaned himself.

"I don't know, Leo," he muttered. "It seems we're looking for a needle in a haystack... We're not really detectives, which seems to be what most of these people need. It was as much luck as cleverness that let us track down the men who attacked your father..."

"How about this?" Leo interrupted, handing a folded paper to his friend.

"Ghostly sightings at the Louvre…?" Robert read. "I don't see…"

"No, not that one," Leo said, leaning over to point at the specific article. "This!"

"A séance?" Robert muttered. "That's what you want to do?"

"Oh course," Leo explained, "I know that most of the mediums out there are harmless cranks, but there are some outright swindlers taking advantage of people. With my ability to see in the dark, I could unmask these scoundrels…"

"I suppose," Robert shrugged. "But most are merely preying on citizens with more money than common sense."

"They're taking advantage of folk so blinded by grief that they're willing to hand over all they have to con men using the cover of darkness and a few conjurors' tricks to lie to them. Nothing would be hidden from me! I could easily separate the wheat from the chaff, spiritually speaking."

"True, and the fellows and I would be at hand if we were to encounter a true villain," Robert said. "But where do we start?"

"That shouldn't be too hard. There are hotels in Paris that have 'medium rooms' for the spiritualists. Séances have become a social event, like hiring a string quartet to entertain at a dinner party. If we check the society pages, I'm bound to spot one of my parents' acquaintances who would be willing to invite us…"

A week passed. Leo and Robert attended two séances and gained invitations to an additional four.

By the end of the second week, the Nyctalope and his friend had exposed three frauds, prevented the robbery of one of the hotels by the accomplices of a fake medium, and gained some notoriety for their actions.

Eventually, Robert decided that Leo was more than capable of dealing with the minor threats they encountered, and found his enthusiasm fading. Leo, on the other hand, filled with the thrill of the hunt, vowed to continue his efforts and promised to meet with his friend the following month to keep him updated on his progress.

"This is going to sound fantastic, but since it's being told to you by a man with an artificial heart, I'm hoping you will accept..."

Leo leaned forward, slowly rolling his wine glass between his palms, watching the red liquid swirl as he prepared to tell his story to Robert. It was exactly a month since their last encounter.

"Leo, you don't need to warn me," Robert interrupted, lighting a cigarette. "Whatever yarn you spin, I'll listen. Get on with it!"

Leo took a sip of his drink and began...

"Thanks to Monsieur and Madame Prillant, two friends of my father, I had been invited to a ceremony held at night in an elegant hotel Rue de Passy.

"After identifying myself, I was escorted through the elegant lobby and to a private located salon on the mezzanine.

"There, I met the Prillants and was given a drink before being introduced to another middle-aged couple.

" 'Leo Saint-Clair, may I present Mr. and Mrs. Baldwin from America,' said Prillant.

" 'Geo Baldwin?' I inquired, as we shook hands. 'The famous philanthropist? My father has often mentioned your name. I'm honored to meet you and your lovely wife.'

"The Baldwins responded amiably and made several minutes of chitchat before excusing themselves. Then, Prillant took my arm and steered me about the room to acquaint me with his fellow travelers in the higher realms of the spirits.

"Upon introducing me to a Miss Rosalyn Thornton, Prillant made some vague statement conveying the impression she was an actress or a singer. Madame Prillant obviously disapproved of the other woman and doubted the stated nature of her profession, but said nothing.

"I sipped my drink, nodding politely as I tried to eavesdrop on the swirl of conversation around me.

" 'I thought the Joneses would be joining us tonight?' Prillant asked Baldwin.

" 'I'm afraid not,' the philanthropist replied, lighting a cigar. 'It seems she took ill. Besides, they're still a bit shaken up after that, er, incident last week. I doubt we'll see much of them before they return to the States.'

" 'Yet, it looks as if the Jones family will be represented tonight after all,' observed Madame Prillant, nodding towards the oaken double doors.

"Two women had just entered; one young, barely out of her teens, though obviously pregnant with auburn hair framing a pale face and sharp black eyes; the other was older and vaguely matronly.

" 'Mrs. Anne Jones and her chaperone, Miss Loveday Brooke.'

"Upon being introduced to Anne, I was gifted with a brief smile and a glance from her dark eyes that gave a hint of something beyond her appearance of a respectable young socialite. I know you would have been tripping over yourself to win her attention and, for a moment, despite her 'condition', I confess that I found myself distracted from my mission.

"Then, one of the nondescript servants indicated that it was time to begin. I hung behind as everyone moved into the main room, in order to gain another chance to better look at the participants. In some of the previous séances I had attended, unscrupulous mediums had an agent planted amongst the guests to assist them with their charade. I pondered who might have been a likely suspect. Miss Thornton was said to be an actress, but that seemed too obvious… I knew the Prillants and trusted them from their years of friendship with my parents. The Baldwins seemed to be cut from the same respectable cloth as the Prillants, but 'philanthropist' was still vague enough to leave me wondering how Mr. Baldwin had made his fortune...

"The séance room was good-sized, done up in dark oak and windowless, dominated by a large rectangular table, set with the appropriate number of straight-backed chairs. At the head was an ornate chair for the medium. Set before it was an old-looking book, with two candles on either side. Two pale servants were drifting about the room, turning down lights, holding out chairs and lighting incense.

"The guests took their places, still chatting quietly as we all waited for the host. I was seated on the right side of the table, between Mr. Baldwin and Miss Thornton. Madame Jones, her chaperone, and Madame Prillant were across from me, with Monsieur Prillant at the end, across from the host's chair.

"Eventually, the medium was escorted in.

" 'Good evening,' he said, in a low tone, as he sat. 'I am Simon Orne. I hope you are all prepared to cross the great divide. Together we may find the answers that you seek.'

"The room was shrouded in darkness. The lights had been arranged to cast a shadow, like a hooded robe, across the medium. However, I could see him as clearly as if it were noon.

"Simon Orne was a middle-aged man of stocky build. His full beard and hair were streaked with grey. His suit, while of an elegant cut, struck me as being a bit old-fashioned. The other thing I noticed about him, which I knew my fellow guests were unable to see, was that while he spoke in a solemn tone, he wore a sardonic grin, and his eyes moved along the table, taking in each guest in a predatory fashion that, frankly, made my skin crawl. I wondered briefly if he, too, was capable of seeing in the dark. As his gazed moved towards me, I quickly shifted mine about, as though if I were struggling to see in the dim lighting.

" 'Please join hands,' Orne intoned, opening the ancient book before him, while his two helpers moved in to light the candles on either side. They gave off a wisp of smoke and a faint odor, hinting of grease and exotic spices. 'Clear your minds of all worldly concerns. Focus on those that have moved beyond that you wish to communicate with. Keep their faces in your minds... remember them... only strong emotions can help the spirits find their way back to this mortal realm.'

"Again, his tone was dead serious, but I could clearly see that he was merely play-acting. Mouthing words that, while convincing, filled his features with contempt.

"The lights were further turned down, until the twin candles were the only source of light in the room. I kept watching as Orne ignored the book in front of him and took a piece of black paper from an inner coat pocket and placed it upon the ancient tome. From across the table, I could see that the paper was brittle with age.

" 'Come, o' spirits, we entreat you,' Orne intoned. He traced a finger across the ancient page and began to move his lips, silently reading off it, while occasionally making an out loud statement to the guests.

"I found Orne's behavior odd, and completely out of character when compared to other mediums I had encountered previously.

"I glanced about the room, thinking that maybe Orne's play acting was mere window-dressing, designed to allow some confederate, one of the servants perhaps, to move undetected among us. But the only sign I could detect was the restless shifting of the attendees.

"By then, I had decided that Orne was a suitable candidate for the 'crackpot' category, rather than the 'criminal' one. But suddenly, a shimmer appeared in the air over the table. It gave off no light, but rippled, like heat haze... Then, reality itself seemed to tear and a hole opened in the air. It all happened in total silence. I only felt a prickling race up my skin and a twinge of pressure in my ears, as if some kind of sound was struggling to come through and my ears were incapable of translating it to my brain.

"I pulled my gaze away and looked around the table, but detected no sign that anyone else had seen whatever was occurring. Orne was still peering down at the ancient page, his lips moving in a silent incantation.

"I felt a deep sense of wonder, mixed with great anxiety, as I realized that, for the first time, a medium had truly pierced the barrier to the worlds beyond!

"There were hints of movement within the opening. I clamped my jaw shut to stop myself from crying out, as a vast bulk moved past the opening, its skin glistening like wet leather.

"I took a deep breath, struggling to stay calm. Whatever fantastic thing was occurring in the room, Orne and I were the only ones aware of it. I had to steel his nerves until I could discover the true nature of the phenomenon.

"The creature shifted its massive body and I found myself staring into a single eye, as large as a dinner plate, sickly yellow in color, and veined with threads of scarlet. Malevolence and hunger radiated from that alien orb. I could feel its emotions like a physical blow I began to notice that the other guests, while still oblivious to the thing's presence, seemed to be reacting as well. They shifted uneasily in their seats, and the hands I held were now damp with perspiration.

"The eye moved, taking in each guest in turn, and then something at the opposite side of the table caught its attention. The immense creature moved, the eye drew back from the opening, and tentacles, numerous and undulating like seaweed caught in the tide, snaked their way through the opening.

"As the first tentacles crossed over, I felt my stomach drop and my mouth grow dry. It was one thing to observe this monstrosity through the opening, as though looking at some denizen of the sea through the glass of an aquarium, but it was almost more than my brain could cope to have it push into the very room with us!

"The tentacles slithered and danced, groping blindly. They hovered over each attendee, coming within inches of touching us, but always holding back. Two things happened, practically simultaneously: the tentacles reached out and touched Anne Jones, causing her to cry out, while another pair lunged towards me.

"I flinched back, letting go of the hands I'd been holding and nearly toppling my chair over backwards. With the chain broken, and the guests startled from their concentration by these two outbursts, the tentacles withdrew back through the opening, which sealed itself shut, leaving no trace whatsoever.

"Two servants entered the room, turning on the lights as they did. I caught a quick glimpse of Simon Orne hurriedly closing the book upon the ancient page he had held.

"I got unsteadily to my feet; my hands were still shaking slightly. I made an excuse of feeling ill from the fish I'd had at dinner and pointed out that Madame Jones seemed in need of attention. Then I made my way to the door.

" 'Most likely still distressed over that horrid business with the attack on his father,' I heard Madam Prillant say before I left.

"I quickly returned home and I've been here since," finished Leo, pausing to gulp down the last of his drink.

"Leo, I… I don't know what to say…" Robert began.

"You might suggest a sanitarium," Leo said, with a bitter chuckle. "I understand there are several nice ones nearby…"

"Stop it," Robert snapped. "I… I need to think!"

"I've been thinking for days now, and it's done me no good," Leo shrugged. "I don't expect you to believe me…"

"But I must, Leo!" Robert muttered, emphatically. "I know you! You could no more lie than you could flap your arms and fly to Mars. It's just, if you aren't lying, then I have to accept this… creature… as real. How do we deal with it?"

"I wish I knew," Leo shrugged. "I've been knocking my head against the wall, trying to make sense of it all…"

"Are you certain it wasn't some kind of illusion?" Robert asked. "A trick, maybe…?"

"For what purpose? I was the only one who could see that thing, and Orne had never met me before. I am convinced the creature was real, and that Simon Orne is a true mystic, either controlling it, or merely setting it loose in our world."

Leo reached for his drink, brought it to his lips, realized it was empty, and, with a sigh, set it back down.

"I've got to admit it, Robert, I feel up against the wall. I'm the only one who knows Orne is up to something bad, but at the same time, I haven't any idea what to do about it. My intuition tells me that his plans somehow involve Anne Jones..."

"The history professor's wife?" Robert asked.

"Yes. I seem to have an advantage, though. Orne doesn't know about my abilities, so he doesn't realize that I know... But what should my next move be?"

Both young men sat in thoughtful silence, Leo toying with his wine glass and Robert blowing smoke and watching it drift upwards and away.

"Maybe," Robert said, "we're looking at this the wrong way?"

"How so?"

"You're getting all stymied, trying to deal with the creature, which seems a pretty hopeless task, but we have shown some talent when it comes to earthly intrigue. What if we get at it from that side?"

"Again, how so?" Leo asked.

"Focus on the other guests," Robert suggested. "Let's find out about Orne and what his interest in Madame Jones is."

"Good thinking, Robert," Leo nodded, his old energy returning. "Yesterday, I received a message from Prillant, inquiring about my health, conveying the concerns of the others, and telling me that Orne had agreed to hold a second séance if the attendees wished it. All the others have agreed, so we have five days to come up with a plan..."

Two days later, Leo and Robert were seated in a private dining room at a fashionable Paris restaurant. Both young men had a sheath of papers by their plates and talked while they ate.

"The good news," Robert said, "is that the Prillants are as noble and upstanding as you'd said. Same with the Baldwins. However, I did discover something interesting about Miss Thornton…"

"She's not an actress?"

"Oh, she is, but Rosalyn Thornton is not her real name."

"Hardly surprising. It's a bit too fanciful for her."

"Her real name isn't much better. It's Lily Flowers, and she's every bit as disreputable as Madame Prillant suspected."

"Maybe we should get Madame Prillant to do our detective work for us," Leo joked. "One can find wonders if one listens to the Paris social circle. So, what makes Mademoiselle Flowers so disreputable?"

"She is suspected of being connected to the criminal gang, the Vampires," Robert replied.

"Interesting," Leo said, leaning forward. "There have been two attacks on the Jones family since they came to France: an attempted robbery of their hotel suite and young Madame Jones was almost kidnapped, attending the opera."

"The plot thickens," Robert added. "Strange they let her go about with nothing but a chaperone."

"Apparently, it's the women we need to keep an eye on. Anne Jones' chaperone is not what she appears to be either." Leo said, glancing at his pages. "Miss Loveday Brooke may look like your maiden aunt, but she is, in fact, an accomplished detective."

"We are surrounded by intrigue," Robert said, shaking his head.

"It's amazing that an American capitalist and a career politician are the most innocent of the lot," Leo added, buttering a roll. "The problem now is, how it all fits together. Everything points to Madame Jones being at the center of it, but is it all connected?"

"How so?"

"The robbery attempt and kidnapping makes sense, now that we know about the Vampires involvement, but what about Orne? Why would someone who can control that monstrosity need to ally himself with a gang of thieves?"

"What do you think we should do?" Robert asked.

"Pay Mademoiselle Flowers a visit," Leo replied, grimly.

Lily Flowers was an attractive woman, if you overlooked the excessive make up, and the fact that her wardrobe was somewhat out of fashion. She strolled down the dimly lit boulevard toward the rundown hotel she called home. Her steps were a bit unsteady as she made her way past the concierge and up the narrow flight of stairs to her room.

No sooner had she closed the door behind her and started to reach for the candle on her bedside table when she heard the key click in the lock.

"Good evening, 'Miss Thornton,'" said a voice. "I wonder if I could have a word?"

She spun and there was the young, dark haired man from the other night, the one with the weird eyes.

"You...?" she muttered.

Despite the darkness he was looking straight at Lily. Her hand trembled as she lit the candle.

"You're in no danger from me," said Leo. "I just want to talk."

"You're not with the police...?" Lily asked, sitting down on the edge of her bed.

"No, but they will listen to me, if I'm not happy with your answers," Leo said. "Tell me what you and Orne are up to."

"Orne?" She asked. "The medium? I don't know what you're talking about!"

"Are you telling me that you attended that séance because of your interest in the spiritual world?" Leo asked, not bothering to hide his skepticism.

"No, it's... we... I've got nothing to do with Orne," she stammered, looking everywhere in the room, but at Leo.

"There have been several attacks on the Jones. Are you also telling me that's also a coincidence?" Leo asked. "I and the police will find that hard to believe."

"Just ask your questions," Lily grumbled, with a defiant glare. "Stop threatening me with the police! Whatever Orne is up to has got nothing to do with me."

"Fine, let us speak plain. You occasionally work for the Vampires. Are you after Madame Jones' jewels? Did your friends attempt to kidnap her?"

"Kidnap... no...!" Lily exclaimed. "We were after her jewels... that's all. I almost pinched her necklace when you and she raised that fuss at the séance."

"Thank you, Mademoiselle Flowers," Leo nodded, as he stood up.

"Is that all?" Lily asked, confused. "You are just going to leave? You aren't going to try to make a deal with me?"

"I don't have to," Leo replied. "You will do two things for me, however: first, you will tell your 'friends' to leave the Joneses alone. Find some other rich family to plunder; second, you will be attending the séance, this coming Tuesday."

Lily Flowers and the Nyctalope locked gazes for several heartbeats.

"My 'friends' won't like this," She said.

"Then, they can come discuss the matter with me," said Leo. "A bunch of theatrical gangsters are really the least of my worries. I look forward to seeing you Tuesday, 'Miss Thornton.'"

The next afternoon, Leo found himself at the café across the street from the Jones' hotel. He sipped his coffee and peered at his newspaper, without really seeing the print. He had left a message, but, after three cups of coffee, was on the verge of giving up and moving on to the next idea on his list.

"Monsieur Saint-Clair, may I join you?" Loveday Brooke asked.

Leo looked up at the lady detective. She was about 30, not tall, not short; neither dark, nor fair; neither handsome, nor ugly. Her features were altogether nondescript. Leo would walk away from his meeting with no strong recollection of her, besides a slight look of disapproval.

"Ah, Miss Brooke, of course," Leo said, standing and offering the detective a seat. 'Thank you for accepting my invitation."

"You had a matter you wished to discuss?" she ignored his greeting and turned to the approaching waiter. "Tea please."

"Er...yes," Leo mumbled, sitting down, wondering why he was more intimidated by this woman than the one connected to the most notorious criminal gang in France. "Well, yes... er... you see, I have been investigating various mediums plying their trade in Paris..."

And so, haltingly, feeling slightly nervous talk, he explained about his investigations (leaving out the otherworldly monster) and his suspicions that Anne Jones was at the center of this diabolical web.

Miss Brooke sipped her tea and listened, showing as much reaction as if she was a statue dedicated to stern schoolteachers.

After he finished, she studied him thoughtfully for a moment, dabbed at the corner of her mouth with a napkin and then nodded.

"I see."

Leo waited several moments, before realizing she had no intention of adding to her previous utterance.

"I'm sorry... you see what exactly...?"

"Monsieur Saint-Clair, I agreed to meet with you only through the respect I have for your father. I have read of your recent 'exploits,' and I must say I have little patience for amateurs," Miss Brooke said. "I am aware of the situation concerning Mrs. Jones; this is why I agreed to act as her chaperone. I, as well as the police, are also quite aware of the identity of Miss Thornton, and what she and her associates are attempting. I am sure you have only the best of intentions, but

67

your efforts threaten a very delicate situation. I would appreciate if you would leave it to me to deal with it."

"Yes, but what of Simon Orne?" Leo sputtered.

"He is a lecherous charlatan, and therefore of little consequence," she said, standing up. "I am sure that Mrs. Jones and her husband would join me in thanking you for your concern. Good afternoon, Monsieur Saint-Clair."

Leo slumped back in his chair as Loveday Brooke walked away.

Robert gave a slight wave as he noticed Leo entering the bar. His friend stalked over to the small corner table, sat and helped himself to Robert's drink.

"Did you enjoy your chat with Miss Brooke?" Robert asked.

Leo sat, arms crossed, grumbling to himself.

"I didn't catch the last part," Robert said, signaling the waiter to bring them another round. "The part after sanctimonious…?"

"Miss Brooke appreciates our amateur efforts," Leo explained, sullenly, "but reassures me she has the situation well under control."

"If she is aware of Lily Flowers, isn't that a good thing?" Robert asked. "Doesn't that mean that we can just focus on whatever Orne is up to?"

"Yes, she's done all the heavy lifting, and all we have to deal with is an unearthly monster," Leo said, with sarcasm.

"Oh, by the way, I'm not sure if this means anything to you," Robert said, reaching into his coat pocket and drawing out an envelope, "but this message was waiting for you at the hotel."

The envelope held a single sheet of heavy, cream-colored paper. Leo read it then handed it to Robert.

"It's suitably vague, but the writer seems to know something about Orne," Leo muttered. "It's worth accepting his offer. He wants to meet with us."

"Who's he?"

"He says his name is Sâr Dubnotal."

Upon arriving at the address they had been given on the Avenue de l'Opéra and introducing themselves, Leo and Robert were taken by the building's concierge into a second, smaller house, built at the back of the property, There, they were ushered into an ornately decorated sitting room, a blend of the homey and the exotic. A grim, dark-haired Italian woman of uncertain age escorted them in and then gracefully drifted out of the room, as Sâr Dubnotal entered.

A slim man of medium height, his skin was tanned, his dark beard trimmed, and his suit of a fashionable cut, but adorned with an eastern sash and a white turban.

"Monsieur Saint-Clair," he said, smiling and giving a slight bow. "My thanks for accepting my invitation. I was hoping I would have the chance to speak with you."

"What is this all about...um...Sâr?" Leo started.

"Please be seated."

Leo settled into an over stuffed armchair, while Sâr Dubnotal sat on a leather couch.

"I wish to speak with you about your recent attendance at several séances over the past month," the Great Psychagogue said. "What has brought about this sudden interest in the spirit world?"

Leo was not sure why, but this eccentric-looking man gave off such an air of knowledge and trustworthiness that he found himself relating the tale of his recent search for adventure and purpose.

The Sâr listened with a look of keen interest and a slight, knowing smile.

"Quite noble, and no less than I would expect of the son of a Saint-Clair."

"You know my family?" Leo asked, surprised.

"I will leave it to your father to relate that story," the Sâr chuckled. "My interest in your recent activities concerns the séance overseen by Simon Orne..."

Leo paused, pondering how to respond, when Sâr Dubnotal raised a hand to gain his attention.

"Please, I do not ask for trivial reasons. This matter is important, and I need you trust me. Tell me all that occurred and be assured that no matter how fantastic your story is, I will believe you."

The two men locked gazes, meeting in a form of silent communion. Whatever Leo Saint-Clair saw in the other man's eyes, it was enough to convince him that he had, at last, found an ally against the otherworldly monster. He told the Sâr the entire story of his encounter and of his struggles to come up with some plan of action before the second séance.

The Psychagogue sat, still as a statue, his fingertips steepled as he took in the younger man's tale.

"It is as just I feared," was his only comment once Leo was finished. "The timing of this could not be worse."

"How so?" Leo asked. "You do believe me then? What is that… creature?"

"I do believe you, my friend. I have been investigating Simon Orne for some time, and was aware he was planning to use his studies of the dark forces, but had no idea he would attempt such a risky move. The creature you saw is known as Baal. It is as powerful an entity as it is malevolent."

"I believe that Orne and this… Baal are after Madame Jones," Leo explained. "But my friend and I are, admittedly, out of our depth here. If you have knowledge of this sort of thing, we would gladly accept your help."

"I will do what I can, but unfortunately, I am involved in some other matters that I dare not put off I must leave Paris tonight. All I can give you at this time is advice."

"I will take whatever help you can give," Leo said. "How do we stop Baal and keep Anne Jones safe?"

"You have the right idea, in that protecting Madame Jones should be your focus. Baal is both unearthly and power-ful. I warn you that attempting to meet him head on would be foolish," the Sâr advised. "Concentrate on the young lady and disrupting whatever ritual Orne is using to summon Baal."

"You mean that strange page?" Leo asked.

"Yes, from your description, it would seem Orne is using a page from that accursed tome, the *Necronomicon*. I'm also interested in those candles. To digress for a moment, tell me about this kidnapping attempt on Madame Jones."

"From what I read, a pair of men attacked her and her husband at the theater," Leo said. "They had knives, but there was a constable nearby…"

"No one was injured?"

"Nothing worth noting," Leo shrugged. "One of the attackers tried to slash Anne Jones. From what I can tell, he ended up nicking her ear and cutting some of her hair…"

"Ah!" the Great Psychagogue exclaimed, snapping his fingers. "A bit of hair! Drops of blood! No doubt, Orne is using that to lure Baal!"

"I'm glad you understand what's going on," Leo grumbled. "I'm still in the dark and feeling quite useless."

"Not at all, my friend," the Sâr said. "You have given me all the information I required. Here is what you must do: Baal is too powerful to be confronted directly by the likes of you, so you must focus your energies on protecting Madame Jones and disrupting Orme."

"Yes, but how…?"

"The page from the *Necronomicon* and… let me think… the candles… yes, the candles must contain the bits of hair and blood," said the Sâr, thoughtfully stroking his beard. "Get them away from Orne and you will disrupt his plans. He is a knowledgeable occult scholar, but also cautious to the point of cowardice. Once his scheme has been exposed, I believe he will surrender the field, rather than risk a confrontation with you."

"If I'm able to disrupt this ritual, what will happen to Baal?" Leo asked, anxiously.

"It is Orne that has allowed Baal to pierce the barriers between our worlds. If Orne is disrupted, the rift will close and Madame Jones will be safe," the Sâr said. He then reached over to an ornate carved wooden box, and drew out a small

71

pouch, made of rough, dark cloth and tied with a piece of twine. He held it out to Leo.

"If you must face Baal," he said, "this may help you."

With a nod, Leo took the pouch, peering at it in thoughtful confusion.

"I am sorry I cannot do more," Sâr Dubnotal said, getting to his feet. "I will be returning to Paris within a week. If all goes well, I hope you will have a story to tell me over dinner."

"Thank you," Leo said, rising and shaking hands with the mage. "If all goes well, I will be more than happy to buy you dinner."

Two nights later, Leo found himself back at the round table with two candles and the ancient book at its head.

Robert was down in the lobby, along with Inspector Milfroid and several policemen, waiting for a signal from the Nyctalope.

Leo mingled amongst the other guests, who were, for the most part, unaware of the sinister drama that was occurring. The exceptions were "Roselyn Thornton," who was looking anxious and distracted, and Miss Loveday Brooke, who seemed as serene as a statue.

Soon, they were once again seated around the table, all in their original places, and the lights began to dim. Leo reached into his coat pocket and touched the small pouch. He was not sure what it contained, and maybe it was meant to have no more effect than to reassure him.

The hushed chitchat of the group faded into silence as Simon Orne entered the shadow-filled room.

"Good evening," Orne said. "I am pleased we can resume our journey into the spiritual world."

He looked about the table, nodding and smiling solemnly at each person. Perhaps it was his imagination, but Leo was sure Orne's gaze lingered longer on him and Madame Jones.

"Please join hands," Orne intoned, taking his seat. "We will begin."

One of Orne's pale servants moved in to light the candles and then all other lights in the room were extinguished.

Leo looked about; the servants had left the room and the others were shifting about a bit. Lily Flowers was looking particularly nervous.

Simon Orne, under the cover of darkness, unseen by all save the Nyctalope, opened his book, placed the page from the *Necronomicon* upon it, and began to speak, keeping the guests focused while he went about his true business.

"Now, focus our minds on those we wish to contact across the veil," Orne intoned.

Leo watched as he silently mouthed the words contained on the dark page.

Again, the air above Orne began to ripple and split, and though he was expecting and braced for the occurrence, Leo winced at the faint, otherworldly smell; his eyes watered as the first streams of unearthly light came through the rift.

Struggling to keep his breathing steady, Leo watched as the huge bulk of Baal moved ponderously past the hole between the worlds. The creature's tentacles, like hungry snakes, undulated through the rift. Leo tensed, preparing to move. Orne was still reciting from the *Necronomicon* and the other guests sat, unaware of the horror that drew ever closer to them.

The tentacles, brown and moist, snaked ever closer to Anne Jones. Even with her eyes closed, the young woman flinched back, sensing the unseen menace hungrily reaching for her.

With both Orne and his inhuman ally focused upon Anne Jones, the Nyctalope sprang into action. He pulled his hands free and leapt across the table, sliding down its length until he had reached Orne. He grabbed the candles and used them to ignite the page from the *Necronomicon*. The mystical items and the old book flared up into a column of flame that scorched the ceiling. The mystic exclaimed shrilly and dove from his chair, scrambling across the carpet to escape.

Leo rolled away from the fire and lunged towards Anne Jones, reaching her at the same time as Baal. Tentacles shot forward, one wrapping itself around her bare forearm; another striking Leo's back like a whip.

He winced in pain, then rolled and came off the table. He clamped his hands together and brought them down upon the tentacle. There was a wet sound and a stinging sensation, like lemon juice poured on a cut, and the tentacles' grip loosened minutely.

Leo scooped Anne up in his arms and lurched away from the table.

"Move away!" he shouted to the others. "Someone get us some light!"

Leo let go of Anne. She swayed on her feet and held onto a sideboard to stay upright.

"Are you all right?" he asked.

"I... think so," she mumbled, rubbing at her arm. "It stings..."

"You had best be able to explain yourself!" Miss Brooke snapped.

"Help your charge," Leo replied, turning back towards the table.

Meanwhile, the edges of the rift seemed to expand and contract. Leo thought it seemed to be getting smaller, but if it was closing, it was doing it so slowly that they were still in danger.

The monstrous Baal was struggling to squeeze through the small, otherworldly doorway, his tentacles pressing against the edges as if to push it open by sheer physical effort. Several tentacles snaked through, thrashing blindly in an attempt to reach their intended prey.

With the candles and page destroyed, Baal was suddenly made visible to the others and panic ensued. The older gentlemen did their best to get their near hysterical wives out; Lily Flowers bolted for the nearest door, having pushed past Leo as she did. (To her credit, Leo discovered later that his pocket watch had gone with her.)

Miss Brooke and Anne Jones were edging towards one of the doors, but were blocked by the whip-like tentacles. Simon Orne, in his attempt to escape, had stumbled and struck his head against the heavy arm of his chair. Stunned, he struggled to regain his feet, a trickle of blood on the right side of his face.

Leo grabbed him by the lapels and roughly dragged the occultist to his feet.

"Close that rift! At once!" he demanded, emphasizing the urgency by shaking Orne.

"I… I can't," muttered the occultist. "The *Necronomicon*… was the only thing that allowed me to hold Baal… without it… it will not listen!"

"Will it close on its own?" Leo said, with another shake. "Can Baal keep it open? Tell me!"

"It… may… I don't know… Baal will not listen!" Orne replied, slapping weakly at Leo's hands. "Must escape… It will be angry with me… I cannot stay!"

With a growl of frustration, Leo hurled Orne away. The mystic stumbled backwards, hit the wall and slid into a senseless heap.

"What do I do now?" Leo asked, looking about the room. He, Miss Brooke, Anne Jones and Orne were the only remaining occupants. The rift seemed to be growing smaller, but Baal still had enough room to maneuver and was close to reaching Anne with the few tentacles he could squeeze through. She and Miss Brooke were huddled down, close to the baseboard, in hopes of remaining out of the creatures' reach and being able to crawl to the door.

Leo reached in his pocket for his gun, doubtful it would be any help, and brushed against the small pouch that Sâr Dubanotal had given him.

"Miss Brooke!" Leo shouted, pulling out his gun. "I'm going to fire at that thing. When I do, you must get Madame Jones out of here!"

The detective nodded her understanding. Leo then turned and fired. Baal squirmed, seeming to feel no more pain than a whale stung by a mosquito. He then turned his gun around and used it to club the tentacles reaching for the women.

As soon as Baal's attention was focused on him, Leo lunged forward, dropping his gun and grabbing hold of two of the tentacles. A third tentacle whipped forward, cracking him across the face, then another wrapped around his right leg and began to drag him towards the rift.

The Nyctalope dug his heels into the carpet, as he struggled to break free. The plan was to keep the creature distracted long enough for the women to escape. But now he was the one in peril. Deprived of his prey, Baal seemed in need of someone upon whom to vent his frustration.

Baal yanked Leo violently forward, and the young hero was driven into the edge of the oaken table hard enough to knock the breath out of him.

Gasping, his eyes watering, Leo pulled one of his hands free and snatched the tiny pouch from his coat pocket. He drew back his hand and threw it into the rift. Upon striking the otherworldly atmosphere, the cloth sparked and burst into flame. It gave out a sickly-sweet odor, which briefly overpowered the smell of Baals' native realm.

Whatever it contained, the contents of the pouch had a visible effect on the creature. The tentacles holding Leo began to tremble and the vibration that drifted through the rift grew to a skull-rattling screech.

Leo pushed off against the table and was able to break free of Baal's grip. With a final throb of frustration and rage, the rift slammed closed. This violent closure cut through two of the tentacles, severing them cleanly and leaving them writhing on the table, like fish flung up onto the shore.

Leo stumbled backwards and fell to his knees. He was now alone in the room. He pulled in a ragged breath and rubbed at his extraordinary eyes, as all the tension and fear drained from him. Somehow he had not only saved Anne Jones, defeated Orne and his monstrous ally, but also managed to survive. He sat back against one of the chairs, drew a cigarette from his surviving coat pocket and with a slightly trembling hand lit it.

"I hope there aren't all going to be like this," he muttered.

Days later, the two young men gathered around a table relating events to Sâr Dubanotal. The mystic nodded occasionally, but mostly stayed silent. Once they had finished the tale, he took a final sip of tea and smiled.

"Well done, my young friends," he said, with a single clap of his hands. "You have done admirably!"

"Yes, once my father smoothed things over with the hotel management, the police, and helped us concoct a suitable cover story," Leo grumbled. "Otherwise, you'd be visiting Robert and me at some asylum."

"Don't mind him," Robert said. "He thought that, as the hero, the damsel would be showering him with affection. Instead, the damsel is soon to be a mother and Miss Brooke and her husband have gotten her as far from Paris as possible, as it's full of lunatics and young ruffians."

"Ah yes," the Sâr chuckled. "Fighting the forces of darkness can be detrimental to one's social standing. I don't know how it slipped my mind to warn you."

"Yes, yes, enjoy your laugh," Leo said, his scowl softening. "Despite it all, we did good. I suppose I should appreciate that. What of Baal?"

"And what about Orne?" Robert added.

"According to my investigations," Sâr Dubnotal said, helping himself to more tea, "Orne has fled France. Whatever he hoped to accomplish by summoning Baal has failed, and with the loss of the *Necronomicon* page he will be lying low for some time. As for Baal, it is not, as some might think, an evil creature. It is no more evil than a shark, or any other predator. Only if it summoned to this world by evil or misguided individuals, can it become a danger."

"So, on the bright side," Leo said, "I can go about my business without fearing its vengeance."

"Baal will not be seeking you," the Great Psychagogue said, gravely. "But should you cross paths again, it may remember you. In Baal and Orne, you have made powerful enemies."

"Not to mention antagonizing the Vampires," Robert reminded him. "You managed to accomplish quite a bit. Luckily, that's the end of it."

"Is it?" Sâr Dubanotal asked, peering over the edge of his teacup.

"Don't get too comfortable, Robert," Leo said, smiling. "I think it's only the beginning."

This story does not feature the Nyctalope, but his arch-foe, Baron Glô von Warteck. In Lucifer, La Hire *writes: "Glô spent ten years [1902-12] traveling for the purpose of study. He discovered all the secrets that a transcendental mind was able to discover, working in the synagogue of Amsterdam, the synod of Dordrecht, the library of San Marco in Venice, the Vatican library in Rome and the Hagia Sofia Mosque in Constantinople. He acquainted himself with the Copts of Egypt, the Maronites of Mount Liban and the monks of Mount Carmel; then he went to Sana'a in Arabia, to Ispahan, Kandahar, Delhi, Agra and finally to Benares, where he lived with the Brahmins for five years." This is an untold tale of one of Glô's adventures...*

Matthew Dennion: *The Angel and the Exorcist*

Giza, 1906

"We pray for thee, in the name of the Father, the Son, and the Holy Ghost. Amen"

The priest made the sign of the cross over the young man as he backed away from him. He removed his handkerchief and dabbed the sweat from his brow. The heat in the tent made wearing the ceremonial robes exhausting, but they were an integral aspect of the ritual.

Father Lankester Merrin took one last look at the man tied to a cot and shook his head, uttering a silent prayer as he exited the tent. It was late in the night and the priest had been inside the tent all day; outside, he was greeted by the gathered workers from the excavation.

The scene was frighteningly reminiscent of what had happened years ago. It was the first time that Father Merrin had encountered Evil. The first time he had been called upon to perform an exorcism. He could still see that young girl being held down by her family as he had driven the demon from her body.

The priest closed his eyes for a moment and silently asked God for strength. When he opened them, he directed his gaze at the group around him. The workers were from various religions: Muslims, Copts and Jews. As he walked past them, they looked to him for answers but he had none to give them. He walked across the campsite to meet with the man funding and supervising the dig.

Father Merrin was the lead archeologist not because of his religious title—a priest was not needed to minister to the workers—but because of his scientific background. He had hoped that reinvolving himself in another archeological expedition, designed to probe the Great Pyramid at Giza, would help him put the events of his past behind him.

The fact that a worker had dared enter the Sphinx was perplexing. First, the government had not given the team permission to explore it, and stealing was a serious offense. The entire dig was in jeopardy of being closed based on the actions of this man. What was even more surprising was that he had entered the Sphinx despite its rumored curses. Most of the Egyptians viewed the Sphinx as a cursed monolith. To them, the thought of entering it was more terrifying than facing a firing squad. Yet, despite these fears, this man had opted to enter the statue...

Late that night, a light had been spotted inside the ancient Sphinx. Father Merrin had led a group of workers to investigate it. When they had reached the structure, they had found the entrance forced open and discovered the man in the first chamber of the statue. He had been searching the walls for something, but when he had seen Father Merrin and the others, his behavior had quickly changed.

He had stepped back from the wall, shrieked in terror, and ran into the wall at full speed. He had fallen to the floor, stunned, his nose clearly broken as blood spattered across his face and chest.

The man had quickly stood up and repeated the shocking behavior. After bouncing off the wall for a second time, he had turned to Father Merrin and had screamed that Lucifer was in his head, causing him to hurt himself.

With the help of the other workers, the priest had restrained the man. Father Merrin had looked into the intruder's eyes and had seen the same look of fear and despair that he had dicovered in the girl, years ago.

The man had been taken to a cot and had been tied down for his own safety and that of the other workers.

While he was being tied down, he had begun to curse at the priest in languages the Egyptian did not know... French, English, German, and even Dutch... All the while continuing to profess that Lucifer was in his head.

Father Merrin had sighed, knowing that speaking in languages unknown to the host was a clear sign of possession.

It was then that their financial benefactor, Baron Glô von Warteck, had entered the tent. The Baron had walked up to the cot and had looked down upon the bloodied worker. He had shaken his head, and had directed his attention to Father Merrin.

The two had spoken in French so as not to cause a panic among the other workers. To the priest's surprise, it had been von Warteck who had first mentioned the Rite of Exorcism, and had asked the priest if he was capable of performing it. Father Merrin had been hesitant until the man tied to the cot had begun vomiting upon himself.

Von Warteck pleaded with him, indicating that, while he did not believe in possession, the workers clearly did. The Baron professed his concern that the workers would not continue the exploration of the pyramid until the man was freed from the demon that possessed him.

Father Merrin recalled the terrified looks on the faces of the gathered workers; it was that, more than von Warteck's pleading, which had convinced him to perform the exorcism.

Prior to entering the Baron's tent, Father Merrin took one more look at the gathered workers, still transfixed around the afflicted man's tent. He felt that his efforts thus far had done little to quell their fears.

The priest took a deep breath and entered the tent. He could feel a strange sense of pressure building inside his head. The Baron was seated in a chair behind a small table, reviewing some ancient scrolls. He seemed in deep concentration and took a moment to notice the Exorcist.

"Ah, Father, how goes your efforts with our possessed worker?"

The priest sat down across from von Warteck.

"Baron, there is something I must make you aware of… I have performed an actual exorcism prior to this…" The priest waited for a response of shock or disbelief from the Baron, but the nobleman simply stared straight ahead, as if in deep thought. After an uncomfortable silence, the priest continued: "I have no doubt that something is in control of that man's mind and body, but the way he reacts to the ritual is very different from my last encounter with an actual case of demonic possession. This man shows some of the same mental symptoms, if you will, but none of the physical characteristics. Demons will often cause a man's skin to lose color and become porous. Writing may manifest itself across the body. Here, none of these things have occurred. Perhaps whatever is afflicting that poor man is some Egyptian deity, over which I have no power."

Once more the priest waited for a response, but the Baron simply stared straight ahead. Suddenly, he sprang to his feet and exclaimed:

"Finally, I have it!"

Father Merrin gave the Baron a quizzical look.

"Forgive me Father, my thoughts were elsewhere. Please, come for a walk… We have much to discuss."

The two men walked out into the night and von Warteck turned in the direction of the Sphinx.

"Look at it, Father. The Sphinx is awe-inspiring, is it not? Do you know that legends claim it contains hidden chambers which are repositories for ancient artifacts of immeasurable power?"

The priest sighed.

"Yes; it is a shame we do not have permission to explore it."

The Baron laughed and continued speaking, giving no credence to the priest's comment.

"In fact, there are texts which suggest that the Serpent Ring of Set is stored inside the Sphinx. The ring was reported to increase the powers of the man who wielded it. The wizard Thoth-Amon was said to have become not uunlike a god when he wore it..."

When the men reached the base of the Sphinx, the priest was shocked to see a group of four workers emerge from within the statue. The priest ran over to the group and asked:

"What in God's name were you doing in there?"

The workers walked past Father Merrin as if they were in a trance and approached the Baron.

"They won't respond, Father, for they are under my control. I can see that you do not yet understand. You see, I have mesmerized them. My thoughts are their thoughts; I control their every action. Much like the man you have been trying to exorcise."

"Baron, why have you mesmerized these people? Why did you have me go through the charade of an exorcism?"

One of the workers handed the Baron a ring shaped like two snakes wrapped around each other and attempting to swallow a jewel. The Baron slid it onto his finger.

"The Ring of Set! You see, I had hoped the first fool I sent into the Sphinx would find it, but he was discovered before I could locate the ring. I then attempted to mesmerize you, Father, but you are a man of impregnable will power and a credit to your Faith. While I could not control you, I was well aware of your past when I hired you, and thought you might prove useful in setting up a diversion, if I needed one. I never really cared about the dig.... Recovering this ring was always my true goal. But mesmerizing thirty men might prove too difficult, even for me. However, mesmerizing one was well within my abilities. When he was discovered, it was easy to make him appear to be possessed, thus diverting both your attention and that of the other workers away from me. After that, with all your attention concentrated on that poor fellow, mesmerizing a few more men and finding the ring was easy."

Von Warteck held the hand with the ring up to his face; the ring began to glow.

"With this ring, I can easily control all of Egypt, and, as my power grows, the entire world will soon bend to my will."

Father Merrin looked past the Baron into the camp, and saw all of the workers pouring out of their tents in the same trance-like state. The Baron smiled.

"I am sorry, Father, but I cannot allow you to live while I am learning to master the ring. Nothing can stand in my way."

The gathered workers began to lumber towards the priest. Father Merrin turned and ran in the direction of the Great Pyramid. He dashed inside as the Baron mocked him:

"You are only delaying the inevitable, Father! My slaves will not tire until you are dead. Make peace with your God, for soon, I, Lucifer, will be the only deity worshipped in this world!"

Father Merrin, quickly lit a torch and began running deeper inside the pyramid. The priest hoped somehow to lose the mesmerized men and then make his way back outside.

He came to an intersection which he did not recognize; he considered which way to go when the horde of mesmerized men began to pour into the chamber. Without further thoughts, the priest ran down the corridor to his right.

As the corridor ran deeper into the ground, it turned left and right at varying intervals. Before long, Father Merrin regretted his choice, feeling that, in attempting to lose the workers, he had lost himself.

The priest ran until the corridor ended in a large burial chamber. He sprinted to the back of the chamber and found a massive sarcophagus embedded in the ground. Even faced with his own demise, the archeologist in him was curious. He dusted off the lid and read the inscription aloud:

The god of justice and protector of the weak.

Father Merrin smiled. Even in this darkest hour and in the bowels of the Earth, God had found and comforted him.

The horde of mesmerized workers entered the chamber chanting, "All Hail Lucifer!"

From behind them, von Warteck taunted the holy man.

"It seems as if you have run into a dead end, Father!"

The priest made the sign of the cross and fell to his knees.

The holy man prayed, not for his life, but for the lives of the workers, asking that, somehow, the Lord save these poor souls from the human demon which had possessed them.

Father Merrin's prayers reached not only Heaven but the sarcophagus behind him. The lid to the ancient coffin slid open. From seemingly nowhere a bat circled the room.

Father Merrin turned around to see a massive golden being with a skull for a face, holding a long staff and adorned with a blood red cape, standing atop the open sarcophagus.

To the ancient Atlanteans, this being had been known as *Ogon Bat*, a protector sent from the past to fight evil. Father Merrin, however, saw the creature through the context of Egyptian history and Christian theology, and whispered to himself: "The Angel of Death."

Ogon Bat turned his gaze on the kneeling priest. The protector nodded at the holy man, and then directed his attention to the workers. They continued to approach the priest chanting the name of the man who controlled them.

The Golden Protector sprang from atop his coffin. As he landed, he slammed his staff on the floor. The moment it touched the stone floor, the entire pyramid began to shake. The mesmerized workers all fell to the ground unconscious. With speed that defied explanation, Ogon Bat flew across the room and grabbed Lucifer by the throat. His powerful grip quickly forced the madman to his knees.

Von Warteck glared in defiance into the empty eye sockets. Lucifer's face strained and the Serpent Ring's glow grew to a near blinding intensity as the mesmerist attempted to force his will on Ogon Bat. But the Golden Protector simply shook his head, proving that the Baron's powers were useless against him.

The madman's eyes rolled into his head as Ogon Bat choked the life out of him.

As von Warteck gasped for air, Father Merrin ran up to his savior.

"Angel, please, spare this man's life. He may be misguided, but he is still a child of God, and deserves a chance at redemption."

Ogon Bat looked into the eyes of the priest and released his grip on Lucifer, letting the unconscious villain slump to the floor. He then grabbed von Warteck's hand and removed the Serpent Ring from it. He held it in the palm of his hand and then closed his fingers. When Ogon Bat opened his hand, the dust that was the Serpent Ring fell to the floor.

The Golden Protector nodded at Father Merrin and then strode back to his sarcophagus. He climbed into his coffin and the lid slid closed, returning Ogon Bat to his long slumber.

The workers awoke free of Lucifer's control and Father Merrin directed them back to the surface. Once there, he would alert the Egyptian authorities to von Warteck's unapproved exploration of the Sphinx. They would know how best to deal with him... Surely, the man had learned his lesson and would never try to pull such a stunt again...

In The Nyctalope on Mars, *Jean de La Hire tells us that Leo spent most of the year 1909 exploring darkest Africa. That's where he met his rival, Koynos, who later became a member of the XV. This second tale by Matthew Dennion is the story of one such encounter, pitting both the Nyctalope and his rival against a world-famous Jungle Lord...*

Matthew Dennion: *Dangerous Territory*

Central Africa, 1909

Taking a deep breath of the hot and humid air, Leo Saint-Clair swung his blade and cut another meter of dense forest out of his way. He had been cutting through the jungle for several hours during the night. Most men would have given up hours ago; the exertion was tremendous and the Dark Continent was living up to its name. Even a better conditioned man would have already dropped from exhaustion or been forced to camp from sheer lack of visibility. But Leo Saint-Clair was much more than a better conditioned man; he was the Nyctalope. His artificial heart provided him with a near endless supply of energy, while his enhanced eyes gave him the perception of the jungle at midday rather than the depth of night. His physical attributes conferred him some advantages in the jungle at night, but it was he sense of adventure that drove him on.

Leo thrived on the thrill of adventure, on the excitement of exploring a land no white man had ever visited. He smiled as he reflected upon the term "white man." This area of the jungle was reported to be totally uninhabited by any humans, including natives. As he crouched down to examine the jungle floor, the terrain told him a different story. The indents in the ground, the relatively new branches which currently barred his

87

way, as well as bits and pieces of sharpened wood and clay, showed that a local tribe had recently been through here. He was sure that, if he continued on his journey, he would find them settled deeper in the jungle, probably near a river or a stream as a source of water. Whether the tribe was a relocated one, or one which was as yet totally undiscovered, made little difference. He would be the one who discovered them; he would be the white man who had delved into the uncharted jungle to make discoveries that were previously thought to be nonexistent. He would have set out to explore that which others were afraid to penetrate, and return with amazing discoveries. Amazing discoveries like the unknown species of primate which he had recently encountered. The mysterious ape species was slightly smaller than a gorilla, but much large than a chimpanzee. Leo was sure of something else: these creatures were omnivores. The group he had found dinning on a boar was proof of that. Leo's artificial heart raced as he dared to believe that these apes may be part of the so-called "missing link" in the evolutionary chain! They might represent one of the many steps nature had taken morphing beast into man. The apes might be a storehouse of secrets which could enhance mankind's knowledge of the human condition.

To Leo Saint-Clair, this was worth more than any monetary treasure. The sense of accomplishment and triumph over nature, the possibility of increasing man's knowledge, were the abstract rewards that drove him into the unknown. This was one of the challenges he would overcome for no other reason than he was the Nyctalope!

Leo stopped in his tracks, his sensitive eyes perceiving a light in the distance several kilometers ahead of him. He could see that it was being partially blocked by some obstruction. He nodded and thought that the first goal in his quest had nearly been achieved. The light was that of a campfire, and it was obscured by a wall. He had found the supposedly non-existent tribe. If any humans knew about the great apes he had encountered, it would be them. Leo could achieve two goals simultaneously: he would record the habits of the tribe, while using their village as a base to study and document the unknown apes. With any luck, their water source would connect to larger river, which he then could use to navigate quickly back to civilization. He hoped that he may even find the opportunity to slay one of the apes and return with its body as proof of his discovery.

Leo hoped the tribe would be friendly. Given his physical appearance, he surmised that, even if the natives were cannibals, they would find his heart inedible and consider him either a demon or a god. As a last resort, should they attack him, a few shots from his pistol should scare them into submission. The Nyctalope calmed his mind for the encounter and began to cut a straight path through jungle toward the village ahead.

Drenched with sweat from the sweltering heat, Leo reached the village shortly after dawn. He examined the exterior of the camp: it was surrounded with large, wooden walls and two large doors which lead into the jungle. It was easy to guess that the walls had been designed to protect the people from the wildlife. Two of the guards spotted Leo from the top of the wall. They became excited and quickly called other members of the tribe to see him.

As the tribe began to gather atop the wall, the large doors swung open and an overweight, elderly man came out, followed by a second man whose head was adorned with feathers. Leo quickly surmised that he was being greeted by the Chief and, most likely, the Witch Doctor. The wind kicked up and blew the still smoldering ashes from the village. As the smoke assailed Leo's nostrils, his head shot back in a reflexive action. He had been exposed to this odor before—it was the smell of burnt human flesh! There were a number of possible explanations, but the most concerning was that he was dealing with cannibals.

The Chief stepped forward and uttered a greeting in a dialect similar to the other tribal languages of the region, which Leo had heard before and basically understood. It lent credence to the theory that this group was a displaced offshoot of a larger tribe, rather than a newly-discovered one.

The Chief bowed down and then addressed Leo:

"Mighty spirit of the jungle! I, Mbonga, chief of this tribe, welcome you to our village. You have heard our prayers and crossed the dread jungle through the dark of night to avenge the loss of our most honored prince."

Leo decided that his best of course of action would be to play the role of the mystical entity in question. If the superstitious tribe thought he was such a spirit, they would be less likely to attack him. So he stepped forward, placed his hand on the shoulder of the chief, and said:

"Arise, Mbonga. I have traveled from afar to answer your prayers. Repay me with food and water while I consider how to avenge the loss of your prince."

Mbonga stood up and took Leo inside the walls of the village. It consisted of some thirty mud huts, decorated with ivory tusks. The Chief's own hut was located at the center of the village, next to the hut containing the remains of what Leo now knew was the funeral pyre of the dead prince.

The Chief escorted Leo into his hut and had food and water brought for them.

After a meal of deer meat and some water, the Nyctalope asked the Chief to fully inform him of the situation regarding the death of the prince. Mbonga told the story of how his son, Kulonga, had crossed a nearby stream to go hunting. The prince was not seen again until his body was found, stabbed through the heart, stuck in a tree. Later that night, a demon of the forest, in the form of a great, hairless white ape, had dropped down from the trees and terrorized the village. Mbonga was sure that it was this same white ape, a demon, which had slain his son and placed him in a tree. He pleaded with the "spirit of the jungle" to avenge the death and free his village from the incursions of this fearsome demon.

The story intrigued the Nyctalope.

"Where in the jungle may I find this hairless ape monster"?" he inquired.

"He has been seen with the great apes on many occasions."

The obsession with adventure and exploration which drove the Nyctalope began to surge again through his veins. His mind was ablaze with thoughts. The creature in question lived with the mysterious great apes he had seen on his journey, and was white and hairless as well... Could he simply be an albino, or some other aberration, or perhaps a further step up the evolutionary ladder...?

Leo looked directly at the chief and said:

"Can you provide me with a guide to take me to the place where the great apes live?"

"Of course, mighty spirit, but..."

The Chief was interrupted by a member of the tribe rushing into his hut.

"Mbonga!" shouted the man. "More spirits are coming! From the waters!"

The Chief's hut quickly emptied as Leo, Mbonga and the Witch Doctor raced to the river which ran across the back of the village. The trio stopped at the river's edge and watched as several men pulled canoes ashore. Leo's face contorted into a look of disgust as he realized who exactly these "spirits" were: It was his rival Koynos and his team, already conversing with one of the natives.

As the trio reached Koynos, it was clear that he had already grasped the situation from talking to the villagers, and had also decided to play upon the natives' superstitous beliefs. He stepped up to Mbonga and said:

"Mighty chief, we, spirits of the river, have come from far away in answer to your prayers. We will assist you in ridding your village of this curse... once the proper tribute has been paid to us."

Mbonga bowed.

"Great spirits of the river, what tribute do you require for ridding us of the white ape demon?"

The numerous ivory decorations had not escaped Koynos's attention. He responded:

"One of my boats will be filled with the tusks of the behemoths you have slain; the other will be filled with five of your women."

Then Koynos faced the Nyctalope and addressed him in French:

"I suspected that, if I paddled far enough up this river, I might find something of value. In addition to the money I'll get for the ivory and the slaves, I'll also be taking credit for discovering this village, and I'll soon have the head of this albino gorilla to mount on my wall. Getting rich is a wonderful thing, but besting the great Nyctalope in the jungles of Africa is truly an exquisite pleasure."

Leo's hatred for his rival, as well as his pride, overcame him. He sprang forward and grabbed Koynos by his shirt.

"You, swine! If it wasn't enough that you would steal the credit for discovering this tribe, you would rob them of women and their treasures as well?"

As Koynos' men aimed their rifles at Leo, Koynos laughed.

"I would not consider it stealing... It is more like natural selection, with the more evolved species taking what the lesser is unable to protect."

Mbonga stepped forward.

"Spirits, please! I can see that you are rivals. The jungle and the river are at constant war with each other. Every year, the rains come, and the river claims a section of the jungle, only to have the jungle claim it back in time, until the next rains. Thus, the spirits of the world battle for supremacy, just as the jungle and the river do themselves. The price requested by the river spirit shall be met, but it will be paid to the spirit who brings me the head of the white ape demon. As the jungle spirit arrived first, he shall attempt to slay the demon tonight. Should he fail, the river spirit will attempt to slay the demon on the following night!"

The entire tribe had gathered around the river at this point. Mbonga turned to his tribe.

"My people! He proclaimed. "Within the next two nights, we shall see the death of the white ape demon!"

A loud cheer echoed through the crowd.

Leo was led to a hut where he could rest, as were Koynos and his men. Leo sighed, musing that at least Koynos's presence assured him of one thing: the river was a route he could utilize to return to civilization once he had examples of the unknown apes. The Nyctalope smiled. Soon, he would not only have the thrill of the hunt, and the exhilaration of a potentially monumental discovery, but he would best his rival as well. With that thought, he drifted off into a much needed sleep.

Night had fallen in the jungle. Leo's native guides had left him after walking for several hours. They refused to go any further for fear of the demon. The Nyctalope crept silently through the dense foliage, sliding between obstacles rather than hacking through them. He did not want to give his prey any advanced warning of his approach. His addiction to adventure had all of his senses operating at peak efficiency. He was fully aware of his surroundings. He could hear all of the sounds of the jungle, from the trumpeting of the mighty elephant to the howl of the elusive monkey and the roar of the terrible lion... It all blended together in a primal symphony through the night.

From the dense trees ahead of him, he heard a terrible call that caused even his artificial heart to skip a beat. It was the call of the bull ape. Leo peered through the foliage and saw the mysterious apes which he had previously encountered moving in the trees ahead. He kept low to the ground; the wind was blowing towards him so he had little fear of the beasts smelling him, but he did not want to test the acuteness of their eyesight. These apes were indeed different from any other known primate. They resembled chimpanzees, but were much larger and walked on two feet for far greater distances.

Leo had been following them for several minutes when a massive figure dropped from the trees into the midst of the apes. His back was toward the Nyctalope.

Leo stared intently at the creature, and mentally sized him up. The beast was large, well over six feet tall, and heavily muscled. The Nyctalope was amazed that he had climbed through the trees and dropped to the ground without causing the slightest sound. At first glance, he thought that this beast was a further step in the long evolutionary journey from ape to man, until the creature turned around.

It was then that Leo saw a human face. It was well defined, with dark black hair that ran down to its shoulders. The man was clearly Caucasian, yet his skin was bronzed as if he had spent the majority of his life under the unforgiving sun of Africa...

As the Ape Man turned toward him Leo could see that he was wearing a loin cloth, and was crudely armed with a large knife that seemed of European design.

There was no doubt in Leo's mind that this was the White Ape Demon who had slain the Chief's son. What astonished him was the apes did not seem to mind that man walking among them! Leo's surprise only grew when the man, through a series of grunts and howls, seemed to communicate with the beasts.

Leo's mind raced back to the story he had heard of a young boy in India who had been raised by wolves, as well as the tale of ten-year-old George Villiers who had been rescued by To-Ho, the leader of a peaceful tribe of ape-men in the jungles of Sumatra. Both boys were reported to be able to run though the jungle and even communicate with the beasts. Leo guessed that, perhaps, this man had found himself in a similar situation and may have been raised alongside the apes...

Leo cursed to himself as he felt the wind shift and blow his scent toward the apes. The White Ape Demon sniffed the air, looked directly at Leo, and once more uttered the war cry of the great bull ape as he beat his chest. He growled at the gathered apes. The simians responded by climbing the trees and fleeing away from Leo's position.

The Nyctalope sprang in pursuit of the group. He watched in amazement as the White Ape Demon scaled a tree, and then jumped from tree to tree with the apes. The speed with which he moved was incomprehensible. The Nytalope's finely tuned muscles strained mightily to keep the White Ape Demon and the great apes in his line of sight. He thought he had a chance to catch up with them as they approached a wide stream which cut through the jungle. Leo could see the Ape Man's body silhouetted against the Moon as the leapt from a tree top and cleared the water in a single bound. Leo dived into the water and quickly swam across.

As the Nyctalope climbed out of the stream, he saw the Ape Man and the apes come to an abrupt stop. The White Ape Demon turned and watched Leo's ascent from the bank of the river, and anger flared in his eyes. He beat his chest and yelled a blood-curdling scream. In a single motion, the Ape Man leapt toward Leo, pulling his knife from his loin cloth.

The Nyctalope's body reacted solely on reflex from years of training. As his opponent hit him, Leo dropped his body flat on the ground, grabbed the Ape Man's hands, placed his foot in this midsection, and used his foe's own momentum to flip him into the water.

The Ape Man had no sooner sunk beneath the surface that he came crawling out of it on all fours with a speed that took the Nyctalope by surprise. The White Ape Demon wrapped his powerful arms around the French explorer and shook him with such fury that Leo's neck nearly snapped from the sudden jolt. The Ape Man then hurled Leo into the trunk of a tree. The Nyctalope bounced off the tree and fell to the ground. He looked up to see his attacker already standing above him.

Leo delivered a quick combination of a right and left to the Ape Man's ribs, followed by an uppercut to the jaw. As his foe staggered back, Leo slid his right leg behind him and tripped him to the ground. Drawing his knife, the Nyctalope sprang on the jungle man. But the White Ape Demon placed his own legs on Leo's chest and, with a powerful thrust, sent him flying backwards. Leo landed in a crouching position, just as the Ape Man crashed down onto his back and sank his teeth into his shoulder. Once more, Leo's body reflexively resorted to his combat training by grabbing his opponent's hand and using a judo throw to send the giant flying into the foliage. The Ape Man tumbled down a hill, which led back to the stream.

It was then that Leo heard the other apes shrieking behind him. He took his eyes off of his foe long enough to notice several infant apes clinging to their mothers.

It was then that Leo realized what he had done.

The apes had fled from Leo until they reached the water. By crossing the stream, he had invaded their territory. It was then that the Ape Man had challenged and attacked im! He must be their alpha male, and was acting to protect his family.

Thoughts raced through Leo's mind. Kulonga had also crossed the river and invaded the apes' territory. Leo shook his head. Could he blame any man for slaying an intruder in order to protect his family—even if that family was comprised of animals?

Leo had come to the jungle seeking adventure and knowledge. He had thought that killing one these beasts, and bringing its body to civilization, was the most effective method of learning from them. As he stood in the dark jungle, waiting for the Ape Man to renew his attack, he saw the she-apes holding their young for protection. He realized that he had already learned much more from their actions than he ever could by killing one of them.

Leo felt ashamed of his pride for a moment, until the Ape Man came out of the jungle and, once more, uttered his battle cry.

Leo dropped to his knees and placed his head on the ground. The White Ape Demon approached and, again, beat his chest and screamed, but Leo maintained his position, head to the ground.

The Ape Man snarled at the Nyctalope, but then took a few steps back. Leo remained in a submissive position and began to crawl backwards, until he felt his feet hit the water. He took a deep breath and slowly backed into the stream, never taking his eyes off the White Ape Demon.

The Ape Man stood on the bank of the river until the Nyctalope reached the other shore and disappeared into the jungle.

Once Leo had left, the Ape Man unleashed his deafening victory cry for all of the jungle to hear.

As Leo began the trek back through the jungle toward the village, he came face to face with Koynos and two of his men. Leo's nemesis laughed:

"The mighty Nyctalope was driven from the jungle by a savage and a group of monkeys! I knew you would find the beast for us if I followed you tonight. You move fast, Saint-Clair, and after you took off after those animals, it took us a while to find you, but I made it in time to see you surrender to a savage!"

Koynos cocked his rifle.

"You were a fool, Saint-Clair, to go after that wild man with only a knife when one well-placed bullet will drop him. I'll take out a few monkeys for good measure as well. Then, it's just a matter of hauling their stinking carcasses back for the Chief to collect my rewards."

Leo grabbed Koynos by the arm.

"For your own sake, Koynos, I am pleading with you to not cross that river."

Koynos pulled his arm free, glared at the Nyctalope, and waded into the water.

Leo watched as his rival and his men came ashore across the stream. The first man had no sooner reached the bank than the Ape Man fell upon him and drove his knife into the man's heart.

Koynos attempted to train his rifle on the White Ape Demon, only to have his foe swat his gun into the water, and knock the explorer to the ground. As the Jungle Lord attacked Koynos' second man, Leo dived into the water. But the second man was already dead before the Nyctalope was half-way across the stream.

Koynos was attempting to rise to his feet as Leo grabbed him from behind and forced him to the ground, head down and arms out, as he himself had done moments ago. Leo commanded:

"Be quiet and stay still!"

Koynos complied as the Ape Man loomed over them. The Lord of the Jungle bellowed his challenge again at the two men. When they remained in the submissive position, he took a few steps back. Leo gestured for Koynos to start backing into the stream. The Ape Man watched as the two men crossed the water and disappeared into the jungle.

For the final time that night, the White Ape Demon's victory cry could be heard echoing through the jungle.

The two explorers wandered into the village the following morning. The natives came out to meet them, led by Mbonga and the Witch Doctor.

"Where are the other river spirits and where is the head of the White Ape Demon?" asked the Chief.

Leo sighed and replied:

"The White Ape Demon has slain two of the river spirits; he is very savage and powerful. Mbonga, I suggest that you give up your quest for revenge and order your people never to cross the water on the other side of these hills. That part of the jungle belongs to the White Ape Demon."

Mobonga shook his head,

"No, spirit! I am Mbonga! I am king of the jungle! I shall go where I please!"

Leo looked Mbonga in the eyes and said:

"Then, great king, you shall die as surely as your son did at the hands of the White Ape Demon."

The two adventurers walked back to Koynos' canoe, boarded it, and headed back down river.

Leo pondered the events that had transpired since he had arrived. He had discovered a previously undocumented tribe. He had thought he had found a missing link—and perhaps he had. The great apes he had just come across certainly did not belong to any of the currently known species. He had come searching for adventure, and he had undoubtedly found that. He had pursued the apes, attempting to learn about the human condition from creatures he had assumed were a step below humans on the evolutionary scale.

He looked over at Koynos, the man who was willing to kill another human for nothing more than ivory and slaves... Leo himself had decided to slay one of the apes for what he had convinced himself were scientific reasons...

He then considered the Ape Man, a supposed savage who had viciously attacked and killed men when his family was threatened. Yet, this man who had been raised by wild beasts, had let the very men who had threatened his family go unmolested when they submitted.

Leo was sure that Koynos would have given no such quarter, and wondered if his own family was similarly threatened, would he not slay the attacker on the spot?

This thought, along with that of the she-apes cradling their young, melded together in the Nyctalope's mind. He had indeed gained some insight into the human condition, and wondered if the apes were truly a step down the evolutionary scale from humans...

This wonderful mini-remake of the 1955 British film classic The Dam Busters *introduces the Nyctalope to Edwin Arnod's classic Martian hero, Lieutenant Gullivar Jones. It also functions as a prequel to our own Gullivar Jones novel,* Egar Allan Poe on Mars, *published by Black Coat Press...*

Martin Gately: *Dam Busters of Mars*

*Dedicated with great affection and respect
to Sir Barnes Wallis, inventor of the bouncing bomb
and real life science wizard, as well as to
Wing Commander Guy Gibson VC and the men of
617 Squadron – the bravest men who ever flew.*
M.G.

The Hither Land Alba Patera, Mars, 1911

The zerlat curled contentedly at Gullivar Jones' feet. Liquorice black and shaped like a deformed bullet, the creature defied precise taxonomic classification, even here on its native Mars. It had seven stubby tentacles and a v-shaped gash of a mouth that was reminiscent of a shark's maw. However, it had proved itself a thousand times to be more loyal, affectionate and courageous than any terrestrial hound could be.

Gullivar tamped some more Red Weed tobacco into the bowl of his pipe and lit it—it had taken years to get used to this stuff—and occasionally he still had a hankering for the taste of some Kentucky fire-cured leaf. As he looked up from his pipe, he saw that his old friend Samoht Yor had gotten served and was returning from the bar. Samoht wove his way skillfully through the crowd without spilling a drop from the two flagons of poiré on his tray. Samoht sat down and passed

Gullivar his drink, then addressed himself to another of his purchases, a paper bag of freshly deep fried Martian elk rinds that was already turning wetly translucent due to the grease coating its contents.

"Well," began the Earthman. "You didn't invite me here to watch you snack... What did you discover on this secretive expedition of yours? Where the Devil have you been these long months?"

The Martian Science Wizard smiled and took a long draught of his drink before replying:

"Myself, and a large number of my colleagues in the Science Guild, plus a full contingent of guards, porters and servants have journeyed beyond the borders of the Hither Land, past the Rock Snake Hills, into the uncharted lands beyond..."

"You never go anywhere without a reason, Samoht. What did you discover?"

"Initially, as expected, we encountered the last of the gargoyle-like insect folk, who are locked in perpetual internecine hive wars. They gave us little trouble; once we had cleared their territory, we were within sight of our goal: The Hinterland Volcanic Range. The nesting ground of the Manta Dragons and their larger, deadlier cousins the Lava Dragons."

"Surely those creatures are pure myth," stated Gullivar flatly. "I've heard tales of them, but have never encountered any during my travels."

"During your time on Mars, they have been hibernating. We found three caves inhabited by the dormant dragons, and two of these contained clutches of eggs."

"Good for you, Samoht! You'll be able to raise your own baby dragons on a Science Guild dragon farm."

"That is not our intention, as well you know, Gullivar. In the ancient tomes of our guild, dragon yolk is said to be a super-explosive. We now know from our tests on the score of eggs that we recovered that this was no idle speculation. The eggs contain the most explosive chemical mixture known to Martian science. And we have need of a super-explosive, do we not?"

"Oh, not this again! I thought I told you to drop it... I want to find a way to free the Hither People enthralled to Ar-Hap, not massacre them all. Your plan was crazy, and worse than that, even you—the most brilliant man on Mars— couldn't figure out a way to make it work."

Samoht fixed Gullivar with the twinkling gaze of his sapphire blue eyes.

"There are some problems that cannot be solved by a lone warrior with a sword; problems which, in this case, cannot be ignored or put off. I have applied all of my ingenuity, and I can see a way through this now. With luck, we will be able to save our society from the monstrous thing that Ar-Hap is growing in the Utopia Planitia Lake."

"What about the Hither People—my people—the ones in the slave camp at the base of the dam? How can we rescue them?"

"We cannot. They are doomed, Gullivar. Their free will has been destroyed by Ar-Hap's mind control device. He was running it at dangerously high levels for months while they constructed the dam. They will be little more than zombies. Your plan to lead a rebellion within the camp was, I am afraid, an impossible fantasy."

"This lake monster that he's growing... What do you call it?"

"The Dagoniah."

"If it comes this way, I'll go out and kill it... Take a whole army with me if I have to."

"Gullivar, even now, with the Dagoniah still in its fetal form it is hundreds of feet long, you would not be able to kill it. In its adult shape, it will be like a walking mountain. A titan under the influence of Ar-Hap. Consuming and sparing only as he sees fit. The lake is its womb; it holds now, not water, but amniotic fluids created in Ar-Hap's factories and directed to the lake via the Thither Land canals. If we destroy the dam, the fluids will drain away in a colossal flood and the monster will be left floundering and helpless like a jelly fish."

"Even so, how are we supposed to deliver ordnance de-rived from dragon eggs to the wall of the dam? You couldn't answer me that last time either."

"Well, now I can—or rather, I'll show you at dawn to-morrow at the town reservoir. But the attack will not be easy. According to our spies, new defenses have been installed on the dam: weapon emplacements that shoot electricity, just like lightning bolts. They call them electro-mirrors."

In the darkness of the alcove next to Gullivar Jones and Samoht's table, the occupant stiffened slightly at the mention of the word "electro-mirrors." The figure sitting there, appar-ently minding his own business, but in reality eavesdropping, was difficult to make out. He wore a black metallic uniform and a black cloak which seemed to allow him to blend with the shadows; at his belt was a long leather holster containing a revolver which fired electric bullets. Atop his head was a pro-tective helmet of an unusual design, which included a combi-nation visor and periscope. At present, the visor was up and this allowed for the display of the man's most striking charac-teristic: his eyes. They could easily have been mistaken for those of some nocturnal predator. These eyes were obviously designed to do only one thing—to see in the dark as easily as a normal man sees during the day.

These were the eyes of the man known to some as the Nyctalope. His real name was Leo Saint-Clair and Gullivar Jones would have been astonished to realize, if he had known, that Saint-Clair was a fellow traveler from Earth. Three weeks before, one of the outposts of Argyre Island—the location of the Nyctalope's base on Mars— had come under attack from an unknown force and, during the conflict, several electro-mirrors had been captured. The Nyctalope now knew that the attacking force was some of Ar-Hap's bestial Thither Folk soldiers. The electro-mirrors were devastating weapons devel-oped by the Nyctalope's one time enemies, the XV.

The politics of Mars were far more complex than the Nyctalope could ever have suspected upon his arrival on the Red Planet. At that time, he knew only of the Martians described by the historian H G Wells—these beings they now referred to as "Kephales." Now, he was aware of the peaceful Hither people and their famous protector, Lieutenant Gullivar Jones; their enemies, the tribute-demanding Thither Folk, led by the dictator Ar-Hap, as well as the various other creatures, such as those his men had nicknamed "roche-serpent" and "les insectes gargouille."

The Nyctalope was deeply concerned about the electro-mirrors being used to commit some kind of wholesale geno-cide and had taken it upon himself to go on a solo mission to recover them. It was not by chance that he happened to be here, in this rather pleasant tavern in the Hither capital. No, he had been following Jones all day. The work of the genius Samoht Yor had greatly intrigued the Nyctalope; there was only one thing to do now, sit here drinking poiré as inconspic-uously as possible and then spy on Jones and the Martian Sci-ence Wizard and see what plan they had in mind for the de-struction of the dam at Utopia Planitia.

The Nyctalope took another swig from his crystal flagon and savored the taste. He had already obtained the seeds from some Martian pears so that his men might enjoy poiré too—fruit trees did not grow naturally on Argyre Island, but he foresaw the building of hot houses that could perhaps be tend-ed by the women—it would be an enjoyable pursuit for them.

A little while later, Samoht Yor had consumed the con-tents of his snack bag; both he and Gullivar Jones had drained their flagons and got up to leave. Their exit was impeded by a group of well-wishers. Jones had been a well-known figure for years; and, by virtue of association, the zerlat was one of the most famous animals in the kingdom and highly popular in its own right. The admirers bullied Jones into being allowed to buy the zerlat a drink—its love of vintage Insect Folk mead was legendary.

"Very well, but only one bottle," chastised Jones.

Everyone then watched as the zerlat used the prehensile suckers on his tentacles to uncork the bottle. He then put it to his lips and glugged away until the bottle was empty, spilling surprisingly little. After this, the zerlat's entire body seemed to vibrate, rather like a tuning fork. This was the zerlat equivalent of wagging its tail. After, Jones went back to his shared royal apartments at Princess Heru's palace, while Samoht headed towards his lodgings near the guild. Not much later, the Nyctalope, too, left the tavern, but it was impossible to discern his ultimate destination. He simply melted into the night.

Dawn broke slowly over the Hither City reservoir. The coral pink sky promised another rainless day, with such clouds as there were scudding innocuously towards the horizon. Gullivar Jones looked around; there was no one here at all. Where was Samoht? It wasn't like him to oversleep. Could some enemy have...?

Gullivar's train of thought was interrupted by a screech from high above. He squinted up into the rosy firmament where he could make out a dark wheeling shape, perhaps a thousand feet up. It was a bird, a massive Martian bird, something like a condor. No, wait. It was a hawk. A malagor hawk, as big as Pegasus, and, like the winged horse, capable of carrying aloft a rider. The hawk swooped lower and lower, circling and looking for a place to land. Gullivar recognized the distinctive purple and gold robes of the rider. It was Samoht Yor all right.

"Good morning, Gullivar! You asked how we would deliver the ordnance. Well here's how... From the air! The hawk has a special harness which holds a Manta Dragon egg and a catalyst fuse... I want to conserve the Lava Dragon eggs for the actual attack. Now watch this!"

The hawk bore Samoht and its deadly payload back into the sky. The bird then banked sharply and lost height until it was about a hundred feet above the water. It looked like Samoht was using the reins and some kind of hook-ended prod to urge the bird lower, but the hawk was having none of it. It maintained roughly one hundred feet on its level approach to the western shore. Suddenly, the great turquoise egg was released from the leather harness. The egg turned end over end as it fell and then struck the water.

Gullivar was astonished to see that the egg's forward momentum caused it to skip across the surface of the reservoir like a powerfully thrown football. It left a trail of splashes behind it and it seemed to be only about twenty yards from the shore when it disintegrated. Sections of egg shell cart-wheeled randomly across the water and the viscous gold and blue contents of the egg spread out from the point of impact. Then, somehow, the catalyst fuse sparked and the yolk ignited producing a blinding white flash followed by a polychromatic flame. The surface of the water blazed intensely and the flames changed hue constantly, as if rotating through the color wheel of the visible spectrum.

Samoht brought the malagor in to land. The bird's wings flapped in a braking motion as it neared the ground throwing up a cloud of dust and dirt. The science wizard dismounted, but kept a tight hold of the hawk's reins for the explosion had served to make it skittish.

"I dropped the egg from too high—that's the main problem I'm facing—the hawks hate water and they're nervous of the sound of the explosion; they learn fast and what they learn is that they don't like the shockwave from the blast either – it bothers their equilibrium in the air. But we've got to try—got to keep training them. If we can train a hawk to get down to sixty feet, my calculations say this will work," explained Samoht.

"Your plan is dead in the water, my friend. Even if you could get a hawk to overcome its fears, it must be well over two hundred and fifty miles to Utopia Planitia. The bird would be totally exhausted. Neither use nor ornament," said the Earthman.

"Gentlemen, I like this plan," said a voice from the rocks somewhere behind Gullivar.

Gullivar Jones spun around already drawing his cutlass.

"Please, do not be alarmed," stated the helmeted figure in black coolly. "Like you, Lieutenant Jones, I am from Earth.

You can perhaps recognize my accent? I am Leo Saint-Clair, the leader of the French Expeditionary Force on the Planet Mars."

"I don't see how that is possible," said Gullivar, his mouth wide with astonishment.

"And neither do I," added Samoht. "The only safe and reliable way to travel between the spheres—short of astral projection—is to make use of the special transport carpets developed by the Science Guild some decades ago. It is unlikely in the extreme that one of those is available to you. I would know about it."

"Well, there is now a new way to journey to Mars—in flying vehicles called radio-planes. Several hundreds of my compatriots are with me here, on Mars, at Argyre Island. But all of that is unimportant right now. What matters is the destruction of our common enemy—Ar-Hap. Forgive me for spying on you just now, but I believe that when the technology at my disposal is added to your plan it would be perfectly capable of succeeding. Come, I want to show you something..."

The stranger's self-confidence and charm were both convincing and infectious. He seemed to be a born leader of men. Gullivar was unsurprised that such a man would be the leader of a vast expedition from Earth. At the same time, he was slightly jealous. He always had to work hard, it seemed, to win people over, and his unique position as the only Earthman on Mars had been instantly and permanently eroded; "flushed down the crapper" was the phrase that sprang to mind most readily, in fact.

Samoht tied the malagor's reins to a stake he'd placed in the ground earlier; then, he and Gullivar followed the black clad stranger to an open area behind a butte. The Nyctalope went over to an object that was almost completely obscured by a covering of cut branches with very dense foliage. He dragged the branches off one by one until the vehicle beneath was revealed. The craft was a metallic grey and obviously constructed from some light steel alloy; there was a cabin with three red leather upholstered seats, one forward for the pilot and two aft for crew or observers. The ship had two propellers and hinged, articulated wings, the action for which was powered by a sophisticated mixed system of hydraulics and pneumatics.

The Nyctalope gestured to the craft.

"This is one of our smaller aerial vehicles, my men call this type 'The Fly,' They are used mainly for reconnaissance. This variant with the two passenger seats is one that I personally requested to be built. Come on inside, I'll take you for a spin."

"There's no gas envelope," observed Gullivar. "What keeps it up in the air?"

"It's an ornithopter... The action of flapping its wings helps to keep it airborne, just like a bird. But unlike your hawks, it can fly very low over water. It would make the perfect delivery system for your deadly eggs. "

Gullivar and Samoht both shook their heads dubiously.

"I suppose it is possible that an alien race might develop working technologies very different from our own," mused Samoht.

"Our machines are not so very different to those of the Kephales," said the Nyctalope.

"Who are they?" puzzled Gullivar.

"I am forgetting that the Hinterland volcano area forms a most effective barrier between your lands and those of your war-like neighbors to the North-East. The Kephales are the Martians who invaded Earth," explained the Nyctalope.

"A lot seems to have happened while I've been away," said the American.

Five minutes later, the Nyctalope's ornithopter was soaring over the Hither City. Saint-Clair took it in lower and Samoht could make out the towering bronze statue of Lu-Pov, the founder of the Science Guild, in the central piazza. Gullivar then tapped the Nyctalope on the shoulder and pointed out Princess Heru's green marble palace. The walled garden in the centre of the complex was large enough for the Fly to touch down in. The black clad pilot set the craft neatly on the lawn, frightening the life out of a couple of gardeners who scurried away. Saint-Clair, Samoht and Gullivar disembarked and headed into the palace proper. The armed guards arriving on the scene recognized Gullivar and Samoht and stood down.

The trio entered the palace and stumbled on Princess Heru just as she was emerging from her personal courtyard ablutions pool. Martian women are not noted for their modesty. In fact, Heru enjoyed both the blush that reddened the face of Samoht and the gaping jaw of the magnificent figure in the black uniform. It would not be an exaggeration to say that the Nyctalope was stunned by Heru's beauty. Her hair was darker than coal and possessed of a natural luster that could have been mistaken for the application of some exotic waxy cosmetic. The Princess's skin was a light golden color—quite distinct from that of the Orientals of Earth—there was an almost metallic shimmer to it. Her jade eyes were almond-shaped and the striking bluish-green tinge to her eyelids was her natural coloring, not the product of a dramatic application of make-up. Hers was the most perfect female form that the Nyctalope had ever seen, exquisitely lovely in every respect, from the soft curves of her hips to the divine flatness of her belly; her breasts were sweet confections topped with... the Nyctalope tore his gaze away. Xavière was the only woman for him! He had travelled millions of miles for the sake of her love... risked everything. His head would not be turned by this brazen, wanton creature.

A serving girl passed Heru a white silk robe which she donned. The material clung to her skin as closely as paint.

"Princess," began Gullivar, "this is Leo Saint-Clair from Earth."

Her face, her mouth in particular, seemed somehow to fill the whole of the Nyctalope's field of vision. There was nothing else in this world worth looking at.

"I like Earthmen," breathed Heru. Her voice was honey and wet velvet.

Somewhere behind him, the Nyctalope could hear Samoht talking.

"Gullivar has told me the tales of your Helen of Troy... of the siege of Ilium... the most beautiful woman of Earth caused a fleet of ships to go to war; but to bring the gods themselves into the fight, it would take a Martian Princess."

After this encounter with Heru, the men repaired to Gullivar's private study where they discussed in greater detail how the reconnaissance craft might be armed with a variant of the egg weapon and used against the dam wall at Utopia Planitia. The Nyctalope suggested that the eggs could be placed within a metal container—possibly a cylinder—that would have a more stable aerodynamic and hydrodynamic shape, and would also protect the egg on its initial impact with the surface of the water.

Samoht had noticed the altimeter in the Fly and wondered if a similar principle could be employed to measure the depth of water; if so, might it not be possible to integrate into the eggs' casings a pressure fuse which resulted in detonation only when the egg sank to a certain depth?

Gullivar wondered how the Fly pilots maintained a very precise height at low altitude. The Nyctalope explained that the XV—the originators of all the advanced vehicles and technology used by the expeditionary force—used powerful electrical lamps mounted on the nose and tail of aerial vehicles to help to help to judge very low altitude; if the lamps were pointed downwards, the height of the vehicle could be calculated from the angle at which the beams met. This idea was so simple and brilliant that it fascinated Gullivar and set him to wondering what other complex problems might have very simple solutions.

The Nyctalope, in turn, was concerned that there were so few eggs to use as weapons. Samoht explained he had used a single Manta Dragon egg at the Hither City reservoir that morning, and two the previous day while perfecting the technique. That left just seven of the smaller Manta Dragon eggs for practice, and ten Lava Dragon eggs for the actual attack. Saint-Clair shook his head. He was sure the pilots would want to do some dummy attacks with the full-sized eggs to get a

110

feel for them. Samoht emphasized forcefully that it would take at least two, probably three, eggs on target to rupture and destroy the dam.

After this long discussion, when it seemed that every detail had been thrashed out, Samoht took his leave and headed back to the Science Guild to start crating up the eggs for transportation to Argyre Island. Gullivar had a prior and ongoing commitment to teach Terran swordsmanship to the Hither militia. He disappeared off, saying that he would be back in a couple of hours. He left the Nyctalope examining a beautifully illustrated Martian bestiary that contained many color plates depicting the megafauna of the Red Planet.

Not long after, the door of the study creaked open and Saint-Clair was surprised to see Heru enter the room. She had dispensed with the bathrobe and her only concessions to "clothing" were ruby encrusted nipple piercings of insufficient radius to properly cover her areolæ and a filmy triangle of gold leaf on her *mons veneris* that could not have been more than two inches across at its widest point. The Nyctalope fixed his eyes back on the book and made a sustained mental effort to find its contents fascinating.

"That must be a very interesting book," said Heru.

"Yes, it is," confirmed Saint-Clair.

"Do you know," began Heru, "how the nobility of Mars choose their lovers?"

"No, I do not," admitted the Nyctalope as he turned a page—the illustration of some sort of colossal white ape on the previous page had not managed to hold his attention. He decided to concentrate harder.

"It is done by way of a lottery," revealed Heru. "And all must abide by the lottery's result, even Gullivar Jones, protector of the Hither People. But I do not allow a princess of the blood to be enslaved to such randomness."

"You cheat," judged the Nyctalope.

"I predetermine the outcome by guile," stated the golden woman. "If you are ever inclined to enter a lottery by which you might win the pleasures of my body, then remember the following..."

She leaned over to him; her sweet breath momentarily washed over his cheek and her lips brushed his ear as she whispered to him, just as she had whispered to Gullivar years before when she wanted him to cheat in the lovers' lottery

"*A golden pool, and a silver fish, and a line no thicker than a hair...* always remember that and perhaps I will be yours... perhaps."

"I am promised to another," smiled Saint-Clair weakly.

"Such things mean little *here,*" she laughed haughtily, and her laugh was harsh and grating, like the crying out of a frustrated she-fox from deep in the woods.

The sooner I get back to Argyre Island the better, considered the Nyctalope as he turned the page once more.

Three days later, Gullivar Jones was solo piloting a Fly reconnaissance plane high above Argyre Island for the first time. Gullivar had heard tell of how the Nyctalope had taught himself how to fly in a single afternoon and had had to be dissuaded from doing the same in order to show that anything a French explorer could do, a US Navy lieutenant could do at least as well. Gullivar had proved himself to his instructors to be a natural pilot with a highly instinctive understanding of the controls of the reconnaissance craft as well as the principles of aviation in general. Flying the plane gave Gullivar a sense of freedom such as he had never before known. He wondered if the Nyctalope would allow him to keep it after the mission against the dam was completed. Somehow, it never occurred to him that he might not make it back from so dangerous an enterprise. Gullivar brought the ornithopter in low and touched down on the esplanade landing strip. He hauled himself out of the cockpit and was immediately met by the zerlat which jumped up at his chest, desperate for affection. Then an amplified voice emanating from the control tower speakers broke like thunder over the esplanade.

"All mission pilots to the briefing room! All mission pilots to the briefing room!" the voice repeated twice in both French and English. The latter language was not purely for Gullivar's benefit since the Nyctalope also had many British allies with him on Mars, such as his good friend Commander Pary O'Brien.

Gullivar bade the zerlat wait outside the white painted concrete cube that was the administration block and headed inside. Two French pilots in the distinctive orange flight suits and white harnesses of the elite Fly reconnaissance group were going the same way. He gave them a jaunty salute, recognizing them as Lieutenants Damprich and Chaland. Inside the briefing room they were met by the Nyctalope himself and his most senior advisor, Oxus, the former leader of the XV, and the senior scientific advisor to the French expeditionary force, Monsieur Flammarion. Samoht Yor was also in attendance and was deep in conversation with Flammarion pointing out details on a scale model of the Utopia Planitia dam.

"The Thither Folk technicians have now run cables from the control chamber inside the dam into the area at the base of the skull of the Dagoniah. The cables connect with the creature's brain and nervous system," elucidated Samoht.

"And the power from these cables will bring the creature to life?" asked Flammarion.

"No, the Dagoniah is already alive. It is a synthetic animal created by the renegade Martian scientist Ras Thavas. The purpose of this connection is to allow Ras Thavas to transfer the consciousness of the tyrant Ar-Hap into the monster. We must attack immediately or we may be too late," concluded Samoht.

The Nyctalope addressed the French pilots.

"Gentlemen, for security reasons, the details of your mission have been kept from you until now. You are to attack and destroy the Utopia Planitia dam in the heart of Thither territory. You have been practicing over water with the dragon egg bombs developed in association with the Martian Science Guild; so you will know that must drop those bombs from no

113

more than sixty feet in height. The aerodynamic features of this ordnance mean that following its release, it will skim the surface of the water and then sink in front of the dam wall. Only a release that lands precisely in front of the dam wall will destroy the dam. The colossal creature gestating in the lake reservoir is the Dagoniah—your bombs will not affect it— it is, to all intents and purposes. indestructible. It is, however, an obstacle, so ensure that your dragon eggs bombs are only dropped once you have cleared it. Master Oxus?"

Following the briefing from the Nyctalope, red-robed Oxus stepped forward.

"We know that the Thither Folk have stolen our electro-mirror technology. These turrets at the extremes of the dam are believed to be armed with electro-mirror barrages. The approach to the dam will be very hazardous. But we have now successfully fitted electro-mirrors to the wings of your Fly craft... So at least you will be able to shoot back," stated Oxus.

"Excuse me, Maître, but will just two hits from the bombs really be enough against that?" asked Damprich as he gestured at the model.

"It will take at least two on target hits to destroy the dam. You will also be accompanied by myself and Lieutenant Gullivar Jones of the United Stated Navy, so there is a possibility of four strikes in all. We'll need to minimize long-range radio chatter, so we'll use code words when we communicate with Argyre Base. The code word for an on target bomb is 'Lu-Pov'—got that?—and the code word for a successful breach of the dam is 'zerlat.' I will see you in the hangar for launch preparation in ten minutes," ordered the Nyctalope.

"Then may God go with you!" intoned Oxus, looking for all the world like the incarnation of an Old Testament prophet.

As Gullivar and Samoht exited the administration block, Gullivar looked around for the zerlat but couldn't see him anywhere.

"Samoht, I've got to get over to the hangar. Can you do me a favor and find the zerlat? Just tie him up someplace and make sure he doesn't get lost, will you," instructed Gullivar, already starting to jog for the hangar door.

"Of course, Gullivar," smiled the science wizard.

Over in the reconnaissance craft hangar, Lieutenant Chaland climbed into his cockpit and checked the alignment of his wing-mounted electro-mirrors.

"This is a story that will be told over and over," he said to himself, but loud enough for Damprich and Gullivar to hear. At that moment, Samoht ran into the hangar looking ashen-faced.

"It's the zerlat, Gullivar!" Samoht began haltingly. "He got too near to a transport vehicle on the runway... He was crushed under its wheels... He's dead."

An icy sensation built in Gullivar's gut. It was a terrible omen. Worse than that he would miss his pet terribly. His eyes stung, but he would not give in to tears.

"Bury him for me, Samoht," instructed Gullivar before pulling the cockpit canopy shut.

They started their engines and taxied out onto the runway with the Nyctalope's plane in the lead; then they took off into the setting sun.

It was well over 350 miles to Utopia Planitia, but the journey was uneventful. The four little planes kept very low, lower than 100 feet for most of the way. Once they reached Thither territory, they navigated by following the routes of the canals westward; all of the canals in this region led towards the great dam. Finally, they saw it: a twinkling expanse of silvery blue that terminated with the hard dark line of the dam wall's masonry. As they drew nearer, the dam looked squat, heavy and unconquerable in the starlight; like some unsinkable battleship. It bristled with armaments. Plainly, it had greater defenses than just the electro-mirrors mounted in its minaret-like turrets.

"I hadn't realized it would be so big," spluttered Damprich over the short range radio.

"No non-essential communication," ordered the Nyctalope abruptly. "I am starting my bomb run."

The Nyctalope broke away from the other three planes and lined himself up with the dam wall. Suddenly, the dam defenses came to life and searing bolts of electricity jumped from the minarets and played across the surface of the water. Then came automated cannon fire; spears of scarlet that tracked the Nyctalope's craft as he was forced to abandon his attack and pull up.

"N for Nyctalope, are you in one piece?" asked Gullivar.

"Hello, G for Gullivar. Minor damage to my fuselage only. Am going around again for a second attack."

"Negative, Monsieur," broke in Chaland. "I am in already in attack vector. Please turn immediately to port to avoid fire from my electro-mirrors."

Chaland set his electro-mirrors to continuous fire and strafed the dam, taking out several of the automatic cannon. Nevertheless, the fire from the turrets and the remaining cannon was withering.

"This is D for Damprich, how many gun emplacements are there on that thing?" broke in the young Lieutenant.

"Estimate about twenty fire-points. Not all of them are on the dam—some are at the sides in the pastures. Watch out for those..." Perhaps Chaland should have heeded his own warning because at that, his plane disintegrated in a welter of white hot metal fragments.

Gullivar noticed that the Nyctalope was being kept busy dodging fire from the turret electro-mirrors—too busy to enter his attack vector. Damprich stole his place in the attack order and started to cross the surface of the lake, but his speed seemed painfully slow.

"Increase your speed, D for Damprich. I'll cut in front of you and try to draw some of that cannon fire onto me," shouted Gullivar into his radio.

The combined efforts of Damprich and Gullivar blasted away several cannon emplacements and the easterly electro-

116

mirror turret. Damprich cleared the kraken-like form of the Dagoniah and pulled the bomb release lever.

The dragon egg bomb's bounces allowed it to clear Ras Thavas' cables by pure fluke, then it continued on its trajectory, momentum diminishing with each bounce until it sank beneath the silvery, amniotic fluid laced waters of the lake. Damprich flew over the dam and the remaining cannon emplacements rotated to try and track him. Gullivar held his breath... and imagined himself to be the dragon egg bomb sinking into the cold waters... pressure fuse ticking, then slowly engaging. A rainbow of fire and light erupted from the water directly in front of the dam wall projecting a mountain of liquid into the air.

"Lu-Pov! Lu-Pov!" cried Gullivar into the long range transmitter microphone.

The message was received and met with jubilation at the Argyre Island communications center where Oxus, Flammarion, Samoht, Xavière and Heru has been waiting impatiently for any sort of news. Heru now wore one of Xavière's simple long white dresses at the French woman's insistence. Xavière had been forced to remonstrate with Heru who seemed to neither understand nor care that her nudity had been distracting the men ever since she arrived on the island.

"It isn't over yet," observed Samoht. "The dam is still not breached."

"N for Nyctalope, are you about to commence your next bomb run?" asked Gullivar urgently.

"Negative, Gullivar. I have a severe problem. Start to line up for your own attack," responded Saint-Clair.

"What the matter, Leo?" demanded Gullivar.

"I'm blind," stated Saint-Clair simply.

Inside the dam control chamber, the bald head of Martian scientist Ras Thavas was beaded with sweat as he worked feverishly to insert various needle-sharp electrodes into the skull of Ar-Hap. It had all become a desperate race against the clock. Not only was there the chance that two years work would be wasted, but there was now the very real possibility that they would be killed. If only Ar-Hap had listened to his advice earlier to evacuate the dam.

"The Dagoniah's current level of physical development is akin to that of newly-born baby. Once your consciousness has been transferred it will take several hours... perhaps a day for it to assert its dominance over the Dagoniah's motor functions," explained Ras Thavas.

"A day!" screeched Ar-Hap. "I'll swat our enemies out of the sky the moment my mind is inside that thing," boasted the tyrant.

"Yes, blind," repeated the now somewhat ironically named Nyctalope. "A burst from the electro-mirror turret struck my canopy a glancing blow—melting it. I think it has overloaded my optic nerve. All I can see is whiteness. It's like being snow-blind. I'll have to circle out of range until it wears off. I've broken the glass on my instruments panel and I'm reading the needles with my fingers. Other than that my plane is airworthy," he concluded.

Gullivar Jones switched on his electro-mirrors and raked the dam wall with needles of destructive energy as his plane shot over the water low and fast. His eyes were fixed on the target and his hand was ready on the bomb release lever as something huge hove into view. The Dagoniah! It was starting to move...

Gullivar pulled up for a split-second to avoid its vast bulk then dropped down and released the bomb. He had dropped it too late! He was forced to bank steeply away from the dam. The dragon egg bounced just a couple of times then smacked into the dam wall and detonated. Not good enough. It had to sink and blow up at the bottom of the wall to stand any chance.

"I messed it up, Leo. We might as well head home," said Gullivar while cursing inwardly.

"No! I've still got a bomb... talk me through it. I know I can do it. You be my eyes!"

"You're crazy. But that thing in the lake is starting to move now. I guess we really have no choice," accepted Gullivar. "Turn to point zero five and drop your height... increase throttle... fire your electro-mirrors..."

Somehow, the Nyctalope had become one with the plane, the sky, the dam and the water. He listened to Gullivar and responded instantly. Flying without seeing ...not even needing to see. All that was needed was faith, confidence and trust.

"Release bomb now!" screamed Gullivar.

The Nyctalope could see what happened next, but only in his mind's eye. A trajectory that was almost poetically perfect... the bomb bounced beautifully, sank and then... the Nyctalope wrestled with his plane as it was buffeted by the shockwave. Then shadows started to invade the whiteness. His eyesight was starting to come back!

"Zerlat! Zerlat!" roared Gullivar triumphantly

The control chamber was hit by a storm of water and masonry. Ras Thavas had just a split second to devise an escape plan. The scientist managed a half smile—the amniotic fluid all around was, in a sense, alive. Could he transfer his sentience into it? Too late; the rushing black water closed in and finished him. Conversely, Ar-Hap's death was exquisitely slow and painful... Weeks would pass before all of the life finally drained out of the helpless Dagoniah, in which his mind was now imprisoned. The creature's body wasn't viable to survive without the amniotic nutrients of the lake.

Lieutenant Gullivar Jones, the fully-recovered Nyctalope and Lieutenant Damprich marched by the massed ranks of the French Expeditionary Force—all in dress uniforms—on their way to the temporary stage where they would be awarded newly struck medals—the Distinguished Martian Flying Cross—by Oxus. Also on the stage were Samoht, Flammarion, Xavière and, of course, Heru. The Nyctalope was pleased to see she was wearing a dress, although it looked like she'd taken her ceremonial dagger and slit the material to the hip. The men received their decorations to thunderous applause from the crowd. Naturally, there was a posthumous medal for brave Lieutenant Chaland.

Then something caught Gullivar's eye. Behind Samoht was something that might almost have been Gullivar's zerlat; except surely it could not have been... It was zerlat-shaped but looked to be composed of something like iron filings rather than flesh and blood... What was it? Samoht saw the look of astonishment.

"If you bury a freshly-killed zerlat, it becomes one with the planet's magnetic field, creates a sort of living ghost. I thought perhaps you knew," smiled Samoht.

"I had no idea," said Gullivar as he stroked the ghost creature's head. "On my world, things tend to stay dead. But you and I need a private talk. Look at all these people, there are thousands of Earthmen on Mars. I'm not needed here now... yet there must be other places where your travel carpets can send me. And I *know* how Heru's eye wanders. She'll soon set up store with someone else once I'm gone," he added confidentially.

"Gullivar, the carpets are powerful. They *could* send you to the future of your own world. You could take part in a war there perhaps... But such journeys are not without cost... cost to both your body and your psyche. You might not even re-member your time here; in your fractured mind, you might come to think yourself as a man of that time period. Another alternative is to send you to the distant past here on Mars. The Martian lineages are long... You will find there other Ar-Haps to fight. Other Herus to love. The choice is yours."

"Why not both?" laughed Gullivar.

"My friend, I'll see what I can do," said Samoht as he slapped Gullivar on the shoulder.

The ill-fated demise of the French Martian colony set up in The Nyctalope on Mars *has become the subject of two later stories: Roman Leary's* The Children of Heracles *and Matthew Dennion's* The Hunters of Mars, *both collected in* The Nyctalope Steps In. *This concept is the subject of a surprising coda in our own story,* The Ides of Mars, *featured later in this volume. In the meantime, Chris Nigro's tale deals with the immediate aftermath of that tragedy, as well as Leo's role in an even greater and bloodier tragedy, the Great War...*

Chris Nigro: *Justice and Power*

Northern France, July 1917

> *Justice and power must be brought together,*
> *so that whatever is just may be powerful,*
> *and whatever is powerful may be just.*
> Blaise Pascal.

Leo Saint-Clair's mind was virtually devoid of coherent thought as he hurtled towards his home planet in a small but sleek spacecraft, powered by a unique energy source known as "heliose," the creation of a mad but brilliant scientist named Korrides. He had pre-set the coordinates to take him from the now dead French colony on the Red Planet to Earth in less than two weeks' time.

The craft shuddered a bit under the spatial equivalent of atmospheric turbulence. That sudden jolt brought the Nyctalope out of his blissful reverie, as he tried—unsuccessfully--to forget the horrific events that had transpired the day after he, his twin children, and his fellow French colonizers had celebrated Bastille Day on Mars, incorrectly believing that it would mark a new era of exploration for his native country. But Mars was named after a cruel deity, and it appeared that the dreaded war god had been lying in wait for those ill-fated colonists.

As a commandant in the French army, and an inveterate soldier, Leo believed he knew war, and could handle anything this merciless deity could throw his way. He was wrong. Dead wrong.

They're all gone now, he mused to himself wearily. *My wife, Xavière... my little children... everyone... gone. We didn't know what infernal forces were waiting for us there. We had no control over our own actions. None of us could resist that overpowering evil... I cannot... I must not hold myself accountable for any of that...*

With the auto-pilot safely on, Leo fell into a fitful sleep, his slumber haunted by the faces of the dead colonists, his two precious children standing in front of all the rest with Leo's own blades jutting out of their abdomens, their internal organs spattered on the marble-like floor before him...

One month later, Leo awakened to a bright sunny morning in the military hospital in Paris, where he had been staying for the past few weeks, being treated for what would someday be called "post-traumatic stress syndrome."

He was under the care of a meticulous physician, Dr. Cerral, who had the annoying habit of not looking his patients in the eye while speaking to them, and instead writing all of his observations down on a pad.

"Bonjour, Commandant," Cerral said in his usual detached fashion. "Did you sleep better last night?"

Stretching and yawning, Leo replied:

"Oui, très bien, Docteur. When can I be released so I can resume my work? I am very aware that there is a war being fought right now, and my talents are no doubt needed."

Dr. Cerral held up a pencil and waved it to emphasize his words.

"Not so fast, Commandant. In my judgment, I believe you should remain here for a bit longer. What you suffered was..."

Leo interrupted the doctor with a stern reply:

"What I suffered is over, Doctor. I am a soldier, trained and experienced in dealing with loss. I want—no, I *need* to return to the front and do my duty. France can no longer wait. Do you understand?"

"Yes, yes, I do, of course, but what occurred to you back on... you know where... was not a typical loss for a soldier, and your, er... participation... in that tragedy may well have left you, er, a bit unwell—from a mental standpoint, I mean."

Leo's iron grip was suddenly around Dr. Cerral's wrist, squeezing so tightly that it caused the physician to drop his prized pencil and yelp in pain.

"Doctor, you may not have heard me clearly enough. I am telling you that I am fine, and eager to return to my military responsibilities."

Before Dr. Cerral could either acquiesce, or protest further, an older French officer entered the room and wasted no time in getting down to business after the customary salutations.

"Commandant Saint-Clair," the officer said, "I am Colonel Gilles Fontaine. Your wish to return to the front is about to be granted. General Foch himself has sent me to recruit you for a clandestine but crucial mission that only someone with your combination of talents could possibly execute."

"Excellent!" Leo exclaimed.

"I'm sorry, Colonel Fontaine," Doctor Cerral said, matter-of-factly. "But as the Commandant's physician, I must protest. I still need to make a professional assessment regarding his mental fitness to serve..."

"That will be enough, Dr. Cerral," the Colonel said with heavy authority. "General Foch himself has decreed this. While your concerns are noted, they must presently be ignored in the interests of France."

The doctor still seemed undaunted.

"I have final authority when it comes to matters such as these..."

"Doctor, your authority ends where the best interests of France, and the troops who so valiantly serve her, are concerned," Colonel Fontaine noted brusquely. "Now kindly take your ministrations to other patients. Commandant Saint-Clair and I have business to discuss. Do not make me say this again."

Visibly withholding the words he wanted to say, Dr. Cerral abruptly walked away. *This is in God's hands now, not mine,* he thought to himself. *May the Lord do what is best for Saint-Clair—and for France.*

Minutes later, Leo sat across from Colonel Fontaine at a table in the hospital commissary. The Officer sipped a mug of steaming hot tea as he briefed the Nyctalope on what was expected of him.

"This will be one of your most difficult missions to date, Commandant."

"With all due respect, Colonel, I've fought some of the deadliest menaces from two worlds. At this point in my life, I doubt there's anything you can throw at me that could faze possibly me."

"You are as brave a man as I've ever seen, Saint-Clair," the Colonel commended. "If only the Hun knew what was coming their way, they would flee in terror."

Leo suddenly displayed a blank expression despite the compliment he had just received.

"Saint-Clair? Are you unwell? Should I summon Dr. Cerral?"

"No, Colonel, I was just... reminiscing. What does the mission entail?"

"This is the situation. Our government is working with Great Britain to launch a third offensive on Ypres a few days from now—a locale that you are quite familiar with, due to your earlier participation in previous military operations there. General Francois Anthonie requested you for a mission of the utmost importance that will be France's contribution to that offensive—a mission that will require all of your legendary skills, and particularly your famed powers of nyctalopia.

"The Germans have recently developed a new type of deadly gas that is worse than chlorine. We call it 'mustard gas' because of its horrific effects on the men who come in contact with it: the color of their blisters all over their skin take on a mustard-like hue. It is invisible and nearly odorless, and its effects do not appear for many hours following exposure. Other effects include swelling of the eyes that results in blindness, frequent regurgitation, and the deterioration of one's mucous membranes to the point that many slowly die an agonizing death over the course of several weeks as their throats close up on them."

"My God!" Leo exclaimed. "Mars never ceases to perfect the horrors he unleashes on the warriors who walk his path."

"Pardon?"

"Excuse me, Colonel, I was speaking in metaphor."

"I see. To conclude, a combined British and French military force is planning to launch an assault on a town in the vicinity of Ypres known as Passchendaele. Recent intelligence reports have revealed that there is a large storage base on the outskirts of that town, filled with over 50 canisters of mustard gas, which is more than enough to wreak bloody havoc on the entire Allied unit when it arrives. That base is well guarded, so a full-scale attack on it would give the Boche ample time to release the gas. This is why we need one man to travel several miles on foot in the dead of night and approach the base surreptitiously, despite all the enemy patrols in the vicinity. It will be your job to neutralize every German before they can release the gas, and to sabotage all the canisters."

"It will be done, Colonel."

"You should know that the meteorological conditions would be atrocious. The entire area has been besieged by enormously inclement weather lately. The ground will be muddy and flooded in many places, thus making travel hazardous in the extreme. However, the overcast skies will ensure that no Moon will be visible. But of course, you won't need a lantern."

"They don't the Nyctalope for nothing, Colonel. The absence of light will be no impediment to me."

"What about the other hazards?"

"I am also called a soldier for good reason too, Monsieur. Overcoming any obstacles—natural or man-made—is what I do."

"Good, good. You will be based at the camp located left of the Ypres Canal, where our men are now sequestered with a new regiment of the French First Army. You will be given the name of a contact answering directly to General Anthoine who will provide you with further instructions upon your arrival. Godspeed, Commandant Saint-Clair!"

"It will be the Boche who'll need to worry about God that night, Colonel."

Leo Saint-Clair sat up on what passed for a bed at the military camp in Ypres, sweating profusely as the result of another one of his nightmares. He could have sworn that he'd seen the bodies of his children lying at the foot of his bed with his blade thrust through their bellies for a brief moment. His abrupt awakening caught the attention of his bunkmate, a fat Belgian wearing glasses named Remy Baudouin, who was unaware of his identity.

"Léon, are you all right?" asked Remy.

"I am. I just thought a scorpion had crawled into my bunk."

"There's no scorpions in Belgium," said Remy, firmly.

"Yes, but…"

"Don't worry about it, soldier. We're all on edge with the way things have been here, especially after the cookhouse was flooded and all the food was drenched. That stuff the cook fed to me yesterday morning looked like something he'd scraped from the bottom of his shoe—and it tasted even worse. It was probably just something you ate, is all."

"I *am* a soldier," replied Leo, stiffly. "I'm accustomed to adverse conditions in the field, and you should be as well. We must all sacrifice comforts for the greater cause."

"Well, yeah, of course, but that doesn't mean some of us wouldn't rather be back home relaxing at the Gai Moulin, watching a revue where the girls shake their cans to the can-can, if you know what I mean."

"Such good things would not exist for anyone back home if not for what we soldiers sacrifice here on the field, Remy. Now, I beg your pardon, but I must get some fresh air."

"I'd bring an umbrella, if I were you, Leon. 'Course, we weren't issued any luxuries like umbrellas, and as soldiers, we don't need any such luxuries, right?"

Ignoring Remy's sarcasm, Leo emerged from his tent in the hope of enjoying the morning air. He saw his fellow soldiers, none of whom enjoyed the benefits of his synthetic heart, diligently going about their various duties while drenched in the rain, their feet ankle deep in mud. Many had a grayish cast to their faces, due to constant exposure to the squally weather; several were visibly shivering, a condition caused by the fact that these men had to wear the same clothing for weeks, and their shirts were infested with lice.

Leo reminded himself again of the necessity for sacrifice. He was a soldier, and knew that it was not his place to question the way of the world; he simply had to perform his duty to the best of his abilities. That was what a warrior did. He told himself that the hardship and suffering that came with war emboldened his nation, and made those who survived all the stronger. He didn't believe in an easy world that bred a soft and lazy civilization. But he couldn't help recalling how many of the high-ranking officers enjoyed comfortable lodgings well away from enemy lines, whereas the enlisted men had had to give up all amenities, many of which they could ill afford even back home.

What are these men truly fighting for? he asked himself. *The liberty of our fellow Frenchmen? Or the continued privilege of the few who make all the decisions?*

Leo quietly admonished himself for thinking such thoughts, and tried to focus on the mission he would be undertaking at nightfall.

As he walked about the camp, the Nyctalope was unaware that another soldier—or at least a man who appeared to be a regular member of the infantry unit—watched his every move, with a concerned and calculating expression on his face...

No sooner had the sun set that Leo began his difficult trek through the rain-filled darkness towards the German base in Passchendaele.

Few men would have had the endurance to make such a trip on foot, and fewer yet could have done so under such conditions. But the darkness was no obstacle to one gifted with night vision. Leo endured the constant rainfall and the frigid wind by reminding himself that every trial just made him a stronger and better soldier.

For the purpose of his mission, he carried a specially modified Luger and a razor-sharp, tailor-made hunting dagger, both ready for use at a moment's notice. During the long trek, the Nyctalope met two German patrols that were wandering about the area, looking for enemy combatants. But they did so under the assumption that these would be subject to the same visual limitations as themselves. As a result, no grenades were hurled at Leo with anything near accuracy as he trod towards his goal. Whenever a German soldier approached him, expecting to find the scattered remains of his human target, the Nyctalope would either put a bullet through his skull or slash his throat, whichever struck his fancy for the moment. He deliberately allowed a few of the Germans the time to scream in agony in order to attract their fellow soldiers, so that they, too, could promptly fall before the fury and might of the night-thriving warrior.

Finally, after a seeming eternity, and with no more than two hours of nightfall left, Leo approached the base where the canisters of mustard gas were being held. Quickly, he dispatched the two sentries who had been unable to detect his approach. Leo savored the thrill of his enemies falling before him with their blood staining his blade as his inner rage built within him like carbonated liquid under pressure in a bottle.

Picking the complicated lock on the front entrance with ease, the Nyctalope entered the base. He found the interior gently lit by several lanterns. He knew that there were eight guards inside, so he proceeded with caution. However, as he moved about, he suddenly found himself plagued with the same visions, as if it were his children whom he had just put killed with his blade, instead of the sentries...

As a consequence of the shock, Leo carelessly kicked a wrench lying on the floor as he strode through the edifice. He might as well have set off a stick of dynamite! Two guards immediately came running in his direction to check the source of the noise.

Leo pointed his Luger at them and let off two blindingly quick shots, killing both as the deadly bullets pierced their chest and skull respectively.

The sound alerted the other six guards, and all of them simultaneously advanced upon Leo. As the Nyctalope turned his gun in the direction of the men to his right, one of the guards, attacking from the left, leapt upon him from behind, drawing a bayonet in preparation for puncturing his left kidney. Leo deftly countered the move by backing into a crate, catching his opponent's arm as he thrust the blade at him, and disarmed the enemy soldier before he could skewer him. He then quickly shoved his dagger into the man's throat, blood spattering from the wound as the man died instantly.

Two other sentries swiftly moved in for the kill, but Leo disemboweled the first with a quick slash of his dagger across the man's lower abdomen, and split open the other's skull with the butt of his Luger before the unfortunate soldier could react.

Now acting in a frenzy, realizing that he needed this conflict as a catharsis, Leo shouted: "I'm here! Come and get me, you boche bastards!"

No longer taking any chances, the last two guards each leapt in front of Leo from a different direction, both expertly aiming their Mauser rifles at him, ready to unleash the full complement of five bullets from each of their magazines. Reacting at the speed of thought, Leo simultaneously fired at one guard with his Luger, killing him instantly, and hurled his dagger at the other, sending the sentry to the ground vomiting a torrent of blood as the blade penetrated his throat.

However, that last soldier managed to get off one stray shot, which failed to hit the Nyctalope, but punctured two of the canisters, sending twin streams of mustard gas into the atmosphere.

The Nyctalope bellowed a scream of victory as waves of adrenaline continued to saturate his system; he then struggled to catch his breath, as his artificial heart had been taxed almost beyond even its formidable limits.

Leo suddenly became aware of an imposing presence behind him. He turned around and discovered a tall, dark-clad figure standing near the entrance to the base. This mysterious man was not dressed like a member of the German infantry, and instead appeared to be covered with a specially designed charcoal-colored outfit intended to protect its wearer from the extreme weather conditions now afflicting the area. He also wore a mask over his face and gloves designed to protect against mustard gas. A distinctive black hat and cloak completed his raiment. Presently, the man was pointing a large pistol of unclear design at Leo.

"I'm afraid I must ask you to come along with me, Commandant," the dark man said in a grim-sounding voice. "You were clearly not mentally fit for undertaking such a mission, and because of your recklessness, this area is now contaminated with mustard gas. You must face justice for these actions."

It was then that Leo realized exactly who confronted him.

"Judex," he said aloud. "The much feared vigilante of Paris. What are you doing here?"

"Let me just say that I, too, have been called to the front," Judex replied. "I know all about your recent travails. I was at the base incognito, and I observed your erratic behavior all day. I know one with a precarious grip on their sanity when I see them. With the use of these special lenses, designed to compensate for the lack of light, I followed you to make sure that you carried out this mission correctly. But you did not. You appear to be harboring some sort of death wish. Allied soldiers can no longer approach this area now, and the threat of mustard gas has not been averted. I cannot sabotage the canisters myself since this mask only gives me limited protection. Come with me now. This is not a request."

"Really? You're hardly a military tribunal. I'm wagering you don't even have a true officer ranking. So I strongly advise you to lower your weapon and go back from whence you came, while I'm still in a good enough mood to give you the option of getting out of here in one piece."

"You wish to escape justice? You think you can intimidate me into letting you walk free?"

"You're not Justice itself, Judex. You're only a man who has the pretentiousness to think he is. You need to be taught the error of your ways, and I can't think of a better teacher than I."

With a lightning swift move, Leo delivered a swinging kick that disarmed Judex, much to the latter's surprise. However, the vigilante trapped Leo's leg after he tried a follow-up kick to the face. Judex lifted the Nyctalope in the air and hurled him to the ground. Leo expertly recovered, landing on his hands and flipping himself back onto his feet, landing in a classic fighting stance. Judex followed suit in a fighting stance of his own.

With a series of blinding moves, the two warriors began facing off, each blocking a flurry of the other's blows, with a few connecting from time to time. The two men soon realized that they each faced a foe the likes of which the other had ever encountered before.

This seeming stalemate went on for several minutes, until Judex managed to dodge one of Leo's blows and struck him hard on the jaw. He then cracked his clavicle bone with a brutal elbow thrust, grabbing the khaki-clad soldier by the collar and smashing him up against one of the crates. Before the vigilante could deliver what he hoped to be the finishing blow, the Nyctalope quickly recovered, blocked Judex's strike, and side-kicked him to the sternum, knocking the wind out of him and sending him sprawling to the ground.

Managing to regain his wits, Judex saw Leo recover his dagger and hurl it at him. Reacting automatically, the vigilante caught it in his left hand and quickly hurled it back at the Nyctalope, who ducked out of the way a microsecond before being skewered in the shoulder.

Somersaulting towards the area where his gun lay on the floor, Judex knew that he had but a few seconds to act. He grabbed his pistol and pointed it at Leo just as the Nyctalope, who had done the exact same thing with his own Luger, took aim at him.

"It would appear we find ourselves at a deadlock, Judex," Leo observed aloud. "So I strongly suggest you allow me to leave, and in return, I will let you do the same. D'accord?"

"Non, Commandant," Judex icily replied. "Despite all you have endured, despite all the good you have done for our nation, and the world itself, I cannot in good conscience let you go on in your mental state and ignore what you did here. You must face justice."

"And you think you have a right to judge me? After all I have been through, all the tragedy I have endured? After all I have accomplished for France? After all the sacrifices I have made? You see yourself, and yourself alone, as being worthy of judging me?"

Judex's bright gray eyes tightened under his face gear. "Yes, for it is what I do."

Judex suddenly rolled out of Leo's line of fire and let off a shot, having very carefully aimed at a thick metal pipe above the Nyctalope's head. Leo shot at the same time, his bullet barely missing Judex due to the latter's suddenly rolling dodge. The vigilante's bullet struck and ricocheted off the pipe in precisely the right direction to crease against Leo's skull, giving him a concussion and knocking him unconscious.

Running over towards the dazed Nyctalope, Judex realized that, despite his foe's injury, he had to act quickly, while Leo Saint-Clair was still unconscious.

"Long ago, I had some very special training courtesy of our common friend, Sâr Dubnotal," Judex said quietly as he pressed his fingers against Leo's forehead and concentrated. "He helped me develop my powers of mesmerism. What I am going to attempt now is difficult, and potentially dangerous, but the risk must be taken. It is the form of justice that I believe should properly be meted out to you. Our country—the very world, in fact—greatly needs one such as you among us, but you cannot be allowed to go about these tasks in your current state of mind. Moreover, you do not deserve to suffer as you have for an act outside of your control. Now, please remain relaxed...

"I am going to suppress all conscious memory of your role in the recent tragedy that occurred on Mars, including the very knowledge that you once had twin children. You will only remember the son who yet survives..."

This memory will not stay suppressed forever, Judex thought, *but it is my hope that it will remain buried long enough so that, by the time you do remember it, you will have gained enough time to be able to properly deal with it.*

A few moments later, the deed was done.

Leo recovered moments later, with Judex helping him to his feet.

"What happened?" the Nyctalope asked weakly. "What are you doing here, vigilante?"

"I was sent here to provide you with some back-up, Commandant. I was able to dispatch the last of the guards, who delivered the head wound you are now suffering from. Regrettably, your mission wasn't entirely successful, as two canisters of mustard gas were breached by enemy fire, and you have been exposed to it. We must get back to the base quickly and have you report to the infirmary."

"I must be really concussed, as my memories of the past few hours are vague at best, and as for the last few months...damn, my head is really pounding the more I try to think back."

The Nyctalope looked at the imposing figure of Judex, smiled appreciatively, and continued speaking.

"Needless to say, I must thank you for your timely assistance. As you said, I had best get back to base now, and hope General Anthoine will show a bit of mercy for my inability to prevent this area from being contaminated. Let us be off."

While returning to the base on the opposite end of the Ypres Canal after another long trek, concern for the possibility of mustard gas infection, and being lamented for the partial failure of the mission, were the only two matters weighing upon Leo Saint-Clair's psyche.

When he was a teenager, Leo spent some time in Russia where his father, Jean, was posted as part of a French diplomatic mission in 1892-94. Jean, who was an Ensign in the French Navy, was likely moonlighting for French Intelligence, as revealed by David McDonald in his story Catspaw, *published in* Tales of the Shadowmen 8. The Girl from Odessa *is a sequel of sorts to* Catspaw *and takes place in the fall of 1919, when Leo was either on his way to, or back from, China...*

David McDonald: *The Girl from Odessa*

Odessa, 1919

Leo Saint-Clair stepped from the train, shuddering as the cold winter wind cut through him. He pulled his fur-lined jacket tighter around his shoulders, and looked around for the attaché who was meant to waiting for him. He cursed under his breath as he noticed the sign leaning crookedly against one of the station walls, *Saint-Clair*, printed in what Leo imagined were the crooked letters of a man used to writing not only in a different language, but a different alphabet. Before he could work up a real head of steam, and get into some of the more esoteric profanities he has picked up in his travels, his attention was pulled away by a commotion further down the platform.

He walked towards the sounds of yelling, taking in a rather odd scene. A shabby-looking porter was cowering in the shadow of an impeccably dressed English gentleman. An oaken cane with what looked like a solid silver head was clutched in his raised hand, the wrist of which was held firmly by a massive figure dressed in a faded but precisely creased set of fatigues.

"Damn it, Ballantine!" The man's face was red beneath his luxurious whiskers, moustache and sideburns bristling. "Let go of me! I'm going to flog this cur from one end of the platform to the other and teach him that an Englishman won't stand for this sort of insolence."

"Now, calm down, sir. I am sure he didn't lose your bags on purpose." The big man's voice was calm and even, and had a soft Highland burr. "Now, laddie, away with you before Mr. Flashman does something both of you will regret."

The porter didn't need to be told twice, and scurried away, throwing a sullen glance over his shoulder before darting into the station master's house. Ballantine released his companion's arm and stepped back.

"Well, sir, let's try and organize some accommodation for you. Hopefully your bags will turn up in the meantime."

They began to walk away, only to halt, startled as Leo yelled after them.

"Mr. Flashman, sir! Wait a moment, if you please."

Leo hurried towards them, only to come to a sudden halt as both men whirled to face him, Flashman's cane gripped tightly in whitened knuckles and the big man's fists clenched.

"And who the deuces are you, man?" For a moment, Leo thought he saw fear on the Englishman's face, but if had been there, it was quickly replaced by anger. "I warn you, I have had enough of botheration today and my patience is almost exhausted."

Leo was too excited to be upset by the harsh words. The man before him matched his father's stories perfectly. He looked a touch younger than Leo would have expected, with only the smallest touch of grey in his thick hair and moustache, still strong and vital looking. But the name and his companion banished any doubt from Leo's mind.

"Forgive me, Mr. Flashman, I have the advantage of you," Leo said, extending his hand. "I am Leo Saint-Clair. I believe you knew my father?"

Flashman looked at him blankly for a moment, then a wide smile spread across his face and he seized Leo's hand, pumping it vigorously.

"You are Jean's son? By Jove, your father and I had more than our share of adventures together!" The smile died slightly. "It's a wonder I survived them, frankly."

Leo was a little surprised by his reaction. "Come now, Mr. Flashman, my father told me many tales of your daring adventures! He told me you thrived on danger and were never happier than when risking certain death."

Flashman choked slightly. "Oh, yes, of course. Faint heart never won fair maiden and all that."

"And, I heard you did well for yourself in the war too?"

"I did my duty, that's all." Flashman seemed uncomfortable with the line of questioning, which confused Leo.

Ballantine broke in, indignation. "Mr. Flashman is being too modest! He won the Victoria Cross and all."

Leo whistled softly. "It seems my father did not exaggerate your bravery, sir."

Before he could ask any questions, Flashman interrupted him.

"Oh, how remiss of me." He gestured to the bigger man. "Monsieur Saint Clair, this is Sergeant Major Ballantine."

Leo shook hands with the sergeant, conscious of the exaggerated gentleness with which Ballantine folded Leo's hand in his. The Frenchman had seen this before, in extremely strong men conscious of not hurting anyone by mistake. He knew that the big man must be formidable and resolved to keep him on his side.

"Pleasure, sir."

Leo turned back to Flashman. "Where are you staying? Shall we take dinner together? I am always happy to hear stories of my father."

Flashman cleared his throat uncomfortably. "That might be a problem, Leo—may I call you Leo?"

"Of course, Mr. Flashman!"

"Harry." He went on. "You see, the damnable thing is that my bags have been misplaced somewhere, along with all my money. I fear that we will have to avail ourselves of the hospitality, limited as it is, of His Majesty's embassy."

Leo was already shaking his head. "Nonsense, Harry! I will not hear of it. I can advance you some funds and when your bags are recovered you can reimburse me."

"Oh, I would hate to impose."

Leo smiled. "My father told me how many times you saved his life. It is the least I can do."

"...So I threw the last grenade into the machine gun nest, and no sooner had it exploded that I leapt in, bayonet in hand, and gave the Boche what for!"

Whatever reluctance Harry had shown when it came to discussing his wartime exploits had long since dissipated, washed away by the copious amounts of champagne he had drunk since they had made their way to Leo's hotel. He reclined on a luxurious velvet couch, holding court amidst an admiring group of simpering young ladies and awe-struck young men.

The Londonskaya was something of an Odessa landmark, one of the last vestiges of Tsarist Russia. Opulent and expensive, it had always been a favored stopping place for wealthy foreigners, and even though the Revolution had swept away the old empire, it had maintained its exclusive air and continued to operate to the same high standards, left alone by a government happy to take its cut of foreign currency.

It had been a very long day for Leo, and he had been happy to sit back and listen. Harry was a natural-born storyteller with a flair for the dramatic, so it was no chore, especially when he was telling tales of his adventures with Leo's father. He had just finished one set in the hills of Afghanistan when Leo felt a gentle tug on his sleeve.

"Begging your pardon, sir, but I just wanted to thank you," Ballantine said. "It's a hard thing, being alone in a strange city with no money and no friends. I am getting a little old for sleeping in the streets."

"My pleasure, sergeant. I am sure Harry would have done the same for me." Ignoring the sergeant's strange, muffled snort, Leo hesitated a moment and went on. "Please forgive my rudeness, but may I ask you a personal question?"

Ballantine nodded.

"According to both Harry's and my father's stories, you were both in your forties when he first met you. That was almost thirty years ago, and you look no more than fifty, and a young fifty at that!"

There was a touch of bitterness in the Scotsman's smile. "Well, sir, being the good soldier that I am, I volunteered for certain extra duties in my younger days. In their wisdom, my superiors used me as a subject for certain experimental procedures. Amongst other things, it seems to have slowed down my aging."

"There are many men and women who would pay a great deal for such a thing!" Leo exclaimed.

"Some things are not worth the price, laddie. Trust me on that." The big man looked away, eyes on some far off place. "They changed me, in so many ways, not just what they did to my body, but the tasks they set me. When you've changed that much... Well, it's hard to ever go back to where you came from."

Leo thought about the way his own life had been changed forever, and the secrets he hid within, and reached out, placing a hand on the sergeant's shoulder.

"You must trust me on this, Ballantine, I, too, know what it is like to be changed like that." Suddenly uncomfortable, he took his hand away and sought to change the subject. "So these stories of Harry's, how much of them are true? No disrespect intended, but they seem quite incredible!"

"Every word, as far as I know. Mister Flashman has a knack for finding himself in dangerous spots." Ballantine's smile was completely free of the earlier bitterness. "Fortunately, he has an even greater knack for getting us out of them alive!"

Both men laughed, and turned back to listen to the next tale of daring, only to find that a deathly hush had fallen across the room, and that Harry had halted mid-sentence, staring ashen faced at the doorway.

Framed in the entrance was an elderly man, dressed in an immaculate black military uniform. His shadowed eyes and flowing white hair and beard gave the impression of great age, but as he walked towards them, his shoulders were square and his back ramrod straight. The crowd gathered around Harry scattered, people hurrying from the room without even a good-bye. The old man stopped in front of them, his lip curling in disdain as he raked them with a withering glance.

"So, it seems we have some illustrious guests." His voice sent a chill through Leo; it was cold and dry and empty and made him think of a freshly turned grave. "I am Commissariat Koschei, head of the Security Services of the People's City of Odessa. I am here to discuss your business in my city."

The way he said "my" reminded Leo of a particularly depraved old lecher saying the name of an innocent young woman who had wandered into his clutches. Its obscene possessiveness made Leo's skin crawl. From the way the Englishman was squirming in his seat, he could see that Koschei's voice and tone had discomfited Harry as well.

"We are merely tourists enjoying a trip to your fair city." Harry's voice had lost any trace of drunkenness, and Leo couldn't help but admire its steadiness considering the baleful gaze of the old man. "A pleasure to meet a distinguished gentleman as yourself, I am…"

Koschei cut him off mid-sentence, his voice cracking like a whip.

"Do not waste my time with your dissembling. I know exactly who you are. You are Harry Flashman, war hero and adventurer, but more importantly, sometime agent of His Majesty's Government. And your companion is Leo Saint Clair, who fulfills a similar role for the French Government." The

140

voice softened, becoming oily in its solicitousness. "But let us not speak harshly. Odessa is something of an open city. We are far enough from Moscow that we do what we please, and it pleases us to allow foreigners to come and go because it makes Odessa the gateway to the Rus. Controlling that gateway gives us a great deal of power. But be warned, this is my city, and if your business in anyway threatens my interests, I will not hesitate to crush you."

Koschei raised a claw-like hand and clenched it into a bony fist. The lights dimmed and the air was filled with the sound of shattering glass as every bottle along the top shelf of the bar exploded at once. Without another word, the old man turned on his heel and strode from the room, leaving the three foreigners staring at one another in shock. When the silence was broken, it was Harry who spoke.

"What a waste of good booze!"

The mood in the hotel bar was much more somber than the night before. There was no crowd of admiring listeners hanging off Harry's every word. In fact, aside from the sullen bartender, who was apparently still sulking from the clean-up job, they were alone. None of them were able to muster much in the way of enthusiasm. Koschei's presence still lingered, casting a chill over them and sucking the very vitality from the room. Harry hadn't even bothered to start telling any of his stories, and was taking a desultory sip of his champagne when the door opened. His eyes widened as he choked on his mouthful. Leo whipped around, heart in mouth, expecting to see the old man,

The young woman walking across the thick, lush carpet could not have been a greater contrast to their unwelcome visitor of the day before. It was not merely her youth—Leo guessed she could not be more than seventeen—but the way she lit up her surroundings, outshining the glittering chandelier that had been grudgingly lit by the hotel manager when night had fallen. Long blonde hair flowed down her back, breaking like golden waves over the shoulders of her black evening gown. Full red lips pursed in slight consternation as vividly green eyes took in the three men, then she took a deep breath and said:

"It is dark outside and the Moon has not risen." Her voice matched her appearance, melodious and with a rich timbre.

"But the light within can be taken wherever you go." Harry and Leo looked at each other in amazement as they finished the response in the same breath.

"What the deuces, Leo?" Harry exclaimed. "How did you know the answer to the code?"

"I could ask you the same thing!"

Ballantine's voice cut through their conversation. "Begging your pardon, sirs, but it seems pretty plain to me. You've both been sent here on the same mission and to meet the same person." He smiled gently at the young woman. "Isn't that right, ma'am?"

The young woman drew herself up to her full height, and tried her hardest to look down her nose at the sergeant.

"The correct term of address is 'Your Illustriousness,' not ma'am. I am Countess Anastasiya Belinskya. I demand an explanation! Only one of you was meant to staying here, the other was meant to be at the Hotel Otrada!" Her voice rose in pitch and volume with each word until she was shouting.

Harry had leapt to his feet and now stepped forward, bowing low from the waist and taking her hand, kissing it gently.

"Colonel Harold Flashman VC at your service, Your Illustriousness. I do apologize for the change in plans, but an unfortunate mix-up at the station precluded me from staying at the Otrada. I thought I still had a day before our meeting to arrange things." He gave her a hopeful smile. "May I offer you a glass of champagne and a more private conversation?"

The Countess disentangled her hand from Harry's. "Never mind that, I am here now and in no mood for pleasantries."

Harry frowned. "Whatever you wish, Your Illustriousness. Let us discuss getting you to Great Britain as quickly as possible. My superiors are very interested in the documents you carry."

"Hold on, Harry." Leo hurried over. "*Enchanté*, Countess, I am Leo Saint Clair and my superiors are also, shall we say, interested in your documents. I was under the impression that an arrangement had already been made for your travel to Paris?"

"Nothing has been decided yet, gentlemen. I want to hear what exactly your respective governments are offering in exchange." There was a faint flush to her cheeks. "You may consider me mercenary and grasping, but these documents are all I have left to my name. Our family's manor was burned to the ground; it was only I who survived. I need to ensure that I am provided for. After all, these documents contain much information of value, and cost much to obtain."

Before either man could reply, a deep voice issued from the shadows by the bar.

"There is no time for bargaining now. If you do not get the Countess out of Odessa tonight, then neither of your governments will get the documents. Koschei knows we are here, and he will not be far away."

"Gentlemen, this is Father Grigor. He has been our family's priest since before I was born, and it was he who saved me from the flames," Anastasiya said.

Leo was disgusted that they had allowed themselves to be distracted by the Countess, and had not noticed her companion. No matter how beautiful she was, a man that big should have stood out in any surrounding. He was as at least as tall as Ballantine, but almost twice as broad across the shoulders. Dressed in simple monk's robes, bound at the waist with a length of rope, his chest was covered with a ferocious black beard streaked with grey. Leo could see Ballantine sizing the priest up, and he wondered whether the sergeant was thinking the same thing that was on Leo's mind and wondering whether he could take Grigor down if needed. Leo thought such a fight would be a sight to see indeed.

"We need to get out of here now," the priest said.

"Too late." Harry gestured towards the street entrance. The door was ajar and, through it, they could hear the sounds of marching feet—a few score of men at least if Leo was any judge.

"I think Koschei has arrived."

The soldiers stood unmoving in the square, unnatural and menacing. The pale light of the Moon glinted from eyes that did not blink and gleamed on teeth revealed by the rictus grins of death. They had no guns, instead carrying the slightly curved swords that had become a familiar sight to Leo as he traveled through the region. His original guess had been off by a considerable margin—there were at least a hundred men, if not more.

"They are corpses!" Leo said.

"You don't say," Harry snapped. "Anything else you want to point out?"

"Go easy, Mr. Flashman. I think we're all a bit rattled." Ballantine didn't sound rattled. He had been the first to move, manhandling a huge cabinet in front of the doors, lifting it as if weighed nothing at all.

Harry stepped back from the windows. "I saw rifles in the manager's office, Leo. Bring back as many as you can carry and ammunition."

Leo didn't argue, happy enough to follow orders that made sense. He knew Flashman had commanded men before, and there was no time for ego. When he returned, Harry and the Countess were arguing nose to nose.

"Dammit, woman, do as you're told!" Harry turned to the priest. "Father, can you reason with her? Take her upstairs. This is no place for a woman."

Quick as a cat, Anastasiya whirled and snatched one of the rifles from Leo. In one fluid motion, she brought it up to her shoulder, sighted and fired through the glass. One of the corpse soldiers staggered, his left eye now a dripping, gory mess.

"I do not need to coddled," she snapped. "I know how to use a rifle and I will not sit idly waiting for Koschei to come for me."

Harry blinked. "Fair enough, have it your way. I am not sure what good rifles are going to do though."

"What do you mean?" Leo asked.

Harry pointed. "Look"

The soldier that the Countess had shot had gotten back to his feet and rejoined the formation, oblivious to the blood running down his face.

"What do you think they are waiting for, sir?" Ballantine asked.

"That." The priest's deep voice was somber.

The soldiers began to move, forming a clear passage through the center of their ranks. A dark shape strode through it, resolving into the terrifying figure of Koschei. He stopped and looked up at them.

"Gentlemen, there is no need for bloodshed tonight. Simply hand over the girl and you can leave unmolested. I do not want to provoke your governments into a rash act." Koschei smiled, a ghastly expression on that withered face. "Send her down and go."

"I'll be damned if I do!" Harry shouted. "Chivalry aside, I'd be barred from my club for life if I folded to a Russkie scoundrel like you."

Leo laughed. "How can I act a coward in front my father's renowned friend?"

Ballantine's reply was simpler, obscene and to the point.

Koschei scowled, his face darkening. "So be it!"

"Thank you." The Countess voice was quiet, stripped of its earlier haughtiness.

"Don't thank us yet, Your Illustriousness," Harry said. "Wait until we are on our way to Mother England."

"Or France!" Leo said.

Their joking was interrupted by Koschei's chants, words spoken in some tongue that was never meant to be heard by men. It rose to a crescendo as he pointed at them, and the dead began to march. A ragged volley of shots rang out as the defenders began to fire into the oncoming corpses. The soldiers staggered, but still kept coming on inexorably.

"Go for the knees!" The Countess didn't wait to see if they were obeying her, but put her words into action.

Each shot found its target, leaving a corpse convulsing on the cobblestones. They did not seem to be in pain, but denied the use of their legs, they were only able to claw their way forward an inch at a time.

"Oh, clever girl!" Leo shouted, receiving a shining smile in return.

His elation was short-lived. There were still scores of soldiers on their feet, and the chanting had started again. As Leo watched, Koschei held his palms about a foot apart, cradling a rapidly growing globe of pitch black darkness. Just before it touched his skin, he flung his hands open and away from himself, sending the globe arcing towards them.

Diving away from the windows, Leo only had time to shout, "Down!" before the world exploded and everything went dark.

Leo could only have been unconscious for a few seconds, but when he came to the entire shape of the room had changed. The windows were gone, and wood and rubble formed a ramp leading down into the square. There was a huge gash running down the center of the room, a gaping crevice that revealed the vast cellars below.

"Is everyone alright?" Leo looked around, and breathed a sigh of relief as his companions each answered.

"We may be in a spot of bother though, old chap," Harry said.

Leo could only agree. The corpses were beginning to move towards the ramp, and it would only be a matter of minutes before they began swarming into the room.

"Countess, grab some rifles, get behind the bar and try and keep them off us as long as you can," Harry snapped over his shoulder. "No arguing, just do it."

"I'm not stupid, I can see what needs to be done," she said. Grabbing the rifles, she vaulted over the bar gracefully, and began to lay out the rifles and rounds of ammunition, looking like she was ready to hold out forever.

The four men stood in loose formation, waiting for the dead. Ballantine and Leo had grabbed lengths of wood, and Leo felt slightly comforted by the sturdy weight in his hands. Flashman had slid a long blade from his cane, and its edges glimmered strangely, unlike any steel Leo had seen.

Harry caught him looking and grinned. "Silver. Remarkably effective in these sort of situations."

"What about you, Father, do you need a weapon?" Leo asked.

The priest held up massive fists. "These are the only weapons I need."

His face began to twist, his features coarsening and thick fur sprouting from his skin. There was the sound of ripping fabric as his muscles started to swell, his shoulders and arms thickening. Fangs protruded from his mouth and claws grew from his fingertips. As the other men watched, he continued to grow until, finally, a huge figure towered over them. Eight feet tall and unmistakably bear-like in appearance, it lifted its head and roared its defiance at the oncoming figures.

"If I'd known priests could do that, I wouldn't have dared draw naughty pictures in the margins of the *Songs of Solomon*," Harry said.

No one replied, as the first dead were climbing through the shattered window frames. As their feet hit the floor, Anastasiya began to fire, coolly picking her targets, kneecaps shattering as she found her mark. But for every corpse she crippled, two more took its place and, soon, the dead were upon them.

Leo swung his piece of timber in a steady rhythm, crushing skulls and shattering bones. To either side of him loomed

Ballantine and Grigor. The priest lashed out with massive arms, talons raking through flesh as he sent corpses flying to all corners of the room. The bodies would lie still for a few moments then drag themselves to their feet and stumble back into the fray. Ballantine was almost as impressive as the priest, far stronger than any normal man should be. Lifting one of the enemy above his head, he sent it hurtling into a group coming towards him, sending them in all directions like a boy playing skittles.

Flashman darted in and out of the pack, his sword weaving in intricate patterns, clashing against the curved swords of his opponents. When his blade bit into dead flesh, it seemed to do a more lasting damage than the wounds inflicted by the other men. Where the soldiers ignored staved-in chests from Leo's weapon or ragged gashes from the priest's claws, he saw one go down with Harry's blade through its heart, and stay down!

"To Flashman!" Leo yelled.

Instinctively, the other men began to herd the dead into Flashman's shining circle of silver and steel, protecting him from being overwhelmed and allowing him to deliver the *coup de grace* time after time. Anastasiya saw what they were doing and added her covering fire to their strategy. The pile of unmoving corpses began to grow, slowly but surely. Leo was just beginning to allow himself to hope when there was a flicker behind him, and the sound of chanting began to fill the air.

Leo whirled to see Koschei behind them, standing at the edge of the gash running through the floor. His chanting was reaching a crescendo, and horror clenched in Leo's chest at the sight of another of the black globes forming between the old man's hands. A wild shout on his lips, Leo sprinted towards the old man and leapt at him, hand outstretched, his only thought being to protect his companions from another of those devastating blasts.

Just before he hit him, he saw a look of surprise and terror on Koschei's face. Then, they were falling into the cellars

148

below, the precariously balanced rubble of timber and stone tumbling into the void with them.

The cellar was not simply dark, it was pitch black. A normal man would not have seen his own hand held in front of his eyes. But that did not bother Leo, the Nyctalope, who looked around in wonder. The cellar was massive, far bigger than he would have thought necessary for even a hotel, even one as luxurious as the Londonskaya.

The roof was vaulted and curved, and he could clearly see the gash they had fallen through, now filled with debris. Ladders ran up the walls to hatches, and strange block and tackles and ropes and pulleys dangled from the ceiling. Directly below one of them, he found the answer to his question. Stacked neatly were barrels of what must be gunpowder, while nearby, in another pile, cannon balls stood in a neat pyramid. All around him were stores of ammunition and weapons. Leo realized that this must be a cache put aside for a time of need.

There was a crash behind him and muffled cursing. Leo turned to see Koschei staggering around, arms outstretched.

"Where are you, Frenchman?" The old man's voice was a shriek. "I will tear out your kidneys and eat them in front of you!"

Leo began to carefully move in a circular pattern around the old man.

"What's the matter, old man? Can't see in the dark?" He moved a bit further around, then spoke again. "How do you plan on catching me?"

Koschei's head moved from side to side as if trying to get a fix on Leo.

"I don't need to see you. I can hear the thumping of your heart." His grin was unpleasant and knowing. "I can hear the way it beats; I can hear your fear."

The old man began to move towards Leo, hands feeling in front of him.

"I'm coming, Frenchman."

Leo concentrated on the beating of his heart, feeling the way that the delicate mechanism pumped the blood through his body. As always, he marveled at its technological artistry as he, gradually, began to slow its beat, until it stopped. A wave of dizziness reminded him that he only had a few moments before the lack of blood flow would render him unconscious and helpless. He picked up a lump of timber and padded noiselessly towards the old man.

"Where are you? Where have you gone?" There was a note of panic in the Koschei's voice that made Leo smile. "You can't hide forever, I will..."

There was a sickening crunch as Leo wrung the timber, catching the old man across his shoulders. With a grunt, the Nyctalope hit again and again, driving Koschei to his knees. But the old man was not finished. With terrifying speed, he lurched up and crashed his fist into Leo's chin, sending him reeling backwards, dazed and hurt. His back slammed into something hard and round, and he heard an ominous shifting noise as something metallic moved behind him. The cannon balls!

"Where are you?" The old man was howling with a mad rage that chilled Leo's blood. "I am going crack your bones and suck out the marrow while you weep for mercy."

Groaning with pain, Leo fought to bring his will to bear on his still silent heart. Finally, he felt the first beat, then another, as it sprang back to life.

Koschei shrieked in triumph. "I hear you! I am coming!"

He launched himself, sprinting towards Leo, arms outstretched and claw-like hands ready to rend and tear.

At the last second, Leo leapt to his right, letting the old man's momentum carry him into the cannon balls. With a terrific crash, the pile collapsed, burying Koschei beneath hundreds of pounds of lead.

Leo walked over and looked down at the monster. His limbs were bent at unnatural angles and blood pooled at the corner of his mouth, bubbling as he breathed laboriously. His eyes snapped open, and glared up at Leo and then, incredibly, he began to laugh.

"Do you think you have defeated me?" Koschei's voice was little more than a wheeze, but it was full of a terrible mirth. "They do not call me Koschei the Undying for naught. You could cut me into a thousand pieces and they would draw themselves together even if it took a thousand years! I may be trapped, but when I am free, I will hunt you down."

"A thousand years, you say? If I blew you into a million pieces, it might take even longer, *non*?"

"What?" Some of the mirth had left the old man's voice. "What are you doing?"

Leo began to whistle a jaunty little tune as he began to gather barrels of gunpowder and fuses, dragging them back to where the old man writhed helplessly.

This was going to be fun.

The fight with the corpse soldiers was over by the time that Leo dragged himself up one of the ladders and through the trapdoor. His companions were sitting exhausted in whatever chairs they had been able to find, surrounded by piles of cadavers.

Grigor had reverted to his human form; wrapped in his tattered robes, he was chatting with Ballantine, while Flashman was drinking a glass of champagne and trying to flirt with Anasatasiya, who seemed rather uninterested. As Leo approached, they all leapt to their feet, gathering around him and smiling in relief.

"Leo, old chap, am I glad to see you!" Harry said. "I was getting a bit worried there for a moment."

Leo felt a light touch on his arm and looked down into the viridian eyes of the Countess.

"That was very brave, leaping on Koschei like that." Her smile was enough to take away some of the sting of his cuts and bruises.

"Yes, well done, laddie!" Leo staggered as Ballantine clapped him on the shoulder. "Koschei wasn't expecting that now, was he?"

"But, where is Koschei?" Grigor asked, worry evident in his deep voice. "I had heard that he could not be killed."

"Koschei is shortly going to find out what happens when you get too close to one hundred pounds of explosive. It may not kill him, but it will be a while before he bothers us again." He looked around at his companions. "But, I'd suggest we get as far away as we can get in about…" he looked at his watch, "…three minutes."

"Sounds like a good plan, Leo." Harry gestured extravagantly towards the front of the hotel. "After you, Your Illustriousness."

As they walked away, as casually as if the were going for a stroll rather than trying to avoid being blown up, Leo could make out snatches of conversation.

"..England is lovely this time of year..."

"...oh, I know all the right people..."

"...with shooting like that, you must come hunting with me..."

Leo swore and hurried after them. He had a feeling that his biggest challenge was still ahead of him.

According to Jean de La Hire, Xavière de Ciserat, whom Leo married on Mars in 1911, was his first wife. Opera singer Laurence Païli (no doubt, the best singer since Christine Daaé!), who fought alongside him against Lucifer in 1921, was his second wife. We know that they had three children together, then separated, but little more than that. Then, Leo met and married his third wife, Sylvie MacDhul, after his battle against Leonid Zattan in 1926, but she died under as yet unrevealed circumstances in 1931. By 1936, Leo was married to Véronique d'Olbans, his fourth wife, whom he met in Le Roi de la Nuit. *Emmanuel Gorlier updates us on Leo's marital situation while bringing in a superheroine who has previously graced the pages of* Tales of the Shadowmen *and appeared in* The English Gentleman's Ball *collected in* The Nyctalope Steps In...

Emmanuel Gorlier: *Una Voce Poco Fa*

Paris, January 1936

"Una voce poco fa..."[2]

The clear, deep voice of Laurence Païli rose from the stage and filled the theater with a poignant melody.

In recent weeks, the singer had triumphed in the leading role of Rosina in *The Barber of Seville* at the Paris Opera. This evening's performance was exceptional, because it was to benefit a charity providing shelter for the poor who suffered from the rigors of winter. All of Paris was attending the gala, to see it as well as to be seen.

---

[2] These first two lines of Rosina's entrance aria from Rossini's *The Barber of Seville* can be translated as "A voice a little while ago," or "Not long ago, a voice echoed in my heart."

153

Leo Saint-Clair, a.k.a. The Nyctalope, was among the spectators. Being a lover of *Bel Canto*, he always listened with great pleasure to La Païli's recitals. Besides, she had been his second wife.

Either because of that, or because she genuinely did not enjoy this type of *soirée*, his current wife, Veronique d'Olbans, had declined to attend when they had received the personal invitation sent by Albert Sarraut, President du Conseil and Ministre de l'intérieur. As a result, Leo had invited the charming Rose Bruyère to be his guest for the evening.

Rose had been the best friend of his third wife, the late and still mourned Sylvie Mac Dhul, whom she had freed from the clutches of her evil stepmother Simone Desroches, better known as "Belphegor," when the latter had tried to steal the fortune of her father, Gregor Mac Dhul. Without her intervention, Sylvie could never have escaped Simone's machinations.

Lately, Leo had tried to reconnect with Rose, partly in memory of Sylvie, but she had been very busy. She had finally agreed to accompany him for this benefit gala, and now sat beside him at the forefront of a balcony situated to the right of the stage.

Earlier in the evening, when they had met again, for the first time in six years, Leo had rediscovered Rose. When Sylvie was alive, the Nyctalope had had eyes only for her, but now, he quickly fell under the charm of this wonderful and vivacious young woman. He had kissed her hand tenderly and entertained thoughts about her that were not proper for a married man!

For her part, it was also the memory of her beloved friend that had made Rose agree to accompany Leo. It didn't take her long, however, to realize the effect she was having on her companion, nor to divine his intentions.

Rose was hiding a secret, unknown to most, even to the Nyctalope. She was not from this era, but had been the victim of a dark, sorcerous spell in the 10th century; she had only been awakened a few years earlier by True Love's Kiss be-

154

stowed on her by Doctor Francis Ardan who had discovered her in her hidden castle.

Very independent in nature, she loved the 20th century and fought crime under a secret identity, that of the masked heroine known to all as the Phantom Angel! Also called "Beauty" by her friends, she had been given a set of papers in the name of "Rose Bruyère" by her associates in the Secret Society of Adventurers.

To her, an evening at the Opera was nothing more than a well deserved break in her adventurous life.

She was, therefore, more than a little surprised when, barely settled in their box, Leo had begun to deploy all his charm in order to seduce her. He used his immense charisma, the powerful gaze of his fantastic and penetrating eyes that could see through darkness as if it were noon, and which seemed to probe the very depths of her soul. On top of that, he made a gallant speech that stirred her feelings.

But Rose quickly made up her mind that she would not yield to his assault. She freely chose the men with whom she had affairs. If Francis Ardan was too disciplined, too tightly in control of himself, the Nyctalope, on the other hand, was far too exuberant and overconfident. She was, after all, the Sleeping Beauty and no man had ever dominated her; she would remain mistress of her actions.

A voce poco fa... From the stage, the insidious song evoking the surrender of a girl to her lover seemed to lend additional power to the Nyctalope's charm offensive. Rose struggled to address Leo with a few words that she tried to make sound as cold as possible, but that only came out as hesitant, something that an experienced seducer like Leo could not fail to notice.

Leo, for his part, had forgotten everything, the opera unfolding on stage before him, Véronique waiting for him at home, even the composed atmosphere of the theater. He suddenly grabbed Rose's hand...

Rose shuddered. *Who does he think he is?* she thought. She was going to pull her hand away brusquely, but her eyes

155

again became lost in his gaze and she felt like a gentle heat in her chest. She was going to tell him, in no uncertain terms, that his actions were inappropriate, when he slowly leaned towards her. *This time, I'm leaving*, she thought. But their lips met.

She turned her head to put an end to this intolerable situation, causing her to take her eyes away from the stage. Meanwhile, the Nyctalope knew that he was in full control of the situation. He looked around to check if they'd been noticed, as he didn't want to create a scandal. In the darkness of the lodge across from theirs, he suddenly caught a movement. A silhouette clad all in black was pointing a Thomson machine gun, of the type used by American gangsters, at them. The mysterious gunman was just about to pull the trigger and fire a hail of bullets at them.

The Nyctalope acted without missing a beat. Grabbing Rose, he slammed them both to the floor, finding temporary refuge behind the balcony. In so doing, he couldn't avoid putting one of his hands across her chest. Unaware of the threat hanging over their heads, and legitimately misconstruing his gesture as one more, bold, amorous advance, Rose angrily slapped him hard ascross the face.

"You pig!" she said. "I'm not that kind of girl!"

Before the Nyctalope could explain, the first rain of bullets hit the spot where they had been sitting only seconds earlier, blowing the gilded moldings of the loge to pieces.

"Who's shooting at us?" said Rose, recovering her aplomb with uncommon speed.

"He's on the loge opposite ours," said Leo. "Right now, I think he's reloading."

It did not occur to him that Rose, rather than he, might be the intended target of the attack!

Rose took a small mirror from her purse and tried to peer into the opposite loge, but it was pitch dark and she didn't have the Nyctalope's miraculous eyes.

"I can't see anything," she finally said.

"There's no longer anything to see; he's gone," said Leo.

"Let's go after him," said Rose. "He had to leave through the roof."

"Or the caves, where Erik used to hide. Stay here where you'll be safe. I'll take care of him."

Rose frowned; she wasn't at all willing to be left behind. Leo stood up cautiously, cast a last glance toward the opposite loge where the perpetrator had stood, and headed for the exit. Rose followed suit.

Together, they walked quickly towards the other side of the theater. Before crossing into the other corridor, leading to the other loge, they paused briefly to make sure they avoided another ambush. Once there, Leo took a quick look inside: the loge was indeed empty. Their enemy could only have taken the stairs up to the roof, or headed down towards the vaults.

"Up or down?" he asked Rose.

Either option presented serious challenges. The roof was an ideal place for the assassin to have another shot at them, but the vaults of the Opera were notoriously dangerous. On the other hand, unless the killer had brought a hot air balloon with him, escaping from the roof would be difficult. So they decided to go down into the bowels of the Opera.

As they ran down towards the vaults, Leo thought he saw the corner of a cloak disappear around the corner just ahead of them. He smiled and rushed forward. Unconsciously he put his hand to his cheek where he could still feel the sting of Rose's slap, but only smiled.

The Phantom Angel, meanwhile, followed the Nyctalope, cursing the narrowness of her dress. She looked forward to a time when women, just like men, would be able to wear comfortable pants at social events!

They arrived in the Vaults. They were in almost total darkness, except for a few, low lights. Rose was humbled by the Nyctalope's ability to move with uncanny precision in that tenebrous environment. However, she noted, not without some pride, that she was able to maintain contact with him.

Suddenly, one of her heels was caught in a crack in the ground and snapped. Rose nearly fell. She quickly discarded the broken shoe. For some reason, she held the undamaged shoe in her hamd as she ontinued barefoot in pursuit of their enemy, Leo still in the lead.

She rejoined him as he was exploring the wall behind a vast wardrobe of costumes, looking for a secret passage.

She joined him in the search and her nimble fingers quickly located a hidden switch. She pressed it and a section of the wall opened, revealing a dark corridor behind it.

In the distance, they could see a faint, but moving light, indicating that they were on the right track.

"That's him!" she exclaimed.

They entered the corridor and ran at a brisk pace. The faint glow had disappeared, but that did not slow down the Nyctalope, and Rose trusted his vision enough to follow him closely. After a turning a few corners, and going down a flight of stone steps, they arrived on the banks of the famous lake located under the Opera.

"We're near the lair of the Phantom," murmured the Nyctalope. "We must exercice caution. I've heard rumors, legends perhaps, that he sometimes returns to this haunted place…"

Rose pointed to the faint spot of light, far away.

"There he is!"

Leo looked and said:

"He's on a flat boat. There's a main connection that leads to the sewers."

"Let's follow him," said Rose.

"How?"

"On this," said the Phantom Angel, pointing out other flat boats stored nearby.

Without hesitation, they got into a boat. The Nyctalope took the oars and moved with determination on the calm waters. As an accomplished athlete, he progressed at high speed and gradually overtook the man in black, despite the latter's repeated attempts to lose them in the maze of the sewers.

The Nyctalope increased his pace. As they approached their enemy's boat, the Phantom Angel, as if moved by some uncanny presentment, told Leo to drop to the floor of the boat. Indeed, they heard a short round of machine gun fire followed by the whistlesof the bullets above their heads.

By the time they started again, their enemy had reached his destination: a pontoon where he had moored his boat. A narrow, winding stone staircase led to a mysterious destination above their heads.

After making sure that the killer wasn't again waiting for them in ambush, Leo and Rose quickly began their ascent.

After climbing the equivalent of three or four floors, they arrived at what was obviously a secret door. They pushed it and found themselves in a cellar filled with crates. They looked around and found another flight of stairs, which led to an ordinary door.

As they came out in a vast, marbled hall, they saw the shadow of a large statue representing a winged woman with no head or arms.

"It's the Victory of Samothrace!" exclaimed Rose. "We're inside the Louvre. And now, I know who our enemy is—it's Belphegor!"

"So the attack was directed against you, not me!" said the Nyctalope, whose vanity was mildly wounded.

"She is very vengeful," said Rose.

At that moment, another burst of machine gun fire resounded on the top floor to their left. Leo and Rose rushed in that direction.

They soon discovered the bloodied corpse of a night watchman who had had the bad luck of being in the wrong place at the wrong time.

Leo was about to enter the room where Belphegor was hiding, when his partner gently pulled him back and showed him a dark silhouette crouching behind a glass display case.

Between the door and the window, there was a zone lit by a streetlamp outside, the light of which filtered through a large window. If they crossed it, they would inevitably be detected—and shot.

The Nyctalope picked up a small chair, of the type used by the museum attendants to sit and rest between shifts.

For her part, the Phantom Angel weighed the shoe she still held in her hand. In her youth, she had often played ball games and won because of her skills at throwing. Did she still have it?

The Nyctalope looked at her and nodded so they could act in a coordinated fashion.

He then hurled the chair into the room. Belphegor immediately opened fire, shredding the piece of furniture. But in doing so, she had stepped out of her cover and exposed herself. Without hesitation, Rose took a step back and threw her shoe at the dark-clad woman.

She had lost none of her accuracy! The shoe struck her enemy's weapon. Belphegor dropped her machine gun and tried to flee. The Nyctalope rushed in after her. Pulling a Browning revolver from under her cloak, the Phantom of the Louvre aimed at Leo, but he was already on her and, exerting pressure on her arm on a specific nerve, paralyzed it. The sound of the gun falling to the ground echoed through the room.

Belphegor was defeated.

Later, Rose and Leo watched the police leave with the Phantom of the Louvre safely manacled between them.

They smiled and turned toward each other. Leo said:

"Shall we return to the Opera? We might still catch the last act."

"I'm not very presentable anymore," said Rose. "Perhaps we could drop by my place for me to change?"

"What a splendid idea" said the Nyctalope, grinning. "We should finish the evening in style!"

They walked away arm in arm.

160

Philippe Ward is a renowned "Occitan" writer from Southern France who has penned several thrillers and horror novels, including Artahe *and the remarkable* Song of Montsegur *(coauthored with Sylvie Miller), both available from Black Coat Press. The following short story places the Nyctalope in his native region and confronts Leo Saint-Clair to the persistent legends of the Holy Grail and the castle of Montsegur ...*

Philippe Ward: *The Hour of the Grail*

Montsegur (Ariège), June 21, 1936

Nestled on the Pog,[3] Montsegur waited. High in the sky, the Moon illuminated the scene, giving it the look of an opera set. The Nyctalope studied the ruins that stood majestically above him. He looked at his watch: 4 a.m. There was still plenty of time; at first glance, he estimated that it would take him less than an hour to reach the top.

He had left Paris three days ago to come to the Ariège; Paris with its strikes, its Popular Front Paris, its various events aimed at celebrating the accession to power of Leon Blum.[4] He had watched distractedly as men and women had expressed their joy in the new régime, but in his heart, he thought that his

---

[3] A term derived from the local Occitan dialect—*puòg*, or *puèg*, meaning peak, hill, mountain.

[4] French politician who was the leader of the left-wing Popular Front and was elected Prime Minister in June 1936. He was the first socialist and the first Jew to serve in that position and was the object of much hatred from the Catholic and anti-Semitic right.

world would soon collapse. France was surrounded by fascist dictatorships: Germany, Italy.... Even Spain now...

The Nyctalope began his climb. With his ability to see in the dark, it wasn't difficult. The slope wasn't painfully steep. He thought about the last few years... The Committee for Information and Defense had largely been dismantled after the tragic death of his wife Sylvie... He had returned to Mars to once again save Earth; then, he had completed a mission in Morocco where he had foiled a plot by Djinn. Finally, he had explored the wandering planetoid Rhea and had married Veronique. But they had recently separated and the pain of that failure was still raw.

Yet, the Nyctalope had agreed to a meeting in this strange place. The message had reached him in Paris. It told him to be at Montsegur on the day of the summer solstice at 6 a.m., and it was signed Otto Rahn. The man said that he wanted to meet him to discuss the future of Europe and, especially, to show him something that could change the face of the world. Rahn had ended his letter by stating that he was speaking on behalf of the "Polaires."[5]

Saint-Clair had questioned his contacts in the French police. He had learned that Otto Rahn was a German academic specializing in the Middle Ages, a Nazi party member who was researching the Cathars of Montsegur in the region. French counter-intelligence agents had been watching him as he had gathered a score of people around him, all revolving around the Cathars, and conferred upon them the name of "Polaires."

The Nyctalope had decided to meet this mysterious character. In the train, he had read a few books on the Cathars,

---

[5] The "Polaires" were a group of French esoteric seekers who shared a common interest in a magical system through which they could contact Agartha and the secret "Masters of the World."

including *Kreuzzug gegen den Gral* written in 1933.[6] In it, he learned that some high-ranking German dignitaries were passionate about everything related to the Occult. He did not understand what the Nazis saw in the Cathars. The Holy Grail, that mythic cup that had haunted the human imagination for centuries, had been, according to Rahn, in the possession of the Cathars, and the Crusade by the Catholic Church and the Louis IX, King of France, in the 13th century had had no other aim than to find it—and steal it. Saint-Clair closed the book, still skeptical and unconvinced by the German scholar's theories.

Once he reached the middle of his climb, Saint-Clair stopped to catch his breath. Without thinking, he put his hand into the right pocket of his overcoat; his gun was there. He had turned down the request of his assistants to accompany him preferring to go to the rendezvous alone. In any event, death did not frighten him. He had already faced it so many times that it had become almost a friend. Besides, if Rahn had wanted to kill him, he would not have made an appointment to see him; he would have shot him without warning.

Saint-Clair continued his progress, all his senses on alert; but other than an owl which greeted him as he passed, there was not a soul around. Even when he had walked through the village at the foot of the castle, he hadn't seen anyone and no cars were parked on the road. He wondered if Otto Rahn would, in fact, be even at the rendezvous.

He finally arrived at the foot of the ramparts. He crossed the threshold and found himself inside a courtyard surrounded by the heavy stone walls of the last Cathar citadel. A shiver ran through his body; he did not know how to interpret it. Here he was, in the middle of a ruin, not unlike thousands of others in France; yet, he felt a strange energy radiating from the ancient stones, almost as if they were alive. He thought back

---

[6] *Crusade Against the Grail: The Struggle between the Cathars, the Templars, and the Church of Rome* (First English Translation by Christopher Jones), 1934.

to the days of the siege of Montsegur by the troops of the King of France, when hundreds of Cathar believers had preferred to die at the stake rather than renounce their faith. Their souls were still present within the walls of the citadel.

"Monsieur Saint-Clair, I'm glad that you agreed to come."

The Nyctalope turned and found himself facing a medium-sized man with a thin nose and pointy chin. His hand was extended. Saint-Clair took it.

"I am Otto Rahn," continued the thin man in almost perfect French, with just a *soupçon* of German accent.

Saint-Clair had been expecting one of those young blond demi-gods prominently featured in Leni Riefenstahl's Nazi propaganda films. Instead, Rahn looked like a meek university professor, a man who would go unnoticed anywhere. That made him even more dangerous.

The Nyctalope looked around and saw a dozen people, including two women, who came out of the main tower and sat down on stones. None looked armed. If these were the Polaires, they didn't look particularly frightening.

"We do not want trouble," said Rahn. "My friends are only here to attend the big day."

"What big day? I thought it was the day of your Führer's accession to power?"

Rahn took Saint-Clair by the arm and led him up the main tower; they climbed some stairs and arrived in a room as deserted as the courtyard. In front of them was a single, narrow window. Rahn invited the Nyctalope to sit on a flat stone bench.

"What do you know about the Cathars, Monsieur Saint-Clair?" he asked.

"Your message intrigued me so I read a book about them on my way here, and I also made some inquiries about you and your Polaires..."

Rahn made a small hand gesture as if to say that that was relatively unimportant. A man and a woman entered and settled near the entrance without saying a word. The woman

164

was in her 20s, brunette, attractive, but she looked shy and kept her eyes down.

"I've been interested in the Cathars for many years. I've read a great deal about their religion, and the crusade against them, and here I am…"

"I've read your book, but I must say I'm not convinced. But unlike you, I'm not a specialist on the Cathars and, frankly, I don't understand the reason for my presence here."

"Don't be so modest, Monsieur Saint-Clair, or should I call you Nyctalope? The *Abwehr*, our intelligence service, keeps a thick file on you and your exploits. You did them a bad turn a few years ago in Morocco…"

The Nyctalope pulled out his gun and pointed it at Rahn, who did not move.

"Do you work for Otto Von Kubitz?" Saint-Clair asked in a harsh voice. "Is it he who has asked you to kill me, in revenge for what I did to him in Morocco?"

Rahn laughed.

"No, I will not deny that I work for the German secret service, but then almost everyone works for them these days. And to publish my book, I had to have an official sponsor, as it were. No, I asked you here today, because there's going to be a phenomenon that will change the face of the world, as I wrote you in my note."

The Nyctalope didn't put his weapon down; he looked at the man and woman, who had not moved an inch, then his eyes returned to Rahn.

"As I said," continued the German, "your record speaks for itself. You are not a mere mortal, you are far more. Almost a superman."

"Let me stop you right here. I'm not the kind of superman that your friends in Berlin seek to create."

"Don't be so modest! You've fought Lucifer, saved the King of Spain, and even tried to assassinate Hitler."

The Nyctalope could not hide his surprise; few people knew about that assassination attempt thwarted by the Time Patrol.

"You are the ideal person to witness this great day. I need a witness whose word will not be questioned."

Suddenly, a ray of sunshine appeared on the horizon. The woman got up and walked to the tiny opening in the wall.

"It's almost time," she said, turning to Rahn.

"Go and fetch the basket," said the German.

The woman left the room immediately.

"Time for what?" asked Saint-Clair, putting the gun back into his pocket. For the moment, it was useless, since no one was threatening him.

Rahn got up and moved to the narrow slit to watch the light that was gradually filling the sky.

"The Hour of the Grail," said the German in a low voice.

He turned to the Nyctalope and stared at him with a look that contained more than a gleam of madness.

"I have not spent my time just reading books; they were only the map which guided me here, to the heart of Cathar country. Then, with my friends, I searched all the sites where the Perfects lived. And I've made some strange discoveries. In this very castle..."

He gestured at the walls.

"I don't see what's so strange about it," said the Nyctalope.

"For someone who has been to Mars, don't tell me that you don't feel the vibrations that emanate from its walls? We're not in a mere castle; we are inside the very Temple of the Holy Grail!"

Saint-Clair was forced to acknowledge that Rahn had a point. Since he had entered Montsegur, he felt as if he was in another world, another dimension, like a bubble outside of space and time.

"The Cathars celebrated the summer solstice," continued the German. "And they built this temple according to that date. I discovered that fact a few years ago, but I could not come back until today to check my theory."

"They weren't the only ones celebrating the solstices."

"True, but they were the only ones in possession of the secret of the Holy Grail.

"You mean, the cup that collected the blood of Christ?"

At that moment, the woman returned, accompanied by two men. They carried a wicker basket which they deposited in front of Rahn.

"The blood of Christ is what matters; the Cathars supposedly threw the cup out the window."

"What about the emerald that fell from Lucifer's forehead during his fall?"

Rahn put his hands inside the basket and pulled out a clay pigeon.

"You can't imagine that the Cathars would worship an object that belonged to Evil. Remember that, for them, Earth is the domain of Evil. The soul must be purified over many reincarnations in order to earn the right to live in the world of Good."

Saint-Clair asked himself if Rahn was not merely eccentric, but actually crazy. Life had taught him to beware of such men, capable of anything, including being right. He decided to take the German seriously. Besides, he had not long to wait now. In less than an hour, he would know if there was anything in Rahn's theory.

The German laid the dove down on a stone, facing the narrow slit. Then, returning to the basket, he pulled out a parchment, which he unfolded with extreme precaution and carefully laid out on another stone. Saint-Clair examined it. The black ink had disappeared in places, but it was still legible. It was written in Latin. He translated the first sentence and began to read aloud:

"Holy Father, who watches over the just spirits, thou art..."

"Stop it!" screamed Rahn. "You're insane! You'll spoil the ritual!"

Saint-Clair drew back. The German's eyes were full of hate, but his face soon mellowed.

167

"Please, excuse me, but reading this prayer is an essential element of the ritual."

"Is it a Cathar prayer?"

"Yes. I first saw it mentioned in the archives of the Inquisition, but there, the copy had been purposefully truncated, whereas this parchment is authentic and complete. I found in a cave that served for the initiation of the Perfects near the village of Ussat. This is probably one of the few remaining Cathar texts in our possession today. Without it, we would be powerless..."

Rahn returned to the basket and pulled out another parchment, which he also unfolded cautiously. It was half eaten by time, and its lower left corner was gone. The German looked at it carefully.

"This scroll was found in the same cave. Do you remember what I wrote in my book? That a treasure had been carried out of the castle of Montsegur the very last night before the Cathars were massacred?"

"But isn't that a legend, like the ones about the Templars' treasure?"

"Not at all!" exclaimed Rahn. "We have three consistent statements about the removal of the treasure, made before the Inquisitors. That treasure did exist, but it was not gold or jewels, but prayers and sacred rituals. And it is I who have found it! This is the great secret of the Cathars!"

The Nyctalope nodded.

"And what is this big secret?"

"You'll discover it at the same time as we do. The hour approaches."

Rahn turned to the woman and said:

"Esclarmonde, prepare yourself."

The woman nodded and knelt before the stone where the parchment lay. She grabbed a stick and traced a huge pentagram on the ground, with the dove at its center.

"The prayer, the pentagram, the dove and the sun. The solstice is almost upon us. Anything that you've experienced until now is nothing compared to what you're about to see,

Saint-Clair. Stand in a corner of the room. You're not pure enough to be inside the pentagram."

The Nyctalope obeyed without question. The men waiting in the courtyard entered; there were five of them, of various ages. Silently, they went to stand at each corner of the pentagram. Saint-Clair understood that they were there purely to make up the numbers. Rahn had reserved the starring role for himself.

The sun now lit the sky and its beams arrived at the foot of the castle walls, progressing towards the narrow slit. In a few minutes, they would enter the room. Rahn might have been right: the Cathars had probably built the castle based on this event.

Rahn checked all the preparations one last time, then entered the pentagram. He stood in the center, facing the window slit. He grabbed the stone dove and held it before him.

The Nyctalope stepped back and stood behind the door leading into room. The sunbeams were now at the bottom of the window. Rahn turned towards the girl and gave her a nod. The ancient Cathar prayer went up the tower and the Nyctalope felt chills through his body as if the temperature had suddenly plummeted. The light came through the window. Saint-Clair's entire body was trembling and he could not stop it. The beam reached Rahn.

Saint-Clair no longer heard the prayer; it was merely a buzz. The light of the sun almost filled the small room. The Nyctalope put his hand over his eyes to avoid being blinded by it. It was only a matter of minutes before the rays of the sun would hit the dove.

Esclarmonde's voice fell silent. And the sun's light struck the dove.

A fireball filled the room. The Nyctalope thought his body was burning, but he felt no pain. He slowly opened his eyes and saw that the room was now bathed in a yellow glow. Otto Rahn was still standing, but the stone dove was gone, replaced by a real bird flying above the participants' heads. The light softened for a short time as the dove alighted on the

169

head of one of the men. All his senses on alert, the Nyctalope watched the scene, trying to understand what was happening, but, apart from the light and the dove, nothing seemed to have changed.

The dove flew and landed on the hand of the girl, who gently stroked the bird. Esclarmonde then walked up to Rahn, but without entering the pentagram.

"You are not worthy to enter the world of Good," she said hoarsely. "Your soul is not pure. But that of the young woman is."

She raised her hand; the dove flew away and the young woman burst into flames. In less than five seconds, she was but a small heap of ashes. In turn, the five men also burst into flames, forming five human torches. A barrier of fire now surrounded Rahn, threatening to engulf him. Saint-Clair vaguely saw the German struggling to escape the deadly trap. Without thinking, the Nyctalope ran through the flames and pushed the German violently outside of the pentagram. They rolled on the ground. When they rose, the sun's light had left the room.

They quickly left the castle of Montsegur, now fully illuminated by the summer sun. They saw the dove flying above them towards the pog, which opened mysteriously, and disappear inside.

"I made a mistake," murmured Rahn, stopping on the way. "It is true that I was not worthy, that my soul was impure."

"Nonsense," said the Nyctalope. "I don't know what happened exactly, but it wasn't the work of a just God. Forget all of this! It's just one more of the Devil's curses to confuse and deceive people."

Rahn replied in a voice that trembled slightly:

"You're wrong, Saint-Clair. Remember what the troubadour said: *seven hundred years hence, the laurel will blossom anew*. I look forward to seeing you here on March 16, 1944—in eight years."

Leo Saint-Clair did not turn back. Other adventures awaited him.

March 16, 1944

The plane flew over the pog at Montsegur. From inside, the Nyctalope looked down at the castle. Eight years had passed. During the war, he had tried to get news of Otto Rahn. A Nazi officer had told him the German scholar he might have committed suicide on an Alpine glacier. This did not surprise Saint-Clair.

He had used all his connections to have a plane and the authorization to fly over the mountain, located in the forbidden zone. Throughout the intervening years, the last sentence uttered by Rahn before leaving Montsegur had haunted him. And he had made himself the promise to return to Montsegur on March 16, 1944. History might have decided otherwise. But today, he was there.

He tapped on the pilot's shoulder and gave him a nod. The man pressed a button and a plume of black smoke appeared in the wake of the plane, which made several turns around the pog.

Finally a Celtic cross appeared in the azure sky. The plane veered again and moved closer to Montsegur. Saint-Clair saw a column of a dozen people climbing the side of the mountain. They were probably Polaires who had come to test Rahn's theories. He wondered whether he should join them, but finally decided that nothing would happen.[7]

He turned to his right.

---

[7] Authentic. At exactly high noon on March 16, 1944, a small aircraft appeared and flew over Montsegur several times, dipping its wings in salute. Then it used skywriting equipment and formed a huge Celtic cross in the sky.

171

A dove was flying a few meters away from the aircraft. A thought crossed his mind: *Thank you for helping the laurel to blossom again.*[8]

---

[8] "After 700 years, the laurel will blossom again on the ashes of the martyrs," is a famous Cathar prophecy.

The shadow of the impending second World War also weighs heavily on this story, which is a prequel of sorts to Jean de La Hire's Night of the Nyctalope. This time, Leo travels to a remote area of Western France to unlock a terrible secret that finds its roots in ancient history...

Julien Heylbroeck: *Blood and Weapons*

October 1938

Paris, Café Chez Lansquine. Leo Saint-Clair opened his newspaper. The headlines were alarming. A dark threat hung over Europe and the world. It was raining in Paris, which added to the ominous atmosphere. The Nyctalope read along with the cadence of the raindrops. Dawn seemed to unfold slowly, sluggishly, as if numbed by the cold. Or by fear. The sky was still more dark than pink. In the shadow-filled room, the silhouette of the CID Chief could hardly be discerned. The owner stuck his head out of the scullery and hailed his customer.

"You must not be able to see a line. Let me turn on some lights!"

"It's useless, my good man. Anyway, I am finished with my reading and my coffee. Would you please summon a cab? Duty calls!"

The bartender, a fellow with a mustache and thick lips overhanging a triple chin, nodded. The motion shook the mass of fat framing his face. Leo Saint-Clair was a regular. He came in to this establishment for two well-packed coffees every morning, even on Sunday, and always at the same time, making him the first customer. It was as if he never slept, or almost never. The innkeeper wondered what news had prompted his customer to leave the café before his second cup. It must have been something very important.

It was still early when Saint-Clair reached the cobbled streets of Montmartre. He paid the driver, then entered the offices of the Committee for Information and Defense after pressing a button hidden in the woodwork of the mansion's elevator. It descended to a subterranean level off-limits to all but a few. In the large main room, just beyond the corridor, his two Corsicans assistants were tinkering with a strange ray-gun that he had recovered on a mission to the ends of the Earth.

"Boss? What's up? A new case?""

Vitto and Soca recognized the signs of anxiety etched on their leader's forehead. The Nyctalope stopped and regarded his assistants with his unique gaze, as piercing as an eagle's preparing to dive on its prey.

"Get me a train ticket, please. The earliest train to Montaigu."

"Will you need our services?"

"I think I'll be able to fend for myself. But you never know... I may send you a telegram. Be ready for that eventuality."

Saint-Clair placed his folded newspaper folded on a table cluttered with several disparate objects, some weapons, a bronze Tibetan statue of the Buddha, an Indonesian mask and a red stone from Mars. The page had been stained and warped by raindrops. While the head of the CID packed his luggage in the next room, Soca threw a glance at the article that graced the wet page. The title was "A new child-disappearance in the Vendée."[9] The article was short and spoke of this wave of disappearances in a dry tone. This was barely news anymore. There had been no ransom demands, and too many disappearances to be written off as runaways (twelve in just a few months). The police and the newspapers weren't advancing any theories.

---

[9] An region in western France.

The train stopped at the Montaigu station with a screech of metal that grated against the eardrums of the few people standing on the platform. The rain had accompanied the train all the way from Paris, and was waiting at the destination. A fine cold drizzle that crept in everywhere, piercing the thickest clothes like countless needles.

Saint-Clair turned up the collar of his coat, straightened his hat and grabbed his leather suitcase. He still had to go seventeen miles to Tiffauges, where he planned to rent a room. A massive car of a familiar French make, yellow and black, all bedraggled with mud, was waiting. The driver spotted him and quickly moved to his side, offering him the tenuous shelter of his umbrella. Saint-Clair had booked the taxi before leaving Paris to avoid having to make the journey in a peasant's cart.

The road was difficult. Cattle had crossed in several places, churning up the ground and mixing it with their excrement. The vehicle nearly slid off the roadway several times.

The Nyctalope took advantage of the trip to talk to the driver and learn more about the object of his visit.

"You came by the Paris train, Monsieur? If I may ask, what brings you to our neck of the woods?"

"I've come to investigate the news reports of disappearing children."

The driver, a man with a ruddy complexion and graying muttonchops, turned his head to talk to his passenger, but his eyes quickly returned to the road. The downpour drew trails on the windshield that distorted and deformed the outside world. The wipers were so overwhelmed that Saint-Clair felt sorry for them.

"Ah, Monsieur, this is a terrible story. Lots of kids have set out in the morning, never to be seen again."

"These children, when did they disappear? On the way to school? At night?"

"It is mostly the little shepherds. There are some who go to school all morning. In the afternoon, they will go to watch the flocks. And this is when they disappear, Monsieur. There have already been many who have vanished, and none of these

175

has ever returned. The police are baffled, no one knows what to do."

"Well, that is going to change! I will he helping the police now, and I promise you that I won't rest until I have found... Ah! I think we arrived. Thank you for the ride, and keep the change, my good man."

The hotel-restaurant was in sight, a small building located on a street that wound from the church to a ruined château.

An old woman greeted him with a sad smile, apologized for her slowness and offered to take his suitcase. Saint-Clair declined and was content to follow her up the narrow stairs to his room. The old woman stopped several times, her face gray with effort.

"Dinner is served at 7 p.m., Monsieur. Tonight, we have cabbage soup and fresh picked mogettes[10] with bacon."

The hotel was mostly vacant. Saint-Clair thought for a moment he might be the only customer, then he saw a man who had also gotten drenched, but was in no hurry to get to his room. Saint-Clair greeted him, but the man breezed past him, not acknowledging the greeting or even pausing to glance at the Nyctalope.

After quickly checking in, and taking a small glass of vodka to warm up, Saint-Clair left the hotel and went to City Hall. As per his earlier telephone arrangements, the Mayor, a man named Bourgaud, was waiting for him, along with Adjutant Mariac from the Gendarmerie. The Mayor's office was spartan. A bust of Marianne, and a framed photo of President Albert Lebrun stood over a functional desk covered by an ostrich leather blotter. The Mayor, a rotund man whose clothes were too tight, sat behind the desk, while Mariac, in his uniform, stood at his side. Saint-Clair shook hands with two men. Neither showed any surprise at seeing the head of the CID—which sometimes worked with local police forces—showing up at Tiffauges.

The Gendarme spoke in a dry tone:

---

[10] Beans.

"We are on the case, Monsieur Saint-Clair, but I must admit that we've been stumbling. These children disappear while they are watching the livestock. I won't lie to you, we thought the first disappearance at harvest-time last September was just a runaway heading to the big city. I forwarded the report to the authorities in Cholet and Nantes. My men have patrolled the area. They have searched the ditches, dragged the ponds, checked all the abandoned barns and ruined buildings. Nothing. And there have been successive disappearances. We increased our patrols and I asked for reinforcements to search the fields. We staked out some sites to catch the kidnappers. Twelve children went missing in two months. No ransom demands, no bodies found, no child showing up in any of the surrounding villages..."

"The community is terrified, Monsieur Saint-Clair," the Mayor added. "No child leaves home. Schools are closed. Foreigners are watched with suspicion. Worse, some Gypsies who had settled on the barrens were chased away by a rock-throwing mob. Some blood was shed."

"It hasn't stopped," the Gendarme said. "Children have even disappeared from the safety of their homes. The parents went to tend their crops and, and when they returned, they found the door or a window broken and the children missing! I have even called on the army, but I was told that I had to deal with the situation myself."

"I need to hear more," the Nyctalope said. "Can I talk to the families of the missing children? How old were these kids?"

"They were between seven and twelve, and mostly boys. All of them were farm-children, living some distance from town. I have a list of the families, and I am at your disposal," Bourgaud said, holding out a folder, held closed by a strip of fabric. "You are welcome to use the car we keep here at City Hall. Can you drive one?"

Though the official's question was innocent enough, it annoyed Leo.

"Of course I can. I piloted a radioplane to Mars, Monsieur le Maire."

The man with massive shoulders, wearing a worn plaid shirt and trousers, poured a glass of home-grown wine. Saint-Clair was in a cellar. Around him, on the stone walls, stood a variety of bottles and old wooden barrels bound with iron bands. A round table and wooden stools completed the furniture. Saint-Clair had come directly to the family of the last child to disappear.

"You say that little Matthieu never returned from the pastures. Can you take me there?"

The man nodded and offered to give the Nyctalope a ride. The rain had subsided, replaced by a light drizzle, which sometimes gave way to mist. Together, they rode up to a field that extended down a slope. Below, a small river wound through a stand of trees. The rain had caused it to overflow at some of the bends, creating large puddles that made the field impossible to cross without wading.

"Please understand, Monsieur. We had no choice. Some have kept their children indoors. They have the priest come and bless their homes. Here, that was not possible. My wife is sick; she has barely been able to walk since her accident. I needed the boy to tend the rabbits and keep the sheep in the meadow. I had to make a sale. I gave him the blunderbuss, just in case. He was a good little hunter, you know? He's often accompanied me in the woods. He is scared of nothing. My wife heard a shot, and then he yelled. She tried to go to him, but she was too weak. I met her halfway there, passed out in a deep furrow in the garden. I thought she was going to die. As for my boy, he was gone. It's the Devil who has stolen my child. We are bewitched. It is impossible!"

The father had tears in his eyes and his shoulders hunched under the burden of his guilt. Saint-Clair could hear the stress distorting his voice. Around them, in the field, stood a few sheep, their wool drenched, indifferent to their master's torment as they grazed. The sepulchral silence was only broken only by the gurgle of water in the stream.

The Nyctalope bent down. His piercing gaze had been attracted by a broken branch. He approached the tree. The gunshot had etched many shallow grooves in the trunk and broken the limb. The boy had fired in that direction. He must have been standing exactly where his father stood now, on a raised flat rock.

The abductor must have arrived and frightened the child, causing him to fire. Most likely, it had been someone that didn't belong in the woods, someone he didn't know.

Saint-Clair took a few steps and crossed the river by stepping on several stones poking above the water. They were slippery, but the investigator was agile and quickly reached the other shore. He was no longer in a field but in a small wood. He waved his hand, signaling the farmer that he was going to explore the surroundings. There were no footprints. The abduction had taken place four days ago. The ground, hammered by rain, had smoothed over, obliterating any tracks. Saint-Clair had questions. The farm was isolated. The dirt road leading to it, remote. The abductor would not have come on foot; that would mean walking miles to capture his prey and then carrying it back. How could he do that? On horseback through the woods, perhaps?

As he considered this possibility, the Nyctalope noticed a small mound of earth, about a meter and a half high. It was covered with moss and brambles grew around it. He walked to the far side and pushed aside some ferns, uncovering a tunnel entrance! He peered into the darkness. It would have been necessary to crawl because the entrance was narrow and even lower than it was wide. The smell of wet earth and decaying humus assailed his nostrils.

The Nyctalope bent his head and leaned in a bit, ignoring the olfactory assault. It was pitch black, as dark as ebony, but the investigator didn't care. Night vision enabled him to detect the details as if it were daylight. There, sheltered from the rain, he spotted traces of crawling. Large clumps of earth had been flattened by someone pushing his way through.

Before venturing further, he straightened up, rubbed his overcoat and the knees of his trousers, which were irreparably soiled by mud, and hailed the farmer. The half-soaked man joined him. He had more difficulty fording the stream, but neither man said anything about that. Saint-Clair pointed to the mound and its dark entrance.

"Did you know about the existence of this?"

"Certainly, Monsieur. These are the tunnels dug by the Chouans.[11] Rumor has it they run all the way to Chavagnes-en-Paillers. This is where our forefathers fought against the Blues, burrowing, hiding their wounded and their weapons. Between that and the windmill blades they used for communications, they had the advantage in the field."

"Do you know where it leads?"

"It's a maze in there. Many of these tunnels have collapsed sections. Nobody really knows where they lead. Some tunnels are dead ends, others have been filled in or flooded with water. Why? Do you think they have taken away little Matthieu through there?"

"It's a possibility. I need to have a map of this network."

Saint-Clair hung up. The departmental archives at La Roche-sur-Yon had not yielded much information. They had no clear plan of the tunnels. The employee had even let slip his exasperation about the detective's request. These fables about tunnels allegedly used by the royalists were only a local peasant rumor. No serious historian gave credence to the existence of this underground network. However, if there were any documents from the period, Saint-Clair had only to turn to Monsieur le Baron Desme d'Esloo, an eccentric old man mentioned by the official. This great collector and antiquarian might help.

---

[11] Royalist who fought a long war of resistance against the French Revolution (the "Blues").

It was a track he had resolved to follow because the Nyctalope, though intrepid, was certainly not suicidal. It wasn't safe to venture into the tunnels without at least an idea of where to go. If he took a wrong turn, he could get stuck or lost for hours of underground crawling. He might as well go see this Baron, whom the archivist said was a little crazy. He just had to find his address.

Saint-Clair opened the door, causing the bell over it to tinkle. The sound called attention to him. The bar was long and narrow, with a counter that ran the length of one wall. The place was full of mustachioed fellows, dressed in coarse linen suits, wearing heavy boots that had been battered and stained with mud. Cap in one hand, a glass of red wine in the other, they drank and talked in low voices. They were all farmers, or almost all. Logically, the room should have been noisy, smoky and filled with laughter, like any self-respecting popular establishment. But here, a tense silence, almost palpable, hung heavily over the scene.

The Nyctalope spotted a man in a suit, stuck behind a table, absorbed in reading a newspaper. He went to the bar and ordered a glass of wine with a gesture. The conversations resumed after a break which the men spent staring blankly. The bartender, a man in his thirties brought him a glass and a bottle of Baco.

"Perhaps you can tell me something, my good man, I'm Leo Saint-Clair, from the Committee on Information and Defense. I'm here to help the police investigate the disappearances of the children."

"We need all the goodwill we can get, Monsieur Saint-Clair, the drink is on the house. It's not every day a guy from the capital shows some concern for our kids. Right, guys?"

Several farmers stressed the correctness of the barman's statement by pushing and grunting, swearing against the police. Leo heard some choice phrases.

"You know the legend of the tunnels? The ones that run underneath the fields?"

"Ah, yes, everyone here knows that. But they are half filled-in, I think, packed with soil to keep them from collapsing."

"I am looking for a Baron Desme d'Esloo. Do you know where I can find him?"

"Ah, the Baron... Are you sure he can help with the investigation? I don't see quite how. He's afflicted with senility. We haven't seen him much since the death of his wife several years ago. That said, if you to go see him, it's his specialty. He lives at the Château de Boisniard, a few kilometers from here."

As he left the bar, Leo Saint-Clair realized that almost all of the customers were staring at him. They continued to talk, but it was only empty words, for use in mock conversations. Some of the looks were suspicious, others frantic with hope. The chime sounded again, and again the Nyctalope returned to the icy downpour that had waited patiently for him to finish his inquiries.

The château, just past an abandoned park, filled the landscape, showing off its two square towers and its main building like a dying old man too vain to acknowledge his decline. The building featured a collapsed roof and decrepit walls, while many shrubs and bushes had escaped the confines of the French garden to spread haphazardly across the aisles, engaging a ruthless struggle for space. The sky was lit with a fleeting glow of a lovely sunset.

Saint-Clair thanked the farmer who had brought him in his cart. The Mayor's car had refused to start, and he hadn't had the patience to call for the region's only taxi. Time was against him. He wondered if some of the children were still alive. It was possible, and that meant there was no time to lose.

A thick fog had followed the rain, which seemed to be taking a break to recharge its moisture. The clouds hung motionless in the low and heavy sky. The dying breeze could scarcely move these gray masses, cottony and menacing. They gave the Nyctalope a feeling of claustrophobia, as if the sky would soon come down to earth, crushing everything beneath it.

The gate was rusted open. It had probably been like that for a long time judging by the weeds that had coiled around the crumbling bars. The gravel crunched underfoot as Leo twisted and turned past misshapen shrubs that his once been cut into decorative squares or spheres. No light escaped from any of the château windows, leading him to believe it was deserted. A bird or a squirrel moved in the foliage, breaking a few twigs. The Nyctalope felt a presence behind him. He turned quickly. There was nothing, not even a wild animal, a fox or a hare. Was he imagining things? He walked toward the main entrance.

Reaching the steps, he climbed a flight, passed a stone pot containing a dried bush, and rang the bell. The noise seemed to echo through the surrounding area, waking up the dozing woods. Then, with almost an air of reproach, the heavy silence returned, broken only by the flight of a flock of birds that had been startled. Leo was about to ring again when he heard shuffling footsteps approaching. An old man opened the door. His skin was leathery and sagging eyelids framed eyes which were jaundiced but still shone brightly. The mouth was a toothless maw and the lips, without anything to support them, had caved inward.

"Who have I the honor of addressing?"

The Nyctalope took off his hat.

"Baron Desme d'Esloo? I'm Leo Saint-Clair, Private Investigator, Head of the Committee for Information and Defense. I would like to speak with you. Please forgive me for not having made an appointment."

"Oh, dear ... An appointment, you say? Pah! I receive no visits from anyone. Not ever."

The Nyctalope entered and hung his coat on the hook near the door. The room was rather large and, at its center, stood a large staircase leading to the second floor.

"I understood that you were a collector of antiques. Don't you have visits from buyers?"

"You do not quite understand, Monsieur Saint-Clair. I collect, yes, but I do not resell anything. Nothing at all. I keep, so to speak, everything I buy or find."

The Nyctalope grasped the implications of this statement as he followed the Baron into the huge main salon. There was hardly enough room to walk. All the furniture: cabinets, bureaus, and bookcases, were covered with an impressive array of knick-knacks. Stacks of books with red, brown, or blue bindings, coats of arms on the walls, hunting trophies, maps both folded and opened, filled the room. It was as if a giant had thrown a snowball whose flakes had been replaced by various bits of junk. He followed the old man along a well defined path between the piled antiques to a small space that seemed like a boudoir, centered around a low table and two armchairs upholstered in frayed red velvet.

"Sit down, I'll get you some tea. Forgive me. I dismissed my housekeeper last year. I have not really been able to afford paying anyone. My passion is ... consuming."

Once his host had gone, Leo Saint-Clair took a few steps into the room. He admired the overflowing library, the shelves that were bowed under the weight of collectibles. He took care not to touch anything, because many of these pieces were precariously balanced. It was dark now and the investigator wondered how he would return to town, but that wasn't the important thing.

Minutes later, the old man returned with a tray topped with a small Japanese teapot and two earthenware bowls.

"I hope you like green tea. I no longer drink it. Or almost never."

Desme d'Esloo accompanied his last sentence in a wink. Then he served the steaming drink by the dim light of two small gas lamps.

"But tell me, what can I do for you?"

The Nyctalope dipped his lips into the hot tea. It was bitter, but strong; a real treat. He smiled thinking that very little escaped the Baron. Saint-Clair was glad to have such good company for this conversation.

"I am investigating the disappearance of a number of children in this region, mostly young shepherds. I think it is possible that the kidnappers have used the old tunnels, at least once, in any case. I was told that they dated from the time of the Revolution or even earlier. They also told me that you would be the only person who might have a map of this network."

"Ah, I see. May I presume you spoke to someone at the archives? They don't like me very much. I often buy beautiful pieces that they want, but can't afford. I bet they told you that such a document probably did not exist."

"Indeed."

The Nyctalope put down his cup and glanced at the old man's bright eyes. He could see the reflection of light dancing there.

"Well, they're wrong. They are just not aware of any. If I dared..."

The Baron tried to rise, but failed. Leo Saint-Clair moved to offer his help but he raised his hand and bracing himself on the arm of the chair, stood up, wincing.

"Old age, my friend... I said, if I dared, I would say they do not know much. Follow me..."

They crossed the room to an ancient secretary with a weathered finish. It didn't take the Baron long to find a box that was hidden in a drawer. He put on thin gloves and opened it, revealing an ancient book. On the red cover was a depiction of the ruins of the Château de Tiffauges.

"This... is priceless. If I wanted I could restore Boisniard just by selling it. But I refuse. Oh, I'm sure that, in a few years, an heir, a cousin or nephew that I have never seen, some stupid uneducated jazz-loving brat may get a good price for it, but that doesn't concern me much."

He opened the book gently.

"Look... This is a historical and geographical study of the château and its surroundings. The book was written just after

185

the Revolution, in the early 18th century. Only a very few copies were ever published and most of those were destroyed by the Church."

"By the Church? A historical and geographical study on an ancient château? But why?"

Desme d'Esloo grabbed a large, circular magnifying glass rimmed with gold.

"Look here. At the bottom of some of the pages... Do you see these symbols?"

He pointed a yellowed fingernail at a long a series of warped drawings that were almost obliterated.

"Yes, think I see a cross..."

"Look closer, my friend, look closer."

The Nyctalope bent. There was little light, but that made no difference to him. He examined the drawing. It looked like a cross, but the crossbar was not at the correct height. An inverted cross. And next to it, was it a star? No, a pentacle. He sat up, surprised. The old man looked at him with a glint in his eyes.

"Yes, it is well hidden, isn't it? This is a book made someone named Alphonse Prelati. This man was an acclaimed expert on regional history. He settled here, in this castle, at the time of Vicomte Hillerin de Boistissandeau, in the early 1800s. Ostensibly, he was preparing the family's genealogy, but his real plan was to explore the underground passages and collect information about Gilles de Rais. He was finally chased out by the Vicomte, who was tired of paying a drunken historian who did nothing but hang out in bars and fields. Prelati disappeared from the region. He wasn't well-liked here and was totally discredited. We find him later in Paris, during the dismantling of a secret Satanist cult. Then we lose track of him. He wrote the book right before he fled and published it with the backing if an anonymous donor. The book is actually a *very* special study."

"You mentioned Gilles de Rais. Is that the same man who was nicknamed 'Blue-Beard,' who was the companion of

Joan of Arc, and who was later arrested, tried, hanged and burned for the murders of many children?"

"Yes, he was the master of Tiffauges."

"Tiffauges? But I thought his château was at La Suze-sur-Sarthe?"

"It was one of his many estates. The most famous one because it was where they found the bones used as evidence in his trial. He also had a château at Champtocé-sur-Loire, and one here in Tiffauges. Prelati's book recounts the terrible fall of the murderer, the story of his château, but not just that..."

"Then the missing children..."

Saint-Clair thought about this and his dark suspicions gave him goose bumps. It made him think of something.

"Remind me, please, why did Gilles de Rais kill those children?"

The old man took a sip of his tea, then resumed his story.

"It is said that the killings began in 1432, following the death of his grandfather, a violent and sadistic man who had abused him. Gilles de Rais, who was then Marshal of France, surrounded himself with a company of murderers and hunters who roamed the woods, capturing peasant children, runaways, and young beggars. They were all from the lower classes, so their disappearance didn't create a clamor. He is said to have abducted 800 children, though the numbers are questionable. They were brought to him in a special room of one of his four castles where they were hung from iron hooks and suffered the worst possible torture. Gilles de Rais committed the abuses himself, laughing as he watched them die. He disemboweled them and preserved parts of the bodies; his favorite was the head. He was assisted by a man named Poitou, who slaughtered his victims, a Parisian named Eustache Blanchet, and a wizard named... you've guessed it: Prelati!"

The ancestor of the book's author, the Nyctalope realized.

"Gilles de Rais' outrages lasted for eight years. Do you understand? Perhaps 800 children killed in eight years? Then he was arrested in 1440 for breaking into a church by force of arms and threatening a priest. During his trial, he finally confessed all his crimes and begged for forgiveness. He was hanged and then burned on October 26, 1440 in Nantes. Gilles de Rais was a practitioner of black magic and alchemy. In his book, Alphonse Prelati claims that he was very close to obtaining some sort of philosopher's stone by using the blood of his innocent victims. He recorded much of his research, various ceremonies and alchemical formulae. Almost a manual, so to speak. Hence the blacklisting of the work by the religious authorities. I said that the French authorities have also banned the sale of the book, but they have not tracked his copies as diligently as the clergy. But that's not all. In this book, there is also a clear map of the facilities that Gilles de Rais used. The author explored the underground passages at Tiffauges and..."

Suddenly, the lights went out. The room was instantly as dark as night. A shot rang out and a jar containing some kind of featherless bird exploded, splattering formaldehyde all around. Saint-Clair threw himself on the Baron, dragging him to the ground.

"Don't move!" he whispered. "Stay on the ground! I'll deal with these thugs!"

There were a lot of them. The Nyctalope could see their silhouettes crossing the hallways. One of them was outside and walked past a window. They had cut the gas to extinguish the lights and plunge the Baron and his guest into complete darkness. But they hadn't reckoned with the superhuman abilities of Leo Saint-Clair. He took a cavalry saber from the wall and unsheathed it, then stealthily moved to the entrance.

"They are there, I think..." one of the attackers whispered from close by.

"Did you get them?"

"I think so," his accomplice said. "They aren't moving."

The beams of several flashlights swept the hallway. One of the men approached. When he was within range, the Nyctalope sprang up like a jack-in-the-box and cut a large gash in his body. When the man started to fall, Saint-Clair lowered him gently so as not to alert his comrades by the

188

sound of his fall. Then he extinguished the light. He could both see in the darkness and blend easily into it. His artificial heart had not panicked, allowing him to assess this situation calmly and professionally. He grabbed the gun from his assailant and moved away, pistol and sword at the ready.

Another attacker appeared in the entrance, following the man the Nyctalope had just eliminated, and proceeded to grope in the darkness. The irony was that, what the attackers thought would disorient him, had actually given him a great tactical advantage.

Saint-Clair allowed him to come closer. The invader was an overweight man of 30 with a mustache who clutched an 1886 Lebel rifle. Saint-Clair spotted sweat dripping from the man's forehead. He positioned himself directly behind him, raised the sword and, with his other hand, tapped the pistol butt against the banister. The man turned and moved forward, impaling himself on the sword's point. He did not suffer. The Nyctalope had targeted his heart.

That left two more assailants, including the one outside. Saint-Clair hoped he hadn't missed anyone. Despite his caution, a sudden ray of moonlight illuminated him, allowing the assailant just inside the front door to spot him. He opened fire. The Nyctalope plunged to the ground as bullets blew holes in the paneling above him. The smell of cordite filled the room. The man was equipped with a flashlight and frantically probed the room with its beam. He aimed at the bullet holes and across the floor, but Saint-Clair had disappeared without a trace. The man walked along the corridor carefully, his back to the wall. Then he spotted the bodies of his two accomplices.

"In the Name of God!" he swore under his breath. Then he began a slow retreat to the entrance, always with his back against the wall.

Obviously, he did not want to be the next to die. They had had planned to find the old man and his guest in the dark, paralyzed by fear. Instead, the man found himself stumbling over the corpses of half of his group, decimated by a silent shadow that seemed to pierce the darkness. He turned as he reached the front door and just had to see a fist flash to meet his nose at high speed. The rest was darkness.

"He's waking up, I think," said the Baron. "What about his accomplice, Monsieur Saint-Clair—the one outside?"

"I haven't managed to catch him. He panicked after seeing his companions disappear and fled. I got as far as the gate but the only thing I saw was a car in the distance. Hopefully, this one will tell us a little more..."

The man was securely tied to a Louis XVIII-style chair. His face was hard, with a flat nose, two rather globular eyes and a thin-lipped mouth, surrounded by an overgrown beard. His head had been freshly shaved.

The man blinked. His initial expression of surprise became more somber when he looked around the room and realized the extent of his predicament. He tried to struggle and break his bonds. He was quite muscular, but Saint-Clair paid him little attention. He had his back turned, and was busy deciphering the pages of the Prelati book. Then, he turned round and, his hands resting on the edge of the table cluttered with various objects, said:

"You will have to reimburse Baron Desme Esloo for the loss of this fabulous bird... What was it, Baron?"

"A rare specimen from New Guinea. Unfortunately, not very well stuffed. He'd begun to rot and I had resigned myself to keep it in formaldehyde. Not that valuable, if you ask me. But I was attached to it. It was a gift from my wife from one of our trips in the wilderness."

"You bastards! Let me go or I swear it'll go bad for you!" growled the prisoner.

The Nyctalope stared at the prisoner. The man accepted the challenge and did not blink. But he eventually turned his head and looked elsewhere.

"I doubt that your threats are frightening enough for us to release you," said Saint-Clair. "Remember that two of your comrades are lying dead on the floor of this castle. Not that I intend to kill you, I do have some principles. But these facts should encourage you not to brag pointlessly. Answer my question: What are you doing here? Who was the target of your attack?"

The bandit spat on the carpet; an angry glow lit up his eyes; he was ready to challenge Saint-Clair again.

"I won't say anything. Our cause is much bigger than me. I will never betray the League!"

Baron Desme Esloo looked at the face of the Nyctalope. Before, it had expressed a certain kind of jovial irony, but now its expression was so cold and merciless that the old man shuddered.

"I assure you that you will speak. Even if I must get my hands dirty. I know your attack is somehow connected with the disappearance of the children. I am determined to shed light on this matter, ven if it means hurting you badly."

The prisoner seemed to weigh this naked threat. He redirected his gaze to the master of the house.

"OK. I'll... I'll tell you what I know. But first, I'd like a glass of water, Monsieur le Baron.

The Baron looked at Saint-Clair, who nodded. The old man grabbed a glass on a shelf and poured some water from a nearby pitcher. He then went around the chair and brought the glass to the mouth of the prisoner and helped him drink. Then he put the glass down and returned to Saint-Clair's side.

Suddenly, the man threw his head back violently. His face became flush. The veins swelled on his neck as if under pressure Then, with a horrible hissing sound, the man's head exploded, letting out a stream of blood and the smell of charred flesh.

All this had taken place within a few tenths of a second. The Nyctalope rushed toward the prisoner, but it was too late. The skull was nothing more than boiled bone and brain and only the ropes binding the man prevented the body from falling. Saint-Clair crouched and looked at the horrible scene. The Baron hurried to open the window; he was very pale, on the edge of collapse.

"A slight smell of sodium. The glass of water... Yes, that's it! He must have coated his mouth with a sodium solution. An explosive substance when it comes in contact with water. A dreadful scheme! Extremely painful, too. To think he was willing to undergo such a terrible death in order to protect his organization... We're facing a tough opponent, Baron! They're extremely determined. The death of this lunatic is undeniable proof of it. It is likely that the stakes are substantial! They've captured the children to find the philosopher's stone. They're in search of wealth. They probably enjoy the facilities and expertise of Gilles de Rais in the vaults of his castle. That's why they came here. They probably followed me during my investigation to see what I discovered. And then, when they saw me meet you, they wanted to stop me... Gilles de Rais, the torturer of innocent children ... This accursed sadist continues to claim more lives almost five hundred years after his death. I think I could use your copy of the Pelati book, Monsieur le Baron... The plans will be useful to me. I just have to go out there and unlock the secrets of this League. Notify the police, ask them to pick up the body and place you under their protection."

The old man said nothing. He was tempted to wish good luck to this strange investigator, who was as brave as a soldier and as deadly as a tiger, but was it really necessary? This Leo Saint-Clair was already so competent that luck seemed to have nothing to do with it. He just gave him the copy of the book, without a word.

"I realize its value," said the Nyctalope, "and I will bring it back. You can count on me, Baron."

"If you must return to Tiffauges, take my car. I'm not using it very much these days."

The return trip went quickly. The Baron's automobile was a roadster and the Nyctalope made the engine roar. He put the pedal to the floor and his goggles protected his eyes from the whistling wind. He slowed down as he reached the town so as not to attract attention.

It was now late in the night. Saint-Clair parked on the lower side of the road, just before the village entrance. Above him, at the top of the hill, the fog shrouded ruins of the château seemed to challenge him. The foundations, made in the typical manner, consisted of large stones, rough-hewn, but solid enough to have weathered the fires of the Revolution and the ravages of time. The building and grounds lay fallow, abandoned for decades. Brambles had climbed the walls, gripping the stones, the vegetation reinforced by many years of wild growth. The ruined keep at the top was filled with stones and had not been usable since the days of Richelieu. There remained only the exterior walls, large and square whose corners were reinforced curves overgrown with weeds. Around these, one could distinguish the remains of a chapel, several towers and some sections of the wall that must once have reached to a great height.

Yes, this château, even mistreated by history and forgotten by men, certainly deserved the respect usually reserved for beautiful buildings. Its imposing nature evoked silent awe.

Saint-Clair opened the book. The binding produced a small creak that sounded like a reproach. After resolving to have it laminated, the investigator located the chapter devoted to the château's underground passages. The entrance was located under a heavy flagstone of one of the sections of the keep. This was the main access to the network of caves and secret rooms.

Saint-Clair continued to unfold the sheets, pasted to the pages of the book, which seemed to be accurate maps. A whole network of tunnels stretched beneath his feet. He sought a second entrance or the equivalent, an underground drain, which would allow the lord to escape in case of siege. Such a passage often ended a few hundred meters away and was hidden by natural features. Finding one here would be useful for it would allow him to enter the former torturer's secret chambers without warning any potential criminals of his arrival. Yes! It was definitely there! A small pipe snaked under the ramparts to run along the hill to an entrance located down near the river Crume.

The Nyctalope walked cautiously until reaching the river that rippled peacefully under a veil of mist. The tunnel entrance was easy to find. It was hidden from view by a small pile of rocks, heavy enough not to be displaced by the river, but light enough so that they could be shifted by human strength. Saint-Clair thought that this passage was quite discreet, but that it would be flooded when the river was high.

That was not the case now and, within seconds, the Nyctalope found himself crawling through the narrow passageway, muddying his custom-tailored suit once again. The darkness in the passage was absolute, but that didn't prevent the detective from pausing to consult the old book for the right branch. The tunnel being about 600 meters, the Nyctalope had to navigate the galleries for almost an hour.

Finally, he reached a chamber where he could stop and plan ahead. Before entering the secret passage, he took out his pistol—a French brand—and a hunting knife. Any bulkier weapon would have encumbered him and slowed his progress. The room was vaulted. Rusty irons hung on the moss-covered walls. Saint-Clair thought he was nearing his goal. This was the entrance to the antechambers of torture.

He crouched, taking time for a look at the book to memorize the different sections. It was like a maze. Some tunnels went away, several hundred meters but most were used as corridors to reach a series of four rooms, themselves situated around a hexagonal central hall built directly under the keep. According to the map, there was even a secret staircase, hollowed into the thickness of a wall, which would allow him to go directly to the surface.

Saint-Clair turned a few pages and came across a drawing of a child hanging from iron spikes and bleeding from several wounds. His blood was collected in golden basins. The precious fluid was then placed into a succession of glass beakers and stills. After being filtered through this apparatus, the blood produced a few drops of a smooth, non-reflective black substance. Once there was enough, one had only to submerge some lead in it and wait a few days. The lead absorbed the *substantia nigra* which transformed it into gold. The hardest part was the processing of the blood. It was required very precise control of the temperature and the addition of a few ingredients at key moments.

The Nyctalope returned the book to its leather pouch after wrapping it in a cloth for protection.

Saint-Clair advanced, his feet sinking into the stony clay. The humidity made breathing difficult. There was no noise, except for the occasionally dripping of water from the ceiling.

After several turns, he neared a section from which occasional flickers of light escaped. He heard moaning and the characteristic sounds of people at work. He advanced cautiously, avoiding the puddles that were more numerous here than at any point since he had entered the tunnels. Saint-Clair infiltrated the room as silently as a shadow, moving forward until he had a good view of its shape and its occupants, but what he heard shattered his careful strategy. A deep, emotionless voice called out an order:

"Bleed him, and quickly! We need to go!"

On hearing a child's panicked cry, the Nyctalope rushed headlong into the room. All that mattered now was saving the boy. However, he had the presence of mind—almost a reflex—to knock over the torch at the entrance, then fired two bullets at the torch on the opposite wall.

The two firebrands fell to the ground where they were extinguished in the puddles with a characteristic hissing. The room was plunged into darkness so dense that it was palpable.

The hall was large and had a higher ceiling than the rest of the underground system. At the room's center, a terrified little boy hung from a set iron hooks attached to chains. All around were laboratory tables on which were placed ornately wrought glass containers. A huge French flag hung on the side wall.

195

The occupants of the room scurried like ants whose mound had been kicked over by a destructive, sadistic child. They moved in all directions, stumbling against each other. Several made their way to a stack of wooden crates as they shouted contradictory orders. The Nyctalope fired at one of them and the retort echoed loudly in the confined space, assailing the gang's eardrums.

The man he had targeted let out a weak groan, clutched his chest and collapsed. Another—the Nyctalope recognized him as the little man in the suit who had been reading his newspaper in the café—groped his way to the child, scalpel in hand. He placed it against the boy's throat, causing a drop of blood to bead on his pale skin.

"Don't come any closer! Don't fire again or I swear, I'll bleed him!"

His voice rose to a shrill pitch, giving testimony to his fear. He tightened his grip on the boy, who began to shiver and sob. The man continued:

"Alfred, turn on the light! Whoever you are, I warn you, if I hear or feel you approaching, I will kill him! Oh, you can always shoot me, but if you do, you will reveal your position. And I advise you not to miss because with my last strength, rest assured, I intend to cut his throat! Henry, get ready to fire if the intruder moves ... Henri? Henri?"

"I believe that I killed him," whispered the Nyctalope who, during the man's discourse, had crept like a cat behind him.

With a Japanese hold that would have done credit to his friend Gnô Mitang, Saint-Clair disarmed him and rapped his temple with the butt of his automatic, knocking him out. The man was right, a shot would have revealed his position. The remaining henchmen had probably had time to seize their weapons. Shielded behind crates and among the tables, they were hidden from Saint-Clair's piercing gaze. He would have to use cunning and his mastery of the darkness.

He spotted a desk on which there was a container of caustic soda and approached stealthily. He laid his pistol—a virtual cannon—on the stone floor and poured the liquid over it. Soon the compound would eat through the metal and explode the powder. He hurried off, pulling out his hunting knife.

Meanwhile, the men talked to each other in whispers. One gave a cry of rage and tried to charge at the Nyctalope. He missed and tripped over a bench with a gasp of surprise. Another tried to relight a torch with his lighter, but again, the Nyctalope spotted him and neutralized him with a ju-jitsu choke. His victim slumped against him, deprived of oxygen long enough to fall unconscious, but not enough to die.

It was then that two bullets exploded, shooting the nearby wall. The gunshots attracted the attention of the thugs who emptied their weapons at the gun. In response, another shot rang out, one of the stills shattered under the impact sending shards of glass in all directions. Now the Nyctalope knew all of their positions. He took advantage of the distraction created by the last shots from his gun, to put criminals out of the way, one by one. He overwhelmed them, knocking some out and killing those who resisted the hardest.

Finally, helpless and terrified, the two remaining bandits cried for mercy and stood almost simultaneously. The Nyctalope ordered them to stand against the wall and bound them. Then he lit the torches, restoring the room's light. It wasn't a pretty sight. There were some acid fumes, debris everywhere and a number of corpses littering the ground. In the center of the room, the child had passed out.

"Now tell me who you are and why you're torturing children like this!"

One man, a bit of a dandy, his upper lip adorned with a very thin mustache, gazed at him, an uncomfortable expression in his brown eyes. Finally he spoke:

"We are the League of the Sons of France! Who are you to dare oppose us?"

"I am Leo Saint-Clair, the Nyctalope, head of the CID. Who is your leader? Why are you taking these children? What

197

kind of research are you doing? Where are the children? Speak, you filthy torturers!"

"I... I will answer you but I'd like a glass of..."

The Nyctalope dismissed the demand with a wave of his hand.

"There's no way I'm going to let you blow yourself up! You will tell me everything. Should I remind you that we are deep underground, you're alone, tied up and I have all the instruments you've used to martyr these poor little ones? Now, where are they? I advise you to answer me immediately.""

The man seemed to think about it for a moment. Then his attitude shifted to a stubborn silence as he gave the Nyctalope a defiant look. The other, a pudgy man with a bald head and round glasses with one cracked lens, squirmed. He spoke, ignoring his companion's reproachful glare.

"We collected the blood from three of them. The others are in a nearby chamber in iron cages. We wanted... We wanted to continue the work of Gilles de Rais and Prelati. The Philosopher's Stone... Changing lead into gold... Wealth!"

"At the cost of children's lives! You're monsters willing to sacrifice youth to enjoy gold made acquired at the cost of innocent blood!"

The mustachioed man spat and looked up. His eyes burned and his features shook with anger.

"What do you know? What do you know about our goals? Do you think we intend us to bask in Morocco or some Mediterranean island with our loot? Ugh! Our goal was far nobler. Are you one of those who shut their eyes to what is happening in the world? Don't you see the situation in Europe?"

"What do you mean?""

As he asked the question, the Nyctalope released the child and placed him on a table he had stripped of its scientific paraphernalia. Then he spread his overcoat across the boy's unconscious body.

"Germany, Monsieur. Hitler's Germany is rearming intensively. She is starting wars just around the corner! She al-

198

ready has her eye on neighboring countries. It won't be long before she wants to avenge the insult of the Great War. And what do we do while this is going on? We dance, we go on vacation! The Popular Front and their Communist cohorts are pushing us toward defeat."

"What is the relationship of this to the murders you've committed?"

"The blood of the children means gold, and gold means weapons. We, the Sons of France, will arm our homeland with the weapons she needs to defend herself when the German eagle moves on us. We have already begun to finance our production with gold ingots. The League watches over the country. Stop us and you weaken France—your country, Saint-Clair—on the eve of the war. Make no mistake, the war will come sooner or later, and we don't have the means to fight against a country that has been preparing for over fifteen years. Which do you care about: strengthening France and preventing our annihilation or the fate of a handful of bumpkins' kids? Are you going to show your patriotism or will you turn your back on your country, like a craven coward?"

The Nyctalope tried to reply but he felt a cold blade slip into his back, then a burning pain, which sliced into his kidneys. He tried to turn but couldn't and let out a cry of pain. He had been stabbed! He didn't have a chance to see his attacker who drew back quickly while the Nyctalope fell to his knees, tears in his eyes.

"Go ahead, Lord Cultnom, bleed the bastard."

He would plant his knife in Saint Clair's throat in another moment. The Nyctalope put a hand on the ground, the other pressed his side which was already wet with blood. It cost him a superhuman effort and nameless suffering, but he threw his right leg back with all his strength, aiming at the man's knee. The shock was terrible. The assailant yelled and dropped his weapon. He tried to retreat, limping and grimacing at every step. Leo staggered to his feet but, before he could turn him around and face him, Cultnom, with a backhand motion, dropped a phial filled with blue liquid to the ground. It broke, releasing thick smoke.

This formed a screen between the Nyctalope and his assailant, who used the cover to hobble away through the gallery. Leo Saint-Clair had turned around but his unique eyes, which could pierce the darkness, couldn't do the same with smoke. All he could see was a male figure with brown hair rushing down the underground corridor.

The two thugs shouted at their leader to come back but the Nyctalope decided to let him go. He was clearly in no condition to pursue anyone. Pushing back the dizziness that assailed him, he reached the surface through the main entrance. It was urgent that he raise the alarm before the criminals could slip their bonds and escape. The staircase seemed interminable and raising the slab he exhausted his remaining strength. He stepped into the open air and nearly sank to his knees. He would never make it up the street to the police!

But Baron Desme d'Esloo was waiting for him, accompanied by Adjutant Mariac and his men. He had contacted them before going to the castle to search for the secret entrance. The old aristocrat rushed to Saint-Clair to help him stand while the police broke into the basement to collect the children and the two killers.

Lord Cultnom was never found. According to the confessions of his accomplices, he had cooperated with the League of the Sons of France, but did not share their "patriotic" aims. The only thing that seemed to interest him was the occult experimentation conducted by Gilles de Rais. In agreement with Leo Saint-Clair, Desme d'Esloo destroyed Prelati's unholy book in the fireplace of the Château Boisniard. The next day he sent a telegram to the CID claiming that the smell of sulfur that emerged from the burning book was so vile that he had to open all the windows.

France declared war on Nazi Germany on September 3, 1939. She was defeated a few months later and signed an armistice on 22 June 1940.

The delicate subject of Leo's collaboration with the Vichy regime and the Nazis is one of the most fascinating aspects of the character, and certainly what makes him unique amongst the pantheon of popular heroes. In that respect, the Nyctalope's fictional life reflects the same ambiguities and conflicted choices that his creator, and indeed France itself, had to make. The Road to Hell, they say, is paved with good intentions. We now present two stories illustrating the tragic moral downfall of Leo Saint-Clair...

Matthew Dennion: *The Road Not Taken*

London, 1942

Rain was falling from the sky in a steady downpour. The alley was wet and smelled of rotting food because the sanitation workers had not yet commenced to pick up the refuse the soldiers had left there.

Leo Saint-Clair perched on the ledge of building opposite the one he was keeping under observation and focused on the task at hand.. Slipping past the guards to get to the roof had been easy. His ability to see in absolute darkness allowed him to shift through shadows which normal eyes could never penetrate.

He stared through the window at his target. The man he had been sent to kill was planning a bombing raid scheduled to take place the next day. The raid was ostentatiously aimed at military targets controlled by the Nazi, but it would be French citizens, not German soldiers, who would be killed. It was part of what Vichy described as a "campaign of terror" by the Allies to dissuade the French to join the Resistance.

Leo pondered again over the great divide that separated so many Frenchmen, and had even alienated him from his own son. Why did so many of his compatriots not see that it was wrong to let France become a bloody battlefield? Hadn't the country suffered enough? Some called him a traitor for supporting Maréchal Pétain, the once hero of Verdun, but it was they whose allegiances had shifted, not him. If, tonight, he could stop a bombing raid that would kill dozens of French civilians, then wasn't he still a hero?

Leo took a deep breath and attempted to regain his calm composure. He surveyed his target once more. He was a World War I fighter ace who had risen to a command position in the current war. There was no record of his real name—he was simply known by his alias: G-8. He and his squad had flown countless missions against the Germans during the Great War. On numerous occasions, they had faced supernatural enemies and fantastic monsters. In many ways, he and Leo were brothers-at-arms. He, too, had fought in the trenches and had had his share of encounters with the Occult.

The difference, however, was that G-8 was still viewed as a hero, while the Nyctalope was reviled by a great number of his own countrymen.

G-8 stood in front of a huge map, addressing the pilots. Leo could see the admiration on their faces as they took in every word he spoke. This was in stark contrast to the stares he received from his superiors who regarded him as some kind of uncontrollable weapon to be used only on suicide missions and never to be trusted.

Leo spat in disgust as anger coursed through his body. How could this G-8 be viewed as a hero while he was a traitor? The ace's friends, family, and countrymen were all safe at home with two oceans between them and the frontlines. Unlike the French, American civilians were not exposed. G-8 could well afford to fight the Nazis since he didn't have to make any of the hard choices Leo had. Everyone Leo knew would have been deported to the camps had he not joined the Resistance. The Nazi had slaughtered entire villages for the rebellion of a single man. Leo used whatever influence he had gained in Vichy to save as many innocent lives as he could. G-8 was not burdened by any of these concerns.

The Nyctalope watched through the window as G-8's men stood and cheered after he finished his briefing with some kind of patriotic speech, and his anger grew as he thought about those who cursed his name every time they heard it.

Leo jammed his fist into his hand. He could have joined the Resistance or fled to England, too. He could be the beloved commander standing there, right now, cheered by his men. He could have been all of those things, but everyone he loved, and more, would have been tortured, starved, or gassed. For making hard choices, his friends had deserted him, condemned him, while G-8 was admired by all.

Leo waited for the room to clear out until G-8 was alone with his two friends, Nippy Westin and Bull Martin. Then he saw his chance. With his judgment clouded by his anger, he passed on the opportunity to shoot the ace from the safety of his ledge. Instead, he jumped over the narrow alley and crashed through the window.

The Nyctalope moved like lighting. A quick roundhouse kick to the temple floored Westin. As his foot hit the ground, he spun around and caught Martin with a spinning back fist. The large man's face no sooner hit the floor than he was kicked in the jaw and lost consciousness.

G-8 threw a punch, but Leo ducked. The Nyctalope dropped to the floor and delivered a kick to the back of the ace's knees, sending him sprawling to the floor. Leo then stood atop the American, repeatedly striking him in the face. With each blow, he saw his fist connecting with everyone who shamed him, and hated him.

Leo pulled back his fist to deliver another blow when, for the first time, he caught a glance of the map of the planned bombing raid.

He saw the targets clearly marked out and a blue line running through. He quickly understood its meaning. The raid was not the "terror attack" his Vichy masters had told him, but only a cover to help the Resistance mount an attack against the

203

concentration camp at Aincourt and free as many civilians as possible before they could be sent to Auschwitz.

Leo's anger quickly turned to disbelief. Once again, they had lied to him! They had sent him to murder the man who was orchestrating the escape of the very people he was seeking to protect!

That brief respite allowed G-8 to regain his senses. Through swollen eyes and a bloody, battered face he looked up at his attacker and recognized him from their common exploits during the Great War.

"The Nyctalope? But why?..." he said.

Leo could hear the soldiers running down the hall towards the briefing room. He sprang out the window, landed on his feet in the alley, and into the cover of darkness.

He now hated himself more than ever, but was it because of what others thought of his choices, or because of what he, himself, thought?

Several allied officers sat around a table in a room with a single light hanging from the ceiling. There were four guards standing at attention, and a young man seated on stool in a corner.

An American general spoke up:

"Gentlemen, we can longer ignore the fact that the Nyctalope is working for the Nazis. Until now, some of us have not believed, or did not want to believe, that this was the case, given his service in the last war as well as the various occasions on which he saved the world. However, his recent attack on G-8 has shown where his true allegiances lie. We all know what a formidable opponent he can be. Furthermore, no one really knows the true extent of the resources he can muster. Therefore, I strongly recommend that we devise a plan to eliminate him."

A British officer stood up.

"Gentlemen, we can't very well send a military unit after him. We need a more surgical approach. The naval officer I brought with me has shown a remarkable aptitude for espionage and assassination. I propose we give him clearance to eliminate the Nyctalope."

All eyes turned toward the young man sitting on the corner stool as he slid a cigarette into his mouth. The American general addressed him:

"What's your name son?"

The young man removed the freshly lit cigarette from his mouth and replied:

"Bond. James Bond."

Like Matthew Dennion, Chris Nigro explores the difficulties the Nyctalope felt in attempting to reconcile his principles and his politics. In this story, taking place during the Götterdämmerung *of Berlin in 1945, Leo must face an even greater evil than that of the Nazis...*

Chris Nigro: *Requiem for a Regime*

Berlin, Early April 1945

Leo Saint-Clair walked purposefully down a secluded side street sequestered within a city that he knew was soon to be under siege.

He was well aware that the Soviet forces were rapidly approaching the heart of the Nazi government, and he doubted that Hitler's remaining forces, which were gathering to defend its municipal borders, would be sufficient to halt the forward progress of Stalin's Red Army. Because of this, it was of crucial importance that he should succeed in a mission that was both essential to the Vichy government, and of a highly personal nature before the Russian ground assault reached the area and turned it into a battlefield: the rescue of the great archeologist Aristide Clairembart.

Clairembart's good friend, the already legendary aviator Commandant Robert Morane, was busy fighting under the auspices of General de Gaulle in the FFAL, and would have had a considerably more difficult time getting into Berlin than an agent of the Vichy government like Saint-Clair did, which is why he had asked the Nyctalope, using back channels, to rescue the archeologist.

Unlike Morane, Saint-Clair couldn't bring himself to fight against the French government alongside the "Free French" that de Gaulle was leading, despite its growing popularity amongst the population of his beloved but occupied nation. These days, Saint-Clair had little respect for Maréchal Petain, the once triumphant winner of Verdun, and even less for the Nazis, whose ideology made him cringe in disgust, but he did understand the notion of pragmatism.

He still believed that the best interests of his beloved France didn't need the kind of civil war that the policies of de Gaulle might foster, especially not at such a precarious point in history. He respected and supported what the Allies were doing, but at the same time, his homeland and its interests had to come first. He didn't like the collaboration between the Vichy government and the Nazi regime, but he felt that working with the latter for the preservation of the former had been a necessary evil. In any event, the Nyctalope was aware that the end was nigh, for his gathered intelligence made it clear that the next few months would determine the final fate of Nazi Germany, as well as the French regime that had supported it.

As he walked down a street littered with the debris of buildings and vehicles, blown to bits by the recent shelling, that cool spring evening just as the setting sun cast portentous shadows upon the wreckage, he knew that he had to get Professor Clairembart out of this hellhole before the arrival of the Red Army.

The Nyctalope looked rather nondescript dressed in an ordinary business suit, approaching a mostly undamaged building. He had taken special precautions to look as inconspicuous as possible since he didn't want it to be known that a Vichy agent was working in Berlin against Nazi interests on the "liberation" of Clairembart. Of course, the archeologist had a knack for getting himself into trouble due to his immoderate enthusiasm for cracking any archeological mystery of extraordinary merit. And what he had been brought here to identify certainly fit that particular bill, if it turned out to be authentic.

Within the fourth floor of the abandoned building, the Professor sat at a heavy table glaring at a black and white photograph that had been handed to him by one of three irate *Wehrmacht* officers. The one that seemed to be in charge, who identified himself as Heinrich Müller, bade the Professor to identify an object he saw in the photo.

"Now, Herr Professor," Müller said sternly, "if you truly wish to leave this place and get back to that comfortable hotel we have provided for you, then you will tell me if the artifact you see in this photo is truly the Spear of Destiny, *Verstehen Sie mich?*"

It would seem that being one of the world's renowned experts in my field doesn't always work to my advantage, the Professor thought as he solemnly glared at the photo. He was well aware that if he identified it as *the* genuine Spear of Destiny, he would never be allowed to leave Berlin alive. He needed to play this carefully, and hope that Bob Morane was aware of his predicament. *Damned Nazis, I hope I live long enough to see Bob—or anyone else!—arrive to put a bullet into their skulls...*

"Rest assured that I am considering this very carefully, Herr Müller," the Professor replied in his best "poker" voice. "But due to the poor quality of the film, I must be certain before I render a professional opinion..."

Müller slapped the archeologist on his shoulder, causing him to wince in pain.

"No more dawdling, Professor. You and I both know that the photo was taken by the best camera German technology has yet to invent. You are privileged to be the man whose expertise has been sought to identify this remarkable find."

"There have been rumors circulating around about a recent German expedition to the Arctic," the Professor hastily responded, trying to keep up his verbal delaying tactics as long as he could, "so perhaps if I knew more about the circumstances surrounding this discovery..."

Müller proceeded to grab the archeologist by the back of the neck and slammed his head on the table with great force, then promptly pulled his face back up so that he could view the photo again.

"You try my patience at your peril, Professor!" the Gestapo officer shouted. "You are in no position to be asking questions instead of answering them, so you had best carry out your task without further banter, or by the hand of Woden, I shall…"

Müller's words were abruptly cut off as a bullet hole suddenly appeared in the middle of his forehead. The Nazi frowned and let out a loud sigh before falling to the ground in a pool of blood.

About damn time, the Professor thought as he wiped blood and bits of brain matter off of his face.

Acting with impressive reflexes, the other two German soldiers quickly raised their firearms and each released a fusillade in the direction of the open doorway from which the shot that had killed Müller had come. But all they could see was darkness accompanied by an eerie silence.

"*Gott im Himmel!*" shouted one of the soldiers. "We must have hit whoever it was!"

"It's too dark to tell for certain," the other replied.

"You Nazis do not consider the dark your ally, as I do," a smooth male voice speaking German with barely a hint of a French accent responded. Then, a second bullet hit the belly of another soldier, who gasped in horror and agony as he collapsed onto the floor.

"*Mein Gott!*" the remaining soldier bellowed, shooting another salvo of bullets into the dark as panic overtook him.

"I don't know who you are, *schweinhund*, but if you don't surrender immediately, I will kill the scientist!"

However, upon turning towards the Professor, the bemused soldier discovered that Clairembard had time to surreptitiously take possession of Müller's own Luger. Before the hapless Nazi could adjust to this state of affairs, the Professor shot him through the head.

Leo's tall, well-dressed form then stepped out of the darkness and into the light of the room, his firearm still pointed in the event of another attack.

"Bonjour, Professor," Leo said, "and good shooting. Bob Morane sent me. My name is Leo Saint-Clair."

Wiping off the dust from his jacket, Clairembart replied:

"The Nyctalope in person? I am impressed. But I knew Bob wouldn't let me down, and if he couldn't come himself, he would send another in his stead. And for what it's worth, I have always known that your true sympathies lie with France, not the bunch of traitors that you serve, or that vermin..." he added, pointing at the dead Nazis on the floor.

"You are correct, Professor," Leo replied, "but we must get you out of here quickly. I'm going to take you to a location where a convoy is waiting for you, which will spirit you out of Europe altogether, until the carnage is over."

"But I must tell you why they brought me here," the Professor stated. "It is of the utmost importance. You have heard of the Spear of Destiny, I suppose?"

"Of course," Leo replied. "It is the fabled weapon said to have pierced the side of Jesus Christ himself during the Crucifixion. It's reputed to have been imbued with limitless divine power as a result."

"Indeed!" the Professor responded. "And should anyone gain possession of it and master the prerequisite degree of will and occult knowledge necessary to access its cosmic energies..."

"...Then that individual shall gain power enough to challenge the gods themselves..." said a new arrival, speaking with a strong, guttural Middle-European accent.

Startled, Leo and the Professor turned to discover a tall, elegantly dressed man with dark hair, dark attire, pallid skin, and a flowing cloak standing in the doorway, with wafts of mist twirling about him. His eyes were like blazing hot coals, and they sent tremors up the spine of even one as ostensibly fearless as Leo Saint-Clair. It was not often that anyone approached him without being detected, so he considered this new player a major cause for concern.

"May I presume that this gentleman is not with you, Commandant?" asked the Professor warily.

"You are safe in making such a presumption," Leo replied, turning towards the chilling intruder. "Who are you, and what do you want?"

The stranger laughed.

"Come now, do you think only the Nazis would learn that the Spear of Destiny has at last been found? I am in Berlin for the same reason as Herr Müller. It is my intention to learn the truth from our esteemed archeologist. As for who I am, you may address me as Count Dracula."

I had heard reports claiming that Dracula was not just a character from Stoker's novel, thought Leo, *but I suppose that after all I've seen, the reality of such a being should not come as too much of a surprise...*

Quickly pushing the Professor aside, the Nyctalope drew his gun and fired off several rounds at the Vampire Lord. However, each slug passed through the dark figure without causing him any discernible harm.

Dracula laughed again.

"It would seem that you do not take folklore seriously, do you, my friend?" Bearing his fangs like an animal ready to attack, the Vampire Lord began approaching the Nyctalope.

Throwing his useless firearm aside, Leo leapt at the Count, pounding him several times with his fists, hoping to stun him long enough to allow the Professor to escape.

However, Dracula withstood the flurry of blows and, equally adept at hand-to-hand combat and far superior in strength to Leo, he grabbed the Nyctalope and hurled him 20 feet across the room and into the wall at the far end.

Leo coughed up some blood and quickly forced himself back to his feet, ready to continue the battle.

"You impress me, mortal," Dracula confessed as he faced his defiant opponent. "You would make a formidable member of my Undead, and would have a place of honor in the new order I plan to create—if you agree to serve me."

"How does one say 'up yours' in vampire tongue, Count?" was Leo's only response.

Dracula gritted his teeth, his face exuding boiling mist as his eyes flared. "You will regret both this decision and your insolence."

"I highly doubt it."

Upon that declaration, Leo resumed his assault on Dracula by launching a brutal but well coordinated barrage of punches and kicks, providing an awesome display of his martial arts prowess in the process. However, Dracula, renowned for his warrior skills, blocked and countered every single one of Leo's blows. Still, the Vampire Lord found himself taken aback when the Nyctalope managed to land a shattering round kick to his jaw. Attempting to follow that kick with a reverse punch, Leo suddenly found his fist caught in Dracula's hand. The Frenchman gritted his teeth in agony as the Vampire Lord exerted a crushing grip upon the bones and muscles of the Nyctalope's hand.

Drooling a thin stream of blood as a consequence of the Nyctalope's blow, Dracula glared down at Leo, who was trembling in pain. "Few mortals have ever been able to strike me so," the vampire snarled. "And fewer yet have managed to cause me pain. But it matters not, because I will have you swear fealty to me and serve in my personal guard. Look into my eyes and acknowledge me as your master, the only true master of all those who call the darkness their home..."

Leo could feel the power of Dracula's mesmeric gaze pouring into his consciousness like a psychic tsunami, but he had studied the Mystic Arts at the feet of some of Tibet's most powerful mages. The Nyctalope's teeth gnashed together as he summoned every iota of his own superhuman will to avoid becoming the thrall of the Prince of Darkness.

"Embrace your inevitable destiny, my formidable friend," Dracula said, redoubling his efforts. "Swear fealty to me, I command you!"

Vacillating like a branch caught in a gale, tears running from his eyes, struggling like never before in his life, Leo proved the proverbial immovable object to Dracula's irresistible force.

"I... will... never yield... to the... likes of you... demon! Never!"

"We shall see, miscreant!" Dracula exclaimed as he continued to redouble his efforts to capture his prize.

But just then, his concentration was suddenly shattered when one of the heavy chairs in the room smashed into his back. Buckling under the impact, but remaining on his feet, the Vampire Lord turned to face the one who had dared to strike him from behind: Professor Clairembart.

Abruptly released, Leo fell to the ground, gasping profusely in both relief and fatigue.

"Ah, I see you are still here, Professor," Dracula said. "You should have made your escape when you still could."

"I'm not about to leave my friend alone with you when he risked so much to save me, monster," the Professor replied. "I may not be a hero, but I don't abandon those who would risk their life for me."

"I approve, Professor," Dracula replied. "Your show of courage will only work to my advantage. Perhaps I shall turn you into one of the Undead, so you can become my personal advisor—after you tell me everything you know about the Spear, that is. Look into my gaze..."

The Professor found himself unable to turn his eyes from Dracula's hypnotic glare as waves of psychic force invaded his mind.

"Tell me, Professor," the Vampire Lord said with great authority. "Did that photo show the real Spear of Destiny? Is it here, in Berlin?"

"I... It looked... I don't..."

"Tell me, you foolish mortal!"

Suddenly, the Nyctalope pounced on Dracula from behind, taking advantage of his knowledge of *chi* and human anatomy to attempt to lock the Vampire Lord in a hold designed to inflict debilitating agony. Dracula found his control over the Professor slipping as he experienced a prodigious jolt of pain. However, the Vampire Lord was more than mortal, and his ability to withstand pain had been considerable, even before he had become the mightiest of all vampires.

"You shall die for this!" Dracula screamed as he tore Leo from his person with supernatural strength, and slammed the

213

Frenchman's body against the ground, knocking the wind from his lungs.

Raising his arm in the air, the Prince of Darkness prepared to sink his hand into Leo's chest and tear out his synthetic heart.

"Let us see how well you recover from *this*, fool!"

But before Dracula's powerful hand could tear through Leo's rib cage to extricate the delicate artificial organ within, a wooden shaft skewered his shoulder from behind.

Howling in pain, his wound sizzling as if it were in contact with a torch, Dracula leapt to his feet and tore the offending weapon from his shoulder blade.

Another combatant had entered the fray: a man of average height but athletic build with longish silvery hair and bright hazel eyes that seemed almost white. The newcomer reloaded another wooden bolt in the crossbow gun he carried and fired it, aiming for Dracula's heart. But the Vampire Lord's uncanny speed enabled him to pluck the lethal shaft out of the air before it could puncture him.

"Ah, Mr. Harker," the Prince of Darkness said. "I should have known you would show up here. Word has been out that you have been trailing me since my revival. Don't you ever learn?"

The man identified as Harker kept his weapon pointed at the Count.

"You're the one who never learns, Dracula. I will never rest until you're permanently laid to rest."

"You and your relatives continue to treat me as prey, when in essence you're only saving me the need to hunt you all down like the vermin you are!" the Vampire Lord exclaimed as mist continued to emit from his pores.

Meanwhile, the Nyctalope was back on his feet and stood beside Harker.

"Shall we take him together, Mr. Harker?"

"By all means," the vampire hunter replied.

The two men charged Dracula simultaneously, only to have him swiftly decorporealize into a cloud of mist. They passed through him harmlessly, and Leo's attempted flying side kick smashed into the wall directly behind the intangible Lord of Darkness.

The swirl of iridescent mist wafted towards the doorway, but before cutting his losses and exiting, Dracula's hollow-sounding and disembodied voice uttered forth the following:

"I no longer have time for this inanity. There will soon be a reckoning for both of you, and I have all eternity to carry it out."

After that ominous declaration, the mist floated outside and quickly metamorphosed into a large bat, which promptly flew out the nearest window and disappeared into the night skies.

The Nyctalope and Harker now looked at each other.

"Thank you for your assistance, Mr. Harker," Leo said sincerely. "I recognized your name, of course, but I thought you were only..."

"Fiction?" the other man replied, smiling. "I'm afraid not. My family has committed its life to destroy that fiend. I have been hunting Dracula for months now. But I believe you have the best of me..."

"My apologies," said the Nyctalope, with the hint of a military salute. "I'm Commandant Leo Saint-Clair."

The expression on Harker's visage suddenly turned hostile.

"You're the Nyctalope! A man I once greatly admired, whose exploits inspired me when I was younger. But I've heard you've become a *collaborateur*... You now work for the Vichy!"

"That is true," Leo said sadly. "I have no love for the Nazis, but I had to do what I did to safeguard the best interests of my country in very trying times, and not jeopardize the safety of its citizens. Did you know that we lost over 100,000 civilians to the Luftwaffe during the Exodus? What would you have done in my place, especially if your Edward had remained King and ordered you to put down your weapons, Mr. Harker?"

"Not bloody well put politics over principles, that's for certain," the Englishman replied hotly.

"That's easy for you to say, but politics do rule the world, there's no getting around that fact. In order to serve the greater good, it is sometimes necessary to compromise."

"There is a fine line between compromise and being *compromised*, Commandant. And I think you crossed it when you agreed to work for those murdering bastards."

"Ah, but I do not work for the Germans! I never have and never will. I work for France."

Professor Clairembart knew that tempers were being frayed and promptly stepped between the two warriors.

"Gentlemen, can we please dispense with the posturing and agree that it's bad form to discuss politics in civilized company?"

Looking at each other with expressions of gloom, the two fighters understood that they could have been allies, but the chasm between them was now far too wide to be bridged.

"I need to ensure that Dracula doesn't get his hands on the Spear," Harker said. "As for you, Saint-Clair, just get the Professor out of here before the Reds come in."

"It will be done," Leo replied in a calm tone.

He put his hand on the archeologist's shoulder and escorted him out of the building. As they exited, Clairembart said:

"Don't take Mr. Harker's words too much to heart, my friend. We both know that during wartime, people are forced to make choices. Things are not always black or white. Such times often bring out both the best and the worst in humanity, as the condition of this city makes abundantly clear."

"Thank you, Professor," the Nyctalope somberly replied, "but Mr. Harker's words were not unjustified. I have always sought to do what was right for my country, but I have realized that I am not infallible, no matter how brilliant I'm supposed to be. I fought in trenches, you know? I was wounded at Ypres. It was unthinkable for me not to support Maréchal Pétain, when he begged for my help. But did I do the right

216

thing? Did I, as Mr. Harker accused me, put politics over principles?"

As the two men disappeared into the Berlin night, Leo Saint-Clair hoped that history would ultimately judge him less harshly than the vampire hunter who may have become his friend had they met at a different time and place...

According to the chronology, the Nyctalope was forced to flee France when its past caught up with him in the summer of 1946. In 1947, we find him in Argentina; at the same time, he was sentenced in absentia by the French courts to ten years imprisonment. Two years later, Leo has now come to America. This story takes place right after Roman Leary's The Children of Heracles, *collected in* The Nyctalope Steps In. *Leo Saint-Clair is still wandering about the Southwestern part of the United States when he stumbles into one of those mysterious encounters that seem to be a regular feature in his adventurous life...*

Travis Hiltz: *Showdown at Steam Town*

New Mexico, Mid-1949

Under the night sky, the highway stretched through the desert like a black ribbon. Without any nearby towns, the only light was the glint of the stars and a sliver of the Moon.

A lone figure walked along the side of the road. He was dressed in denim with a much-abused looking rucksack slung over his broad shoulder. His black hair was streaked with silver and his yellow-green eyes glanced about as he walked, giving the impression that the darkness was no barrier to his journey.

After several minutes, the walker paused as a distant sound caught his attention. It was the low rumble of an approaching automobile. He soon caught a glimpse of its headlights; one was brighter than the other, and the way they moved gave him the impression that the driver was not having much success staying on the road.

Speeding down the road was a black Hudson, a big car decorated with the dirt, dings and scratches of a lifetime on the road.

It swerved a bit, then straightened out, then slowed down as it caught up with the walking man. The window rolled down and a young man leaned out. He had a rugged face, with ears that stuck out a bit, a heavy jaw and a smile that bordered on a sneer.

"Hey, man," the young driver said. "Little dark to be out for a stroll?"

"Day or night," the older man shrugged, "don't make much difference to me."

"You want a lift? I could save you some shoe leather."

"Sure. Why not."

The older man climbed into the back seat, dropping his rucksack on the floor. The car took off on its speedy, if slightly erratic, way.

There were two men in the front: the big rangy man who had offered the walker a ride, dressed in a work shirt and jeans, the steering wheel clutched with one hand, a cigarette in the other and, in the passenger seat, a thinner man, also dressed in a t-shirt and jeans. He had neat, dark hair, an open face and an apologetic smile.

"Evening," he said, leaning over the front seat to offer the older man a hand. "I'm Sal, and your pilot for this trip is Dean."

"Leo," the other man said, accepting the offered hand. "Thanks for the lift. What brings you fellows out here this time of night?"

"Gonna get us some pie!" Dean announced, looking over his shoulder to give his new passenger a manic grin.

"Pie?"

"Dean got into an argument with a fellow in Arizona over where to find the best pie," Sal explained. "He told us bout a place in New Mexico and Dean won't rest till he's tried some."

"Gotta know, man," Dean added. "Can't sleep with such an important issue unsettled, you dig?"

"Well, I've heard worse reasons for hitting the road," Leo said.

"Cool. Come along, we'll get you a piece," Dean said. "Say, you've got a bit of an accent there, Leo! Mind me asking where you from? Ain't British, are you?"

"No. I'm French," Leo replied. "Not fond of the Brits?"

"Don't mind him," Sal said. "Dean's got some problems with his family on his Pops side, and he gets a bit tense when he meets anyone from the 'old country'."

"France, huh?" Dean muttered. "That's supposed to be some mighty pretty country, full of some mighty pretty girls. You are a long way from home, man."

"You have no idea," Leo muttered, settling back in his seat.

"Wanted to see the world?" Sal asked. "That's what got Dean and I out here."

"Big old world," Dean muttered, happily. "Gonna drive from one end to the other!"

"Something like that," Leo said, quietly. "More like, I'm looking for a way home."

"Ain't everyone?" Dean said. "That's what we are all trying to do... Wanna run away, but also need to find our way back. My old man's out there... somewhere... every now and then I get lucky and find him. Sal here is running away from his bad dreams and a girl that wants to lead him to the altar."

"It's not exactly like that," Sal interjected. "I'm a writer and I figured I needed to see some of the things I want to write about."

"What about you, Leo?" Dean asked.

"Me? A long time ago, I made a mistake and had to leave home," the Frenchman said, his voice quiet, his gaze on the distant, horizon. "Since then, I've been looking for a way back, or maybe a way to make up for what I did."

He shrugged and looked back at his traveling companions. A sad smile played across his weathered features.

"Well... um... I hope you find what you're looking for," Sal said.

"You too," Leo nodded in reply.

"I hope we find some pie first," Dean said. "I'm so hungry you could poke me in the belly and feel my backbone... Hey! What's that noise? You playing with the radio again, Sal?"

"What would be the point?" Sal replied. "You'd get more noise out of Harpo Marx. With all the noises this chariot of yours makes, how is it possible you can hear a new one?"

"Hope it ain't the fuel pump," Dean muttered. "No pie's worth walking for... What the Hell is that...?"

A massive dark shape loomed out of the night, right in front of the Hudson.

Leo lunged over the seatback and grabbed the steering wheel, sending the car swerving off the road and out of the path of whatever it was.

The desert was less smooth than the highway and the big car bumped and jostled its passengers around before Dean was able to wrestle it under control and bring it screeching to a halt.

All three men were soon standing outside, peering around anxiously at the surrounding darkness. Sal was leaning against the trunk; Dean was stalking around in front of the car, swearing and trying to light a replacement for the cigarette he had lost in the chaos. Leo stayed by the back door, as alert as a trained soldier.

"Man!" Dean raged. "What the Hell was that?"

"I dunno, man," Sal shook his head. "Big is all I saw... Must have been a train...!"

"There aren't any railroad tracks," Leo said, peering around. "Or any signs or crossroads."

"Yeah, then what else could it...?" Sal started, then stepped back as Leo stepped into the light of the headlights. "Where'd you get that gun...?"

221

"What? This?"Leo asked, looking down at the gun as though he just noticed it himself. "It's a Browning. I got it during the war...Sorry, force of habit."

He tucked it into a shoulder holster under his denim jacket and he and Sal joined Dean at the hood of the car.

"Car OK?" Sal asked.

"Not great," Dean muttered, tossing away his cigarette and immediately lighting up a new one. 'That fender is bent in. We keep driving on it and it'll tear that front tire all up. What was that thing? A truck? We got smugglers driving us off the road?"

"It didn't move like a vehicle," Leo said. "It moved like an animal."

"An animal?" Sal exclaimed. "What, one of the famous wandering elephants of New Mexico? We on the migration path?"

"I don't know, but this is probably not the best place to be discussing it," Leo said. "We need to get your car back on the road. Maybe we can drive to the nearest gas station?"

"Where would that be, man?" Dean asked. "We've seen an abundance of nothing out here."

"You fellows having car trouble?" A new voice asked.

All three men spun, Leo once again with his gun in his hand.

Stepping into the cone of light was an American Indian. He was short and dressed in plain work clothes. His grey hair was done in a single braid that reached between his shoulder blades, and his forehead was adorned with a thin band of rawhide. A crude quiver was slung across his back, and he held a wooden bow in one hand. His face, brown and worn as old leather, was set in an expression of mild curiosity.

"Yeah, something like that," Leo responded, replacing his gun in its holster.

"How!" Dean said, with a grin and a raised hand.

"We swerved when something ran in front of the car," Sal explained.

"Lots of jackrabbits round these parts," the Indian nodded.

"Oh man, what do you feed the rabbits in these parts?" Dean exclaimed. "Thing was big as the damned car."

"That's not good," the Indian said, thoughtfully. "You fellows should get off the road. Not safe to be out driving."

"The car got banged up," Leo said, his expression neutral, but his eerie eyes watching their new acquaintance intently. "Is there somewhere nearby we might get it fixed?"

"Yeah, there is, about a mile back down the highway. Can you get it that far?"

"Yeah, she'll last that long," Dean replied.

"I can guide you there," the Indian said, going around and getting into the back seat. "I know the family that runs the place."

The other three men shrugged and climbed back into the car.

"So, do you have a name?" Leo asked, sitting next to their stoic new passenger.

"It's not important. Once you get up on the highway, head back the way you came and keep an eye out for a dirt road on the left."

Sal made introductions, to which the Indian responded with a friendly grunt and no further information.

They almost missed the turn off in the dark, but much to the others' surprise, Leo spotted it, earning him a thoughtful glance from the Indian.

The dirt road snaked through the desert for another quarter mile before coming to an end at a collection of ramshackle buildings. They were arranged to form a rough plaza, framing a packed dirt clearing. There was a barn that seemed in the process of slow collapse, a small house, clean but plain, a garage decorated with a vast collection of car parts, and then what looked to be some kind of combination of a general store and diner. All but the garage showed no sign of life or habitation.

Dean pulled the car into the square, close to the garage. Their Indian guide climbed out and walked over to a hubcap hanging from a chain, by the garage door. He picked up a piece of pipe and gave it a couple of whacks.

"What's that all about?" Sal asked.

Leo shrugged, busy trying to decipher the faded and dirt-covered sign hanging over the garage door.

"Steen town?" he muttered. "Or maybe that's an 'A'...? Steam Town...? Sounds familiar..."

"What?" a voice shouted from inside the garage. "Can't a person get some work done?"

A side door was flung open and a young woman in a pair of dingy overalls came storming out. Her auburn hair was done up in a ponytail, dirt smudges and freckles covered her cheeks. She wasn't much over five feet in height, but gave the impression that a lot of energy was packed into that small frame.

She had a wrench in one had a six-shooter in the other.

"Well?" she asked, looking around. She then spotted the old Indian. "Little Beaver? What do you and your friends want?"

"Little Beaver?" Leo asked. "That's your name?"

"I told you it wasn't important," Little Beaver muttered, then turned toward the young lady. "These fellows went off the road and need some work done on their car..."

"Whoa, there man!" Dean exclaimed. "She's the mechanic?"

"Here we go again," the girl muttered, raising her gun.

"Hold on!" Sal shouted, stepping in between the two. "Don't take it personal, Miss... Dean doesn't like anybody touching his car. You seem busy, if we can just... uh... please borrow some tools, we can take care of it and be out of your hair."

"They shouldn't be on the road tonight," Little Beaver said. "They said something ran them off the road."

"Again?" the lady mechanic said, lowering her gun and moving her gaze to the older Indian. "You think...?"

He nodded in reply.

"OK," she sighed. "I'll get you some tools and lights so you can get your car fixed. Kind of tight on spare rooms, but there's fresh hay in the loft and I can dig up some blankets."

"What's out there?" Leo asked.

"I want a Coca-Cola," Little Beaver said, ignoring the question and wandering off towards the old diner.

"Better put the coffee pot on too," The lady mechanic said, before turning to Dean. "Come on, big man, let's get you some tools."

Dean shrugged and followed, leaving Leo and Sal alone by the car.

"What is going on here?" Sal asked.

"No idea," Leo replied. "But, I get the feeling they'll tell us when they are ready. Nothing to do but wait till then."

"Too bad Dean didn't think to toss a deck of cards in the glove box."

"You and Dean seem like very different people," Leo said. "Hard to imagine you sharing the journey together."

"Not that different," Sal explained, leaning against the hood of the Hudson. "We both want to see the world, both of us are looking for…something. It's just while the thoughts swirl around my brain they tend to stay there, only coming out when I put pencil to paper. With Dean, there's nothing to keep the ideas in. It's like… I guess everyone has that friend that drags you along, you put up with them because you know no matter how crazy it gets, and you won't be bored. Plus, somebody needs to keep an eye on them. You've gotta have a friend like that."

"Actually," Leo chuckled, "I think I am that friend."

He glanced away from Sal, as he noticed Little Beaver emerging from the dilapidated diner. The elderly Indian still had his bow and quiver and there were two green glass bottles of Coca-Cola in his hands. He wandered off into the shadows, toward a trio of low dunes.

"I think," Leo said, turning back to Sal, "that I need to have a chat with our Indian guide."

He walked off and found Little Beaver, seated cross-legged on the middle dune. He nodded a greeting to Leo and offered him a soda.

"See anything out there?" Leo asked, sitting down in the sand.

"I thought you could tell me," Little Beaver replied.

"What do you mean?" Leo asked, concern and suspicion creeping into his voice.

"You seem to me to be a man who can see farther and see things other men don't."

"You might have something there," Leo nodded, taking a sip of cola. "So, tell me, where are we?"

"New Mexico."

"I was aware of that. I meant here... Steam Town?" Leo asked, gesturing back towards the collection of buildings. "Who is our young hostess?"

"Fran, Fran Reade," Little Beaver replied. "Her Grand-daddy built this place... He was an inventor and a traveler who decided to settle down out here..."

"So, Steam Town is the family business and estate all in one," Leo mused. "Where's the rest of the family?"

"Scattered. Some moved back east, one got married and is in San Francisco, I think... Fran inherited her Granddad's gift for tinkering. I met the family back in my traveling days... We crossed paths a couple times and when they finally settled down here, I sort of settled with them. They closed the store. Not too many people come through since they built the high-way to the east."

"So, now that we've met Miss Reade," Leo said. "What drove us off the road?"

"This is an old land," Little Beaver said, looking not at Leo, but off into the night. "The Indians, Mexicans and the Europeans came and they all brought their own...myths and magic, I guess you'd call them. Then, the white man came here with atomic power."

He took a sip and then gestured off into the distance.

"Los Alamos, White Sands, Gamma Base...they are all out there, and all have had an effect on the land... changing the soil, the people and the animals."

"Are you trying to tell me there are monsters prowling out there?" Leo asked.

"There are things you might not want to believe..." Little Beaver began.

"Actually, it's a bit of a relief," Leo said, pausing to take a swig of his cola. "I've faced my share of monsters."

He paused and for a moment his uncanny eyes seemed to be looking across, not just the distance to the far horizon, but through the years. "It's only the evil that men do that truly frightens me. In comparison, monsters are easy."

"You are a very unusual man, Leo," Little Beaver said, shaking his head. "You remind me a bit of a man I knew..."

"Really? I guess I was arrogant enough to think I was unique."

"He was a traveling man too. He took me in when I was very young and alone in the world." Little Beaver said, his leathery face creasing in a smile. "He knew there were good people in the world and bad, and both needed to be taken care of."

"I was worried for a moment there you were going to cast me as a noble cowboy," Leo smiled, "but I do agree with your friends' philosophy. Though, my judgment on good and bad leaves something to be desired"

"Someone is coming," Little Beaver muttered.

Leo nodded. Both men moved with casual purpose and had let go of their bottles and put hands on their weapons.

Sal came jogging up the dune, paused to catch his breath, as the two older men moved their hands away from their gun and bow.

"We... huh... got something making... noise in the barn," he said, straightening up. "So, unless Fran has a dog, you've got mice... big goddamn mice...!"

227

Leo and little Beaver were quickly on their feet and trudging down the dune after Sal, their bottles forgotten and abandoned.

In the plaza, Dean stood by the car, looking anxiously at the old barn. The other three men came to stand by him. Little Beaver and Leo shared a glance and a shrug, as they heard nothing.

"Don't be making with the parental looks of disapproval," Sal remarked. "We both heard it. Sounded like something was taking a crowbar to the back wall, then…"

"Then…?" Leo asked.

"Weird noise," Dean muttered, not taking his eyes off the barn.

All four men stopped, their expressions moving between curious and anxious as a sound drifted from the barn. It was a high-pitched trill, which moved up and down the scale, like some surreal and demented musical recital. There was something hypnotic and disturbing about it.

"What is that?" Leo asked.

"Don't know," Dean replied, anxiously. "Anybody wanna volunteer to go look?"

Nobody seemed eager to peek behind the barn door.

"What's going on out here?" Fran Reade asked, coming out of the garage. She had a shotgun in the crook of her arm. "What was that noise? Why are you all standing around… what's with the guns…?"

"Dean… Where'd you get that gun?' Sal asked, surprised.

"Always had it, man."

"Always? Since New York?"

"Yeah, I think. My daddy gave it to me, long time back, when he realized I had the same wanderlust as him. There can be some bad people out there, get it? I kept it stashed under my seat. Guess I should have mentioned it before…"

"Not sure if I would have felt better knowing you've been sitting on a gun the whole way," Sal muttered.

"Not that this ain't an entertaining tale," Fran interrupted. "But, what in Sam Hill is in my barn…?"

"What do you keep in there?" Leo asked.

"Just storage and ends and odds from when we closed up the diner and grocery. Left over car parts, kindling, some sacks of flour, coffee and sugar…"

"Really don't want to go in there without some answers," Leo muttered.

One problem was solved and a new one arrived as the barn door began to buckled, the wooden cross bar keeping it closed made a harsh creaking noise, like a shriek and then both bar and door began to crack.

"Everybody get back," Leo barked. "And nobody shoots till I say so! We need to see what we are up against."

"Did I miss the vote that put you in charge?" Fran Reade asked, sarcastically. "Just walk into a woman's home…"

"Fran, shush," Little Beaver interrupted. "Listen to Leo."

Leo had no time to thank the old Indian for his support before the door shattered and the group dove behind the shelter of the Hudson to avoid a shower of splinters.

Little Beaver had guessed right and monsters did walk the Earth in New Mexico. The creature was massive, dwarfing the Hudson, and closer in size to the locomotive engine they had originally mistaken it for.

Its massive body sported an armored shell, that seemed to glint in the light from the garage and the Hudson's' headlights. It had six legs, each as thick as a fence post. A pair of tiny eyes peered down on the group, studying them with unearthly intelligence, while the pincers on either side of its mouth twitched hungrily.

It was a horror that almost defied words to describe it.

"That's a goddamn big ant…!" Fran breathed, wide-eyed.

"Oh good!" Dean exclaimed. "I was worried I'd might be the only one seeing it."

"Afraid not," Leo said.

"How'd it get so big?" Sal asked. "What's it after?"

"Common theory seems to be radiation made it that way," Leo replied.

"It's probably a scout, looking for food," Little Beaver added.

"Barn full of sugar and flour," Fran muttered. "Probably drew it like a magnet. What now?"

"Anyone know anything about ants?" Leo asked.

"They have a shell that holds them together, instead of a skeleton," Sal said. "So, being that sized, the thing is probably built like a tank."

"Don't they hunt by smell?" Fran asked.

"I thought it was by sound...?"Leo added. "The antenna seems to move when we talk."

"So, what do I shoot at?" Dean asked.

"Jesus, Dean!" Sal said. "Don't shoot at anything till we figure what the Hell's going on. If the thing's just scouting for food, it might to just wander off and leave us alone..."

"We can't let it go," Little Beaver said. "If it's a scout, then there's more."

"Which means it'll tell all its friends where the good chow is to be found," Fran said.

"If it didn't already," Little Beaver told her. "We don't know what that noise it was making before was for."

"Or the way it's looking at us," Fran added. "It might well have said 'Oh look, we've got rats in the pantry'."

"So, do we shoot or not, man?" Dean asked.

Leo and Little Beaver exchanged a glance.

"Antenna and eyes?" Leo asked.

The older Indian nodded in response.

The ant scuttled forward, pushing through the shattered remains of the barn door and causing the wood of the front wall to creak ominously.

"Maybe if we're lucky, it'll collapse the barn on top of itself?" Sal suggested hopefully.

"We can hope," Leo said. "As we aren't going to be able to stop it with a handful of pistols."

"I might have something that'll work," Fran Reade said. "If one of you gives me a hand in the garage."

"I'll volunteer," Sal said. "I seem to be the only one who didn't bring a gun to this party."

"Whatever you've got planned, make it quick," Little Beaver said. "We can't hold that thing off for long."

"Just be careful, old man," Fran said, patting his shoulder as she got to her feet. Sal gave Dean a nod in farewell and then followed after her.

Antenna twitching, the giant ant's head moved to observe their progress.

"Oh man, here it comes!" Dean breathed. "Crazy, crazy...!"

"Ready?" Leo asked, getting to his feet.

"I don't want to die tonight, if that's what you mean," Little Beaver muttered, fitting an arrow to his bow.

"So much for my image of the stoic Indian warrior," Leo said, with a faint grin.

The three men stood up and all at once began firing at the colossal insect. Dean's shots were as wild as his driving and speech, raining down on the ant's massive head.

It flinched a bit, but did not slow its progress through the wall of the barn and into the bare dirt plaza.

Little Beaver's first arrow buried itself in the ant's right eye.

The creature reacted with a wince-inducing shriek and flung its head from side to side. Because of this, Leo's first shot missed, skidding across the ant's protective shell.

"Bullets aren't doing much," Leo said, firing again and taking the tip off one of the antenna. "If we rammed it with the car, we'd have a chance of knocking it down!"

"Ramming it?" Dean exclaimed, not pausing from shooting at the ant. "With my car? Get another plan, man!"

Dean's gun was soon producing nothing but clicking noises.

Another shot from Leo severed the damaged antenna, but as yet none of their shots seemed to have slowed down the creature.

As it lunged forward, Leo dodged its mandibles, dropped and rolled out of its reach. He lunged for the Hudson, ripping open the back door and grabbing his rucksack.

"I need to reload! Keep it busy!"

Little Beaver's next arrow sank deep into one of the ant's front legs and it reared up momentarily, like a wild horse, and when it came down, the ant lunged forward, butting the Hudson with its head.

"Hey! Get off my car!" Dean yelled, standing up and throwing his empty pistol at the unnatural insect. It struck right between the antennas. The creature shook its massive head and gave off another high-pitched trill.

Leo leapt out of the car, reloading as he moved and fired off three shots into the ant's already wounded front leg. The ant stumbled striking its chin against the hood of the car.

"That's it!" Dean shouted, stalking around from his side of the car. As he came around, he spotted a pile of assorted junk and grabbed a length of pipe. Swinging it in a wild over hand attack, Dean brought it down on the mandible nearest him. Upon impact, the ant flinched back and the shock caused Dean to drop the pipe.

"Man, that stings!"

Dean was preoccupied, shaking feeling back into his hands. The ant swung his uninjured front leg and struck Dean hard enough to send him flying back several feet.

Little Beaver fired off two quick arrows, more in an effort to distract than injure, and quick as his old legs would move him went to Deans' side.

Leo continued to fire at the colossal creature, but it seemed somehow fixated on seeking revenge for the injury Dean had visited upon it. The ant shouldered its way past the Hudson, ignoring Leo as he emptied his gun into its side.

"This is not going well," Leo muttered, as his gun clicked empty. He ran to put himself his new friends and the ant, holding his arms out. The insect was momentarily startled, but then raised its front leg to brush him aside. Leo grabbed hold of the leg, wrapping his arms around it. He dug in his heels and his whole body trembling with the effort brought the huge ant to a stop.

"You aren't... going... hnn... any further...!" Leo snarled, through gritted teeth. Deep within his chest, his heart, a wondrous organ constructed of steel, rubber and wires, had kept Leo active and alive for decades. It operated on a level that more closely resembled alchemy than science. This unique device not only kept Leo's blood pumping through his body, but also seem to contain a spark of life energy, or essence, that some believed was the secret of his longevity.

Whatever was at the center of his miraculous heart, Leo tapped into it and was able to hold his own in this bizarre wrestling match.

The ant pushed him forward several inches, but he then ground to a halt, and even attempted to dislodge Leo by striking him with his other front leg. But it pnly tore the cloth of his denim jacket and scratched the skin underneath.

"I am the Nyctalope!" Leo grunted, digging his fingers into the flesh and muscle of the ant's leg. "I've walked alien sands and faced the worst this world has to offer. You may be big, but in the end, you are nothing but an insect to be swatted!"

With a cry of anger and pain that mixed with the high-pitched screech of the creature, Leo tore the ant's leg from its body. As he stumbled, he swung the massive limb and struck the ant with it, driving it to the ground.

Leo dropped the leg and fell to his knees. Little Beaver used a discarded burlap sack as a makeshift pillow for the dazed Dean and then hurried over to his other fallen comrade.

"Pretty impressive," the old Indian commented, helping Leo back to his feet.

"Yes, I wish I could attribute it to clean living," Leo rasped in reply.

'You're going to have some bruises come morning," Little Beaver said, steering him towards where he'd left Dean.

"You should see the other guy." Leo said, wincing. "So, wasn't Mademoiselle Reade supposed to rush to our aid…?"

"Gotta say man," Dean added, weakly. "Isn't the cavalry supposed to show up before the cowboys get the snot kicked out of them?"

"At this rate," Leo added, sitting down on a dusty barrel, "she'll show up past the point that we need saving."

"Wouldn't be too sure about that," Little Beaver breathed. "Look!"

Poking its massive head around the edge of the general store was a second giant ant.

"I'm out of bullets," Leo said, getting to his feet.

"I lost my gun," Dean said, struggling and failing to get up.

"I've got a couple arrows. I can keep them busy," Little Beaver suggested, half-heartedly. "Do we want to try for the car, or maybe the garage…?"

"I ain't leaving Sal," Dean muttered.

"I don't think anybody's going anywhere," Leo said, tucking his empty gun into his belt and flexing his hands. He grabbed a length of pipe and a broken piece of board from the junk pile they'd been resting against. "I'll try to keep the healthy one busy. Put a couple arrows into the other one, then help Dean to shelter."

Little Beaver nodded grimly, and drew his last two arrows. One he strung on his bow, the other he held with his teeth.

"Welcome to the Alamo," Dean muttered, using a broken plank as a makeshift cane.

Leo and Little Beaver stood back to back, as Dean hobbled for the questionable shelter of the garage.

Just as he was reaching for the garage door, it flew open and nearly knocked him to the ground. An amazing creature raced out into the plaza.

It stood close to twelve feet tall and resembled a heavily armored, stout Victorian gentleman. Its eyes were two head-lights and from its iron top hat poured dense grey steam. Its metal, jointed limbs were thick as telephone poles and its blunt-fingered hands wide as shovels. There was what looked like a metal knap sack on its back, decorated with numerous valves and pipes.

Perched on the metal mans' shoulders was young Fran Reade, goggles over her eyes. She wore heavy work gloves and a manic grin. She seemed to be steering the metal giant by way of two levers, one built into each shoulder.

The metal gentleman emitted a shrill whistle, like a train engine and its young pilot let out a triumphant yell.

"On any other day," Dean muttered, as he sat down hard on the packed earth, "that would seem really strange..."

Sal came running out of the barn, behind the steam pow-ered giant.

"Leo! Catch!" he yelled, throwing the shotgun to the older man, before dodging behind the steam man to reach Dean.

As the giant trudged past him, Leo caught the gun, spun and fired both barrels into the mouth of the injured giant insect that was limping towards him and Little Beaver. The back of the creature's head erupted in a shower of shell and flesh as the massive insect fell to the ground for the final time.

Fran drove the steam man toward the other ant and punched it full in the face. There was a crunching noise and the giant ant staggered. The steam man then caught it in a headlock.

Smoke poured from its top hat and over the sound of the giant insects frantic trilling could be heard the screech of straining hydraulics. Atop his shoulders, Fran Reade gritted her teeth and struggled to hold onto the shaking control levers. With a creak and the sound of a bursting metal seam, the steam man twisted the ant's neck till its head tore loose from its' body.

235

With a high-pitched whistle of triumph, the steam man lifted the severed head above its head and then threw it away.

Fran Reade then steered the steam man over to the others. One of its arms hung loosely at its side and oil was leaking profusely from its right knee joint.

"Everybody still alive?" she asked, sliding to the ground.

"What the Hell...?" Leo muttered, staring up at the steam mans' face.

"I can't believe you got that thing running!" Little Beaver exclaimed.

"Yeah, well, Granddad built things to last," Fran smirked, patting the side of the giant steam man. She then flinched back, as its torso was still hot. "Damnit!"

"Everybody in one piece?" Leo asked, moving away from the steam man and slumping to the ground next to Dean.

"Looks like everybody survived," Sal observed, looking around the plaza. "And the car's in one piece... I'm impressed, I'd started to believe this desolate little oasis was going to be where my bones came to rest for good."

"So, what in the world is that?" Leo asked, pointing at the steam man.

"My great Granddad built him," Fran said, smiling up at the clunky automaton. "He got mothballed when granddad built his own version, and then when my family started playing around with electricity and then got obsessed with airships and doing work for the government... I'm what you'd call the packrat of the family and when I took over this place, I inherited a lot of Reade family... 'heirlooms,' some might call them..."

"Junk is what all the rest of us call it," Little Beaver said. "What are we gonna do about them?"

He had wandered a bit away from the group to gather up his arrows and gestured towards the giant corpses.

"Guess I'll have to call into town," Fran shrugged. "The Sheriff will never believe me, but I think I can get hold of one of Daddies government friends and we can..."

236

"Sheriff?" Dean said, with a frown. "Government men? That's my cue to go, man, go...!"

He got unsteadily to his feet. Sal rolled his eyes and offered him a hand up.

"Sorry, bout this, but I've got to agree with Dean. Both of us are not really big fans of the law and we do have 'miles to go before we sleep.' Nice meeting you all though. Been quite a night...!"

"You gonna put this in your book?" Dean asked as Sal helped him hobble over to the car.

"Nah, I don't think so. Who's going to believe this?" Sal said, pausing to turn and wave good-bye to the others. "Think tonight goes to the back of the notebook..."

"What about you, Leo?" Little Beaver asked. "You going to stay?"

"Me? I don't know... I feel I should help with the clean up, and part of me does not want to walk away before getting some answers on those monsters, but like Dean, I'm not exactly on friendly terms with your government. My being here could help or hinder whatever happens next... It's a coin toss..."

He sighed and looked around the plaza, battered, dusty and homey.

"Though, it has been awhile... too long even... since I've stayed in one place for very long... or found a place where I felt maybe I could belong..."

The Hudson did a tight doughnut, kicking up a cloud of dust and screeched to a halt by Leo. The window rolled down and Dean, grinning once again like a maniac stuck his head out.

"Hey, Leo! You still want pie?"

A few months after Leo's peregrinations around the South-west, we find him in New York for a story that sees him cross the path of boxing legend Marcel Cerdan and cross swords with an old enemy...

Emmanuel Gorlier: *Madison Square Garden*

New York, October 1949

"Jab!... Jab!... Jab!... Straight left!... Watch your foot-work!... Now an uppercut!..."

Inside the ring, the two boxers watched each other care-fully and alternated their blows, under their coach's vigilant stare. The men were very different. One was heavyweight, tall, dark, muscular and blue-eyed; he must have been well over forty and yet still moved very fast for his age. His technique was a bit rough, but he appeared to be a formidable opponent. His adversary was lighter, faster on his feet, and displayed a much higher technical level. His friendly face with its broken nose would have been recognized by most French as that of Marcel Cerdan, the so-called Moroccan Bomber or Casablan-ca Clouter, former World Champion in his middleweight cate-gory, on his way to regaining his title.

The coach commented on his every move and seemed satisfied with his performance. His protégé was ready for his match against qualifying champion Tino "Lightning Bolt" Cardona. This encounter would decide, if Cerdan won, wheth-er he would be entitled to a return match against Jake "Raging Bull" LaMotta, who had taken his title three months earlier.

Watching the two boxers, the coach again reflected that he had been right in handpicking Steve Costigan to be Cerdan's sparring partner. Indeed, the Texan's style of boxing resembled that of LaMotta. He was a tough guy, a true "iron man," on whom it was virtually impossible to land a serious blow. Cerdan could practice his endurance on him. The coach had heard of Costigan years ago, while traveling in the South Seas. At that time, the Texan was a famous boxer in the ports of Asia. The coach had been particularly impressed when he had witnessed the match in which the sailor had fought "Tiger" Valois, the champion of the French Navy.

Moreover, and this had come as a happy surprise, the two boxers had quickly become friends and that enabled Cerdan to better withstand his separation from his girl-friend, Edith Piaf, who had remained behind in France.

The sparring match continued, allowing Cerdan to improve his combos. Costigan seemed to be marking time when, suddenly, with an unusual movement of the chest, he managed to break through the Frenchman's guard and deliver a perfectly executed uppercut to his chin. The power of the blow lifted the Moroccan Bomber, whose feet left the ground. Flung against the ropes, Cerdan remained there for a moment, getting his wind back.

The coach didn't believe his eyes. Steve slowly approached Cerdan and inquired:

"Are you OK, Marcel? Do you need a hand?"

Shaking his head, the Frenchman replied:

"No, I'm fine! I'm still a little dizzy, but I recover quickly. I've never seen such a blow! You've got to show me how you did it. It might come in a handy."

"No problem! I learned it when I was sailing on the *Sea Girl*!"

The training session continued throughout the afternoon, but at a slower pace, small bouts alternating with instruction sequences during which Steve taught Marcel some tricks that he himself had learned in ports around the Pacific in the 1930s. They practiced them endlessly, so that the former world champion could, when the time came, use them without hesitation.

At around 5 p.m., they called it a day. While the coach was getting his things, the two boxers headed to the shower and the dressing-room. When they were halfway there, three men entered the gym. The first was a young man of medium build, light brown hair, with blue eyes, elegantly dressed, who moved with comfortable ease. The other two were massive; both had dark eyes and dark complexions, and appeared to be his escort.

They approached the two boxers. The elegant man first addressed Marcel Cerdan:

"Good afternoon, sir. Do I have the honor of talking to Monsieur Cerdan?"

"Yes, that's me," said the Frenchman. "Good afternoon, gentlemen."

He looked at the newcomers questioningly. The man continued:

"My name is Tom Hagen. I'm an attorney representing Mister Vito Corleone who manages the affairs of Tino Cardona, your next opponent. Could we find a quiet place to talk business? My client would like to make you an offer of, shall we say, the type you can't refuse."

Marcel Cerdan hesitantly looked around the gym, then pointed at an empty office located at the back of the room.

"I suppose we could go in there," he said.

"Excellent," said Hagen. "Please, lead on."

Seeing that Steve Costigan was following them, Hagen immediately added:

"It would be better if my conversation with Monsieur Cerdan was held in private."

Costigan looked at Cerdan significantly, and the latter told the lawyer:

"I don't have any secrets from my friend Steve. I'd like him to join us."

"As you wish."

They went into the office. After closing the door, Cerdan pulled the blinds down and said:

"Let's sit. We'll be more comfortable that way."

Hagen sat down and began speaking:

"For years, my client has been following Tino Cardona's career and was greatly pleased when he was chosen by the World Boxing Federation to fight in this match. However, we recognize that you are, by far, the odds on favorite. Your defeat by La Motta hasn't affected your confidence, and I can only congratulate you for the thoroughness of your training. This has led my client to make you the following proposal, which I think might prove to be of mutual interest. What if you were to lose the fight, after considerable, heroic resistance, of course? In exchange, we would offer a very comfortable consideration that would allow you to lead the good life you seek, plus we would have time to organize a new match, that you would then win against the odds, and that would pave the way towards a new world championship title. You'd be rich and help your career at the same time—a win-win situation, surely. What do you think?"

Hagen was all smiles as he finished his pitch.

Marcel Cerdan sat speechless for a moment. It was due more to his surprise than his serious consideration of Hagen's suggestion that he throw the match. He glanced at Costigan. His face was attentive but not broadcasting any clues as to his thoughts. Cerdan concluded that it meant that the choice was his and his alone. After a minute of silence, he replied:

"I don't think so. The match will take place normally. I have never thrown a match before, and I don't intend to start now. I'd be grateful if you left now—and I don't want to see you again!"

Tom Hagen grinned and added in a harsher tone of voice:

"You know, Monsieur Cerdan, we could compel your cooperation..."

"I wouldn't try that if I were you," replied the boxer.

"Rocco!" said Hagen, turning to one of his two companions.

The big man put his hand under his coat, as if he were grabbing a gun in a holster, but did not have time to complete his action. Costigan had gotten up and grabbed him by his lapels. He held him so strongly that the mobster's hand remained stuck inside his coat. The second man made a gesture, but stopped as soon as he took notice of Cerdan. He figured that the man hadn't been nicknamed the "Moroccan Bomber"" for nothing. Before the situation could escalate further, Tom Hagen intervened:

"Gentlemen! Gentlemen! Let's all calm down. My friends and I will go. I won't rebuke you, Monsieur Cerdan, but I shall warn you: you'll lose this game no matter what, and you will have lost an opportunity to earn a large sum of money for little effort. Good evening, Monsieur Cerdan, and you too, sir. We'll meet again on the night of the match. I won't bother to wish you good luck, of course".

The three men rose and left the gym. Cerdan turned to his companion and said:

"Thank you, Steve. If you hadn't been here, I might have had a tough time convincing them to leave."

"I've always got your back, pal. But I don't think you've seen the last of them. That Hagen fella seemed mighty sure of himself..."

"I don't see what they can do. Still, I'll be careful. Now, I need to take a quick shower and call Edith..."

Several hours later, Tom Hagen entered the office of Don Vito Corleone located in a large house on the outskirts of New York. The room was dark. The "Godfather" was sitting behind a large desk, staring distractedly into empty space. Since the attack that had almost cost him his life, he had aged. No doubt, he was thinking of his son, Michael, who had been forced into exile in Sicily to escape the vendetta of the other families. Upon the entrance of his *consigliere*, the old man sprang back to life and said in a broken voice:

"So, what happened?"

"He turned us down and asked us to leave. We'll need to call our... specialist."

"It is unfortunate, but the stakes are too high to hesitate," said Corleone with a nod towards the phone.

Hagen dialed a number. Then, he said:

"Good evening, Madame. May I please speak to Mister Cultnom."

Two weeks later, on an early evening, a crowd had gathered at the entrance of Madison Square Garden to watch the big match that was the high point of the season, pitting former World Champion Marcel Cerdan against Tino Cardona, Champion of Atlantic City.

The public had come from every borough of New York, from the poorest neighborhoods to the highest society. There were even a few French fans that had crossed the Atlantic to watch this match, so crucial for Marcel Cerdan. Among them was a man quietly following the crowd heading towards the entrances. Nothing distinguished him from anyone else, except that he wore dark glasses, which was peculiar for the time of the day.

The man bought a Coke and settled into a good seat, only a few rows from the ring. These were expensive seats usually reserved for local personalities: New York Mayor William O'Dwyer was there with two senators; there were also Humphrey Bogart and Lauren Bacall, Frank Sinatra, and several prominent tycoons...

Behind the dark glasses lurked Leo Saint-Clair, a.k.a. the Nyctalope, once one of the most famous champions of France, one of the most adored celebrities, now a fugitive, a man wanted in his own country for collaborating with the Nazis, who had only managed to escape by fleeing, like so many others, to South America. Since then, he had had to leave Argentina as well, and had sought refuge in the United States, a country he had always wanted to visit and explore at greater length.

He had been unable to resist the lure of attending the fight of his most famous compatriot.

Leo distractedly followed the opening match between two lesser boxers and only began to pay attention when Cerdan and Cardona walked onto the ring.

243

He scrutinized the two men; Cerdan appeared to be in great shape; his opponent was relaxed and even made a superior smile at the French champion, which surprised Leo, given the fact that the Moroccan Bomber was an adversary to be feared, not mocked.

The referee climbed into the ring, introduced the two men, and made his usual announcements. Then, each boxer went to stand in his corner until the gong sounded. The fight began. The two men approached each other slowly and began to circle around the ring, each exchanging a few cautious punches to test his opponent. Gradually, as the match progressed, the blows became more accurate and powerful. At the end of the first round, Cerdan seemed to have the advantage over Cardona and, due to his superior speed, even managed to land a powerful blow just before the gong sounded.

The Nyctalope thought that the Frenchman had a small advantage, but not a decisive one. Cardona had an impressive endurance record when it came to being able to take punches and still manage to strike back. The match was over twelve rounds, so anything could still happen.

The second round began. Cerdan quickly took the upper hand. He was definitely faster and had nothing to envy from Cardona in terms of his punching power, as evidenced by his previous 61 victories by knockout. A series of powerful body blows and punches to the face followed, quickly backing the Atlantic City champion into the ropes. Cardona raised his guard to parry the Frenchman's next right blow to his face, but instead was caught by surprise by a blow to the liver. He almost folded in half, and fell heavily to the ground. The referee pushed Cerdan back and began the countdown. At 8, Cardona rose painfully to his feet and the fight resumed, but clearly, he wasn't fully recovered and managed only to defend himself until the gong signified the end of the second round.

The Nyctalope had remained very quiet, in contrast with the rest of the public which had been particularly loud during the round. He thought that Cardona would struggle to finish the third round. While the coach was sponging Cardona's swollen face, Leo noticed a strange expression on the face of the boxer. He wasn't looking at his coach or his opponent, but at some spot in the audience near where the Nyctalope was sitting. Curious, Leo looked in that direction, but saw nothing other than the faces of the public still excited by the fight. There was one man, however, who had remained calm, too, but as he was lost in the crowd, the Nyctalope failed to notice him.

The gong sounded. Both boxers picked up the fight again. Cardona seemed tired. Cerdan approached him with the intention of finishing him off. But suddenly, he stopped, as if he were frozen on his feet. His gaze became fixed. Cardona took that miraculous opportunity to deliver a series of blows to his foe, but they weren't as powerful as they might have been, had he not been weakened by the previous two rounds. Cerdan defended himself, but more by reflex than design. It was now obvious that his opponent had the upper hand. The former World Champion's eyes seemed drawn to the same spot that Cardona had watched earlier.

The Nyctalope followed Cerdan's line of sight and, this time, noticed the quiet man. He seemed very focused on Cerdan, and Leo wondered if he wasn't exercising some kind of nefarious influence over the French boxer. However, he couldn't quite distinguish the man's features until the spectator next to him stood up in his excitement. Then the Nyctalope finally saw his face and recognized it! It was Godfrey Cultnom!

Suddenly, everything made sense. Cultnom was a powerful practitioner of the Dark Arts whom Leo had already defeated in Paris in 1941. During that first battle, the evil sorcerer had used his power to remotely enslave a young woman. Obviously, he had somehow managed to escape from the French prisons, and was back at his old tricks—probably even more powerful now—and Cerdan was his latest victim.

His "prey" was now helplessly tossed around the ring. Cerdan's mind, clouded by Cultnom's powers, no longer enabled him to protect himself from the blows of his opponent, let alone fighting back. He received a straight left to the temple and was violently thrown into the ropes, before collapsing on the mat. This time, it was his turn be be subjected to the humiliating countdown. Cultnom redoubled his effort to prevent the Frenchman from getting up. But suddenly, the bell rang before the referee could reach the fateful 10. Cerdan, as the saying went, had just been saved by the bell. His return to his corner was sheer torture.

Now, no one else gave the Frenchman the slightest chance of winning the match. No one? Not the Nyctalope! Leo used the pause to concentrate. If he wanted Cerdan to have a fair chance of winning the fight, he had to break the unholy hold that Cultnom's occult powers had placed over the champion.

As the gong sounded, announcing the fourth round, Leo got up as discreetly as he could and walked towards Cultnom, approaching him from the back. The sorcerer was so focused on exerting his influence over Cerdan that he didn't sense the Nyctalope. As Leo reached the sorcerer, he spilled the ice from his soda on the back of his foe's neck. Cultnom jumped from his seat. His concentration broken, his hold over Cerdan was over!

Quickly, Leo put both his hands over the sorcerer's shoulders and, combining pressure over certain *chi* points with his own, powerful mental powers, caused Cultom to doze off in a state of semi-consciousness.

Everyone around him was so captivated by the fight that no one had noticed his maneuver. In the ring, Cardona had begun the round clearly determined to finish his opponent. But freed from Cultnom's spell, Cerdan began to mount an effective counterattack. Puzzled, Cardona quickly sought Cultnom to find an explanation for Cerdan's unexpected recovery. But instead of the sorcerer's gaze, his eyes only saw the stare of the Nyctalope who had taken off his dark glasses to better focus his mental energy over the sorcerer.

Upon seeing those eerie eyes, and Cultnom almost unconscious, Cardona understood that he was now alone with his opponent. If he still wanted to win, he had to give it his all before Cerdan could react. He launched a series of powerful body blows which he thought might end the fight. He wasn't entirely wrong, because Cerdan, still weakened, staggered back. The Frenchman might have been on the verge of collapsing when, suddenly, though the fog in his head that had clouded his thinking but was now almost entirely dissipated, he heard a loud voice from ringside screaming:

"Don't forget the *Sea Girl*!"

The evocation of his friend Steve Costigan's boat provoked in him the reaction for which the Texan had hoped. With an unusual movement of his chest, Cerdan picked up his strength and surprised his opponent with that unusual uppercut to the chin that Costigan had taught him to do earlier. Had that punch been delivered by any other boxer, it would have only shaken its recipient, but Marcel Cerdan wasn't "any other boxer," he was a born puncher capable of "blowing out the lights with a single blow" as the saying went. Cardona fell to the mat like a sack of potatoes. Cerdan had won and now had a chance of regaining his world title.

Later, amidst the brouhaha caused by this surprising victory, three men quietly left Madison Square Garden.

First, the Nyctalope, smiling, reflecting that this had proven to be a most entertaining evening after all.

Then, a recovered Godfrey Cultnom now afraid of his old enemy, whose presence he had finally recognized, but even more afraid of the wrath of the Godfather, to whom he had cost a lot of money.

Finally, Tom Hagen, who had attended the match, and thought that the Family had been dealt a blow at least as powerful as the one that had knocked Cardona down that night. The Don should never have relied on that charlatan Cultnom, who had clearly deceived them. He would pay. But he also worried about the Godfather... Maybe it was time for Michael to return from Sicily and assume power...

After listening to Hagen's report, Don Vito Corleone grabbed the telephone and said:

"We will settle accounts with those who thwarted us." When his correspondent picked up, he added: "Is this Mister Roman Orgonetz? This is Vito Corleone. A few years ago, you came to see me for a service. I then told you that, some-day, I might call on you to reciprocate. That day has come…"

On October 27, 1949, the Lockheed Constellation F-BAZN carrying Marcel Cerdan to Paris crashed on the Pico de Vera, a mountain on the island Sao Miguel in the Azores.

After his New York interlude, the Nyctalope is back in California, again undercover, still on the trail of mysterious space invaders. The reasons why will be revealed in The Ides of Mars *later in this volume, but in the meantime, enjoy this prequel to the 1958 classic* I Married a Monster From Outer Space...

Roman Leary: *The Devil You Know*

California, 1950

The monsters from outer space met for their weekly poker game in the back room of Dan Tally's bar. At first, the game had merely been a convenient cover for clandestine meetings. It afforded them an opportunity to speak freely among themselves and, if only for a few hours, relax the suffocating restrictions imposed upon them by their masquerade. Pretending to be human could be a taxing exercise, especially during the transition phase, and the game provided a necessary outlet for the unrelenting pressure.

There were six monsters in the Harrisville cell. The one who wore Dan Tally's face was the eldest and highest ranking. The game had been his idea, and he considered it to be one of the best command decisions he had ever made. Not only were the weekly gatherings an invaluable curative for the grinding stress, they were also...fun.

For the monsters, *fun* was an unfamiliar (not to say alien) concept. They were a tough, practical race, and they tended to limit their activities to strictly utilitarian endeavors. They saw no tangible benefit in the pursuit of pleasure, and therefore considered it a worthless, even subversive, waste of time.

Time, unfortunately, was something that the men of Earth seemed to enjoy wasting. The monsters felt as if they

249

were under a never-ending barrage of opportunities for leisure. They discovered, to their profound dismay, that their unsuspecting human spouses expected them to fill much of this "free time" with conversation. This cruel and unexpected burden had prompted the monsters to demand – and ultimately receive – full combat pay for their mission. They were prepared to have sexual intercourse with the females, but to constantly *talk* with them...well, if the briefings had been more complete, there would have been even fewer volunteers.

The sex, at least, was tolerable. Some of them even enjoyed it. Reproduction on their own world had been a cold, clinical affair viewed by both sexes as an unfortunate necessity. The contrast was a frequent topic of discussion, especially with monsters new to the cell.

"Does your wife drape herself on you at night?" Dennis Kirk asked one evening. The question seemed to be directed to no one in particular.

"I'm not sure what you're talking about," said Frank Lyle. He was the Harrisville chief of police, and, among the monsters, was second only to Dan Tally in rank.

Dennis spoke without looking up from his cards: "Does she crawl on top of you while you're trying to sleep?"

"Oh, you mean *cuddling*," said the chief. "Yes, mine does it, too. I rather like it."

Dennis discarded and looked up with a frown. "You do? I find it uncomfortable. I asked her to stop, and she was angry about it for days."

"Mine's angry all the time," muttered Vince Hallam. He was the youngest member of the cell. He had replaced the human Hallam five months earlier and was having a lot of difficulty adjusting. There was a general murmur of sympathy from his fellow monsters. It was well known that Cindy Hallam was a tempestuous and passionate creature, the very antithesis of an ideal mate. She was also the sister of Dan Tally's wife.

"I keep telling you to relax," Dan Tally said. "Remove your pride from the equation, and you'll be surprised how quickly things level out. Just be patient."

"I'm running out of patience."

A stillness fell over the gathering. "What's that supposed to mean?" Dan asked.

Vince looked up and saw that the others had fixed him with cold, analytical stares. He stuck out his chin in a very human gesture of petulant defiance. "I am merely giving voice to my frustrations," he said. "Do I not have the right? I was given to understand that that was one of the main purposes of these meetings."

"You are correct," Dan Tally said.

Vince laid down his cards. "Very well, then. Allow me to speak freely. This insolent harpy that you have seen fit to pair me with is making my life miserable. I am weary of being counseled to show patience and forbearance. I think that we should be allowed to teach these wretches the discipline of…"

Dan cut him off with an upraised palm. "Stop," he said.

"But I…"

"Not another word."

Vince frowned darkly, but kept his tongue still.

"You were not sent here to experience conjugal bliss," Dan Tally said. "You are here on a mission with specific objectives that must be met if our race is to survive. Your personal happiness is irrelevant. If you cannot accept that, then I will replace you with someone who can. Do I make myself clear?"

Vince did not reply.

Dan's eyes narrowed. "I asked you a question."

"Yes, sir. You have made yourself clear."

Dan flashed a humorless smile. "Excellent. Let's return to the game, shall we?"

They did so, and they played for another two hours. The evening's big winner, oddly enough, was Vince Hallam. This seemed to brighten his mood and he was almost cheerful when the game broke up at midnight.

Dan gestured for Frank Lyle to remain, and the two of them bade good evening to the other monsters as they exited through the back door into an alley behind the bar.

"What's on your mind?" Frank asked after the door was closed and barred.

"Can't you guess?"

Frank sighed. "You're overreacting. He'll come around. You said exactly the right things to him tonight."

"You think so? I'm not so sure. That talk about discipline…"

"He's young."

"He's arrogant and insubordinate. If I don't see some changes soon, I'm getting rid of him."

Frank sat down at the card table and poured himself a glass of water. Dan kept beer and liquor in the room for appearance's sake, but that was merely window dressing. The monsters could not abide alcohol. It was one of the few flaws in their imposture. "While we're on the subject," Frank said, "there's something I need to tell you."

"Yes?"

"He sent me a telepathic distress."

"Vince? When did he do that?"

"Two weeks ago. He was afraid Cindy was going to leave him."

Dan growled a curse in his native tongue. "What did he want you to do about it? Loan him money to buy flowers?"

"He thought that she suspected."

Dan walked over to the chair next to Frank's and sat down heavily. "How did you handle it?"

"I had a little talk with her. She's known me—well, she's known Chief Lyle—all of her life. She trusts me."

"That's helpful. How much trouble are we in?"

"None, I think. Oh, she can sense that he's…changed…but she's not sure how. I told her that what she was feeling wasn't unusual for a young newlywed. I said that she needed to give Vince time to mourn the loss of his bachelorhood."

"You actually said that?"

"Yes. I thought it was pretty clever."

They looked at one another for a silent moment, then broke into laughter. After a few moments, they sobered and Frank Lyle said, "I was actually surprised she didn't go to your wife."

"They've been estranged for years. Cindy didn't approve of her sister's marriage."

"She doesn't care for you, eh?"

"She should give me another chance. I'm a changed man these days."

Frank chuckled. "That is true. What should I do if she persists?"

"She won't, if that idiot will do his job. Why didn't you tell me about this earlier?"

"I was afraid you would feel obligated to include it in your next report to the Council. We really don't need that kind of grief right now. Besides, I felt that I could handle it."

"Without my knowledge?"

"Without adding to your troubles. If you feel that I merit disciplinary action…"

Dan waved it away. "Forget it. Spilt milk, as my wife calls it. Notify me immediately if there are any more complications. Do not hesitate to use our telepathic connection."

"All right. If you don't mind, there's something else I want to talk to you about."

"Yes?"

"The engineer's assistant is pressing for a field assignment."

"No."

"Respectfully, I would submit to you that…"

"He needs to stay where he is. If the duplicating machinery on our ship were to fail, even for a few minutes, the bio-feedback surge would kill us."

Frank was steadfast. "There are others who can handle that, as you well know. Be reasonable. There is a great deal of pressure to increase the level of our infiltration. Other cells have done so, and the Council can't understand why ours hasn't."

"Oh, very well. Let's meet tomorrow to discuss possible candidates for replacement."

"I already have the perfect one in mind."

"Really?"

"Yes. Your bartender."

"Leo? He isn't suitable."

"He's ideal! He's strong, handsome, and single. There's a young woman in my office who would marry him tomorrow!"

"He isn't suitable."

Frank favored his commander with a skeptical eye. "May I ask why you…"

"My decision is final. I will brook no disagreement. Is there anything else?"

Frank made no effort to hide his annoyance. "No, sir."

"Then you're dismissed. We can discuss other possibilities tomorrow."

"Yes, sir," Frank said, and he left without another word.

Four months before he was declared an unsuitable candidate by Dan Tally, Leo Saint-Clair, once better known as the Nyctalope, walked into the town of Harrisville in dire need of a drink. He wasn't a very impressive sight. Dirty, disheveled and hollow-eyed, he drew hostile stares from more than a few worthy townsfolk as he wandered the immaculate streets. He was not offended. In fact, he found the irony amusing. In his celebrated youth, he had been the object of countless admiring glances whenever he strutted the Parisian boulevards. Now, staggering with exhaustion among these bourgeois American villagers, he felt like an invading virus about to be attacked by white blood cells.

Thus it was with no small amount of relief that he spotted a picture window emblazoned with the words, *Dan's Bar & Grill*. It was mid-afternoon, and when he stepped inside he found that the place was nearly empty. He sidled up to the bar and was greeted by a short but powerfully-built man with a towel draped over his shoulder. "How can I help you?" the fellow asked.

Leo started to speak, but his voice came out as little more than a dry rasp. Lord, he was tired.

The bartender leaned forward. "You okay, pal?"

Leo cleared his throat. "May I please have a glass of water?"

"Water?" said the bartender. He blinked in surprise, as if Leo had uttered an unexpected password.

Leo smiled in bemusement. "I'll pay for it, if necessary."

The man seemed to recover himself. "No, no, of course not. Water, coming right up."

Leo drained three large glasses before ordering food and beer. The fare was palatable, if ordinary, and Leo soon began to feel more like a man and less like the husk of one. By the time he finished his meal, the place was empty save for himself and the burly barkeep.

"You're not from around here, are you?" the man asked as he removed Leo's empty plate.

"I'm practically from another world," Leo said.

The barkeep's muscles tensed beneath his shirt. A second later, he relaxed and turned back to Leo. The man gave him a long, searching look, and said, "No, not another world. Another country. You're from…France, aren't you?"

It was Leo's turn to be surprised. The flat, mid-Atlantic accent he affected while abroad in the States had never been questioned by anyone. "You have a sharp ear," he said. "May I ask what gave me away?"

The barkeep shrugged. "Nothing in particular. I'm just a good listener, I suppose." He extended a hand. "I'm Dan, by the way. Dan Tally."

Leo gave the hand a firm, friendly shake. "My name is Leo. I am pleased to meet you. Have you been in this town for very long?"

"Yes and no," Dan said. "Why do you ask?"

"As you say, I am a stranger here. I could use a little advice from someone who knows the area."

"Oh, I know it very well," Dan said. "You could even say I've studied it. What kind of advice do you need?"

"I've been through Hell recently, and I'm exhausted and almost out of funds. Frankly, I'm at the end of my tether. I could use a place to stay and a way to earn some money. Can you offer any suggestions?"

"I see. A temporary arrangement, right?"

"Just until I'm back on my feet."

Dan scratched his chin and gave Leo an appraising look. "I don't know," he murmured. "You might clean up good..." He looked into Leo's eyes. "Have you ever tended bar?"

Leo allowed himself a wry smile. "Not professionally, but I have the requisite skills."

"Hm. Are you a decent cook?"

"I have been told so."

Dan pulled a pen from his shirt pocket and scribbled a note on a piece of paper. "There's a hotel four blocks south of here," he said. "It's run by a guy named Dennis Kirk. He's a friend of mine." Dan presented the note to Leo. "Walk down there and give this to him. He'll give you a room for the night and charge it to me."

Leo shook his head. "I would rather you didn't."

"Let me finish. Go there and get yourself cleaned up. Be back here at five. You can work the grill until nine, then tend bar until closing. If I like your work, I'll take you on for a while. If not, well, you still get the one night, but after that you're on your own. Deal?"

Leo considered it. "I don't have any suitable clothes..."

"Do you see me wearing a tux? What you've got on is fine. Just get your duds laundered at the hotel while you're resting up. You can worry about a new outfit if I hire you."

Leo grinned. "Very well. I accept your offer."

"Good," said the barkeep. "I have a feeling you're going to be very useful to me."

256

After Chief Lyle's angry departure, Dan Tally turned out the lights and spent a few quiet minutes cleaning up the back room. He found this to be very relaxing. The monsters from outer space could see in pitch darkness with perfect clarity. They uniformly hated artificial light, and relished every opportunity to be without it. *Why are you sitting in the dark?* was a question almost all of them had fielded from a bewildered spouse at one time or another.

Whether or not to run the lights during the game had been a major point of discussion at the beginning of the weekly ritual. Eventually, the "lights on" side of the debate had carried the day. It simply wouldn't do for a nosey human to find them playing cards in a room as black as the bottom of an inkwell. What had been left unsaid – primarily as a gesture of respect to Dan Tally, who didn't want to discuss it – was the fact that only one human had access to the back room of the bar: the man named Leo.

After he was finished, Dan checked to make sure the alley door was secure, then stepped out of the room, walked down a short hallway, and entered the bar. He was not surprised to see that Leo was still at work, wiping down the tables one final time before returning to the hotel room that he called home.

"Give it a rest, will you?" Dan said, taking a seat at the bar. "Who the hell are you trying to impress, anyway?"

Leo chuckled. "I'll slack off when my probationary period ends."

"That ended months ago. If I fired you now, the place would go out of business. The whole damn town thinks you're the best cook in California."

"The secret is in the spices," Leo said.

"Right. You want a nip before you go?"

"Why not?" Leo went behind the bar and fixed himself a vodka martini. "Care to join me?"

"No, thanks."

"You know, I don't believe I've ever seen you take a drink."

"Never touch the stuff. Not anymore. I realized I was hitting it a little too hard and decided to quit while I was ahead."

Leo nodded and sat down on a stool opposite Dan. He raised the glass. "To quitting while you're ahead," he said. "May God grant that we always know the right time."

"Amen," Dan said.

There was a moment of contemplative silence, and then Leo said, "There's something I've been meaning to ask you."

"Yes?"

"Why did you give me a chance? That isn't something many people would have done."

"Oh, I don't know. Sympathy for a stranger far from home, I guess. But you shouldn't give me too much credit. My main reason was purely selfish. I was working on something that I thought you could help me with. I was only planning to keep you on board long enough to get you in the program."

Leo smiled. "What was it? Some sort of Ponzi scheme?"

"Not exactly."

"What made you change your mind?"

Dan took a deep breath and slowly exhaled. "I'm beginning to have my doubts about the project. I'm afraid it isn't going to end well."

"Anything I can do?"

"No. This thing...It's something I'd rather not involve you in."

Leo's eyes hardened slightly. "Dan, if you're in any kind of trouble, you should tell me. I can help you. It would surprise you, how much I can help a friend in trouble."

"It's precisely because you're a friend that I don't want you involved." Dan Tally shook his head. "I shouldn't have said anything. Do me a favor, just forget this conversation. Don't bring it up again, okay?"

Leo hesitated for a moment, then nodded. "If that's what you want."

"It is."

Leo shrugged. He took a few minutes to finish his drink in silence, and then he washed out the glass.

Dan smiled at him. "You know the main reason I kept you on? The reason I like you so much?"

"I give up," Leo said.

"You know when to talk, and when to stay quiet. That's a skill almost no one in this universe has mastered."

"The entire universe?" Leo said. "Has anyone ever told you that you have a peculiar way of putting things?"

Dan turned up a palm. "What can I say? I'm an eccentric. Maybe one day I'll tell you some other peculiar things. But not right now. Let's talk about something else. I have some good news for you, something you'll really like. Susan wanted me to invite you over for dinner Sunday night. Can we expect you around seven?"

"Of course. I would be honored."

"Good. We'll be looking forward to it."

Susan Tally was a petite woman with short auburn hair and alabaster skin. She had a certain fragile elegance that inspired Leo's protective instincts. She seemed like someone who could be easily broken. "I'm pretty nervous," she said as she lifted the cover from a steaming meatloaf. "Dan says you have sophisticated tastes. I sure hope you like this."

Leo took a sip of water and arched an eyebrow at Dan. "Sophisticated tastes?"

Dan grunted. "I'm pretty sure you're the only grill man in California with a copy of *Larousse Gastronomique* behind the bar."

"They'll get around to printing an English translation eventually. Then everybody will have one."

"Right. Don't keep my wife in suspense. Let's hear your verdict."

Susan served Leo a generous portion of the meatloaf, along with some mashed potatoes and green peas. Her large, dark eyes gazed at Leo with real trepidation as she set the plate before him. She seemed to genuinely fear his disapproval. *Good heavens*, Leo thought. *Does she think I'll throw it at her if I don't like it?*

Leo sampled all three of the items on his plate, then took a few extra bites of the meat. "The glaze is spicier than I expected," he said at length. "You've added hot pepper sauce, and also honey for sweetness." He took another bite. "I think this is perfect. A triumph."

Susan grinned. "Thank you! I really wanted you to enjoy it."

Leo gave her a smile and a little salute. It really was a satisfactory dish. He was glad that he hadn't had to lie.

They passed a pleasant hour at the table. The conversation was banal but enjoyable, and Leo decided that this was easily the most agreeable evening he'd had in months, perhaps even years. For most of his life, he had taken for granted the pleasures of food and fellowship. Now, having endured the privations of an exile, he appreciated how wonderful these simple things really were.

Later, after the table had been cleared, Susan offered Leo a glass of wine. "I picked out some for you. We usually don't keep any in the house, not since Dan…" She bit the sentence off, as if catching herself in a dreadful faux pas.

"Since I went off the sauce," Dan said with a smile. "It's all right to talk about it. It's not that big a deal."

Susan chewed her lower lip. "I think it is. I think it's wonder…I…I'll go get the bottle." She walked briskly toward the kitchen.

Dan looked at Leo. "Thanks for telling her the food was good. It meant a lot to her."

"I was only telling the truth. Is that what she's been so agitated about?"

"She really wanted it to be a special evening. You're the first person we've had over since I stopped drinking. I…didn't like to have guests. When I was drinking."

"I see."

"Yeah."

Susan returned with a glass and a bottle of cabernet sauvignon. "I'm sorry," she said. "I went ahead and opened it before I remembered that you would probably want to do that

260

yourself. Isn't that something connoisseurs like to do? Open it and sniff the cork?"

Leo smiled. "Only if you like the smell of cork. Here, let me…"

She handed him the bottle as if she were passing him a live snake. He took it and poured a small amount into the glass. As he was about to take a sip, he glanced over at Dan. What he saw made him freeze.

Dan Tally had raised his right hand and was pressing the tips of his fingers against his temple. His eyes were closed, and his mouth was curled into an angry snarl.

Leo set down his glass. *What the Devil? What's wrong with him?*

"That damned fool," Dan whispered. He opened his eyes. "I have to go. I have to go right now. I'm sorry."

Susan gawked at him. "What are you talking about? Where do you…?" She was talking to his back. He was striding out of the dining room, heading for the front door.

"I'm sorry," he called over his shoulder. "Stay as long as you want, Leo." The front door opened and closed and he was gone.

Susan turned to Leo. Her lower lip was trembling. "What just happened?" she said. "Was it something I did? Oh, God, please don't tell me that I –"

"Calm yourself," Leo said. "You did nothing wrong. There's something going on here."

"What do you mean?"

"Dan said something to me a few nights ago, something about a project that wasn't going well. Do you know anything about that?"

"Project?" Susan shook her head. "I don't know what you're talking about. He hasn't said anything to me about…"

Someone was pounding on the door. Susan jumped at the sound. Leo reflexively laid a comforting hand on her shoulder. "I'll get it," he said. "Stay here."

He detoured through the kitchen on his way to the door, grabbed a long blade from a block of kitchen knives, and slipped it up his right sleeve. By the time he reached the front entrance, the pounding had increased to a frenzied tattoo that was shaking the door on its hinges.

"Open up, dammit!" someone cried. It was a woman.

"Who is it?" Leo demanded.

"Cindy Hallam! Who are you?"

Leo opened the door. He was acquainted with the voluptuous redhead on the stoop. "Leo!" she exclaimed. "Thank God! I know *you're* a real man!"

"I beg your pardon?"

She looked around nervously. "Is Dan here? If he is, then I'd probably better go. I'm not so sure about him."

"He just left."

Her eyes snapped to meet Leo's. "Did he? Did he say anything about where he was going?"

"As a matter of fact, he didn't."

She bared her teeth in a humorless grin. "Well, I'll be damned! That clinches it! He's one of 'em too! Look, you've got to let me in. I need to talk to my sister."

"I'm not sure if that's a good idea."

"Don't argue with me, Leo! This is serious business. I'm in real danger, here. So is Susan. So is everybody!"

Leo's curiosity decided the question. He stepped aside and allowed Cindy to bustle in. He turned and saw that Susan had not obeyed him. She was standing in the hall. She stared at Cindy Hallam as if the woman were a Fury come to deliver judgment.

Cindy rushed to her and grabbed her shoulders. "Susie," she said, "I need you to listen close to what I've got to say. It's going to sound crazy, but I swear it's the truth. I swear it! Doctor Noyes will back me up. He's seen the proof. He's seen the ship! We saw it!"

Susan was visibly shaking. "W-What?" she stammered. "What ship? What are you talking about?"

"*The spaceship*!" Cindy Hallam barked. She released Susan and actually started pulling at her own hair in frustration.

"My husband is *not* my husband, and neither is yours! They're monsters from outer space!"

Susan's face was a perfect portrait of stunned incredulity. "Have you completely lost your mind? We've barely exchanged a word in three years and all of a sudden you come storming in my house yelling at me about...about...*monsters?*"

"Yes! That's exactly what I'm doing!"

"You really are crazy! Get out of here!"

"No," Leo said. Both of the women looked at him. He closed the front door and locked it. "I think we should hear what she has to say."

Cindy had known something was wrong since the honeymoon. At first she thought Vince was simply pining for his days of carefree bachelorhood. At least, that was what Chief Lyle had told her was happening. She had wanted to believe it, but that explanation had proven too thin a skein, and had quickly unraveled. The thing pretending to be Vince knew all the things he was supposed to know, and said all of the things he was supposed to say, but Cindy wasn't fooled. He knew the words, but not the music. He wasn't Vince Hallam.

She started to spy on him. If he worked in the garage, she watched him. If he went for a walk, she followed him. If he talked on the phone, she listened in.

One night, eavesdropping on an extension, she heard a conversation that Vince had with Dennis Kirk. Vince was unhappy. He wanted Dennis to tell him if there was any news on when the scientists were going to perfect the fertilization process.

"How much longer before I can finally impregnate this cow?" he whispered. "I used to think the females on our world were tiresome, but *these* creatures..."

"I would prefer it if you would not speak of our females," Kirk said. "Their memory is sacred. The disaster that killed them —"

"You sound like all the others! Why did I even call you?"

"I was wondering that myself."

Vince slammed the phone into the cradle. Cindy held on to the extension for several long minutes, staring into space, listening to the silence of the broken connection.

Later that evening, Vince slipped out of the house. He thought Cindy was asleep, but she wasn't. She slipped out behind him.

She was careful. She hewed to the shadows, following Vince at a distance of about one full block, never closing the gap. Eventually, they came near the edge of town. Vince rounded a corner, and few moments later a pair of headlights came up behind Cindy. The car slowed, and the driver called out to her.

"Cindy Hallam!" said Dr. Noyes. "What on Earth are you doing out here in the middle of the night, and dressed in that flimsy thing? You're going to catch your death, child!"

For a moment, Cindy was completely flummoxed, but then she had an idea. "Oh, thank Heaven it's you!" she exclaimed. "I'm following Vince. He's sleepwalking! Will you walk with me? We can be there to help him when he wakes up."

The doctor found it hard to believe, and he was none too eager to get out of his car, but Cindy knew how to be persuasive. The flimsy nightgown probably helped.

They caught up with Vince at the city limits. Instead of staying on the road, he turned into the woods and, with a few purposeful strides, disappeared among the trees. At that point Cindy almost lost Dr. Noyes. He protested that she simply wasn't dressed for tramping around in the forest at night, and for that matter neither was he. Vince was a big boy. He would find his own way home.

Cindy countered that her husband could get seriously injured out here, and then how would the doctor feel? He conceded the point, and into the woods they went. They hadn't gone far when they saw Vince standing alone in a clearing.

And then they saw something else...

"There was a sort of *shimmer*, and that thing stepped out of Vince's body like he was taking off a Halloween costume. Come to that, I think that's all it is; a costume. The real Vince—*my* Vince—is on that ship!"

"The spaceship," Leo said. He took a sip of his wine. They had moved to the dining room and they were all sitting at the table, listening to Cindy.

"It's there!" Cindy said. "It's in the clearing. They've hidden it with trees. We saw the thing disappear into it. I thought Noyes was going to have a heart attack!"

"What did you do then?"

"I grabbed the old man and we got the hell out of there. I managed to get him calmed down by the time we got back to his car. He wanted to call the governor or some stupid thing, but I told him I had a better idea."

"What was that?"

"I remembered what Vince and Dennis had said to each other. These things, they want to have children, but they're not able to get women pregnant. At least not yet."

Leo nodded. He saw where she was going.

"I told Dr. Noyes to call every man in town who had a pregnant wife. Those are the men we can trust. I sold him on it, and he's getting a posse together right now. They're going to raid that ship and get my...get *our* men back!"

Susan Tally struck the table with her fist. She glared at Leo. "Why are you encouraging her? Why are you talking to her like anything she's saying makes sense?"

Leo was patient. "Susan, I have been far and seen much. Trust me, I have known stranger things even than this." He turned back to Cindy. "You told me earlier that I was a *real man*. Why did you say that? I haven't fathered any children since I came to this town. How do you know that I'm not one of these invaders?"

Cindy pointed at the wineglass. "They can't stand alcohol. That was one of the first things I noticed when Vince

265

changed. I called Dennis's wife and she told he stopped drinking eight months ago." She looked at Susan. "Right about the same time Dan miraculously dried out."

Susan's face flushed. "My husband…" Her voice dwindled into an inaudible whisper. She swallowed and tried again. "My husband stopped drinking because he loves me."

Cindy rolled her eyes. "Oh, for God's sake! He loves you? Your husband was a monster even before he got replaced by an alien! Y'know, Susie, I can't say I blame you if you like the phony Dan better. At least this one doesn't get plastered and slap you around every night. If you had just listened to me when I tried to talk you out of…"

"That's enough," Leo said. His voice was low and even, but it struck Cindy like the crack of a whip. She looked for a moment as if she wanted to argue the point, and maybe she would have, but the window behind her exploded and the conversation ended in a shower of glass, wood, and flame.

The women fell to the floor screaming. Leo gripped the edges of the heavy dining table and flipped it over to form a makeshift shield. He crouched behind it and firmly took each sister in hand. "Have either of you been injured?"

Cindy was the first to speak. "I've got some slivers of glass stuck in me, but I'll be okay!"

Leo looked at Susan. "And you?"

"I'm…yes, I'm all right. What was that? What happened?"

A bolt of yellow lightning screamed through the air over their heads. It crashed into the far wall and traveled left to right across the width of it, carving a black and smoking scar into the plaster.

From outside the broken window, a voice called out. "Cindy? Are you still alive in there?"

"Vince!" Cindy gasped, wide-eyed with terror.

"You've been a lousy wife, Cindy," Vince Hallam said. His voice was getting closer. "I'm afraid I'm going to have to file for a divorce."

The yellow lightning came again, and the wall began to burn.

Leo lifted the table in front of the window. "Run for the back door! Both of you! Now!"

They obeyed, scrambling clumsily over the broken glass. They were just out of the room when the table was blown to pieces. Leo had been expecting the blast and was thoroughly prepared for it. He rolled with the force of the impact, turning a somersault and coming to rest in a kneeling position. He was facing the ruined window, and he found himself looking directly into the eyes of Vince Hallam.

Vince regarded him with casual contempt. In his outstretched hand was a small cylinder he wielded like a metallic magic wand. "Hi, Leo," he said.

"Hello, Vince."

"Where's Cindy?"

"She left."

"That's too bad. I guess she told you all about me. About us."

Leo shrugged. He used the movement to cover a slight shift of his body, so that Vince would not see the knife slip from his sleeve.

"Everything would have been fine," Vince said, "if she had been more like her sister."

"But she wasn't. Now your plans have fallen apart. Why don't you just cut your losses and get out?"

"It isn't that simple. Our ship has already been damaged by that moronic rabble that Cindy stirred up. It's only a matter of time before they fight their way inside. When they do, they'll discover our human counterparts and free them from the duplicating machinery."

"Then Cindy was right. The men are imprisoned on your vessel."

"She guessed that? Ha! Clever bitch. Yes, they are, and when they are freed, we will surely die. But not before I've avenged myself on *my wife,*" he practically spit out the words, "and as many of you disgusting vermin as..." His statement was cut short by the knife he found suddenly buried in his throat. Leo's throw had been swift, expert, and unerring.

Leo pressed the attack, charging and leaping through the window, slamming into Vince with a flying tackle before the impostor could recover enough to squeeze off another blast from his weapon. The alien was driven to the ground, a spray of blood exploding from his mouth upon the impact. Leo grasped the hilt of the knife and gave it a sharp, brutal turn in Vince's neck, practically decapitating him. The monster from outer space gave a final, gurgling cry of agony, and then was still.

Leo rolled from atop the creature, pulling the knife with him. Almost immediately, the thing began to decompose into a putrescent mass of steaming, viscous goo. Clenching his teeth, Leo reached out and plucked the deadly metal cylinder from the remains. He took a moment to examine it, and easily found the stud that functioned as the trigger mechanism. Behind him, he heard someone make a retching sound. He turned and saw Susan clutching at her midsection, her face twisted with revulsion.

"Where's Cindy?" Leo demanded.

Susan pointed at the curb, and Leo saw the redhead climbing into a late-model sedan. She called out to Leo. "Come on! I'm going out there! I want to be there when they get Vince!"

Leo ran to the car.

They could hear the gunfire when they reached the woods at the edge of town. Cindy didn't spare Leo a word or even a glance before jumping from the car and running for the trees. He did not try to keep her back.

He advanced steadily but cautiously toward the sounds of the conflict. The percussive cracks of the rifles and pistols were occasionally drowned out by the electric scream of the invaders' weapons, and the less audible screams of men and monsters. He had almost made it to the clearing when he caught a movement at the corner of his eye.

He dropped to a crouch and scanned the surrounding wilderness. Like the monsters, Leo Saint-Clair could see through the darkness as if it were day. To him, the pale shafts of moonlight that lanced through the leaves were not unlike the brightest rays of the Sun. It took only a few seconds for him to fix upon the figure stalking through the trees. He pulled the cylinder from his pocket and stealthily closed on the man (monster?) until there was only a few yards between them. "Please do not make any sudden movements," he said in a calm voice. "I have a weapon trained on you. Raise your hands and turn around."

Dan Tally turned and gave Leo a sad smile. "I'm sorry dinner got ruined."

"Drop that weapon."

Dan let the cylinder he was grasping fall to the ground. "I wasn't going to use it anyway."

For a moment, neither of them spoke. From the clearing, there rose a chorus of exultant shouts, followed by a fusillade of gunshots.

"It's almost over," Dan said. "Soon, they'll find the prisoners, and when those men are disconnected from our machines..." He shook his head and leaned back against a tree.

"Are they all right? The men you kidnapped?"

Dan was offended. "Of course! They're perfectly fine. We're not monsters, you know."

"Why didn't you replace me, too? That's the real reason you hired me, isn't it?"

"Yes, but I decided not to. I liked you too much. I enjoyed being your friend."

"But you were only playing a role."

"To an extent, but not completely. Not with you. And not with Susan." He closed his eyes and sighed. "That poor woman. Nothing can save her now."

Leo frowned. "What's that supposed to mean?"

"Dan Tally is a violent and abusive drunkard. He's put Susan in the hospital twice. He probably would have beaten her to death by now, if I hadn't taken his place."

There was another chorus of shouts, but no more gunfire.

Dan winced and made a sharp intake of breath that hissed between his teeth. "It's over," he said. "They've killed the last of my men. What a stupid, pointless waste."

"Then it's all true," said a soft, quavering voice. Leo looked over his shoulder, and saw Susan emerge from the trees. She walked past Leo as if he were air, and stood in front of Dan Tally. She reached up and cupped his face in her hands and slowly turned his head from side to side. "You're not...him?"

"No. I am sorry I deceived you."

Tears began to flow from Susan's eyes. "It's not fair," she said. "It's not fair. I thought he had really changed. I thought that he...that you really loved me."

"I do care for you."

Susan fell forward and wrapped her arms around Dan. "I don't want him back," she cried. "I want *you*. You've been so kind to me...so kind...so...gentle..."

Dan wrapped his arms around her trembling body and held her close. Suddenly, he gasped in pain and pushed her away. "The connection's been severed," he said in a strangled voice. "Turn away...I do not want you to see..." He went to his knees, fell face-forward to the earth, and disintegrated into a liquid mass draped in the clothes of a man.

Susan knelt beside the remains and wept. Her tiny body swayed and shook as if she were being pounded by fists. Leo was moved. Out of respect for her grief, he averted his eyes.

A few minutes passed. Susan's weeping subsided into small, choked sobs.

"Susan," Leo said, "would you like for me take you home?"

"She can come with me," said a familiar voice, and Dan Tally lurched out of the shadows. He had lost a lot of weight. His hair had grown long and unkempt, and a thick, tangled beard hung from his sunken cheeks. Leo and Susan regarded him in startled silence.

The man pointed at Susan. "I thought I heard you up here. What the hell are you doing? Are you crying over that goddam thing?"

Susan's mouth worked, but no words came forth.

Dan turned and spit, then looked back at his wife. "You and me, we're gonna have a little talk later." His eyes moved to Leo. "As for you, I know who you are. Those machines they used to steal our faces and suck our minds, they were a two-way street. I know everything that happened while I was gone."

"Is that a fact?"

"Yeah, and I don't need some nancy-boy frog working at my bar. You can get lost."

"Dan," Susan said.

"What?"

Susan raised her hand. Clenched in a white-knuckle grip, she held the metal cylinder that had earlier been dropped by the false Dan Tally. There was a flash of yellow lightning, and her husband was enveloped in a burnt-orange aura that soon reduced him to a pile of smoldering ashes.

The lightning faded, and darkness fell. Susan dropped the cylinder. Leo stepped forward, and gently helped her to her feet. She looked steadily into his eyes. "The monsters killed my husband," she said.

Leo sensed a question there. He answered it with a single nod. As a friend had once observed, the Nyctalope knew when to talk, and he knew when to stay quiet.

A logical follow up to the theme of the occupation of France by the Germans, is that of the occupation of Algeria by the French, which had begun in the 1830s. The so-called French-Algerian War, or War of Independence from the Algerian viewpoint, had turned violent in the early 1950s, and lasted until the Evian Accords of 1962. With a great deal of sensitivity and historical perspective, Emmanuel Gorlier takes us to the heart of this troubled period of French history...

Emmanuel Gorlier: *The Algerian Dilemma*

French-occupied Algeria, July 1959

To J.-C. Vaury, military orderly,
Conscripted during the Franco-Algerian War

The perimeter had been secured by an entire section of French infantry, deployed around the two trucks involved in the accident.

The road was an ordinary country road near Algiers. One of the trucks was a GMC troop transport; the other an old, weather-beaten vehicle carrying poultry. Four victims were lying on the ground: three soldiers who had been thrown from the back of the troop transport, and the driver of the poultry truck who had been trapped under his vehicle when it had flipped over.

Four military ambulances arrived, preceded by a jeep from the army's medical corps. Inside was Commandant Rougeot, the Chief Medical Officer for the area.

At each end of the road, there was a long line of vehicles carrying a motley crowd, waiting to be allowed to pass the scene of the accident and continue on their journey. Most of these belonged to locals who were going into the city on business, or returning to their farms. A few newer vehicles belonged to the "Algerian French," who were not afraid to complain loudly about the delay caused by the accident. There was also a bus, waiting patiently for normal traffic to resume. Inside, the passengers were mostly native Muslims, sweating profusely under the hot sun. They were traveling to Algiers from the hinterland and were used to delays and the need to be patient.

Among them was a European of medium height, black hair with graying temples, wearing a light-colored shirt and linen trousers. He wore sunglasses despite the fact that it was dark inside the bus. He seemed interested in what was taking place on the side of the road and didn't seem to mind the delay. However, his interest did not stop him from turning his head slightly from time to time to keep an eye on another one of the passengers sitting two rows ahead of him.

That passenger was a native who differed from the other passengers because he had a pair of piercing blue eyes; he, too, stared closely at the events unfolding on the road.

The orderlies had gently placed the three French soldiers under the shade of a wall; the medical officer was now examining them.

A little to the side, a male orderly approached the poultry merchant who had been removed from the wreck of his vehicle, but was lying in the sun, one leg almost torn from his body. The orderly leaned forward, looked at the wounded man, and took his pulse.

Just then the medical officer stood up and, pointing to two of the soldiers, issued an order:

"Take these two to the Military Hospital. I'm afraid there's nothing more we can do for the third one."

He then walked back to the jeep and prepared to leave. The orderly approached him and asked:

"Commandant, what about the driver of the other truck?"

"He'll die soon. There's nothing more we can do for him either," replied the officer, stepping into his jeep.

"Excuse me, Commandant," said the orderly, "but I took his pulse; it's quite strong. We could still…"

The Commandant shrugged and said:

"Look, if you feel you've got the time to take care of him, then take him to a civilian hospital."

Nodding, the orderly summoned two of his colleagues and, together, they carried the poultry farmer to another ambulance.

The ambulances left, slowly at first, then moving at full speed once they were past the secured perimeter, their sirens blaring in the distance.

The European had followed the chain of thoughts transparently displayed on the face of the man with the piercing blue eyes as he had watched the scene.

At first, he'd been angry at the medical officer, but then he'd been pleased by the orderly's intervention, and finally had felt appeased when the ambulances had driven away.

Minutes later, the bus resumed its travel toward Algiers. While the man with the blue eyes gazed indifferently at the landscape, the European kept thinking about what he'd just witnessed.

His sunglasses hid a pair of eerie, blue-green eyes, eyes that belonged to Leo Saint-Clair, better known as the Nyctalope. Struck in the face by a bullet when he was still a young man, he had been mysteriously transformed and had acquired the extraordinary eyes that allowed him to see through the darkness as if it were the middle of the day. However, they had the disadvantage of making him easily recognizable and, therefore, he was often driven to hide them behind tinted glasses.

As the bus entered the outskirts of Algiers, the Nyctalope mentally reviewed the chain of events that had led him there.

Everything had begun a few weeks earlier when he had landed in Algiers to help the Government with the spiraling violence that threatened to engulf French Algeria. His attention had soon been drawn to a mysterious rebel who had caused the French authorities much trouble. He was a terrorist known only by his "nom-de-guerre" of Djinn, who had masterminded a series of spectacular bombings, destroying several military and administrative buildings. The nature of the explosives he had used remained a mystery, as no traces of known substances had been detected, and yet, the buildings had been taken apart and their occupants buried under the rubble. Another mystery was that the buildings had been under close surveillance; yet no one had witnessed anything suspicious beforehand.

In addition to these two mysteries, the very name of the terrorist had attracted Leo's attention: Djinn. In the 1930s, he had fought a woman in Morocco who had used the same pseudonym, before being killed by local mystics who hated her European origins. Was there a connection between the two? Both Djinns fought against French rule, but with very different means.

The Nyctalope felt obliged to take on the case, as the mystery surrounding Djinn was starting to create a panic and stir up the natives against the French.

Leo approached some old friends from French Military Intelligence with whom he had been working on and off since the 1930s, and most recently during the Antekirtta Affair.

Unfortunately, these contacts knew no more than he. Nobody had seen anything. There was, however, a report from old *harki* who claimed to have seen a giant demolish one of the buildings, a police station. Understandably, no one had taken it seriously.

Leo then decided to go and personally inspect the sites that had been destroyed. He was surprised by the extent of the damage. To facilitate his investigation, he had assumed the ordinary disguise of a farm worker who had allegedly lost a brother during the attacks. His bronzed face and perfect knowledge of the various local dialects made his story totally believable. He even managed to hide his extraordinary eyes behind a pair of shades.

Under this disguise, his investigation was much easier; people trusted him and began to share information that they would never have given to the police. Soon, he learned that the same man had been seen near each site before the attacks. What had made him memorable was that his eyes were of a striking blue. Of course, that eye color was not unknown, even amongst native Algerians, but in this particular case, witnesses also remembered the fact that the stranger carried a small suitcase, about the size of a hat box, everywhere he went.

The Nyctalope's investigation had achieved a breakthrough, but how to find such a man in the vast expanse of French Algeria, not knowing where he next planned to strike? Leo reflected that his targets were getting progressively more ambitious, and he had gradually increased the importance of his objectives. He had begun with a small police station in an isolated village; his latest attack had been military barracks with over a hundred soldiers. The Nyctalope tried to guess what Djinn's next target might be, but his choices were inconclusive, and his enemy remained just as elusive. Leo shared his information with the French authorities, but when a sentry reported seeing the man with blue eyes in Oran, he still managed to escape by vanishing inside the local cashbah.

Leo had reached a deadend when a newspaper article caught his eye.

On July 14, 1959, a grand reception was to be held at the Prefecture of Algiers under the auspices of General Bigeard himself. All of the city's high society, as well as key members of the General Staff, would be present. *That would be a target worthy of Djinn*, thought the Nyctalope.

Still in disguise, he began to carefully monitor the Prefecture. Sitting under a palm tree, pretending to doze in the sun, he didn't lose a single detail of everything happening around the building.

To play it safe, a platoon of infantry and a light-armored vehicle were also providing security. On several occasions, Leo himself was forced to move at the request of patrols annoyed by the beggar who was too close to their security perimeter. But that did not prevent the Nyctalope from conducting his careful surveillance.

276

On the eve of Bastille Day, his patience was finally rewarded. He saw a man with blue eyes approach the building. He wasn't carrying a box, but sported a significant hump on the left side of his back. *Perhaps he, too, is disguised?* thought Leo.

The hunchback made a few back and forth trips on the square, paying particular attention to a palm tree situated about twenty yards from the Prefecture. Then, he walked away.

Leo got up and began following him. This was how he had found himself in the bus that first dropped them in a small village near Algiers, where the suspected Djinn stayed overnight, then brought them back to the White City.

Leo ended his reminiscences when the bus arrived at its terminus. The passengers got out slowly. The Nyctalope continued to tail his target who limped through different sections of Algiers during the day. Leo was afraid that he might give him the slip during his occasional visits inside a building or a café, but that fear proved unfounded because, inevitably, after a visit lasting between fifteen minutes and one hour, the man he suspected of being Djinn came back to the street and headed towards his next appointment.

At nightfall, the suspect was still doing his rounds—whatever they were. They were in a poorer and more sinister section of town, full of dimly-lit alleys. The Nyctalope, of course, had no problems following then man thanks to his night vision. Suddenly, he saw four men, who thought themselves invisible in the darkness, come out of an adjacent alley and walk towards him.

Leo acted as if he had not noticed them. From watching the grim expressions on their faces he realized immediately that they had been lying in wait for him. Obviously, Djinn had noticed his tail = and had organized this surprise.

The four men were armed with knives. Two stood before him blocking his path, while the other two had moved stealthily behind him to strike from the back. One of the men in front of him suddenly lunged forward, trying to stab to stab him in the neck. The Nyctalope bent forward, grabbed his attacker's arm and, using jiu-jitsu, sent him flying over his head onto the two men who stood behind him. He then turned to the right to face his last opponent. Before the man could react, Leo delivered a powerful blow to his neck, which hurled him violently against the wall, where he collapsed, unconscious.

Smoothly, the Nyctalope then turned to face his earlier three adversaries who were getting back to their feet and preparing to attack again. Leo saw a gleam of disbelief in their eyes. They had been stunned by his ability to respond so swiftly and in such a devastating manner.

The three men looked at each other hesitantly and decided to attack all together. But in this narrow alley, such a tactic played to the Nyctalope's advantage. They obstructed each other and lost precious speed. Still, three against one was not a threat to be taken lightly!

Leo's mastery of the martial arts, and the long training sessions he'd spent with Gnô Mitang, once again proved useful. He first struck his opponent on the left, who was still dazed from having had his comrade fall on his head earlier. Then, he quickly stepped back to avoid a murderous knife thrust and delivered a back kick to the attacker's face. The man stumbled backwards, almost into the arms of the third aggressor. While they were trying to regain their balance, Leo quickly moved in and simultaneously pressed one of their vital nerve centers. They both collapsed immediately.

When the Nyctalope left the alley, there was only silence. His four opponents lay motionless in unsightly poses, faces grimacing in pain, on the ground.

Leo looked around him. Djinn had obviously taken the opportunity to slip away, hoping to have gotten rid of his bothersome tail. *But he is unaware that he is dealing with me*, thought Leo. *I know where to find him, however, and I'm ready for the final act.*

A hundred meters from the Prefecture, the hunchbacked form of Djinn had stopped in front of the palm tree he had spotted the day before. He watched the comings and goings around the building entrance. A group of soldiers carrying musical instruments had just arrived.

The fanfare for the Marseillaise, thought Djinn. *This is a perfect, symbolic moment to act. At five minutes to midnight, the Prefecture will be destroyed. And to the tune of the* Marseillaise!

Djinn clutched his hump and, from under his garments, pulled out an ancient oil lamp.

Once again, the genie will strike. At the first strains of the Marseillaise, *I'll rub the lamp, like Aladdin once did, and order him to destroy my enemies.*

In the distance, the band started playing. Djinn raised the lamp and... stopped. He stared at the entrance of the Prefecture.

Just there stood the large orderly who had taken care of the truck driver earlier. He was carrying a folder and was arguing with the guards at the gate to be admitted inside.

Djinn froze and hesitated, facing an inner turmoil that he had not anticipated. His hand almost touched the magic lamp, then backed away from it.

Aux armes, Citoyens... resounded loudly and clearly from inside the Prefecture.

Suddenly, Djinn felt something hard and cold against his neck—the barrel of a gun—and head a voice:

"The show's over," said the Nyctalope. "Put your hands up very slowly, and without touching that lamp!"

The Nyctalope watched carefully as his foe obeyed his orders.

"Now give me the lamp, again without sudden moves!"

The Nyctalope took the lamp, and then looked at Djinn.

"Can it be? Aladdin's Lamp! I always thought it was a legend! Where did you manage to find it?"

"I recognize you now," said Djinn, avoiding the question. "These eyes... You're the Nyctalope... I was hoping to meet you one day to settle our accounts..."

"But I don't know you. How can you have a score to settle with me?"

"I'm the son of Ou Skouti and Helen Parsons—the original Djinn—whom you fought, oh so long ago..."

"I remember Helen; she died in my arms! But I wasn't responsible for her death. She was killed by a bunch of Moroccan mystics—the very people for whom she fought. You've got the wrong enemy, son!"

"No! The French have destroyed my family, imprisoned my father, caused my brother to die, lost in the desert. I only owe my life to the providential intervention of Tuareg nomads who saved me from certain death. And you, Nyctalope, you represent the very empire that has enslaved Northern Africa for over a century!"

"I've had many native friends in Morocco. I have never sought to enslave, subjugate or humiliate anyone—I've only sought to help build a better world, for everyone. But perhaps our views are too different to be easily reconciled. Still, a short while ago, I saw you hesitate before unleashing your genie. Why?"

"Didn't you see the orderly at the gate?"

"Yes. Wasn't he at the scene of that traffic accident this morning?"

"Yes, he was—and he saved the life of that poultry farmer. It is because of him that I hesitated. I want to liberate this country from the yoke of the French, but if I kill a Frenchman who saved an Algerian's life on that very day, then am I not the same as our oppressors? I fight for the freedom of my people, Nyctalope, like the French against the German occupiers. But perhaps, you can't understand that either?"

In the silence that followed, they heard the band reach the last stanzas of the *Marseillaise*: *Liberté, Liberté chérie...*

Now it was Leo Saint-Clair's turn to hesitate! He did understand what Djinn had said but the burden of having chosen to stand by Vichy while his own son had joined General de Gaulle's forces in England, was still a heavy burden on his soul. But now, de Gaulle's forces were in Algeria... The tables had been turned...

Still, Djinn was a terrorist and a murderer.... His duty was clear... But as he pondered, Leo had unconsciously lowered his gun. Surreptitiously, Djinn put his hand under his robe and... disappeared!

Leo was stunned. How had his enemy managed that trick? Upon reflection, he came to the conclusion that, if Djinn had located Aladdin's lamp, he might also have found the ring of invisibility mentioned in the legends...

Well, at least I have the lamp, he thought. *It's too dangerous to be entrusted to anyone. I'll neutralize it by using the method of the Seal of Solomon taught to me by my friend Jules de Grandin.*

After a final glance around, the Nyctalope went inside the Prefecture where he was invited.

A few streets away, Djinn suddenly reappeared. He took off his ring, and shook his head. *Too bad the effect is so short,* he thought. *I missed my target, but ultimately it wasn't a wasted evening. I crossed paths with the Nyctalope and managed to escape to fight another day. Better yet, I shook his confidence. He now doubts the justness of his cause. And if the Nyctalope doubts, can the rest of France be far behind? Yes, Algeria will soon be free!*

This present-day story features the Italian comic-book hero Martin Mystère (created by writer Alfredo Castelli), who previously met Colonel Bozzo, the seemingly immortal godfather of Paul Féval's Black Coats, in the story we co-plotted with Alfredo for the Almanacco del Mistero 2012. *It also foreshadows the events of our forthcoming novel,* The Return of the Nyctalope, *to be published in 2013...*

Jean-Marc Lofficier: *The Ides of Mars*

for Alfredo Castelli

Los Angeles, 2012

The sky was the color of rust, and so was the sand beneath his feet.

Martin Mystère looked up and saw a white dot, barely larger than the size of a nickel, up in the sky. The landscape around him was hilly, desertic, totally barren. He knew at once where he stood because he had often looked at the photographs with awe.

He was on Mars—and specifically, near the Columbia Hills.

But if he was truly on Mars, how could he still be alive? Breathing?

He lifted a foot off the ground and took a tentative step forward. The surface gravity on Mars should have been only 38% of that of Earth. So if he wasn't really on Mars, then, where was he?

He didn't have time to ponder this mystery because he heard a small cough coming from behind him.

An old man, leaning on a cane, had mysteriously appeared. He was tall, with a wizened yet still strong face, long

282

white hair and dark eyes that were full of a strange energy. He was dressed in a black frock coat reminiscent of late 19th century fashion. Next to him, holding a ridiculous umbrella, as if to shield the old man from the dangers of the hostile environment, stood a huge, burly man with a short beard and closely cut hair.

Martin recognized them both at once.

"Colonel Bozzo and the Marchef," he said.

Colonel Bozzo was the preternaturally ancient godfather of a criminal empire once known as the Brotherhood of Mercy, or the Black Coats, which was now operating under the name of BlackSpear Holdings. Martin had met him and his associates only a few months before.

"Good afternoon, Professor Mystère," said the Colonel. "As you have undoubtedly surmised, you are not on Mars itself, but on a very accurate holographic simulacrum built from NASA's very own data. My lovely associate, the Countess de Clare, could tell you exactly how it works—she is our science specialist—but I'm afraid I can't."

"Where are we, I mean, really?" asked Martin.

The Colonel shook his head. "I'm sorry I can't tell you that either, Professor, but I can tell you *why* you are here."

Martin smiled. "That's a start I suppose. I'm listening."

The Colonel pointed with his cane towards a pair of tracks in the rusty sand, heading up a small hill a hundred or so yards away.

"Do you see these tracks? They're made by one of the NASA's two Martian rovers—*Spirit*. You may have heard of it?"

"Yes, of course. It was damaged by the Martian winter and stopped broadcasting in March of last year."

"Ah. That's what the US Government told everyone, but *Spirit* is, in fact, doing fine and still broadcasting images."

"I don't understand," said Martin, genuinely perplexed. "Why...?"

"Let's follow the tracks to the other side of that hill, and you will have the answer to your question, Professor, although I doubt it will satisfy you."

Treading on the sand-which-wasn't-there, Martin Mystère, Colonel Bozzo and his bodyguard walked up the simulated Martian hill. Martin couldn't help but notice that the Colonel was not winded in the least when they reached the summit.

There, in front of him, he saw *Spirit*—and the ruins of the city.

When he got off the Air France flight at LAX, Los Angeles' international airport, the Nyctalope knew that he didn't have much time to act—a couple of days at the most, if his information was correct.

Avoiding the curiosity of Homeland Security was easy. His papers, conveniently updated by the French intelligence department which occasionally employed his services, could withstand even the harshest scrutiny. They didn't even have to change his name, just his birth year, as there were too few people alive today who remembered the name of Leo Saint-Clair.

He hailed a yellow cab and gave his destination: a discreet hotel in La Cañada. As the taxi negotiated its way onto the 405 freeway, Leo reminisced about the last time he had been in California. It was in 1949 and 1950... There had been that incident in the desert involving an ancient Martian capsule... Then, he had had to stop John Parsons from building a rocket to Mars... He had to kill Parsons and the Martian, whom had once been a man called Damprich, but had posed as the entity "Bartzabel." Disaster had barely been avoided. Earth had again been saved, without anyone being aware of it.

Now only one Martian remained, intent as ever to destroy Humanity.

But not if Leo acted in time.

For once in his life, Martin Mystère could not believe his eyes. It was astonishing enough to discover an ancient city on Mars, spread before him, partly buried beneath the sands of the red planet, but the ruins didn't even look alien.

He had expected golden spires, strange alien shapes, perhaps a decadent and crumbling architecture, straight out of Ray Bradbury's or Leigh Brackett's imaginations. But instead what he saw could have been designed by Gustave Eiffel. It was clearly of Earth manufacture.

He ran down the hill, careful not to stumble, followed by Colonel Bozzo.

Martin approached the first girder and saw some writing on it: *Fabriqué par les Aciéries Schneider – Le Creusot.*

"French? *French??*" he exclaimed. Then he turned towards the Colonel and, pointing at the ruins, shouted: "Is this another of your tricks, Bozzo?"

The Colonel made a calming gesture with his hand. "No trick, I promise you, Professor. This is a totally faithful simulacrum of the same corresponding spot on Mars, which has been secretly studied by the Americans since *Spirit* stumbled on it last March. Of course, they don't know what I know..."

He chuckled, a dry sound like two bones knocking each other, something which Martin found extremely annoying.

"And what do you know?"

"You are a lover of mysteries, Professor Mystère," replied the Colonel, not responding directly to Martin's question. "There is perhaps no one on Earth who knows more about the secret history of our planet than you. And yet, this, perhaps the greatest secret our world has ever known, has totally escaped your notice until now. Strange, isn't it?"

"I research the past, Colonel, not science fiction stories," said Martin, curtly.

"Ah, but this started in the past... A long, long time ago, in fact... You are aware, undoubtedly, that our planet was visited by extra-terrestrial beings several times during its pre-cataclysmic days?"

"Yes, of course. There are conflicting legends, myths about the Elohim who walked on Earth and married the Daughters of Man…"

"Suffice it to say that at least some of these beings came from the fourth planet of our Solar System, when it was still inhabited by powerful civilizations… Whoever they were, no one knows for sure, but they were, for the most part, evil, and left deep scars in our collective psyche… Whether in the West, China or India, Mars, Mangala, Yinghuo, came to symbolize the Enemy of Earth… The god Ares was often depicted as a villain, and today is still, even in your comic-books… Its color red came to represent blood, violence, aggression…"

"An interesting theory."

"More than a theory, Professor, for myths aren't the only things the Ancient Martians left behind on our planet; they also left some of their technology—I guess you might call it 'rocket science,' although it didn't involve the combustion of propellants, like our own primitive spacecrafts."

"How do you know all this?"

"Because some of their technology was found in the Gobi desert in what appears to be an ancient spaceport, by Kiang-Ho of the Golden Belt, a mad Mongol who was defeated by Rama Rundjee, the man nicknamed Doctor Mystère, after whom you yourself are named. This is where I became involved…"

"You?"

"I was interested in space technology even before that discovery, because I had read the works of Messieurs Verne and Wells, and I foresaw a day when Man might be driven to go out in space and explore other worlds…"

"You mean, plunder and loot?"

"Please, Professor! I also invested heavily in the Conquest of the American West. Manifest Destiny is what made your country the greatest in the world. I similarly believe it is man's destiny to subjugate the Heavens. Doctor Mystère, I knew, would crush that Mongol upstart, once alerted to his mad plans of world conquest, and so he did, leaving me to hire one of his assistants, a man named Oxus, whose research I then financed. Oxus gathered a group of like-minded men around him, which he christened the Fifteen. A few years later, they established the first human colony on Mars..."

"You're kidding me?"

"I am not. Unfortunately, one of the Fifteen, Koynos, fell in love with the beautiful Xavière de Ciserat, who at the time was fianced to the notorious French explorer Leo Saint-Clair. Koynos kidnapped Xavière and took her to Mars. Somehow, Leo found a way to follow them. What happened after that is not entirely clear. Koynos died. Leo reclaimed Xaviere and eventually wrestled the control of the colony away from Oxus. Then, some kind of catastrophe struck. They all died—but for one—and every trace of Man's first organized venture into Outer space was expunged from the records of Human History."

"But why?"

"That's what I want you to find out, Professor Mystère."

From his hotel window, the Nyctalope had a perfect view over the 210 freeway and the Jet Propulsion Laboratory, supposedly of Pasadena even though it was really located on neighboring land belonging to the incorporated city of La Cañada Flintridge.

The last Martian had succeeded in avoiding him for almost a century now, but tonight, their long standoff would come to an end.

Leo's mind returned to 1917 and the tragic events that had precipitated the death of the Martian colony.

The Ancient Martians had not perished. Sensing the slow, agonizing death of their world, losing its atmosphere, turning into a barren desert, they had mutated into a microorganism, a collective intelligence, buried in the sands, waiting, waiting...

Waiting for the day of the Earthmen...

For the technology they had left behind on Earth was but the sweet bait of a lethal trap.

When Oxus and the Fifteen had set foot on Mars and built their colony, the organism had struck and stealthily invaded the bodies of the humans, lodging itself inside their hearts, from which it could command its host, after having destroyed anything that made him or her human.

It wasn't a simple task. Many had died; others had succumbed to a sort of genocidal madness. Those who had not been possessed were killed by others, who had expired in turn.

During the Martian onslaught, Leo had lost Xavière, by then his wife, and their two children. It was a tragedy which he still felt today, a century later, with just as much pain as he had experienced then.

One man, however, had proved invulnerable to the alien attack: he, Leo Saint-Clair, because of the accident of fate which had conferred upon him that damnable artificial heart that also made him immortal. He had experienced a bout of temporary madness, but had quickly recovered.

Against the Nyctalope, the Martians themselves could not prevail.

Three Martians—for they were no longer humans—only three—had managed to escape, fleeing back to Earth in one of the rockets built by the Fifteen with Martian technology. They had gone to Earth, hoping against all odds to either return with more victims, or bring Martian seeds to our world. Either way, their success would spell doom for Earth.

But the Nyctalope had followed, a wrathful angel bent on vengeance, determined to save Earth from the Martian menace.

He had killed the first Martian—once a man named Jolivet—in 1932, pursuing him all the way back to Mars and destroying his ship.

The second Martian—Damprich—had tried to manipulate Parsons, in 1950, to build another rocketship to Mars, and Leo had killed them both too. There remained only one Martian, who had been behind many attempts at enticing Men to travel to the Red Planet. Leo had been forced to assume the role of the "Great Galactic Ghoul," destroying or causing the failure of more than 10 launches towards the Red Planet, and preventing five of the missions which had land on Mars from transmitting their data back to Earth.

But his Martian enemy was nothing if not patient, and resourceful. The latest mission, christened *Curiosity*, included, unbeknownst to the public, a plan to bring Martian soil samples back to Earth. The deadly microorganisms would at last be released on our planet where, in its oxygen-rich atmosphere, they would proliferate. Most of the population would die; the rest would become Martians.

That could not—would not—happen. Leo would see to it.

It was his destiny.

"Wait a minute," said Martin Mystère. "I know the story you're telling me. I read it when I was a kid. It's *Le Mystère des XV* by a French writer... Jean de La Hire. That Leo Saint-Clair—the man you're talking about, it's his hero... The Nyctalope!"

Colonel Bozzo pretended to poke at some sand with his cane.

"Like many famous persons, the Nyctalope had his biographer. Holmes had Watson, Rocambole, Ponson du Terrail, Greystoke, Burroughs, and even I had that *feuilletoniste* Féval, until I was obliged to silence him... La Hire embellished some of the Nyctalope's exploits, of course, and made up stories when Monsieur Saint-Clair did not deign tell him what really happened. If you remember *Le Mystère des XV*, you will recall that it has no proper ending. Why? Because Saint-Clair did not tell La Hire what had really happened on Mars. So he just made things up."

"And what did happen on Mars?"

"That is precisely what I want to know.

"I take it the Nyctalope was the one man whom you mentioned who survived the death of the colony?"

"—and managed to return to Earth, yes."

"But surely, for a man such as you, with all your power, your organization, it would have been child's play to…"

"…To capture, even kill Leo Saint-Clair?" interrupted the Colonel. "Yes, I guess I could have. But no one in over a century has ever defeated that Devil of a man, and I haven't reached my age by taking unnecessary risks… Besides, I know I couldn't have broken him and made him talk, whereas he will confide in you."

"In me? Why me?"

The Colonel's gaze became veiled, absent, as if he was peering into another time. Martin Mystère could almost see the tendrils of the past breaking through and trying to grasp him and pull him back into the mists of History.

"I knew your ancestor Rémy d'Arx very well, you know… Everything he learned about my organization, he found out by talking—and listening. He had the same gift as you do: the ability to elicit confidence… My gift is to make and protect secrets; yours is to expose them and learn the truth. You are the greatest truth-seeker of our age, Professor Mystère. If anyone can learn the Nyctalope's secret, it is you."

Buying a gun in Los Angeles was ridiculously easy. Leo had found what he needed right away on Del Mar: a Lorcin L-380, purchased for $100. It was a fairly well-made gun. It had pretty good heft and balance, although the craftsmanship was poor, and some of the materials and internal parts would not hold up, but for the short-term, it was an adequate weapon and would kill his target just as quickly as a .45.

He then had stalked the Martian until the Invader had gone, alone, into the multi-storied JPL car park. Leo knew that killing his foe would not be enough; he also had to destroy her *Curiosity* project—or at least, the secret part of it. But he had played "Galactic Ghoul" before and was confident that he would. What mattered was to put an end to this cat-and-mouse game once and for all.

With a few, quick moves, he shut off the electricity in the car park, which was suddenly plunged into total darkness. The

Nyctalope had chosen hia night well: there was no Moon up in the sky, and the lights from the outside street lamps only outlined the edges of each floor, but provided no light inside.

Of course, the Nyctalope did not need lights!

Stealthily, moving like one of those great jungle cats he had hunted in the past, Leo neared his prey. The Martian kept moving towards its car undisturbed as if it, too, was nyctalopic. Leo pointed his gun and fired a shot.

The bullet hit the Martian squarely in the back. The creature fell to the ground; its legs twitched, then it remained still.

Leo sighed. It was all over, at last.

He took a step forward, planning to take the body to the station wagon he had rented earlier and parked in the car park, intending to bury it in the Mojave Desert. It was the least he could do, he thought.

As he bent forward, the bullet hit him in the chest.

Martin Mystère was not a Nyctalope, but anticipating some kind of situation like this, he had borrowed a pair of night vision goggles from Colonel Bozzo.

He had awakened in the backseat of a limousine driven by the Marchef. The Colonel had told him they were now in Los Angeles, driving towards Pasadena where BlackSpear's agents had spotted the Nyctalope. The rest was up to Martin.

Before he left the limousine, the Colonel had handed Martin a disposable cell phone, to contact him, a set of keys to a Dodge parked nearby, and a gun, which Martin had refused. Instead, Martin had asked for the goggles, which the Marchef had pulled out of the trunk.

Then Martin had discreetly tailed the Nyctalope, until he saw him getting shot in the car park.

Leo Saint-Clair fell to his knees, clutching his chest. His opponent stood up, casually removing a bullet from the bullet proof jacket hidden under her coat.

Until then, Martin had not had a clear view of Leo's prey, but now he saw that she was a tall, stunningly beautiful woman with long, black hair. Her face was somehow ageless, but her dark eyes were full of ancient malice.

She delivered a kick of her foot to the Nyctalope, who was still moving, and breathing raucously.

"This time, you have lost, Leo Saint-Clair," she said. "The only way to get rid of you for good was to draw you into this elaborate trap. I knew you could not miss this opportunity. I have only one regret: that you will not live to see my world rise again out of the ashes of yours, your species replaced by mine..."

The woman now aimed her gun at the Nyctalope's head.

Martin pulled his own stun gun and fired a paralyzing bolt at her.

The woman stopped, then turned and saw Martin. Moving slowly, as if in slow motion, she advanced towards him, raising her hand to point her gun at him.

Martin had never seen his stun gun fail before but then the woman had just identified herself as not human. Could she be—a Martian? he wondered.

He fired another stun blast, without any better results. In a matter of seconds, the Alien would shoot him. He had to run.

Martin jumped to take cover behind a car when he heard the shot. Surprisingly, he didn't see the bullet fly by and hit the concrete column behind which he had stood.

He bent forward to take a peek.

The left side of the woman's head had just exploded. Though his goggles, Martin saw a phosphorus-bright corolla of blood burst from her broken skull and splatter around.

The Nyctalope, leaning on one knee, his gun firmly in his hand, had just fired the fatal shot.

Martin rushed from behind the car he had used for shelter. Leo was getting back on his feet.

"We need to get you to a hospital," said Martin. "You took a bullet in the chest."

"My circulatory system has already repaired itself," said the Nyctalope. "I'll get the bullet removed later. Thank you for saving my life…" Then he took a long, hard look at Martin. "I've seen you somewhere…" he added.

"I'm Martin Mystère. I…"

"Ah yes. I've seen your program on TV. Perfect. You're just the man I wanted to see…"The Nyctalope pulled a small spiral-bound notebook from one of his pockets. "Give this to Colonel Bozzo. It will tell him everything he wants to know—and warn him about Mars."

"Colonel Bozzo? How did you know that I…?"

"Don't you work for him?"

"Not exactly, no, but…"

The Nyctalope forced the notebook into Martin's hand.

"Give this to him. And tell him that Man will conquer the Heavens—just, not his kind of Man. I've taken steps already."

"I don't understand," said Martin.

"He will," replied the Nyctalope, with a grim smile. "Now help me load this body into that station wagon there… I'll go and bury it in the desert."

"Don't you think we should leave it here for the police? Or the scientists perhaps?"

"No," said the Nyctalope, opening the station wagon. Martin helped him pull the body inside. "Besides, she deserved better than that."

"She?" asked Martin.

The Nyctalope sat behind the wheel and turned the key in the ignition. The vehicle started right away.

"Once, she was Xavière de Ciserat. My wife."

As the station wagon drove away in the darkness, Martin Mystère understood why no one in over a century had ever defeated that Devil of a man.

Credits and Sources

First Steps

Also Starring:
Robert Champeau
The Prillants
The Baldwins
The Joneses
Loveday Brooke
Simon Orne
Lily Flowers
Sâr Dubnotal
Baal
Inspector Milfroid
The Necronomicon

Created by:
Jean de La Hire
Jean de La Hire
Louis Feuillade
George Lucas
Catherine L. Pirkis
H.P. Lovecraft
Louis Feuillade
Anonymous
Renée Dunan
Gaston Leroux
H.P. Lovecraft

© 2012, Travis Hiltz.

The Angel and the Exorcist

Also Starring:
Father Merrin
Glô von Warteck
Ogon Bat

Created by:
William Peter Blatty
Jean de La Hire
Takeo Nagamatsu

© 2012, Matthew Dennion.

Dangerous Territory

Also Starring:
Koynos
The Ape Man

Created by:
Jean de La Hire
Edgar Rice Burroughs

The Great Apes	Edgar Rice Burroughs
The Indian Boy	Rudyard Kipling
George Villiers	Jules Lermina
To-Ho	Jules Lermina

© 2012, Matthew Dennion.

Dam Busters of Mars

Also Starring:	Created by:
Gullivar Jones	Edwin Arnold
Ar Hap	Edwin Arnold
Samoht Yor	Martin Gately
Princess Heru	Edwin Arnold
Oxus	Jean de La Hire
Camille Flammarion	*Historical*
Ras Thavas	Egar Rice Burroughs
Damprich	Jean de La Hire
Chaland	Jean de La Hire
Xavière de Ciserat	Jean de La Hire

© 2012, Martin Gately.

Justice and Power

Also Starring:	*Created by:*
Korrides	Jean de La Hire
Dr. Cerral	Maurice Renard
Colonel Fontaine	*Historical*
General Anthoine	*Historical*
Rémy Baudoin	George Lucas
Judex	A. Bernède & L. Feuillade

© 2012, Chris Nigro.

The Girl from Odessa

Also Starring:
Harry Paget Flashman II

Sgt. Ballantine
Koschei
Countess Anastasiya
Belinskya
Gregor

Created by:
based on George
MacDonald Fraser
based on Henri Vernes
Russian folklore
based on Kazuo Ishiguro

David McDonald

© 2012, David McDonald.

Una Voce Poco Fa

Also Starring:
Rose Bruyère (Phantom Angel)
Véronique d'Olbans
Sylvie MacDhul
Simone Desroches (Belphegor)

Created by:
Randy Lofficier
Jean de La Hire
Jean de La Hire
Artrhur Bernède

© 2012, Emmanuel Gorlier;
translation by Jean-Marc & Randy Lofficier.

The Hour of the Grail

Also Starring:
Otto Rahn

Created by:
Historical

© 2012, Philippe Ward;
translation by Jean-Marc & Randy Lofficier.

Blood and Weapons

Also Starring:
Gofrey Cultnom

Created by:
Jean de La Hire

The Road Not Taken

Also Starring:
G-8
Nippy Westin
Bull Martin
James Bond

Created by:
Robert J. Hogan
Robert J. Hogan
Robert J. Hogan
Ian Fleming

Requiem for a Regime

Also Starring:
Professor Clairembart
Bob Morane
Heinrich Müller
Dracula
Harker

Created by:
Henri Vernes
Henri Vernes
Historical
Bram Stoker
based on Bram Stoker

Showdown at Steam Town

Also Starring:
Dean Moriarty
Sal Paradise

Created by:
Jack Kerouac
Jack Kerouac

Little Beaver .... Stephen Slesinger
& Fred Harman
Fran Reade .... based on Harry Enton
& Luis Senarens
The Steam Man .... Edward S. Ellis
The Giant Ants .... Ted Sheredman, Russell Hughes
& George Worthing Yates

Madison Square Garden

Also Starring:	*Created by:*
Marcel Cerdan	*Historical*
Steve Costigan	Robert E. Howard
Tom Hagen	Mario Puzo
Don Vito Corleone	Mario Puzo
Godfrey Cultnom	Jean de La Hire
Roman Orgonetz	Henri Vernes

The Devil You Know

Also Starring:	*Created by:*
The Aliens	based on characters and concepts by Louis Vittes

The Algerian Dilemma

Also Starring:	*Created by:*
Djinn	based on Jean de La Hire
Jules de Grandin	Seabury Quinn

The Ides of Mars

Also Starring:	*Created by:*
Martin Mystère	Alfredo Castelli
Colonel Bozzo	Paul Féval
The Marchef	Paul Féval
Doctor Mystère	Paul d'Ivoi
Kiang Ho	Philip Reade
Oxus	Jean de La Hire
Xavière de Ciserat	Jean de La Hire
Damprich	Jean de La Hire
Jolivet	Jean de La Hire
Rémy d'Arx	Paul Féval
John Parsons	*Historical*

SF & FANTASY

Henri Allorge. *The Great Cataclysm*
Guy d'Armen. *Doc Ardan: The City of Gold and Lepers*
G.-J. Arnaud. *The Ice Company*
Charles Asselineau. *The Double Life*
Cyprien Bérard. *The Vampire Lord Ruthwen*
Aloysius Bertrand. *Gaspard de la Nuit*
Richard Bessière. *The Gardens of the Apocalypse*
Albert Bleunard. *Ever Smaller*
Félix Bodin. *The Novel of the Future*
Alphonse Brown. *City of Glass*
André Caroff. *The Terror of Madame Atomos; Miss Atomos; The Return of Madame Atomos; The Mistake of Madame Atomos; The Monsters of Madame Atomos*
Félicien Champsaur. *The Human Arrow*
Didier de Chousy. *Ignis*
Captain Danrit. *Undersea Odyssey*
C. I. Defontenay. *Star (Psi Cassiopeia)*
Charles Derennes. *The People of the Pole*
Georges Dodds (anthologist). *The Missing Link*
Harry Dickson. *The Heir of Dracula*
Jules Dornay. *Lord Ruthven Begins*
Alfred Driou. *The Adventures of a Parisian Aeronaut*
Sâr Dubnotal *vs. Jack the Ripper*
Alexandre Dumas. *The Return of Lord Ruthven*
Renée Dunan. *Baal*
J.-C. Dunyach. *The Night Orchid; The Thieves of Silence*
Henri Duvernois. *The Man Who Found Himself*
Achille Eyraud. *Voyage to Venus*
Henri Falk. *The Age of Lead*
Paul Féval. *Anne of the Isles; Knightshade; Revenants; Vampire City; The Vampire Countess; The Wandering Jew's Daughter*
Paul Féval, *fils. Felifax, the Tiger-Man*
Charles de Fieux. *Lamékis*
Arnould Galopin. *Doctor Omega; Doctor Omega & The Shadowmen*
G.L. Gick. *Harry Dickson and the Werewolf of Rutherford Grange*
Edmond Haraucourt. *Illusions of Immortality*
Nathalie Henneberg. *The Green Gods*
V. Hugo, P. Foucher & P. Meurice. *The Hunchback of Notre-Dame*
Michel Jeury. *Chronolysis*

Gustave Kahn. *The Tale of Gold and Silence*

Gérard Klein. *The Mote in Time's Eye*

Jean de La Hire. *Enter the Nyctalope; The Nyctalope on Mars; The Nyctalope vs. Lucifer; The Nyctalope Steps In; Night of the Nyctalope*

Etienne-Léon de Lamothe-Langon. *The Virgin Vampire*

André Laurie. *Spiridon*

Gabriel de Lautrec. *The Vengeance of the Oval Portrait*

Georges Le Faure & Henri de Graffigny. *The Extraordinary Adventures of a Russian Scientist Across the Solar System* (2 vols.)

Gustave Le Rouge. *The Vampires of Mars The Dominion of the World* (w/Gustave Guitton) (4 vols.)

Jules Lermina. *Mysteryville; Panic in Paris; To-Ho and the Gold Destroyers; The Secret of Zippelius*

Jean-Marc & Randy Lofficier. *Edgar Allan Poe on Mars; The Katrina Protocol; Pacifica; Robonocchio; Tales of the Shadowmen 1-8*

Xavier Mauméjean. *The League of Heroes*

Joseph Méry. *The Tower of Destiny*

Hippolyte Mettais. *The Year 5865*

José Moselli. *Illa's End*

John-Antoine Nau. *Enemy Force*

Marie Nizet. *Captain Vampire*

C. Nodier, A. Beraud & Toussaint-Merle. *Frankenstein*

Henri de Parville. *An Inhabitant of the Planet Mars*

Gaston de Pawlowski. *Journey to the Land of the 4th Dimension*

Georges Pellerin. *The World in 2000 Years*

J. Polidori, C. Nodier, E. Scribe. *Lord Ruthven the Vampire*

P.-A. Ponson du Terrail. *The Vampire and the Devil's Son*

Henri de Régnier. *A Surfeit of Mirrors*

Maurice Renard. *The Blue Peril; Doctor Lerne; The Doctored Man; A Man Among the Microbes; The Master of Light*

Jean Richepin. *The Wing*

Albert Robida. *The Adventures of Saturnin Farandoul; The Clock of the Centuries; Chalet in the Sky*

J.-H. Rosny Aîné. *Helgvor of the Blue River; The Givreuse Enigma; The Mysterious Force; The Navigators of Space; Vamireh; The World of the Variants; The Young Vampire*

Marcel Rouff. *Journey to the Inverted World*

Han Ryner. *The Superhumans*

Brian Stableford. *The New Faust at the Tragicomique;The Empire of the Necromancers (The Shadow of Frankenstein; Frankenstein and the Vampire Countess; Frankenstein in London); Sherlock Holmes &*

The Vampires of Eternity; The Stones of Camelot; The Wayward Muse. (anthologist) *The Germans on Venus; News from the Moon; The Supreme Progress; The World Above the World; Nemoville*
Jacques Spitz. *The Eye of Purgatory*
Kurt Steiner. *Ortog*
Eugène Thébault. *Radio-Terror*
C.-F. Tiphaigne de La Roche. *Amilec*
Théo Varlet. *The Xenobiotic Invasion; Timeslip Troopers* (w/André Blandin); *The Martian Epic* (w/Octave Joncquel)
Paul Vibert. *The Mysterious Fluid*
Villiers de l'Isle-Adam. *The Scaffold; The Vampire Soul*
Philippe Ward. *Artahe*
Philippe Ward & Sylvie Miller. *The Song of Montségur*

MYSTERIES & THRILLERS

M. Allain & P. Souvestre. *The Daughter of Fantômas*
A. Anicet-Bourgeois, Lucien Dabril. *Rocambole*
A. Bernède & L. Feuillade. *Judex*
A. Bisson & G. Livet. *Nick Carter vs. Fantômas*
V. Darlay & H. de Gorsse. *Lupin vs. Holmes: The Stage Play*
Paul Féval. *Gentlemen of the Night; John Devil; The Black Coats ('Salem Street; The Invisible Weapon; The Parisian Jungle; The Companions of the Treasure; Heart of Steel; The Cadet Gang; The Sword-Swallower)*
Emile Gaboriau. *Monsieur Lecoq*
Steve Leadley. *Sherlock Holmes: The Circle of Blood*
Maurice Leblanc. *Arsène Lupin vs. Countess Cagliostro; Lupin vs. Holmes (The Blonde Phantom; The Hollow Needle); The Many Faces of Arsène Lupin*
Gaston Leroux. *Chéri-Bibi; The Phantom of the Opera; Rouletabille & the Mystery of the Yellow Room*
Richard Marsh. *The Complete Adventures of Judith Lee*
William Patrick Maynard. *The Terror of Fu Manchu; The Destiny of Fu Manchu*
Frank J. Morlock. *Sherlock Holmes: The Grand Horizontals; Sherlock Holmes vs Jack the Ripper*
P. de Wattyne & Y. Walter. *Sherlock Holmes vs. Fantômas*
David White. *Fantômas in America*